The
DOCTOR
of
ALEPPO

The
DOCTOR
of
ALEPPO

A NOVEL

DAN MAYLAND

BLACK STONE
PUBLISHING

Printed in the United States of America

First edition: 2020
ISBN 978-1-982622-15-2
Fiction / War & Military

1 3 5 7 9 10 8 6 4 2

CIP data for this book is available
from the Library of Congress

Blackstone Publishing
31 Mistletoe Rd.
Ashland, OR 97520

www.BlackstonePublishing.com

Then he will say also to those on the left hand, "Depart from me, you cursed, into the eternal fire which is prepared for the devil and his angels; for I was hungry, and you didn't give me food to eat; I was thirsty, and you gave me no drink; I was a stranger, and you didn't take me in; naked, and you didn't clothe me; sick, and in prison, and you didn't visit me."

Then they will also answer, saying, "Lord, when did we see you hungry, or thirsty, or a stranger, or naked, or sick, or in prison, and didn't help you?"

Then he will answer them, saying, "Most certainly I tell you, because you didn't do it to one of the least of these, you didn't do it to me."

—Matthew 25:41-45,
World English Bible

In the spring of 2011, protests erupted throughout the Middle East. Governments were overthrown in Tunisia, Egypt, and Yemen.

In Syria, the regime of Bashar al-Assad shot, beat, and tortured protesters, but instead of crushing the opposition, it sparked a civil war. By July of 2012, that war had breached the walls of Syria's capital, Damascus. But to the north by the border with Turkey, in what was then Syria's largest city, an uneasy peace still held . . .

Author's note

Although a work of fiction, every effort has been made to depict the war for Aleppo in a way that aligns with the actual history of the conflict. To that end, the major combatants and institutions I portray should be assumed to be real—except, however, for the European Development Service and aid group known as Bonne Foi, which are my own creations.

2012

PROLOGUE

Aleppo, Syria

At the members-only Club d'Alep, as women wearing cocktail dresses and pearls played buraco at baize-topped card tables, a waiter in the back of the club paused before a wall of freshly laundered linens.

He looked left, then right, then slipped a black tablecloth into his leather satchel.

Minutes later, not far to the south, a sixteen-year-old girl stood poised on the threshold of a silk shop in the souk, anxiously observing a young salesman as he wrapped a brilliant red scarf around his neck with theatrical flair.

Her hand trembled as she let her backpack slip from her shoulder. Her mouth was dry.

"Come, come," said the salesman when he saw her, welcoming her in with a wave of his hand and speaking loudly to be heard over the clatter of sewing machines. "I have your mother's order." Turning to a customer behind him, he added, "This will only take a moment."

And a moment truly was all it took for him to hand the girl a package that had been wrapped in brown paper and tied tight with twine.

"Only green and white," he whispered.

———

Across town, in one of the Kurdish districts, a young mechanic slid out from underneath a Hyundai sedan.

"Done," he said. Although it was only two in the afternoon, he had finished his last oil change of the day. Business had been slow of late.

"No later than seven tomorrow," said the garage owner without looking up from the car engine he was repairing. "We paint the Kia."

"Six forty-five," promised the boy, then he stripped off his coveralls, hung them on a peg, and exited the three-bay garage via a door in the rear. Before starting off down the garbage-strewn alley that paralleled the back of the building, he reached his hand into a bald truck tire that lay near the door.

The boy felt some shame that the small Nescafé tin he pulled from the tire was only half-filled with red paint, but it was all he could steal without raising suspicions.

———

Facebook and regular phone lines were monitored by the government, but Skype was not, so that was how everyone knew to take their packages to a middle-class neighborhood on the western side of the city and hide them inside a white bucket, on the periphery of an overgrown garden.

At three that afternoon, a fifteen-year-old boy named Adel retrieved the packages and snuck them up to the attic above his third-floor condominium. There he rolled out the fabric, pulled a needle, thread, and scissors out of a dry water tank, and began to cut the cloth into strips.

The sewing part took him a long time, and he was unsatisfied with his inconsistent stitching, but he felt a bit of pride at the way the painted red stars turned out.

"Where are you going?" demanded his mother after he had crept down from the attic and was running out the door.

"The mosque."

Which was true in that he did walk straight to the nearby silver-domed Rashid Mosque. And he even made a show of praying with the rest of the congregants—of which there were hundreds more than usual that evening.

But when the imam finished his service, an uneasy silence settled over the crowd until a lone voice shouted a single word: "*Takbir!*"

"*Allahu Akbar!*" Adel roared in unison with all the others who had been waiting for this moment. Then he pulled his orange T-shirt up over his nose so that it covered his face like a mask and ran for the exit.

As the congregants spilled out, Adel unwrapped his five homemade flags from around his waist and began to give them away.

It was the green, white, and black flag of independence, marked in its center by three red stars. It was the flag that Syria had flown when the French had finally left sixty-six years ago, and it was the flag that Adel was determined to see flying from the Presidential Palace in Damascus when the dictator Assad was gone.

"Get out, Bashar!" he cried as he handed out the flags.

"Get out, Bashar!" cried a gap-toothed boy as he grabbed the last of Adel's flags.

Side by side, the two boys raced to join the throng of protesters who were already marching in the street, chanting, "The blood of the martyrs is not cheap. Pack your things and get out! Get out, Bashar!"

When the Mukhabarat attacked moments later, firing bullets and tear gas into the crowd, it was as though they had been lying in wait. As though someone on the inside had tipped them off.

Adel sprinted to an alley down the street. Just before ducking into it, he glanced over his shoulder and saw two men in black, backlit by the sun, batons arcing high over their heads, pummeling the gap-toothed boy.

CHAPTER 1

Monday, July 16

The clinic lay just a short walk from the University of Aleppo Hospital.

Its wide glass entrance doors proclaimed the doctor's name—Samir Hasan, MD—and opened to a carpeted waiting area where the air was cool, the seats upholstered with leather, and the glass coffee tables cluttered with bowls of Turkish delight and sugar-coated chickpeas.

The doctor sat at a pedestal desk in his office. Behind him, diplomas in gilded frames hung from the wall. In front of him, the deputy minister of irrigation, who had just flown in from Damascus, was wedged into a wingback chair. They were discussing the minister's knee.

"You suffer from osteoarthritis," Sami announced as he leaned back in his swivel chair and zoomed in on a digital X-ray image on the laptop in front of him. "In a young person, the femur bone is separated from the tibia by a cushion of cartilage we call the meniscus. In your case, the cartilage has deteriorated to such a degree that in your right knee, bone is grinding against bone. That is the source of your pain. The joint should be replaced, of course."

Ordinarily, Sami might have turned his laptop around to show the patient an X-ray image of the knee in question and pointed out where the meniscus had deteriorated. He might also have brought out a skeletal model of a knee joint and specified exactly what would be replaced. But Sami harbored no love for government bureaucrats and made a point of doing as little as possible for them without giving obvious offense.

"Does that mean—"

"There is also the matter of your weight," Sami interjected.

The Damascene minister exhaled loudly through his nose and shifted in his seat. Sami caught a whiff of rosewater perfume.

"I do have large bones."

"Your bones are neither larger nor smaller than they should be. The issue is that you are obese." Sami steepled his fingers on the top of his desk. "This is a clinical observation," he continued, "based upon your height and corresponding weight. Your obesity is relevant because it has doubtless contributed to your underlying condition, and it will certainly affect your recovery and the durability of the implant. I recommend you lose thirty kilos."

"Thirty kilos! But that could take a year to accomplish!" The minister raised his eyebrows and made a small *tsk* sound.

"At a minimum. Either that, or you must be prepared for a subopti-mal—" Sami paused, interrupted by knock on his office door. "Yes?" he called, annoyed, thinking it was probably someone from the minister's security detail, asking for some special privilege or another. As if clearing out his clinic during prime business hours wasn't privilege enough.

His receptionist, a twenty-five-year-old brunette, who also happened to be his second cousin, poked her head in. The minister diverted his eyes to his lap.

"I asked that we not be disturbed," snapped Sami.

She smiled weakly. "The hospital is on line two, Dr. Hasan. One of your patients has suffered a setback."

Sami frowned. "Dr. Issa is on call. Surely he can handle it."

"They said it was an emergency. And that they just need a minute of your time."

"Surely—"

"Please, Doctor." She gestured with her eyes that it was important Sami comply.

"My apologies," said Sami to the minister. He opened the bottom drawer of his desk and pulled out a model of a knee that had been fitted with an implant. "Evidently I must offer a quick consultation. In the meantime, this might interest you."

———

As soon as they were out of earshot of the minister, the receptionist thrust the phone into Sami's hand.

"Sorry," she said.

"What is it?" he asked.

She placed a hand on her heart and gestured to the phone. "Tahira will explain."

He stepped into an empty exam room, closed the door behind him, and listened as his wife, who was in tears, explained that her sister's eldest son, Omar, had hurt his arm—badly—while working at the soap factory owned by Tahira's family.

"So bring him to the clinic," said Sami calmly.

"No! You must come to the factory."

The deputy minister of irrigation had shut down the whole street outside the clinic. As a result, Sami was already running an hour and a half behind schedule for his evening appointments. He would make the time for Omar, of course, but the boy needed to be brought to the clinic. He told Tahira as much.

"Sami, think for a moment. Why would I ask you to come to the factory?"

"I have no time for riddles, Tahira."

"Sami, please!" she cried. "You know Omar. You know he has these ideas . . ."

Her voice trailed off.

And then suddenly Sami understood, or at least thought he did.

"His leg is injured too," whispered Tahira. "And there is bleeding."

Sami cursed under his breath then looked at the ceiling.

"Give me twenty minutes," he said quietly. He wanted to ask questions, but the government could be listening. Especially with the deputy minister inside the clinic.

After hanging up and standing dumbfounded for a moment, he gave the phone back to his receptionist.

"I need to leave," he said quietly.

They stared at each other without speaking.

"Please reschedule the rest of my evening appointments," he added. "On Wednesday we will remain open for an additional hour. More, if need be."

"What should I tell him?" She gestured with her chin to the office.

"Leave him to me."

———

"I suggest we schedule the operation for October," Sami said, addressing the deputy minister. "In the meantime, here is the name of a nutritionist I have used in the past, who may be able to help with the weight loss."

"Doctor, thirty kilos—"

"Is ideal," Sami said briskly as he transcribed the name, "but all I ask is that you do your best, okay? You lose as much as you can before the operation, the rest after."

He recited the bare minimum of information regarding what could be expected in terms of recovery after the operation, then handed the minister off to his nurse for blood work.

Once Sami heard the minister laughing with the nurse in the next room over, he opened a series of cupboards in his outpatient operating room and hastily filled a soft briefcase with supplies he thought he might need: bandages, scalpels, latex gloves, liquid bandages, a suture kit, a small bottle of Betadine antiseptic, a cautery pen, an assortment of syringes and needles, two flexible splints, and anesthetic drugs—fentanyl and ropivacaine.

Moments later he was racing out the back door of his clinic, his satchel bouncing on his hip with each long stride he took toward his Honda scooter.

———

The midday heat was stifling, and the city smelled of car exhaust and burnt dust. His forehead was covered in sweat before he even reached Saadallah al-Jabiri Square, where he observed a collection of young soldiers lounging around a canvas-topped Ural transport truck, AK-47s slung across their shoulders, some of them staring at traffic, others at their phones. They were just kids, he knew that. But they were kids with the power to search him, and if they were to do so, and question him about the contents of his satchel . . .

He was too tall for this kind of deception. He stood out, always had.

As he made his way from the wealthy neighborhood that surrounded the University of Aleppo and into the walled old city, the roads grew narrower. Upon reaching the periphery of the central covered market, he nosed his scooter down a narrow, stone-walled service alley, then parked and ducked through a low doorway.

Tahira was waiting for him. She wore stretch jeans, gold flip-flops, and a loose-fitting white blouse that accentuated her bosom. Her black hair was uncovered, her eyelashes long, and her face lined with worry. Gold bracelets jingled on her wrists. Florescent lights hung from an arched ceiling.

She grabbed his hand.

"Was he protesting?" demanded Sami as he allowed Tahira to lead him to one of the arched alcoves where a pallet of pastel-green soap, partially illuminated by an open skylight near the apex of the arch, lay drying.

"Of course."

Sami cursed.

"Aya came to me," pleaded Tahira. "What could I do?"

"Who knows he is here?"

"Only Aya. I think."

Sami was not reassured. What if, in the days to come, his sister-in-law, Aya, or her son, Omar, were to be arrested and questioned? Of course, neither would willingly confess that he had provided treatment, but when the interrogations turned violent—as they inevitably would—and loved ones were threatened, what then?

He recalled the medical student whose mutilated remains had been found in a burnt-out car, and the dermatologist who had been found dead on the side of the road with half his bones broken. Both had been accused of aiding protesters.

Aya was seated behind the pallet of soap, where the sweet smell of laurel-leaf oil was being fouled with the chemical, bleach-like smell of tear gas residue. Four years older than Tahira, she was a slight woman, with slender arms and high cheekbones. Her shoes were missing, revealing socks with holes in them. One ear was bleeding where an earring appeared to have been pulled off her lobe.

In front of her, on a tarp, lay her son. His nephew.

Sami dropped to his knees beside her. "Hello, Omar!" he said loudly, even though the boy's eyes were closed. "It is your Uncle Samir! I have come to help you."

He gently tugged on Omar's ear, and the boy's eyes briefly fluttered.

"How long has he been unconscious?" he asked as he leaned down, ear to his nephew's mouth. The boy was still breathing.

"Unconscious? No, he is not unconscious, I just told him to close his eyes and to save his strength for when you got here. Omar!" she called. "Your uncle is here. Tell him where it hurts."

Sami placed a hand on Aya's forearm.

"For now, leave him be."

"We were walking by the Rashid mosque," Aya said, crying. "And Omar saw the flags, he heard the chanting. I tried to stop him, but he ran from me, and then we were both . . . they beat him . . . I tried to stop them, but . . ."

She bit down on her bent index finger, unable to continue.

Sami assumed she was lying. The Rashid mosque was nowhere near her home. She had gone there to protest and had brought her son with her. Stupid.

He turned back to Omar. The boy was fourteen years old. Slight and short, like his mother. Gap-toothed. Too young to have more than a hint of facial hair. One of his bare arms indeed was misshapen—likely a break of the humerus, Sami guessed—and his right foot lay at an angle that suggested trauma. Blood had seeped through his jeans, but it was the runny nose that worried Sami.

He dipped his index finger into the clear fluid that was dripping out of Omar's nostrils then brought his finger to his tongue. The texture of the liquid was thin, the taste metallic and salty. Not mucus, he determined. Cerebrospinal fluid.

He took the boy's pulse. It was rapid and terribly weak. The brain fighting for oxygen.

"Can you fix his arm?" asked Aya.

"Yes."

She sighed, relieved.

Sami unbuttoned the boy's shirt and examined his chest and ribs; seeing no signs of trauma that would impede breathing, he turned to the head. Near the back was bruising, matted blood, and a sunken area of sponginess where the skull had fractured. He imagined the swing of a club, the club connecting with the skull, the pressure inside the skull rising, the cerebrospinal fluid breaching the dura mater.

But the arm was far more noticeable. That would have been what Aya's eyes had been drawn to. She didn't know. She didn't know what a mess this was.

Knowing the psychological pain he was about to inflict, Sami paused, then placed a hand on Aya's forearm and said, "Omar is showing signs of traumatic brain injury."

"*Auzubillah*," she said turning from him. I take refuge in God.

"Which means he should be put on a ventilator—immediately—because that will help him breathe, and his brain needs all the oxygen it can get. And we may need to relieve the pressure in his skull. You must bring him to the emergency room. I cannot treat him here. Not properly."

He examined Omar's eyes. There was no sign of blood seeping into the tissue beneath them, but it was too early for that.

"The emergency room?" asked Aya, incredulous.

"I know."

"But you know what they will do to him there! You have to fix him here!"

"You must tell them he was in a car accident."

"They will not believe it. They will know."

"But you at least have oxygen at your clinic, no?" asked Tahira. "You can give him that?"

"He needs more than oxygen, Tahira!"

He needed a lumbar drain to take pressure off his brain and steroids to decrease the swelling and a CAT scan to determine the nature of the injury—there was a scanner at the university hospital, but only one—and an intracranial pressure monitor, and—

"Do either of you have a car?" Sami demanded.

Tahira did. But it was parked outside the alleys of the old city. She said she could run to get it though, and she would park at the factory's narrow loading dock.

It would be faster than calling for an ambulance, Sami calculated, and less dangerous. If they were lucky, no one would see them moving Omar. He resolved to do what he could for the boy at his clinic. And hope that would be enough, and that no one would question Aya in the days to come.

"Go." said Sami. "Go!"

Tahira ran off.

"I need something we can lay him on," Sami told Aya. "A cot, or—"

He remembered the tall hand trucks that were used to move boxes of soap that had been packed for shipping. Though they were not long enough to accommodate an adult, Omar was short and lithe. Aya brought him one, and he lay it upside down on the ground. The lip at its base caused it to settle at an angle, which Sami thought would work well because it would be better for Omar's head to be raised.

"I will need you to help me move him," he told Aya. "We must do it carefully. Very carefully."

But at that point, Omar's body stiffened slightly, and his head, arms, and fingers began to tremble. His brown eyes cracked halfway open. Spittle drooled out of the corner of his mouth.

Aya cried out. She grasped her son's hand and asked what was happening.

Sami tried to stabilize the boy's head, to angle it slightly to the side in case he vomited. "Perhaps a small seizure."

"Is that okay?"

"It is . . . not uncommon," said Sami.

"Can you stop it?"

"No."

The trembling quickly became less pronounced, as though the boy were tiring. Sami noted that the cerebral spinal fluid draining out of his nephew's snub nose had increased to a small trickle. He took the boy's wrist again.

What had been a weak pulse was now nonexistent.

"Omar!" Sami said. "Omar!"

"What is it?" asked Aya.

Sami stuck his fingers in Omar's mouth and inspected his airway to make sure he hadn't choked on vomit.

"What is it?" Aya demanded again.

As he felt for a femoral pulse on Omar's upper thigh near the groin, Sami also bent his cheek to Omar's mouth, feeling for breath.

There was no pulse. No sign of respiration.

Kneeling over the boy, Sami placed the palm of his right hand in the center of Omar's chest and intertwined the fingers of his left hand with those of his right. He thrust down sharply and rapidly on Omar's chest, again and again. Omar's ribs cracked, but he kept going. After counting thirty compressions, he pinched Omar's nose and blew two lungfuls of air into the boy.

His nephew's lips were smooth, his cheeks bare save for a few barely visible wisps of downy blond hairs.

Aya grabbed her son's hand and brought it to her cheek, and she began to wail.

CHAPTER 2

The next day

Tucked away as it was at the end of an exceptionally narrow hall on the second floor of a shabby two-story, cash-only hotel, there was little to recommend the tiny room.

Its tile floor was cracked, its ceiling low, and even though an air conditioner mounted up near the ceiling was rumbling like a diesel truck and madly dripping water into a plastic bucket underneath it, the air was stale and hot.

Still, twenty-four-year-old American Hannah Johnson was relieved to be in it.

She flopped down, fully clothed, on the twin bed that took up half the room. Oskar Lång, her Swedish boyfriend, joined her. Because he was a tall man, his feet extended past the edge of the mattress. They were both sweating.

"It's not so bad," she said. By which she meant it wasn't so bad considering it was only a five-minute walk away from the auto repair shop where they'd left their car. "Don't you think?"

The bed sagged, and a spring was poking into her back, but she was encouraged by the clean smell of the sheets beneath her. And the one window afforded a magnificent view of the Citadel, a medieval hilltop fortress that loomed over central Aleppo.

"Could be worse," he allowed.

"You won't miss your flight. We'll hire a driver if we have to."

"I'm not worried."

"Yes, you are."

The early evening summer sun had dipped to a point in the sky so that it was streaming through a gap between the faded lace curtains and the window. They lay in the sun's glare for a minute, then Hannah sat up, rolled over, and straddled Oskar.

"We just have to roll with it," she said, gently poking him in the chest as he pretended to fight her off. "We're stuck here for the night whether we"—she snuck in another poke—"like it or not. Which means"—she bent down and he flinched, but instead of poking him she kissed his upper lip—"we may as well enjoy ourselves."

"You make a fair point," he said, and then he kissed her back.

Even though she suspected he was still thinking about the broken transmission on their car and the flight he had to catch tomorrow, she felt him stirring beneath her.

Then the chanting started. Voices in Arabic, not far away.

Get out, Bashar! Get out, Bashar!

Hannah exchanged a look with Oskar. He cursed; she climbed off him and approached the window.

From behind the dusty curtains, she watched as hundreds of protesters poured into a busy intersection just down the street. Some held the flag of Syrian independence. Others clutched signs in English and Arabic that read *Bashar the Butcher* and *Revolution Until Freedom*. Most of the protesters were young men, but Hannah's eyes fixed on three women wearing homemade dresses fashioned out of green, white, and red fabric. The word *freedom* had been scrawled in magic marker on headbands they wore over their hijabs and they were holding their arms high as they marched, flashing the V for victory sign and chanting with the crowd.

Hannah cracked the window so she could hear the protesters better. Oskar climbed out of bed.

"Don't even think it," he said as he wrapped his arms around her and pressed his rough stubble against her cheek.

Hannah scanned the crowd again, and this time noticed two women on the periphery. Both wore their hair uncovered. One was in tight jeans and heels. Another wore big, pink sunglasses more suggestive of an attempt at fashion than a disguise.

She guessed they were university students, around her age.

"I don't see any police," she said.

"Hannah."

"I know," she said.

Their supervisor at the Brussels-based development organization they worked for—Hannah as a community liaison officer, Oskar as a field engineer—had warned them against getting involved in political demonstrations.

"But still," she added.

Hannah had been working in Aleppo for nearly two years—at first living in the city, and then when the protests had started to heat up, commuting every other day from a satellite office in Turkey. In that time, she had grown to detest the regime and she knew Oskar had too.

Without waiting for him to try to stop her, she grabbed her sunglasses, slipped out the door to their room, and ran down a flight of tiled steps.

"Miss!" cried the receptionist as she left. "I would not go out there!"

"I'll just be a minute!"

The parade of people at the end of the street had swelled and come to a stop at an intersection where a bearded man with a megaphone had climbed on top of the roof of a car and was leading the crowd in a song-like call and response.

Get out, Bashar!

Get out, Bashar!

The blood of the martyrs isn't cheap. Pack your things and get out! Get out, Bashar!

Get out, Bashar!

You are nothing but a thief!

Hannah began to chant with the crowd, which was filling in so quickly behind her that soon she was no longer confined to the periphery, as she'd intended, but in the thick of it.

In front of her, a woman covered head to toe in black had affixed an oversized photo of a boy to a mop handle and was pumping it up and down. The name at the bottom of the photo read Omar Seif; someone who'd been killed by the regime, Hannah assumed. To her right, a man with Elvis-style sideburns held a banner that read *Down with the Little Dictator.*

The volume of the chanting rose as the crowd continued to swell. To her right a group of gangly teenage boys, still dressed in their school uniforms, shook their fists in the air.

The Syrian people will not be humiliated! Get out Bashar!

And yet every day there were new humiliations. Police barging into homes and businesses. Young men stopped on the street for no reason, and God help them if they had forgotten their state IDs—unless they had connections or money. Just last week, a Syrian friend of Hannah's had been jailed and beaten simply because she had dared to sign a petition demanding the regime hold local elections that were truly free.

"Get out, Bashar!" she yelled with the crowd. "Get out!"

When she felt a hand on her waist, she startled momentarily, but then she saw Oskar standing behind her, his shock of wavy brown hair rising far above the crowd. She smiled at him, and he smiled back.

"Get out, Bashar!" he yelled.

———

Minutes later, when the *pop-pop-pop* of automatic gunfire sounded from somewhere behind her, the chanting stopped, the screaming and cursing started, and the crowd surged forward. Hannah was shoved into the woman in front of her. To her left a girl's long hair got caught in the zipper of a man's jacket, and as the force of the crowd pulled the two apart, a clump of the girl's hair was ripped from her scalp.

"Oskar!" called Hannah. She tried to swivel her head to look for him but was being jostled on all sides and almost lost her balance when she stepped on someone who'd fallen.

The crowd swept her into the intersection where the man with the megaphone had been. The bodies thinned out. Not far away, she observed an open-walled, khaki-colored tent standing next to a small cemetery. A larger-than-life photograph of a smiling, gap-toothed boy named Omar Seif had been hung from the cemetery fence.

Hannah cursed.

Of all the protests, the ones centered around funerals for fallen protesters were the most dangerous because the Mukhabarat—the regime's secret
police—could anticipate when and where they'd take place.

And indeed, hordes of Mukhabarat were piling in, as though they'd
been lying in wait. They were clad in black and armed with batons and
AK-47s. Some wore helmets with visors. Over by the funeral tent, they
were smashing folding chairs, sending shattered fragments of plastic seats
skidding across the pavement. One pummeled a veiled woman over the
head with a baton.

Head down, Hannah sprinted away as tear gas canisters were fired,
enveloping her and everyone who was running with her in a white cloud.

She covered her mouth with her shirt and tried not to breathe in the
gas, but she was too panicked to hold her breath for long. Everything
burned—her eyes, her nose, even the skin on her face. Stumbling on the
curb, she fell to the pavement and scraped her hand and smashed her
sunglasses. Sparks flew off a nearby metal trash bin as bullets pinged off it.

Someone grabbed her elbow and hauled her up to her knees. She
thought it might be Oskar, but when she turned, she saw a young man
using a homemade flag of independence as a mask. He motioned her to
the edge of the cloud of tear gas.

"Run!" he cried.

She did. Down one block, and then another, until her lungs were
bursting, and she could go no more. Doubled over and moaning, she
rested her hands on her knees. Her eyes were blinking uncontrollably and
tearing so much she could barely see. Her nose felt as though someone had
stuffed hot coals up into her sinuses.

Someone thrust a piece of onion into her hand and told her to rub it
underneath her nose. She started to, but it did nothing for the pain, and
she threw it away when the smell began to make her sick.

Bleary-eyed, she half ran, half staggered away from the sound of
renewed gunfire, all the while calling out for Oskar. Fifteen minutes later
she'd finally managed to loop nearly all the way back to her hotel.

Crouched behind a silver, cat-infested dumpster, she eyed the street in front of the hotel. It appeared to be deserted, as did the intersection where she'd first joined the protest. Rusted steel roll doors had been yanked down over storefronts, as though it were the middle of night. The table outside the general store next to her hotel had been overturned, and loofah sponges and toilet plungers now littered the street. On the sidewalk, a watermelon vendor had abandoned his cart; melons lay smashed on the pavement. A butcher's refrigerated display case had been shattered, exposing the beef sides within to the hot air.

The smell of tear gas, acrid and bleachy, lingered.

Sporadic gunfire still sounded in the distance, but she saw no sign of the Mukhabarat or protesters. And the entrance to the hotel, which lay behind a waist-high wrought iron fence topped with spiked tips, appeared to be undisturbed.

She sprinted to it, but the door was locked.

"Let me in!" she cried, as she pounded on the door. There had been only one key, and Oskar had taken it when they'd checked in. "I'm a guest!"

Although her eyes were still blinking uncontrollably, she saw something move on the periphery of her vision. Glancing down the street, she observed a single Mukhabarat officer patrolling the intersection. He wore a helmet with a tinted visor; she couldn't tell whether he was looking at her or not.

She flattened herself against the door.

"Let me in!" she whispered as she rattled the handle.

When the door opened, she nearly fell to her knees, but Oskar caught her.

"One of them is out there!" she cried as she pushed past him.

Oskar slammed the door shut and locked it. Hannah leaned against the cracked stucco wall in the shabby reception room and began to cough uncontrollably. She felt Oskar's hand on her shoulder.

He was just as blinking and bleary-eyed as she was, and his tight black jeans were ripped, exposing his left shin.

The receptionist, a woman of perhaps sixty with painted nails and bright red lipstick, stared at them for a moment, then disappeared into a back room without saying anything. Moments later, she returned with a can of Coke.

"For the face," she whispered.

"For the face?" asked Oskar.

"It helps stop the pain of the gas."

———

Hannah's face still burned, and the stink of the tear gas on her clothes was making her throat convulse, so once in the room, she immediately stripped off her clothes and opened the cold-water valve in the shower all the way.

Oskar joined her moments later. Naked, they cracked open the cold can of Coke and poured it in each other's hands and scrubbed their faces with it. Whether it was the soda neutralizing the lingering effects of the tear gas, the cold water, or simply the passage of time, Hannah found she could breathe normally again. After holding her eyes open and rinsing them with water, the pain and blinking began to abate.

She leaned back into Oskar's chest, eyes closed, allowing the cool water to cascade over her face.

"That was crazy!" he cried, half laughing and half crying because of the lingering effects of the gas.

Hannah agreed, but also felt exhilarated by what they'd done. Get out, Bashar, she thought. *Get. Out.*

She turned to face Oskar and explained how the crowd had pushed her into the center of the intersection and of her run-in with the Mukhabarat officer at the car.

Oskar told of how he'd lost her in the crowd when the shooting started. "When I couldn't find you, I ran back here."

She clasped her hands around his waist, grateful that they were both safe and began to recall where they'd left off in bed before the protest had erupted.

Her thoughts were interrupted by the sound of knocking. Heavy, violent knocking that rattled the door. They both froze.

"Oh, God," whispered Hannah, thinking it couldn't possibly be the receptionist. "He must have seen me."

"Who?"

She explained about the Mukhabarat officer who'd been in the intersection while she was trying to get back inside the hotel.

Oskar's eyes widened. Then he cursed.

"We'll show him the work slip for the car, tell him we walked near the protest by mistake," Hannah whispered.

"If he sees your Syrian passport, he'll arrest you anyway."

Hannah was born and raised in New Jersey. But her father had been Syrian, and before coming to Aleppo she had applied for a Syrian passport so she wouldn't have to deal with constantly having to renew a work visa.

Both her US and Syrian passports were in her purse.

"I'll hide it," she said.

"Where? He'll search the room to make sure we don't have any anti-regime stuff. And if he finds it and realizes we tried to lie to him—" There was more pounding on the door. Oskar bolted out of the shower, grabbed his clothes from where he'd left them on top of the toilet, and silently gestured for Hannah to follow him.

She did, then called, "Who is it?" loud enough so that whoever was on the other side of the door could hear her.

"Open up!" said a male voice, followed by more pounding.

"A minute of privacy, please," said Hannah. "I must dress."

Oskar threw on his clothes in a matter of seconds, padded silently to the street-facing window, threw open the lace curtains, and quietly raised the sash. A blast of humid air hit Hannah as she struggled to step into her panties. As she was forcing her wet arms through her blouse sleeves, Oskar stuck his head out the window and looked left, then right.

"Street's empty," he whispered. "Grab your purse and come right after me, I'll catch you."

"I don't know about this . . ." Hannah whispered back.

"There's a reason everyone runs from these assholes. We'll just get a different hotel."

"Are you sure it's clear?"

Oskar took one more look out the window, flashed her the thumbs up, then awkwardly slipped one leg through the window followed by the other. For a moment, he lay with his belly half in the window, half out. Then he positioned his big hands on the sill, as though preparing to lower himself to the ground.

Instead of a controlled descent, however, he just fell. One second he was there, the next he was gone.

Another series of raps on the door sounded.

"Oskar!" Hannah cried.

She ran to the window.

The entire wooden sill had given way and lay on the concrete pavement. Oskar was a bit higher up, tangled up in the wrought iron fence and moaning. Protruding from a rip in his khaki slacks was what looked like a bloody bone.

"Oskar!" she cried again.

A key rattled in the door lock. Hannah turned from the window.

Paralyzed with indecision, she just stood there eyeing the door handle. Oskar weighed far more than she did. She couldn't move him by herself.

Better to throw herself on the mercy of the Mukhabarat, she decided, than to try to attempt the impossible.

"Hold on!" she called to Oskar, then she threw on her pants, hid her Syrian passport between the box spring and the mattress, unlatched the lock, and yanked the door open.

It took her a moment to process just how foolish she and Oskar had been to panic.

For standing in front of her was the owner of the hotel; the same man who'd shown them their room when they'd checked in. His thick, calloused hands gripped a can of Coke and an onion.

"For the gas," he said brusquely, but not unkindly, offering his gifts to her.

"I need your help," she said.

Hannah ran down to the street and out the door, with the owner trailing in her wake. Upon seeing Oskar still tangled up in the fence, the owner's eyes widened. "Ahh! Ahh!" he blurted as he dropped the onion.

Oskar was still moaning. Blood dripped down from his wounded thigh and was puddling on the pavement beneath him. Hannah noticed a smaller bloodstain near a rip in his light blue shirt.

"Help me get him down!" Hannah said. When the owner remained transfixed, she yelled, "Now!"

Hannah took Oskar's good leg and heaved up on it as the owner lifted Oskar's torso. Together, they slid him down to the sidewalk, at which point Oskar appeared to notice the extent of his leg injury for the first time and cried out in horror.

"Call an ambulance," said Hannah. As the owner pulled out his cell phone, she applied pressure around where the bone had broken through his thigh.

Doing so prompted Oskar to scream, but she didn't want to risk letting him bleed out on the sidewalk, so she kept up the pressure until the ambulance finally arrived.

CHAPTER 3

Two hours later

Sami was in a foul mood.

Upon learning that Aya was determined to advertise her son's funeral in a way that almost guaranteed it would be co-opted by protesters, he had tried to get his wife to intervene, or, at the very least, not to attend.

Did Aya not realize she was putting the whole family at risk? A private funeral for the family, yes, of course. But this? This spectacle?

Sami grieved for his nephew and was furious about what had happened, but he had children of his own to worry about. Surely they should not have to suffer because of what had happened to Omar.

By the time he began his final rounds at the hospital, he had learned that the funeral had gone ahead as planned and had indeed been marred by violence—but also that his wife was safe and Aya had not been arrested, at least not yet. Still, his nerves remained on edge.

It showed.

A woman named Mrs. Hadad, whose hip he had replaced and who was now recovering in a room packed with five other patients, wanted to know if Dr. Hasan could arrange for her to be given a hot bath. Because she very much thought that might alleviate some of the pain.

He most certainly could not, he informed her. Nor should she do so at home until the incision was fully healed. What Mrs. Hadad should do is follow the instructions she had already been given regarding her post-operative care. Had she read those instructions, as she had been told to?

"Of course, Doctor," she said, which Sami knew meant exactly the opposite.

He directed her to read them now, without delay.

Two rooms down, a Mr. Qureshi peppered him with questions unrelated to his fractured tibia. What was the best remedy for bunions? And could foot fungus spread to one's hand or mouth, because if it could, he was going to force his wife to sleep in another bed.

As Sami brusquely informed Mr. Qureshi that he was an orthopedic surgeon, not a Google search engine, he received a call from the emergency room: a twenty-six-year-old male suffering from a chest wound and compound femoral shaft fracture had just been admitted. Significant soft-tissue damage should be expected.

Sami cursed. Mr. Qureshi averted his eyes.

"Comminuted?" asked Sami into the phone, referring to the fracture.

"Not visibly," said the ER nurse. "But I have not seen the X-rays."

Sami exhaled. Over the course of the day, he had performed one planned hip replacement, one unplanned anterior cruciate ligament repair, administered five cortisone shots, and had conducted more evaluations than he could recall. All this on only a few hours of sleep. He was ready to go home.

"And his current condition?"

"Conscious. Vitals stable."

"The chest wound?"

"It's stable."

Sami hesitated. A femoral fracture in which the bone had pierced the skin needed to be handled by an orthopedic surgeon. At least, if the patient ever wanted to walk normally again. Which meant either he did it or they asked Dr. Issa, the orthopedic surgeon who was on call that evening, to come in early.

But Dr. Issa had covered for Sami on multiple occasions. And the sooner they began debriding and irrigating the open wound, the better.

"Do we have a room?" he asked.

"7B."

"I must wash, give me ten minutes."

———

The patient had already been anesthetized, intubated, and fitted on a radiolucent table so that his broken left leg was exposed, his left hip raised slightly, and his left arm drawn across his body to provide Sami unimpeded access to the injury. The skin around the wound had been shaved and sterilized. Leaded blue blankets covered his genitalia and torso. His large head was shrouded behind a leaded screen where the anesthesiologist had set up a monitoring station.

The patient was ready for surgery.

But Sami, upon entering the operating room and reading that the patient was a Swede, decided he wasn't ready.

"He smells of tear gas," Sami informed the nurse. The smell was faint but undeniable when one got close; it lingered in the hair. Gesturing to the patient's upper thigh, Sami added, "And this did not happen tripping on a sidewalk."

He wondered whether it had happened at Omar's funeral. The timing would have been right.

The nurse explained that the Mukhabarat had already cleared the patient.

"No one cleared it with me," said Sami, prompting the nurse to crack open the operating door and call to another nurse. Minutes later, a uniformed Mukhabarat officer appeared, but advanced no further than the doorway.

"*Ya Rab!*" he exclaimed upon observing the patient. And then, referring to the holiday when lambs were slaughtered, "Is it Eid al Adha?"

He laughed.

"You told him?" Sami asked the nurse.

"Yes, yes, we know." The officer raised a surgical mask to his mouth, coughed violently, glanced at the patient's leg again, grimaced, then said, "He was staying in a hotel near one of the protests, but he is not one of them. Swedish engineer, this one. Involved with building that park by the Qinnasrin Gate—he and his American girlfriend. It has all been investigated." After another coughing fit, he said, "These foreigners, they panic. He heard the noise from the protest and got scared, that is all."

"So, the operation is approved?"

"Of course."

Sami frowned, as though he disapproved, but it was an act. He had known the Mukhabarat would not want to provoke the Europeans by withholding treatment from a Swedish citizen, even one who had attended a protest. But the assistance he had rendered to Omar, paired with the possibility that his sister-in-law, Aya, could be broken under interrogation were she to be arrested, meant that the opportunity to make a harmless show of loyalty to the regime was not one he could pass up.

"He does not look well, Doctor," said the Mukhabarat officer. "I suggest you begin."

———

On a stainless-steel table next to the operating table, the nurse assembled an array of instruments: scalpels, scissors, retractors, forceps, pins, brackets, long bars, short bars, wrenches, screws, a drill handle . . .

Sami donned his leaded gloves, collar, apron, and glasses. His focus narrowed; his worries receded.

After reviewing a CT scan of the Swede's pelvis and confirming there was no femoral neck fracture and inspecting the chest wound to confirm it had been bandaged properly and could be safely addressed later, he began cleaning and irrigating, cutting away damaged tissue, and cauterizing blood vessels.

Once he was done with that, he and the nurse pushed and pulled on the Swede's thigh until the bone had slipped back inside the leg and was at least close to the position in which it should be. More cleaning followed, then Sami cut holes through the soft thigh tissue and, using guide brackets, screwed large pins into the femur. The pins he attached to clamps, which he in turn attached to a guide bar.

As Sami fiddled with his external fixation device, his eyes darted from his hands to the fluoroscope monitor, allowing him to see the changing position of the bone. He yanked on the Swede's thigh then whacked it with a rubber mallet. The swollen flesh wobbled.

"Pull," he said to the nurse, and as she strained to do so, he tightened one of the several clamps on the guide bar. After checking the monitor, he said. "Pull harder!"

CHAPTER 4

Forty-two-year-old Mukhabarat officer Rahim Suleiman trudged slowly up the steps that led to his third-floor condominium, holding his black helmet in one hand and resting the other on the grip of his holstered Makarov pistol. He had twisted his knee while kicking over a chair at the funeral protest, so he took a moment to rest on the second-floor landing, outside his brother's open door.

His double-chinned mother was seated in the living room, fanning herself with a newspaper while watching his brother's two young sons wrestle on the floor. "You are late. Ahmed already left," she said, referring to his brother.

"I told him I would help him tomorrow."

"He needed help today."

Rahim waved her complaint away with his hand—Ahmed's water heater had been dripping for a month, the world would not end if it dripped for another day—and continued up the stairs.

Upon entering his home and removing his shoes, he observed his wife standing in front of the kitchen stove, wearing a baggy, black, sleeveless blouse and looking squatter than usual as she stirred a pot of what smelled to Rahim like the lamb meatballs she used in her *labanieh* soup.

"May food such as this always be abundant," he declared as he waved the scent to his nose, adding "*Mashallah*." God has willed it.

She ignored the compliment, and when he attempted to kiss her, turned her cheek.

THE DOCTOR OF ALEPPO

Shrugging, he opened the refrigerator, pulled out a bottle of Cola Turka, drank a sip, and settled into a chair at the kitchen table.

"Why do you act like this?" he demanded after a minute of silence had passed between them.

She gestured with her chin to the living room. "I suggest," she said as she stirred the pot violently enough so that it rattled on the stove, "you ask Adel."

Too tired to argue, Rahim heaved himself up and padded to the living room, where his fifteen-year-old son, Adel, and his thirteen-year-old daughter, Zahra, were seated in the center of a couch that was sagging even more than usual. He should have paid for real wood instead of letting himself get talked into a pressboard frame, Rahim thought as he eyed the couch.

Adel wore an orange T-shirt that was too small for him and exposed his spindly arms. The hijab headscarf Zahra had worn to school had fallen to the floor by her feet. They were both staring at a small laptop, playing The Sims 3 video game.

Rahim told Zahra to pick up her hijab or wash it herself—was her mother a servant?—then turned to his son.

"Why is your mother upset?" His intention was to sound threating enough so that his wife would appreciate that he was taking the situation seriously, but he was too tired to really pull it off.

Adel briefly made eye contact with his father.

"We will talk outside," Rahim called to his wife.

"He is not to smoke!" she said as they were leaving.

———

They sat side by side at the base of the concrete steps behind the building, looking out over a weed-strewn garden. Rahim tapped out a Marlboro cigarette for himself then offered one to his son.

Adel took it and leaned in as his father flicked his lighter.

"She is angry about my math scores," offered Adel eventually.

Rahim rested his forearms on his knees. "How bad?"

"Seventy-four percent average."

"But that is not bad at all!"

"Yes, it is, Baba. I need ninety percent to qualify."

Adel had been taking a summer course in algebra in hopes of being accepted into a government school for exceptional students.

"Then you should study harder."

"I will."

They smoked in silence for a time.

"And the photos?" asked Rahim quietly, as he looked past the steps to the weedy garden.

Adel took a drag off his cigarette, then pulled his cell phone out of his back pocket and showed it to his father. The screen was shattered. "Sorry," he said.

It was hard for Rahim to hide his disappointment. Posing as a protester, Adel was supposed to have photographed real protesters gathering for a funeral in a neighboring district. Rahim had promised to bring those photographs to his commanding officer in Military Intelligence.

But he was also concerned.

"I told you to leave before the march started," Rahim said.

Rahim had been clear on that point. Adel was not to be anywhere near the protest once it actually got underway.

"Yes, but after it was disrupted, everyone ran. I was bumped, but I should have been watching. It was my fault."

Rahim draped an arm over Adel's shoulders. "It is of no matter. You were brave to try."

"I will do better next time," said Adel. "When is the next protest?"

Rahim studied his hands and sighed. "It will take place at the Bilal Mosque, after sunset prayers. Freedom Torches," he said, referring to a local group of protesters, "has planned it."

"How do you know this?"

Upon observing the look of adulation in his son's eyes, Rahim raised his eyebrows, then pulled Adel close. "An informer of course," he whispered.

"You have infiltrated Freedom Torches?" asked Adel, sounding incredulous.

"What, you think your father simply sits behind a desk all day?" said Rahim with pride, giving his son an affectionate squeeze. "Of course I have an informer. So yes, go to the mosque. Use your sister's phone but protect it! Photograph what you can without endangering yourself. But you must find a reason to leave before the service ends. On this point there can be no compromise. We will not wait long before attacking. You understand?"

"I understand."

Rahim and Adel smoked their cigarettes in silence. When Rahim ashed his butt on the concrete steps, Adel stood. "I am going to the store. Mother needs mint."

"Do not be long. She will want to see you studying your maths tonight."

———

Rahim had intended to walk back up to the third floor but then thought better of it and tapped out another cigarette.

As he smoked, he massaged his knee and absentmindedly regarded the overgrown garden that extended out from the base of the steps. The widow who owned the first-floor condominium—and with it the garden—barely ventured outside anymore. Her late husband's garden tools were rusting next to an unsightly white bucket, the lemon tree had not been pruned this year, the lentil beds had not been weeded. Rahim felt sympathy for her plight of course, but he had offered to help her, and she had refused his assistance.

His feeling now was that if she was not going to use the garden, she might as well sell it to him.

Next month he would make her an offer, he resolved. Perhaps his brother could be persuaded to go in with him.

Rahim's thoughts were interrupted when, just outside the garden, he heard the squeal of car tires, an engine revving, and—seconds later—a crash. Upon limping out to investigate, he observed a red Toyota pickup truck down the street, backing away from a dented garbage bin.

The truck's tires were smoking as they spun on the pavement.

Rahim drew his pistol. Then he saw a figure next to the garbage bin struggle to pick himself off the street. It was a skinny kid with jet-black hair and an orange T-shirt, and he could barely stand.

"Adel!" called Rahim. "Adel, get back!"

But his son seemed frozen in place. The truck came to a sudden stop then roared forward as the driver threw the engine into gear.

Rahim's hand jerked up with each shot as he emptied the five rounds still left in the magazine of his Makarov. The back window of the truck shattered.

Adel had always had fast reflexes, and Rahim could tell that his son tried to jump at just the right moment so that he would roll over the car. And indeed, instead of being hit square in the chest, the hood of the pickup truck only hit Adel on the right side of his hip. But it was enough to send him spinning over the hood, arms flailing, head flopping.

He landed in the center of the street, head facing the sky.

As Rahim charged, forgetting the pain in his knee, someone from inside the truck shot at him. Rahim kept his eyes focused on his son. Adel's mouth was wide open, as though he were struggling to breathe.

The truck skidded to a stop then backed up. One of its wheels rolled over Adel's legs, the other narrowly missed his head. Then it shot forward.

Rahim tried to grab the tailgate but was too slow. He wailed as he dropped to his knees beside his son, watching the truck disappear. Around him, people were shouting.

For a moment Rahim just looked up at the sky, praying to God, unwilling to face the reality of what had just happened.

And then he heard his son's voice. It was barely a whisper.

"Baba, I am hurt."

Rahim turned and saw that the lower half of Adel's body was horribly twisted. A thin trickle of blood dripped from his mouth. Rahim forced himself not to react to what he saw and instead, simply said, "Yes, you are hurt. But I am here, and I am going to get help, and everything will be all right."

CHAPTER 5

Sami cut an incision in the Swede's hip, just above the femur.

As the nurse pulled it open with retractors, he used a scalpel and scissors to cut through the soft tissue beneath the skin.

Upon exposing the top of the femur, he touched the bone with his finger as he eyed the fluoroscope monitor.

"There," said the nurse.

"Quiet," said Sami.

When he was sure he had found the right spot—a process made easier because the Swede was thin, what a nightmare it would be to perform this surgery on that fat Damascene!—he inserted a guide wire into the incision and tapped it into precisely the right place on the top of the femur.

"Drill with the 15.5 bit," he said.

The nurse placed the tool in his hand as he finished speaking.

He drilled open the top of the femur, reamed out the inside of the canal that ran the length of the bone, then hammered an intramedullary nail—an extra-long one, because the Swede was so tall—down the center of the bone. After checking that the nail was positioned correctly, he screwed it into place by cutting and drilling more holes through the Swede's thigh, leaning into him at times to get a good purchase on the screws. Finally, several hours after starting the operation, he used a ratchet wrench to affix a cap to the hole he had drilled in the top of the Swede's femur, and then he stitched everything up.

Post-surgery, as he was standing in front of a utility sink, stripping off his leaded surgical gloves, one of the emergency room nurses tracked him down and told him they had yet another patient who required an orthopedic surgeon.

"Then you need to page Dr. Issa," snapped Sami. He was hungry, had already missed his children's bedtime routine, and had gone back to brooding about Omar and Aya and that whole mess. He was done.

"Dr. Issa is already here. He needs your help."

The nurse explained the nature of the new patient's injuries.

Sami sighed, thinking he would be lucky to be able to leave the hospital by dawn.

"Tell Dr. Issa I will join him shortly."

CHAPTER 6

Hannah spent the night on a cushionless chair in one of the waiting rooms, shifting in her seat every few minutes, barely sleeping.

By the time she was permitted to see Oskar, it was seven in the morning the next day. She practically ran to his room.

The hospital bed he lay on looked as though it might qualify as an antique, but it had been fitted with clean blue sheets, and his broken right leg had been braced, elevated, and secured in a way that suggested a degree of competency on the part of the hospital staff.

"Oh, Oskar. I'm so glad you're—"

She put her hand to her throat, unable to finish her sentence.

Gauze covered the puncture wound to his chest. Behind his head a tangle of electric cords was plugged into a wall-mounted receptacle strip. An IV drip led down to his arm, and a pulse-oxygen monitor had been taped to his right index finger—the real-time results of which were being displayed on an old computer that was mounted on a stand to the left of his bed.

His eyelids looked heavy; for a moment, he appeared not to recognize her. Then a lopsided smile appeared.

"Hey," he said.

Hannah exhaled. "When I saw you down there, outside the window, I thought you were . . . you know." She swallowed hard and fought back tears. She'd never considered herself to be squeamish, but she couldn't shake the image of that bone sticking out of his leg.

She dropped the two small, soft suitcases she was carrying—his and hers—and approached the bed. His big left foot stuck out over the edge, not covered by the sheet. She gave it a squeeze, then moved to the front of the bed and lightly kissed his forehead. A sour collection of chemical odors masked his natural Oskar smell.

He opened his mouth as if he were going to speak then winced in pain. Moments later, his voice raspy and dry, he asked in English, "Where am I?"

"Aleppo University Hospital."

He glanced around the cramped room, as though seeing it for the first time.

It had been outfitted with two beds, one of which was empty. The only windows were up near the ceiling, and they were covered with an opaque privacy film that made them look dirty. A tiny bathroom with a cracked tile floor opened off the main room.

Oskar sighed.

"I think you're getting the favored guest treatment," Hannah said, recalling that some of the other recovery rooms she had passed had been packed with five or six patients and had no privacy curtains. Then she explained what had happened after he'd fallen out the window.

"God, I'm a moron," he said.

"You didn't know."

"You're okay, though?"

"I'm fine." Hannah said, and looked at her hands. "You were a good diversion," she whispered. "They never searched the room or me."

Oskar attempted a smile then grimaced. "Thank you. For everything. If it wasn't for you, I might still be on that fence."

"If it wasn't for me, you never would have fallen. I should have stayed inside the hotel."

"You have nothing to be sorry for, Hannah."

But she did. And not just because she'd lured him down to the protest. For nearly two years, she and Oskar and a half dozen of their coworkers at the European Development Service had been partnering with the Syrian government to develop a park in downtown Aleppo. If it had been up to Oskar, instead of moving EDS's Aleppo office to Turkey when the protests in the south of Syria had really taken off, they would have applied for a transfer to somewhere else in the world. He'd stayed because of her. Because she'd been so dead set on keeping the park project in Aleppo on life support.

Glancing at his leg, Oskar asked, "Do you know what they did to it?"

"Repaired the break, I think. But no one's talking to me. It took me forever just to get someone to figure out what room you were in. It's as bad as dealing with the permitting office." She grasped his hand. "I've called Greta," she added, referring to their boss back in Turkey. "And I texted your brother, so your family knows you won't be flying to Paris tonight. If you can tell me where your flight information is, I can see about getting you a refund."

"Screw the refund, I'll just shift the dates."

"Oskar . . ." Hannah gestured to his leg.

"Did they say when could I fly?"

"No."

"I only put in for two weeks' vacation."

"You don't have to worry about that."

"Well, I do worry."

"Even if the protests settle down, you can't commute from Turkey with a broken leg, and it's not like we can get another field engineer to step in at this point, which means there is no project." She hesitated, then added, "Greta officially killed it last night."

"No," said Oskar, incredulous.

"She had to. I don't blame her."

In fact, the decision made her sick. As a community liaison officer, she'd been the one to spread the news in the neighborhood that a park would be built, that construction workers and surveyors and engineers would be paid, that money would flow to the community and neighboring schools.

People had rearranged their lives and invested money they couldn't afford to lose, because they'd believed in her.

"I'm sorry, Hannah."

Oskar sighed—whether out of relief or frustration, Hannah couldn't tell. Then he winced as he tried to lift his head off the pillow. "Do we know what all this stuff is for?" he asked, gesturing to the equipment next to his bed, and the tubes going into his body.

Hannah examined the IV bag that hung from a stand next to his bed. A sticker on the bag had Oskar's name on it, and the name of a medicine—cefazolin—that she didn't recognize; the writing on the bag itself was in Cyrillic instead of Arabic. "I don't know," she said. But it occurred to her that, if she really wanted to help him, she should know.

What Oskar needed, she determined, was someone to look out for him. Someone to make sure he was getting the right treatment. To translate the Cyrillic, to figure out what cefazolin was and why it was going into his blood.

You couldn't just rely on the doctors nowadays, you had to take matters into your own hands.

Hannah picked up Oskar's satchel and pulled out his laptop.

"I left my computer in Antakya," she said, referring to the border city in Turkey where they shared an apartment, "so I'll need to borrow yours. What's your password?"

CHAPTER 7

Sami arrived back at the hospital at eight, having showered, shaved, and slept for three hours. He entered through the emergency room entrance instead of the main entrance—it was faster that way—and took the stairs to the second floor because the line for the two small staff elevators was too long. Although breakfast in the cafeteria was served from eight to eight thirty, he was too pressed for time to take it. The first patient he checked on was Adel Suleiman, the fifteen-year-old he and Dr. Issa had operated on the night before.

The boy had suffered femoral shaft and intracapsular hip fractures on both legs, a broken tibia on his left leg, a shattered right ilium, six broken ribs, and a concussion. He was still on a ventilator in the intensive care unit and in for what at best would be a long, painful recovery. But Sami confirmed that the boy was alive and likely to stay that way.

From the ICU, he navigated through a labyrinth of hallways in need of a new paint job to the room where the Swede was recovering. Upon knocking and entering without waiting for a response, he saw that the patient, who was sleeping, was accompanied by a woman. Her head was down, and she appeared to be concentrating intently as she tapped away on a laptop.

The Swede's chart was affixed to a clipboard that hung at the end of the bed. Sami picked it up.

"Oh, hi!" said the woman brightly—too brightly, thought Sami. She stood. "I'm Hannah! Hannah Johnson. Are you the doctor who operated on Oskar?"

"Has he urinated yet?" asked Sami, as he examined the chart. They spoke in Arabic, although it was immediately clear to him that Arabic wasn't her first language.

"Ah . . . not that I know of." Hannah pulled back her hand. "Is that a problem?"

Sami picked up the plastic urinal that lay on a shelf underneath the bed and inspected it. Dry.

"It is not unusual for someone in his condition, especially given the effect of the morphine. When he does attempt to urinate or defecate in the toilet, the act of getting up will be painful. As will attempting to sit on the toilet. A nurse must help him. Will you be here often?"

"Yes. Yes—absolutely!"

"Watch how the nurses help him so that if you need to, you can as well."

Sami pulled up a chair and sat down next to Oskar. Hannah remained standing on the opposite side of the bed.

"He has been given morphine?" she asked.

"Yes."

"Is that going to be addictive? I read, you know, that . . ."

Sami stared at her as she fumbled for the right words. At first, it was a stare of thinly veiled disdain designed to convey that his time and patience were limited, but he also noticed that the woman, however annoying, was also was distractingly attractive—large wide-set eyes with long natural lashes; shiny, straight, black hair tucked behind small ears. Bright teeth, wide lips, prominent forehead. Much shorter than he was, but so was his wife for that matter.

"You have read what?" he demanded.

"That it can sometimes be . . . a problem?"

"We will be tapering him off of it soon and transitioning to oral pain-killers," said Sami, then he turned his attention back to Oskar. Placing one hand underneath Oskar's thigh and another on his ankle, he gently bent the leg at the knee.

Oskar's eyes opened wide. He cursed in Swedish.

"Good morning, Mr. Lång," said Sami loudly, as though speaking to a half-deaf grandparent. "This might hurt a bit."

Oskar gritted his teeth and cursed again.

"When will he be getting a cast?" asked Hannah.

"Never."

"Won't he need one?"

"No."

"I'm sorry, and who are you?" Hannah asked.

"Dr. Hasan."

"Oh. Why won't he need a cast?"

"Because I inserted a metal rod through his femur. It holds the bones in place, obviating the need for a cast."

He released Oskar's leg.

Oskar unclenched his teeth and exhaled.

"How are you feeling, Mr. Lång?"

Oskar, in between hyperventilating, managed to say with something approximating a polite tone, "In a bit of pain, actually."

"Unfortunately, that is to be expected. And, in fact, you can expect much more of it. Every day you will work on the flexibility. The nurses will teach you. I have given them instructions. You are experiencing light-headedness?"

"Some."

Sami checked the chart again then felt Oskar's hand. It was on the cold side. "Your hemoglobin count was low this morning. I will order a transfusion. One of the nurses should be by to administer it." To Hannah, he said, "Make sure he eats and drinks plenty of fluids today. In the meantime, deep breathing and coughing is advisable. It helps prevent pneumonia. In two, three days, maybe we will try walking with crutches."

Sami stood up, withdrew a pen from the front pocket of his white coat, and noted the need for a transfusion on Oskar's chart.

"Crutches?" asked Hannah. "With a broken leg?"

"As I have already informed you, the fracture has been repaired. The rod I inserted will prevent the bone from moving. He will be unable to walk normally for many months, but some movement early on is important."

"What I would really like to know," said Hannah, "is whether he has been receiving the proper antibiotics. I read about different treatment plans in the United States, and—"

"You are American?"

"Yes."

Sami nodded. That explained it. "I see. And given your expertise with these treatment plans, as you call them, could you please inform me what antibiotics you think he should be receiving?"

"Well, I am not sure, but I have been trying to make out the Cyrillic writing on the"—at a loss for words, she gestured to the IV bag— "on that."

Sami read the list of medications that were being administered.

"And is that . . . ahh . . ."

"Is that what?"

"Appropriate?"

"Yes."

"You do know his bone was exposed? All I am saying is that I think we need to be worried about infection."

As she spoke, it occurred to Sami as strange that, even though the words coming out of her mouth were inane, and he was happily married and had already passed along his genes to two beautiful children, that something so simple as a pretty face could affect him this way—the same way a bright flower might attract a bee.

"And that," said Sami, "is why he is receiving the antibiotic I have prescribed him. And why I spent all the time I did last night irrigating and debriding the wound. And why I intend to monitor it in the days to come for infection."

"Oh. Thank you."

Sami turned to leave.

"Wait, I mean, Doctor, please—"

Sami stopped but didn't fully face her.

"When do you think he can leave? Or at least be transported to Turkey?"

"One week."

"A week!" cried Oskar, in English. "I can't stay here a week."

"That is my recommendation," responded Sami, in passable English. "But this is not a prison, Mr. Lång. If you choose to make other arrangements and accept the consequences, that is your business."

CHAPTER 8

Over the course of the day, the bruises on Oskar's leg darkened, and the swelling increased. Blood seeped out from the sutures. Hannah called for a nurse, who assured her it was fine.

When the transfusion was delayed, Hannah complained. Politely at first, then less so. When she tried to find Dr. Hasan, she was told he was at his clinic. After the transfusion was finally administered at eight that evening, Oskar perked up, but his increase in energy was paired with an increase in pain, and for the rest of the night he was moaning and gripping the metal rails of his bed.

That night Hannah slept in the empty bed that lay on the other side of the room. Instead of a sheet, she used a towel from the bathroom.

At six in the morning, she was awakened by a team of three nurses—all women. They wheeled her bed out of the room and a new bed in.

On it lay a patient who appeared to be unconscious. Oxygen tubes led to his nose. IV lines and wires sprouted from his arms and torso. His head had been shaved and bandaged. One of his legs had been placed in a cast from the knee down, and both legs had been fitted with black braces.

Hannah took a seat on the folding chair next to Oskar's bed. She couldn't see the new patient directly because the nurses had pulled a privacy curtain between the beds, but a mirrorlike chrome paper towel dispenser hanging above a common sink afforded her a distorted view of the man's face.

Only as she studied him, she realized he wasn't so much a man as a boy. Smooth cheeks, curly, jet-black hair, thin arms.

Poor kid, she thought.

———

Unable to see more than hints of daylight through the opaque, ceiling-level windows, the passage of time failed to exert its usual influence on Hannah. The fluorescent lights looked the same at noon as they had at six in the morning. The hospital was air conditioned but still hot.

Oskar grew irritable. His body itched. He spent a lot of time on his phone, texting with his family back in Sweden, trying to sort out the logistics of when and how he'd get back home.

Hannah took a walk outside, just so she could see the sun, and returned to the hospital in far better spirits—only to find Oskar being helped to the toilet.

A powerfully built bald man in black slacks and a gray blazer held him under one shoulder, a pear-shaped middle-aged nurse under the other.

"Go!" Oskar shouted when he saw her, his face contorted with pain.

"Let me help."

"I don't want your help!" He grimaced and hopped on his good leg as the man in the blazer opened the bathroom door. "Not with this. Please, Hannah. Give me some space."

She wanted to tell him it didn't matter. She wanted to say she didn't think less of him just because he was human and needed to shit.

She just wanted to help him.

"Go!" he cried.

———

When Hannah returned half an hour later, the man in the blazer who'd helped Oskar to the toilet had been joined in the room by his wife, daughter, mother, brother, and six children of varying ages and sizes. They were all talking over each other.

"Do not touch him!" a man shouted.

"It was only his hand! Surely a mother can touch her son's hand!"

"He is so pale. Why will he not he wake?"

Hannah felt like an intruder, the way she was eavesdropping on them from the other side of the privacy curtain. Oskar seemed not to even hear them as he tried to eat a bit of thin leek-and-chicken stew.

That afternoon, the family left but Rahim—as Hannah had learned the man in the blazer was named—stayed. By watching his distorted reflection in the towel dispenser, she saw him remove his shoes, wash his face, arms, and the tops of his bare feet in the bathroom sink, then roll out a red prayer mat. First standing with his arms at his sides, then alternately bowing, kneeling, and raising his arms, he prayed. By the end, he was breathing heavily, his forehead glistening with a thin film of sweat.

He struck Hannah as a kindhearted man, clearly devoted to his son, whom she gathered had been in some sort of traffic accident.

The folding chair on the other side of the curtain creaked when Rahim plopped his heavy frame down on it.

She glanced at Oskar and saw that he'd fallen asleep, so she stood and ducked her head around the curtain. Rahim was rubbing his knee.

"I wanted to thank you," she whispered in Arabic. "For what you did earlier. To help my friend."

He glanced up at her, then quickly averted his gaze, stood, placed a hand over his heart, and said, "You are most welcome."

"And I am so sorry about your son," she added. "I do hope his recovery goes well."

Keeping his hand over his heart and performing a little bow with his head, he said, "*Inshallah*. And for your loved one as well."

Hannah wanted to ask him about his son, and whether he was satisfied with the treatment he was receiving at the hospital, but she sensed he was a traditional-minded man who would be uncomfortable talking to a woman for very long—especially one who wore her hair uncovered as she did.

So she simply thanked him and turned back to her side of the room.

But Rahim stopped her. "Wait," he said, and then he grabbed a box from a bag on the floor and said, "Please, my wife, she brings these pistachio *karabij* for my son. They are his favorite biscuits, but he cannot eat them."

"Then you must, of course," Hannah said.

"Oh, for me there are far too many. My wife, she brings so much."

Rahim continued to hold the box out with two hands. "Please," he said.

Hannah took it, because she didn't know how not to without giving offense. "You are most kind," she said.

CHAPTER 9

They came from everywhere and nowhere. From mosques and apartment houses, from the cars and buses that spilled off the M5 highway, from the backs of spice shops and cafés. They didn't form so much as swarm.

They wore jeans, dress slacks, camouflage pants, and cargo pants. Oxford shirts, camouflaged combat vests, T-shirts, hoodie sweatshirts, black headbands, baseball caps, and red kaffiyeh headdresses.

Some wrapped scarves around their mouths to hide their faces. Others wore aviator sunglasses. A few were too proud or reckless to disguise themselves.

Everyone carried a rifle. Russian-made AK-47s. Chinese, Yugoslav, or Romanian AK-47 knockoffs. A few next-generation AKMs and AK-74s. Some of the rifles had steel folding stocks, some wood stocks, some no stocks.

A few men waved the flag of Syrian independence, but they hadn't come to protest and be shot at in the streets. They'd come to fight.

Because he served in the Shu'bat al-Mukhabarat al-'Askariyya, the military intelligence division of the regime's secret police, Rahim Suleiman got the warning before anyone else at the hospital. It came in the form a call from his commanding officer.

There was trouble brewing in the Salaheddine district.

"How much trouble?" he asked, still standing at his son's bedside.

No one knew for sure. But it was bad. Come straight to headquarters. It was not a request. To refuse would be to refuse an order. Men had been shot for less.

Rahim called his wife as he retrieved his ten-year-old, Iranian-made Samand sedan from the hospital parking garage. Believing the attack on her son was somehow tied to his profession, she hung up on him before he could finish explaining that he was being given a chance to avenge what had happened to Adel. But he knew she would hurry to the hospital, so at least their son would not spend the night alone.

———

The headquarters of the Aleppo division of the Military Intelligence Directorate lay just east of the Aleppo University Hospital, behind high walls topped with silver concertina wire. The building itself was a dun-colored monolith, five stories at its highest, unremarkable save for the entrance which was flanked by an enormous Syrian flag on one side and an equally large flag imprinted with a photograph of the Syrian president Bashar al-Assad on the other.

The photo of Bashar looked out onto a traffic circle, in the center of which loomed a statue of Bassel Assad, Bashar's late brother, riding a leaping horse into battle. As Rahim sped around the circle, the Assad brothers staring down at him, he saw that BTR armored personnel carriers and 6 X 6 armored Ural troop transport vehicles had taken positions outside the walls of the headquarters building. Regular army troops, dressed in camouflage uniforms and looking top-heavy because of all the magazine pouches strapped to their chests, were assembling. In the parkland that lay between the traffic circle and headquarters, a T-55 tank had left a path of crushed shrubbery in its wake and was now belching out black clouds of diesel smoke as it aimed its big gun down Abu Al Shuhada Street.

Rahim eased his Samand into the gatehouse checkpoint funnel and manually rolled down his driver's-side window to flash his ID. Not far south of the headquarters, shooting and explosions sounded. Past the gatehouse, scores of military intelligence soldiers, all dressed in black riot gear and armed with assault rifles, were piling into civilian cars, packing them absurdly tight like clowns at a circus.

Rahim double-parked at a rear lot. As he jogged to the entrance, he was intercepted by Major Akhras, a short man, ten years his junior, but far more influential because he was distantly related to President Assad's wife.

"You will be outfitted in full combat gear and ready for transport within five minutes," the major ordered.

"The protesters, they are rioting?" asked Rahim.

"These men are not protesters."

Rahim's eyes widened. "Free Syrian Army?"

"They are not an army, Lieutenant. They are criminals, and that is how we will treat them."

The major began walking toward the headquarters building, and Rahim jogged a few steps to catch up.

"Reinforcements are coming," the major added, "but for tonight, we must hold them back ourselves." In case his point wasn't clear, he added, "The rebels are within a kilometer of this building. They already control Salaheddine and they are moving into Sakhour. I also hear reports of skirmishes at the border crossings. Five minutes, Lieutenant. Be ready!"

The hairs on the back of Rahim's neck tingled. The rebel Free Syrian Army was no disorganized criminal gang. Comprised of thousands of defectors from the regular Syrian Army, and backed by Islamist groups, they had already taken over large swaths of land on the border with Lebanon and Turkey, and there was open fighting in Damascus and Homs. But Aleppo was the largest city in Syria, the economic capital of the country. Textiles! Pharmaceuticals! Food for the whole nation was processed here. If the Free Syrian Army was able to take Aleppo in a surprise attack, they might very well win the war.

"And my squad?"

Rahim had six men under his command. But they were not real soldiers. They were the eyes, not the fists, of Assad; the men who secretly patrolled the stores of the souk and infiltrated the student groups and yes, put down the protests, but none had ever been in a real battle.

"They are already here."

———

Rahim and his men received their orders: hold a narrow residential street not far from the epicenter of the fighting. But nobody really knew where the epicenter was. There was no front line. The rebels were like ghosts, appearing for a moment and then disappearing just as quickly, as though they had never been there.

To get into position, his squad pushed through a countercurrent of mothers clutching the hands of crying toddlers in one hand and rolling suitcases in the other, of fathers carrying tube television sets and computers. Once there, Rahim didn't even know which way to tell his men to face.

Windows behind them rattled, rocket-propelled grenade explosions echoed off steel roll doors in front of them. Puffs of black smoke curled up above the rooftops. A rebel pickup truck, with a Dashka machine gun bolted to the back bed, raced down a nearby cross street. Police and ambulance sirens blared.

Rahim positioned one of his men behind a wrought iron gate that blocked an alley and two more behind an exterior staircase that stood in front of a ridiculous mural of a cartoon cat. As he rushed up the stairwell of an apartment house with his remaining three men, headed for the roof, he was cursed at by people rushing in the other direction.

When a rebel fighter ducked his head around a corner at the end of the street and fired a rocket-propelled grenade, Rahim and his men on the roof fired off a few shots; when two more rocket-propelled grenades were fired in quick succession, they took cover behind a rusty water tank.

Gunshots, followed by cheering, erupted.

Rahim crawled to the edge of the brick parapet that ringed the roof and slowly raised his head. He caught glimpses of the rebels below him, partially shrouded by smoke. They wore civilian clothes and were screaming *Allahu Akbar!*—God is the Greatest—as they stripped the three men he had posted to the street, now dead, of their weapons. One of the rebels was dancing as he filmed the crime with a cell phone. Another scanned the roofs on the opposite side of the street.

Rahim held up a fist, signaling that his remaining men should wait. Then he waved them forward, so that all three were crouched with him right below the parapet that ran along the edge of the roof.

"When I command," Rahim whispered.

As he waited for the smoke to clear, and for three more rebels at the end of the street to cautiously creep forward, he recalled hearing stories of army snipers in Damascus who had made a game of shooting at rebels. One would shoot for a specific body part, and over the course of the rest of the day, other snipers would compete to see how many others they could hit in the same spot. Rahim had always thought the game to be depraved and ungodly. What kind of man did such a thing? But at that moment, he thought of Adel and the men in the pickup truck who had tried to kill him—rebels, like the men below him—and he whispered, "Right temple."

"Sir?" asked the soldier closest to him.

"You will fire when I do. Aim for the temple. We will see who shoots best."

Rahim failed to hit anyone in the right temple. His AK-47, though reliable, could hardly be described as accurate. Its sights were useless. But it mattered little.

The gun hammered against his shoulder, the muzzle flashes in the weak light hurt his eyes, and the gun smoke in his lungs left him light-headed. The magazine contained thirty rounds. He fired them all, then reloaded and emptied the new magazine. His men did the same.

The rebels below wobbled and fell and crawled and then were still.

CHAPTER 10

Sami had just started his final rounds of the day when rumors began to ripple through the hospital. Multiple gunfights had broken out in Salaheddine! The police station had been overrun! The Mukhabarat were fleeing! The liberation of the city was near! Thousands of rebel fighters were gathering by the new soccer stadium!

There was jubilation—the ultrasound technician he passed in the hall could not stop smiling, the cafeteria custodian blew by Sami with his chest puffed out. But there was also panic. Three of his patients demanded that he release them immediately, before the fighting spread to the hospital. Sami impressed upon them that if they were determined to leave, there was nothing he could or would do about it. But people should not jump to irrational conclusions simply because they could hear a few explosions. Besides, he told them, it was probably just rumors.

When the helicopter gunships began buzzing the city, however, flying so close to the hospital at times that they rattled the windows, Sami concluded at least some of the rumors must be true.

He called Tahira. "Get the children inside. Lock both doors."

She had already done it. She could hear the explosions perfectly well, she informed him, adding, "Now they will pay for what they did to Omar."

Sami hoped she was right, but he cringed to hear her speak in such a fashion on the phone. He hoped that the rebels and government alike would be hesitant to take the fight inside the old walled city, where his house lay and which had been designated a world heritage site. Surely there was a shared interest in protecting a shared heritage.

Tahira wanted to know when he was coming home.

"Not tonight. Maybe tomorrow."

"Treat none of them," she said. "Those thieves deserve nothing."

"Tahira," he said. "Please."

"They will not be around much longer to worry about anyway," she added.

Sami hung up. Maybe she was right and maybe not, but for now, it still was not safe to talk that way.

———

Many of the doctors and nurses abandoned their posts. Farrah al-Mahmoud, a middle-aged nurse who had been assigned to the orthopedic recovery wing that evening, was one of them.

Sami found out during his rounds, when the American woman named Hannah tracked him down in the hall to tell him that her boyfriend Oskar hadn't been given his final course of intravenous antibiotics. She knew everyone was busy, and she had heard about the fighting, but could he please, please give Oskar his antibiotics? Immediately, if possible?

Always it was something with this woman, always charging toward him, as though her forehead were a battering ram. A constant river of words spilling out of her mouth—and she was not even the patient!

But after checking the medical administration record affixed to Oskar's chart, he conceded that she *did* have a point.

"I know you are short-staffed," she said. "And I can hear what is going on outside. If there is anything I can do to help, I will."

"There is nothing you can do."

He would likely have to give the other patient in the room his medications, too, Sami realized. And check on all the rest of the patients this nurse had abandoned . . .

Had the medicines even been delivered from the pharmacy?

He rubbed his head, thinking he could not do it all, that someone had to find another nurse for the floor. Minutes later, he retrieved two saline bags, a vial of cefazolin, and a vial of ciprofloxacin from the medicine cabinet at the nurses' station. Back in Oskar's room, he double-checked the medication administration record, then reconstituted the cefazolin with 10 cc of saline, added it to the saline bag, and set up a drip. That done, he checked Adel's medication administration record, reconstituted the dry ciprofloxacin, and set up Adel's drip. The cipro would not have been his choice, Sami thought, but given that other alternatives were in short supply, he supposed it was a reasonable decision on the part of Dr. Issa.

CHAPTER 11

Hannah had gotten in the habit of checking to make sure that whatever was going into Oskar was what was supposed to be going into him because over the past five days, she'd learned from experience that mistakes were often made: the wrong dosage of morphine, almost doubling up on an anticoagulant medicine, forgetting to mark down when Tylenol had been given and then offering new pills too soon.

So, while she hadn't wanted to imply that her trust was less than absolute when Dr. Hasan had been in the room, she had no compunction about pulling the medicine vials out of the garbage after had left. And she noticed the mix-up right away. Both bottles had originally been labeled in Cyrillic, but the pharmacy had covered up the Cyrillic labels with new labels in Arabic. By looking through the back of the vials, though, she could see the original labels. And because she had learned to distinguish between the Cyrillic words for cefazolin and ciprofloxacin, she saw that the Arabic label for ciprofloxacin had gone on the cefazolin bottle, and the Arabic label for the cefazolin on the ciprofloxacin.

"What's wrong?" demanded Oskar, as he observed her holding the empty vials up to the light to inspect them.

"Nothing you have to worry about," she said, not wanting to feed his anxiety any more than he appeared to be feeding it himself. Besides, she knew ciprofloxacin was just another antibiotic, so she wasn't that worried. At least Oskar and Adel were both getting something.

She ducked her head around the privacy curtain and that was when she noticed that, for the first time she could recall, no one was sitting with Adel. At a glance the boy seemed okay.

"We need to think about getting out of here, Hannah!" Oskar called after her as she left to try to catch Dr. Hasan.

He could hear the fighting. Everyone could.

"I *am* thinking about it, Oskar," she called over her shoulder.

Dr. Hasan wasn't in any of the adjacent rooms, and the nurses' station at the end of the hall was empty, but twenty minutes later, in the next hall over, she nearly ran into Farrah—the very same night-shift nurse who'd supposedly left earlier in the evening.

Around the age of her own mother, she was wearing banana-yellow scrubs and a black headscarf. Between that and her pear-shaped body, Hannah thought she looked a bit like a bumblebee. Hannah was particularly well-disposed to her, though, because she'd helped Oskar get to the toilet twice.

"Oh," said Hannah, surprised to see her. "I thought you had gone home?"

She explained that she had, but her adult daughter had left Aleppo to stay with her extended family outside the city, so she had come back.

When Hannah told her about the mix-up her eyes widened. "*Ya Allah*," she said as she clutched her throat.

"Is it unsafe?" Hannah asked.

"Not for your boyfriend. But for the other boy . . . Oh, I must fix this immediately."

———

"Wonderful," said Oskar, upon learning that he'd received Adel's medications and that Adel had received his. "That's just wonderful."

"Hey," said Hannah, putting a hand on his shoulder. "What's wrong? You're not acting like yourself."

"What's wrong is that doctor gave me the wrong meds. He would never make it in Europe. Never."

"Actually, I think he's pretty good," said Hannah. The truth was, she liked Dr. Hasan. All her research suggested that up until today, he'd done exactly what he should have done to treat Oskar. And while he might have just mixed up the medications, it was really the pharmacy's fault for mislabeling them. Besides, Dr. Hasan was a surgeon, not a nurse, and at least he hadn't panicked and run when the explosions had started up. He was doing his best. "He's just stressed. I would be, too, if I had his job."

"He's an asshole even when he's not stressed," said Oskar, with uncharacteristic venom. "I've seen the way he treats you."

"He treats me fine," said Hannah.

CHAPTER 12

Hannah tried calling several private ambulance companies. None would transport Oskar to Turkey while there was still fighting going on in and around Aleppo. She tried her Syrian acquaintances, hoping to find someone willing to drive her and Oskar to the border. Most didn't answer their phones. The few who did didn't have cars and didn't know anyone who would be willing to loan or lease one to her.

Maybe when the fighting let up, they said.

She tried calling the airport and was told that even if Oskar were physically capable of boarding a plane, all the outbound flights were booked, and no inbound flights were coming in—which meant soon there wouldn't be any outbound flights at all.

Around the hospital, the taxi drivers had either gone home to avoid getting caught in the fighting or were already ferrying other people out of the city. When she finally found one outside the Pullman, a modern seven-story hotel just north of the hospital, the driver refused to take her and Oskar into Turkey out of fear the border crossing would be shut and he wouldn't be let back in.

Around midnight, though, an EDS colleague in Turkey called her back with an offer—if Hannah could get Oskar to the border, this colleague would drive them the rest of the way back to Antakya.

"Done," Hannah said.

She'd hire a taxi at the Pullman to take them to the border, and they'd cross on foot—Oskar would just have to suck it up and use crutches.

Oskar said he was game.

"I can't thank you enough," he said. He took her hand in his.

She kissed him on the lips. "Don't thank me yet. The ride to Antakya is going to be awful."

"I mean for everything. For staying here and looking out for me. I've been a pain in the ass, I know. I'll never forget it."

"I'll call you when I get a taxi. Then we'll get you back to Sweden. We'll figure this out."

———

Hannah jogged back to the Pullman. The taxi that had been there earlier was gone, but the concierge said it was expected back soon from the airport.

Two hours later it still hadn't arrived. Explosions sporadically brightened the night sky, and the sound of gunfire just to the south of her was relentless. Military trucks roared by every few minutes.

At three thirty in the morning, four hotel guests climbed out of the taxi in question, having just returned from the airport where their flight had been canceled.

For five times the normal fare, the driver—an ill-tempered older man with a Saddam Hussein mustache—reluctantly agreed to bring her to the border. Hannah used the ATM inside the hotel to take out extra money on her credit card.

From the back of the taxi, she tried to call Oskar, to let him know she'd be there soon, but the call wouldn't go through. While she was sending him a text, the taxi pulled to a stop in front of a haphazardly erected barrier made of corrugated steel roofing panels and adorned with Syrian flags. Government soldiers, dressed in camouflage uniforms and wielding assault rifles, stood in front of it.

The driver cursed.

"Checkpoint," he said, adding, "It was not here twenty minutes ago."

"Will they let us through?"

He tapped his steering wheel, looking antsy and nervous. "*Inshallah.* How much money do you have?"

"How much do I need?"

The driver tapped the steering wheel again, peered through the windshield, then said, "Maybe one thousand."

Hannah slipped a thousand Syrian pounds—the equivalent of about fifteen dollars—into her US passport. Moments later, the driver handed his Syrian ID and Hannah's passport to a soldier.

They let the driver through but not before they told him fighting had broken out at the border crossings north and west of Aleppo and that it was not safe to go anywhere near them.

Hannah, her bribe notwithstanding, was detained.

CHAPTER 13

"Dr. Hasan! Dr. Hasan!"

Sami heard the nurse but kept walking. Having just operated on a woman who had been hiding under her bed when a stray bullet had shattered her tibia, he was now needed to help stabilize a patient who had been shot in the hip. Meanwhile, the emergency room was filling with patients faster than they could be treated.

"Dr. Hasan, I must speak with you!" said the nurse, trying to catch up. "It concerns one of your patients."

"So speak," said Sami, still not breaking stride.

"It is about a matter that would best be discussed privately."

"I do not have time"—Sami stepped out of the way, his back to the wall, to avoid colliding with a bed-bound patient being wheeled down the hall at race-car speed—"for a private discussion."

"Dr. Hasan, I beg of you!"

The nurse—Farrah was her name, Sami recalled—leaned closer.

"One of your patients has died," she whispered. "The one in room 142."

"The Swede?"

"No, no—the other one."

Sami took a moment to process the information.

"I am sorry," said the nurse.

"Adel Suleiman," said Sami.

"Yes."

"Thank you for telling me." Sami began walking again.

"Doctor, that is not all. The reason I am here is because the pharmacy distributed the wrong . . ."

The nurse had lowered her voice to the point where Sami could not hear what had been said.

"The pharmacy distributed the wrong what?"

Sami stopped walking. The nurse stepped in close.

"The wrong medication. There was a mix-up. Between the medicine for the boy and the Swede."

"No. I checked the labels," Sami said. "And the MAR," he added, referring to the medication administration record.

"Of course you did, Dr. Hasan. And yet, with the war in the south, we have been low on the usual medications, and some replacements have come in from Russia. The pharmacy relabels them, but this time there was an error. The American girl, she noticed it and told me. I fixed it, but it was too late. The boy had a reaction—"

Sami raised his eyes and clucked his tongue. "No."

"—to the cefazolin," said the nurse. "A bad reaction, he was allergic."

"I knew he was allergic to cefazolin," snapped Sami. "I read the MAR. And besides, I helped operate on him. He threw a rash when administered cefazolin, became hypertensive. Dr. Issa ordered the switch to cipro."

"He had a worse reaction this time, Doctor. Much worse."

Sami leaned back against the wall and took two deep breaths. He knew what cefazolin and ciprofloxacin looked like when spelled out in Cyrillic. He would have been able to tell the difference if he had been as careful as he should have been. There was no excuse for not checking; no good excuse at least. The nurse knew it, too, but she was simply allowing him to save face by placing all the blame on the pharmacist. "You administered epinephrine?"

"It was too late."

Sami lifted his head. It was possible—unlikely, but possible—the nurse had misjudged the situation.

"Get me a .5 milliliter dose of epinephrine, meet me in the room!"

Moments later, Sami, slightly out of breath, ran to Adel Suleiman's hospital bed. He felt for a pulse, but the second he picked up the boy's hand and felt how cold it was, he knew. The computer monitor, which displayed the boy's vital signs—or rather, lack thereof—confirmed it.

He slumped into a bedside chair and cradled his head in his hands, his confidence shaken. He had been distracted. Worried about Tahira and his children. But that was no excuse.

Still, the odds of the boy going into anaphylactic shock and dying instead of just breaking out in a rash were incredibly low! In surgery, he had become hypertensive, yes, but when the medication was changed, his blood pressure had returned to normal and his flushing had receded.

Stop it, Sami admonished himself. He cradled his head in his hands again. The odds were irrelevant. There were always outliers. The boy's body had been under stress. It would not have taken much to kill him. Maybe a second hypertensive incident had led to a stroke. The boy had, after all, suffered a concussion.

———

"The epinephrine you requested, Dr. Hasan," said the nurse. "Shall I administer it?"

"No." From where Sami sat, he could see Adel's toes. They were pale. He touched them. They were already cold. "You were right. Has the patient's family been informed?"

"Not yet. I thought it best to speak to you first."

"We should call them. Now." He checked the time on his phone; the woman with a bullet in her hip was waiting for him in the emergency room. "This is not news that will get better with time." Sami considered what his reaction would be if one of his children had landed in the hospital, and some pharmacist and an absentminded doctor had accidentally killed him. He would be devastated. And furious.

Sorry was not nearly enough.

"I can look up the phone number for the parents," offered the nurse.

"Bring it to me in the emergency wing. Have you informed the pharmacist?"

"She left not long after the fighting broke out. This would have been one of the last scripts she filled. The nurses that remain are filling their own scripts."

"I see."

Sami stood. It was then he noticed that the Swede—and all the Swede's belongings—were gone. Even though he had not been discharged.

"But I was wondering . . ." said the nurse, as Sami stared at Oskar's empty bed.

"Wondering what?"

"Wondering what the use would be of telling the family about the medicine issue."

Turning to the nurse, Sami said, "They deserve to be told the truth."

"And you believe they would want to know it?"

"You think I should lie to them?" Sami posed the question as an accusation—even though he knew that most doctors at the hospital would lie. To admit an error was to admit weakness, and while such an admission might be looked upon admirably in the hospitals of Paris and London, it would not be here.

Sami had been fighting against that attitude for years now. Arguing at staff meetings for better reporting standards. If no one admitted their errors, how could future ones be prevented?

"All I am saying, Doctor, is that the family might be better off not knowing that the boy died as a result of something that could have been prevented." Lowering her voice, she added, "We must also consider that the patient's father is Mukhabarat and will likely think more kindly of you, and me, if he believes his son died as a result of an act of God. An embolism, perhaps."

Sami stood perfectly still for a moment. The Mukhabarat—a catchall name that could apply to any of Syria's myriad domestic intelligence services—were not to be trifled with. Most likely it was the Mukhabarat who had killed Omar. He had not realized Adel Suleiman's father was one of them. He further considered that, with the possibility that Aya could be detained and questioned by the Mukhabarat, his situation was already exceptionally precarious.

"No," he said.

"No?"

"There are protocols that must be followed. I helped write them. I made a mistake, and now I must—"

Sami stopped in midsentence as he observed a woman, squat and dressed in a black abaya robe embroidered with silver thread, enter the room looking anxious. Adel's mother.

"Dr. Hasan," she said. "*Subhanallah.*" Glory to God. "How glad I am that you are here. My husband was called away because of the troubles, and I was worried that Adel would be alone."

She stared at the floor as she spoke, as though Sami were royalty. Her Damascene accent reminded Sami of his own mother.

"Please." Sami gestured to the chair beside Oskar's empty bed, hoping that if she sat there, the privacy curtain would continue to block her view of Adel.

But she was already stepping forward and trying to see around the curtain. Sami tried to block her.

"I am so deeply sorry to have to tell you this," he said, "but your son—"

Before he could speak the words, she slipped past him and after a moment of pained silence, began to wail. She kissed her son's face and forehead; she pulled him up into her breast, and talked to him, calling his name again and again and again.

Sami waited, intending to confess his role in Adel's death before he left to operate. But as he watched her suffer, he began to think perhaps the nurse was right, that it would be better if she never learned that her boy had died because of a stupid, entirely preventable error.

Which is why when Adel's mother began bawling, "Why? Why? Why did this happen?" and the nurse responded, "It was *eraadat Allah*, sister,"—What God wanted—"a stroke as a result of his injuries. He died peacefully," that Sami, instead of correcting the nurse, simply walked away.

CHAPTER 14

It was undeniably true, Hannah admitted to the army officer who questioned her, that she had been in the streets of Aleppo, in the middle of the night, on the very same night the rebels had launched their attack on the city. It was also true, she conceded, that she was one of only a handful of Americans who were still in Aleppo.

She didn't deny it. Just as she didn't deny that the Americans were probably using the CIA to secretly funnel arms to the rebels. But she very much did deny that she, personally, was doing any of the funneling, which is what they were accusing her of doing.

She showed them her European Development Service badge and her American passport; she explained that she had been working in Aleppo for almost two years trying to help the Syrian government—the Syrian *government*, did they understand?—build an urban park and revitalize the neighborhood that surrounded the park. She helped people get small business loans. She arranged for grants for elementary schools. She compiled community feedback. She wasn't here on some absurd secret mission!

Along with a list of local people who would vouch for her, she gave them the names and numbers of EDS directors in Antakya and Brussels.

"Or call the university hospital! Talk to Oskar Lång—room 142. I work with him; he is an engineer. Talk to the engineers Oskar works with in your government."

"Please calm yourself," said the officer, in a way that served only to infuriate her. "We are checking everything."

A female soldier searched her. When they found her Syrian passport in her purse, she explained that technically she was a dual citizen—her late father had been Syrian—but that she considered herself American. They said that if one of her passports said she was Syrian, then she was Syrian, and they locked her in the back of an army-green van.

Night spilled into morning. The sun beat down on the roof of the van, and the temperature inside spiked. She wanted to call Oskar, but they'd confiscated her phone. She heard men yelling orders, explosions, and helicopters.

At 8:00 a.m., a young private she'd never seen before unlocked the back of the van, handed over her belongings, and told her she was free to go.

She didn't know or ask why, although she did ask whether the university hospital was safe.

It was just around the corner, but the roads were nearly empty. An eerie quiet, punctuated only by the occasional sound of gunfire, had settled over the university district. The air smelled of smoke.

The soldier shrugged. "Nothing is safe."

"But the hospital is not overrun?"

"That is my understanding, but the situation is changing rapidly."

———

Hannah jogged down Fatih Sultan Mehamed Avenue, consoled by the sight of an ambulance careening toward the emergency-room entrance, sirens blaring; a sign, she reasoned, that the hospital was still functioning.

And it was. As she made her way to Oskar's room, the halls were a frenzy of activity, the influx of wounded raising the normal din of managed chaos up to a roar as patients cried out, family members called for doctors, and nurses shouted over each other.

Upon entering Oskar's room and seeing that the bed was unoccupied, she checked the bathroom; it, too, was empty.

His satchel was gone.

Stay calm, she told herself. The hospital was in a state of upheaval. They must have moved him, she reasoned. They must have known he was going to leave anyway, and proactively moved him to make space for a new patient. Then she ducked her head around the privacy curtain and saw that Adel was gone too. That, she thought, was strange. He hadn't been anywhere near ready to leave.

The women at the reception desk had no record of Oskar having been moved or discharged, but they were so overwhelmed that Hannah put little stock in what they told her.

She texted Oskar.

Where are you???

Then, determined to find someone who could tell her what had happened, ran back to his room, intending to question the nurses or Dr. Hasan.

Instead, she found a soldier, dressed in full battle gear, in the room. His face was smudged with dirt and blood and peppered with stubble. He smelled of body odor and burnt plastic. Pouches were clipped to his tactical vest, an assault rifle slung across his back. A holstered pistol hung from one side of his belt, a knife from the other. His thick boots were covered with dust. Beneath it all was the black uniform favored by the Mukhabarat when they were putting down protests.

Hannah startled, then realized it was Rahim, Adel's father, and that he was in the process of stuffing books and sweets that his son had never been well enough to appreciate into a plastic bag. His movements were sharp. His gear rustled. He didn't acknowledge her.

"They moved Adel," she said.

"Yes," he said, after cramming a few more things into his bags.

She eyed the assault rifle, hoping he had engaged the safety or whatever it was one did with those things when they weren't being used.

"Why?"

Rahim finished gathering his son's things as though he had not heard the question.

"Oskar is gone too," Hannah blurted as Rahim was walking toward the door. "Do you know where he is?"

"No."

Hannah just stood there, confused. Then she remembered about the medicine mix-up. And she wondered. The nurse had said both Oskar and Adel would be fine. But things clearly weren't fine.

"Was it the medicine?" she asked as Rahim stepped out into the hall. He turned.

"There was a mix-up," she added. Her intention wasn't to cast suspicion on Dr. Hasan. Besides, he hadn't been the one that had mislabeled the vials. She just wanted to know what had happened to Oskar and Adel.

"What mix-up?"

"With the medicine. Between Oskar and Adel. I am only wondering whether that is why Oskar and Adel . . . whether something went wrong."

Rahim glared at her.

"I told the nurse about it," Hannah continued, and then briefly explained what had happened, adding, "The nurse thought everything would be all right, but now Oskar is gone, and Adel—"

Before she could finish, Rahim stormed away.

CHAPTER 15

Rahim had left his car at military intelligence headquarters, so he commandeered a Peugeot hatchback from a university student who was pulling out
of the parking garage.

As he careened past the gold-domed Ibn Abbas mosque and into
the Bassel al Assad traffic circle, an Mi-24 helicopter gunship screamed
down the 214 highway, rapidly gained altitude, then released two black,
seed-shaped objects from its weapon wings. Moments later, an explosion
rocked the city as undulating waves of light gray smoke rolled over the
rebel-held section of Aleppo, and a darker smoke cloud shot up from the
impact point and curled up into the wind.

Rahim, consumed with rage—at the rebels, at Dr. Hasan, at his wife
who would not even speak to him—hardly noticed. He passed quickly
through the gatehouse checkpoint and headed straight to the second floor.

A veiled, middle-aged secretary, whose name Rahim could not
remember, was typing at a metal desk in Major Akhras's office. Because
the one window in the office faced the front of the building, and therefore
was covered by the flag that depicted Bashar al Assad, a portion of the
president's thin mustache was projected onto the wall above her.

"I need you to retrieve a file," Rahim said, slightly out of breath. "The
name is Dr. Samir Hasan. He works at the University of Aleppo Hospital."

They were alone. Nearly everyone else had been deployed.

The secretary squinted at him. "The major told me nothing of this."

"Because he knows nothing of it yet."

"Then I will have to call him."

Rahim inclined his head. "Do as you must."

"And yet, he asked not to be disturbed."

Major Akhras and his men, having been relieved by army reinforcements, had been sent home to sleep for a few hours. Indeed, Rahim had been ordered to get some sleep so that he could be ready to fight again that evening, but his daughter had called him with the news about Adel, and he had instead run straight to the hospital, hoping to see his son one more time before the body was brought to the morgue. He had been too late.

"I guess you will have to decide whether this is an emergency!" said Rahim.

He had not intended to shout, but that was how it came out.

"You are okay, Lieutenant?"

Rahim took a moment to collect himself, then said, "Of course."

The secretary eyed him, then tucked a wisp of hair back under her headscarf. "This doctor. You are sure he has a file?"

"Yes," Rahim lied. But he felt confident in his answer, as it would be unusual for a man of Dr. Hasan's prominence not to have been investigated over the course of his career.

She frowned then asked Rahim to spell the name, which he did. "Wait here," she said.

Ten minutes later, she returned from the basement bearing a manila folder. Rahim snatched it from her hands. On a bench outside Major Akhras's office, he read as fast as he could.

Born in Damascus to a prominent thoracic surgeon, permitted to leave the country to study medicine in Paris, applied for an only-child waiver from military service—no surprise there, the coward—had operated on countless high-ranking air force and army officers at his expensive clinic . . .

As Rahim considered how the doctor had breezed in and out of Adel's room the day prior, spending two minutes—no more!—with his son, he imagined all the attention the doctor must have lavished on his more important patients at his clinic. His frustration boiled over and he smacked the file as hard as he could on the bench. By treating Adel as though he were nothing more than a bothersome dog, Dr. Hasan had insulted the whole Suleiman family!

Moments later, Rahim picked up the file again and resumed reading.

No hint of subversive behavior. Had signed no anti-Assad petitions. Had sent no private letters to President Assad—a fellow doctor—entreating him to show more mercy. No record of him having treated protesters. When he had been approached by air force intelligence in 2010 and asked to keep an eye on the chief of surgery at the University of Aleppo Hospital, he had agreed to do so, but had apparently seen nothing that merited filing a report.

Typical, Rahim thought with contempt. Everyone knew the vast majority of doctors—and especially the medical students—were against the regime. But they hid their true allegiances, protested anonymously, covered their tracks.

Disappointed at not finding any direct evidence of sedition, Rahim flipped to the end of the file, where Dr. Hasan's familial connections were listed. There, he only had to read the name of Dr. Hasan's wife—Tahira Seif—to know that all was not lost.

Seif, he recalled, had been the last name of the boy whose funeral had devolved into a protest just three days ago. The same funeral protest Rahim had helped to put down. The same funeral protest that Adel had attended, just hours before he had been attacked.

It was a common name and possibly a coincidence, but Rahim doubted that was so. After sending Major Akhras's secretary back down to the basement to pull more files, he was certain of it.

———

Major Akhras was not pleased at being disturbed. "What are you doing at headquarters? I sent you home to rest."

Rahim explained that not only had the renowned Dr. Sami Hasan intentionally killed his son, who, even though he was only fifteen had been a member in good standing with the local *shabiha* and—

"Lieutenant Suleiman, please!" interrupted the major. "You and your family have my deepest sympathies, but a medical error is not—"

"I assure you, Major, this is about more than my son and defending the honor of the Suleiman family. I must humbly tell you that I have discovered that Dr. Hasan is related to a boy named Omar Seif who was killed at a protest three days ago. This boy's funeral was held two days ago, at which there was another protest. The sister of Dr. Hasan's wife would have been brought in for questioning yesterday were it not for the hostilities. Dr. Hasan is working with the rebellion, Major, I am sure of it. His whole family is filled with rebels!"

Major Akhras sighed. "Of course, this Dr. Hasan, he will have people—patients—that will try to protect him."

"A man like Dr. Hasan could be of great use to the Free Syrian Army," Rahim countered. "If we allow it."

Silence, then, "Take one of your men and bring him to headquarters. But you will wait to question him until I have time to investigate this further."

CHAPTER 16

As the wounded flooded in and the staff drained out, the University of Aleppo Hospital had descended, if not into anarchy, then something on the verge of it. Patients crowded into the halls wearing only hospital robes and pulling their IV stands behind them, clamoring for doctors or medicine, complaining that they were hungry because the cafeteria had failed to deliver the usual breakfast trays of bread, eggs, and olives. Overburdened doctors and nurses rushed from room to room, but never fast enough. Over the loudspeaker, calls went out for surgery residents to report to the emergency room.

For Hannah, it meant navigating a moving obstacle course as she searched for Oskar. She checked the intensive care unit, pushing her way past a nurse who insisted she wasn't allowed in. She ran through the cardiology unit, which was an attached building, thinking maybe Oskar had developed a blood clot. She snuck past the nurses' station in the maternity wing, in yet another adjacent building, reasoning that they might have opened the rooms there to trauma patients.

She tried to call him, twice. After checking the morgue, it occurred to her that it might be worth trying to get into his email account. Just in case there were clues within it as to where he'd gone.

She'd never done it before—she wasn't a snooper—and she never would have done it now if she hadn't been so worried about him. She wasn't even sure she knew his password. But she knew he used a Gmail account, and she knew the password he used to protect his laptop. It was just Oskar1234. She was betting that he'd used the same password for his Gmail account.

He had.

The first thing she noticed was a purchase confirmation for a flight from Antakya to Copenhagen—with a stop in Istanbul on the way.

The existence of such a confirmation didn't alarm her so much as the fact that it had been made an hour and a half ago. For a flight that was scheduled to depart in a half hour. Which meant that boarding for the flight had probably already started.

It took her a moment to process. Was he really at an airport in Turkey? Right now? That would mean he had left the hospital hours ago. Last night even. But he would never . . .

She texted him again. This time he texted right back.

> Sorry, seeing texts/calls now, bd reception.
> Farid bring Turkey, crossed Yayladagi, hope
> Istanbul tonignt Germ tomorrow. Pls forgive,
> Farid can't wait. Where you?

She stared at the garbled message, hoping she'd misinterpreted it. She checked the number to make sure it was really from Oskar.

It was.

Had he really left Syria without her? How else to interpret a text like that?

She stared at it again, tempted to reply, but what would she say? She shook her head in disbelief, too angry to be hurt.

The hospital hadn't even been overrun. If Oskar and Farid—a Syrian engineer Oskar had been working with—had waited even just a few hours, she could have gone with them.

Yes, Oskar was hurt and probably not thinking quite right. Yes, he was probably scared. But to leave her like this . . .

She never would have left Aleppo without him. Never. She was here now, wasn't she? Why would he do such a thing?

After closing out the messages app on her phone, Hannah returned to the emails displayed on her phone's browser. The newest had been from Turkish Airlines, and that's what her eyes had initially been drawn to. But now she noticed that underneath that email were more messages than she could count from someone named Elsa.

Elsa?

Oskar had a brother named Nils, and his mother's name was Marie. He'd never mentioned anyone named Elsa.

Goose bumps broke out on her arm. Her throat constricted. Close it out, she told herself.

She kept reading.

The emails were written in Swedish. But between what little of the language she'd picked up from dating Oskar, Google Translate, and the English-language links to an Airbnb apartment in Paris—with only one king bed—she was able to piece it together well enough.

Oskar hadn't been planning on going on a family trip to celebrate his mother's sixtieth birthday. He was seeing someone else in Sweden. And evidently had been for some time. And until he broke his leg, he'd been planning on vacationing with her in Paris.

Biting her lower lip, Hannah looked up at the ceiling, then down at her hands. They'd only been dating for five months. No permanent commitments had been made. But still.

That son of a bitch, she thought. That selfish, cowardly, lying son of a bitch.

CHAPTER 17

Treating facial wounds was not Sami's specialty. But there had been no other surgeon available, so he had numbed the wound with a local anesthetic, irrigated it, and was about to attempt to remove a piece of windshield glass that had nearly severed the facial nerve of a Syrian Army soldier.

"Remain still," he ordered the soldier, who was still conscious and had a face that, even if it had not been marred by a laceration that stretched from the base of his right ear to the underside of his lip, would have been considered ugly.

The soldier mumbled that he was remaining still.

"No, you are not," said Sami quietly. "Speaking involves moving. And if you ever want to smile again, you will stop speaking." Sami adjusted the loupe magnifier that was affixed to his surgical glasses.

The last time he had seen the buccal branch of the facial nerve was when he had been doing his residency in Damascus.

"Wider," he said to the nurse who was holding the sallow, fatty tissue underneath the soldier's cheek open with a pair of retractors.

She pulled the cheek open wider. Sami identified the masseter muscle and parotid duct.

"Stop breathing," he said to the soldier.

The soldier did, remaining perfectly still, so that even his ear hairs stopped quivering. Sami used forceps to extract the glass fragment. It clanged when he deposited it in a stainless-steel bowl.

"Is it out?" asked the soldier.

"I told you not to—"

When the door to the operating room burst open, Sami looked up. Observing one of the emergency room intake nurses, he scowled beneath his mask.

"They are here for you, Dr. Hasan," she whispered.

As Sami stared at her, his annoyance morphed into concern. "Who?"

"Two men. They have ID. Military Intelligence. One is a lieutenant. They say they want to speak to you."

Sami inhaled sharply. He considered running, but to run now would consign himself to running forever. No, he would face them and let the truth be his defense. He was no rebel. Yes, he had treated Omar, but would they not have done the same for a member of their own family?

"I need twenty minutes. Tell them."

"They will not wait."

"They will have to!" Sami gestured to his patient with his suture needle. "Because I am busy."

"I can finish," said the nurse who stood next to him.

Sami clenched his jaw then sighed. "There was some intraoral penetration," he said, "so make sure you prescribe him cefazolin." Turning to the emergency room nurse who was still standing in the doorway, he said, "Have them meet me in the cafeteria in five minutes."

It was too late.

From behind the emergency room nurse, two black-clad Mukhabarat officers pushed through a set of double doors. The one in the lead wore a tactical vest stuffed with ammunition magazines. He had an assault rifle slung across his back and a pistol lodged in his belt holster. Although his face was sweaty and smudged with dirt, Sami recognized Rahim Suleiman.

"Go!" whispered the nurse to Sami.

But Sami held his ground. The Mukhabarat had not come to question him about treating Omar, he realized. This was about the boy, about Adel. Somehow Rahim had found out about the medicine mix-up.

He would speak to him, Sami resolved. As one father to another. He would tell him the truth about his son, as he should have done the day before. And maybe—if he were brave—he would even mention

Omar, that perhaps the Mukhabarat should spend less time killing other people's sons.

He handed his suture needle to the nurse as Rahim pushed through the door.

"Mr. Suleiman!" called Sami. "Please wait outside the operating room." Hand on heart, he said, "I beg of you, this is a sterile room, I will join you shortly."

A stainless steel instrument table clattered to the floor as Rahim threw it out of his way.

Sami stepped back from his patient. Before he could remove his surgical glasses, Rahim shoved him.

Shocked, Sami teetered backward. Rahim, who was a bit shorter than Sami but far broader, kept barreling forward. He shoved Sami again. Hard.

"Calm yourself!" Sami stammered, attempting to hold his ground. He had never been a fighter. But to be challenged like this in front of the hospital staff was untenable. "We must talk."

"I do not want to talk, Doctor."

"It was a mistake," said Sami. "And one that was quickly addressed. I will—"

Rahim shoved Sami again, only this time it came so quickly, it knocked the wind out of him. "A lie is not a mistake!"

Struggling to breathe, Sami said, "I can understand—"

Rahim threw Sami back against the hard tile wall of the operating room then pummeled him in the head. As Sami lost his footing and slipped to the ground, Rahim produced a pair of plastic zip-tie handcuffs.

"Help me with him," Rahim called to his associate.

The second Mukhabarat officer entered the operating room but hesitated because the patient on the operating table was partially blocking his path.

Then Sami noticed the scalpel.

Along with a few other tools that had scattered when Rahim had overturned the instrument table, it lay within arm's reach. As Rahim glanced over his shoulder to see what was holding up his associate, Sami grabbed it.

He could have plunged the scalpel into Rahim's inner thigh, right below the groin, perhaps severing his femoral artery—a wound that, even when inflicted in a hospital, could lead to death. Instead, he thrust it straight forward, into the meat of Rahim's thigh, directly above his kneecap.

The scalpel was sharp and went deep. Rahim roared as he stepped back, colliding with the second Mukhabarat officer.

Sami ran out of the operating room and into the staff prep rooms, throwing chairs and hazardous waste bins into his wake. He heard shouting behind him, then a gunshot. When he came to the door that led from the imaging hall to the lab rooms, he locked it behind him and sprinted through the pediatric intensive care unit, into the cafeteria, and out through the loading dock in back.

He had a Mercedes C300 sedan parked in the employee lot but did not dare retrieve it. The scooter he used to get to and from work was behind his clinic. He left that too. When he got to the Omar Abu-Riche thoroughfare and heard gunfire behind him, he forced himself to keep sprinting for a bit longer.

His house was southeast of the hospital, but he could see plumes of smoke rising from near the new soccer stadium to the south, so he headed straight east, hoping to skirt the many raging, amoeba-like battle lines that were advancing and retreating all over the city.

At the nearby al-Razi hospital, out of breath and dripping with sweat, he stripped off his bloody surgical gown, shoe booties, and hair net and threw them into a garbage bin. Dressed now only in his green scrubs and dress shoes, he walked at a fast clip through the public park.

It all seemed so normal. Water still arced from fountains, the palm trees were as green as ever, cars in the expansive Saadallah al-Jabiri Square just south of the park still honked their horns. One street vendor was selling grilled corn cobs, another cotton candy.

Sami recalled the crazy popcorn vendor who camped outside the medical school library every evening—everyone knew he was Mukhabarat, was it the same with these vendors? Were they watching him now?

The fast food shops that bordered the park were still wrapping calorie-bomb *döners* packed with French fries and mayonnaise for customers. To the east, outside the Club d'Alep where his mother liked to play cards on Saturday afternoons, two BMWs and a yellow Hummer were idling. They couldn't all be Mukhabarat.

Upon reaching one of the Christian districts in the old city, he took a hard turn to the south and for the next fifteen minutes, bobbed and weaved through crowds and narrow alleys, skirting the Great Mosque and cutting straight through the covered alleys of the al Madina souk where the spice shops were still open.

He didn't have his keys, cell phone, or wallet, but his wife always left spare keys for her extended relations under a loose cobblestone in the stone-walled entrance corridor that led to their home.

He retrieved them. One opened the tall, solid-steel gate that he had paid to have installed the year prior. The other opened the original four-hundred-year-old oak entrance door.

Sami slipped through both, locking the deadbolts on each as he shut them back up tight. His chest was heaving. God, he was out of shape, he thought. He wanted to slide down to the cool marble tile floor in his foyer, but instead, he leaned his back against the stone wall and took a few deep breaths, collecting himself.

Sweat dripped from his brow to the floor. He took a few steps forward and forced himself to sit down on the tulipwood foyer bench.

As he swapped out his shoes for slippers, he reminded himself that the eyes of his family would soon be upon him. The eyes of his children. He could not let them see him rattled.

Minutes later—he wanted to wait longer, but they would have heard him come in—he entered the sunny courtyard.

Tahira's sister, Aya, stood with her two remaining young children underneath the two-story-high pointed iwan arch that overlooked the courtyard. His own mother sat behind them. In the middle of the court-yard, by the marble fountain, his brother-in-law Rafiq appeared to be using the fountain water to perform his preprayer ablutions. Tahira's mother was resting on a nearby bench, veiled, back arched, lips pursed in disapproval as she clicked through her prayer beads.

They turned to him as one, their collective alarm evident.

THE DOCTOR OF ALEPPO

He was still a bit out of breath. His scrubs were stained with sweat and—below the knee, where his surgical robe had ended—blood. His right eye was throbbing from where Rahim had punched him; he suspected it was swollen.

"Baba, Baba, Baba!" called his daughter, Noora, as she toddled over to him. She wore a frilly pink dress and the gold earrings Tahira had bought her for her second birthday.

Sami ran his hands over the top of her hair, as his mother and Tahira's relations continued to stare.

Straightening himself to his full height, he greeted his relations and told them they were welcome, more than welcome, to take refuge here at Beit Qarah for as long as they wished—there was plenty of room. And now, if they could just excuse him for a minute . . .

———

"But surely this man will find you here!" gasped Tahira, when they had retired to the formal reception room and Sami explained what had happened.

"Will he? I receive my mail at work. Yours comes to the factory."

"Sami."

"There is also the issue with the title."

When they had purchased Beit Qarah—which was what the house was called, having been built by a spice merchant by the name of Qarah some four hundred years ago—Sami's lawyers had said it would take years for his and Tahira's clear title to be recognized by the government, if it ever was. The real law was that occupancy equaled ownership. Even the utility bills they paid every month were still in the name of the prior owner.

"Sami, for a smart man . . ." Instead of finishing her thought, Tahira said, "I will call the hospital and try to fix this. Give me your phone."

"What will you tell them?" Sami asked just as Adam, his four-year-old son, walked into the room.

Tahira, looking frustrated upon seeing Adam, sighed, then brushed a lock of hair out of her son's eyes as he climbed onto the leather couch and rested his head in her lap.

"Things that a young boy would do well not to hear," said Tahira. "Where are Rima and Maysoon?"

"I have no idea."

Sami's understanding was that his receptionist and nurse both worked elsewhere on their days off from his clinic, but he was not so familiar with their lives that he knew where.

"I must coordinate with them. If they are questioned . . ." She held her hand to her throat, then shook her head, looking deeply distraught. "Either way, we must tell the hospital something that they can tell to the Mukhabarat and this terrible man." She bit her lip. "Something that will give us time."

"Time for what?" asked Sami.

"God knows, not I."

But they both did know, and Sami suspected Tahira was being circumspect only because she did not want to frighten Adam.

"If we were going to do it, we should have done it last year," he said, as he regarded the reception room. It was marked by little alcoves filled with incense burners, dried flowers, and his mother's old china plates. A seventeenth century brass scale that may or may not have been used by the Qarah family. His father's medical books, and his own, sat inside bookshelf niches with glass doors. A backgammon set inlaid with satinwood, mother-of-pearl, ebony, and camel bone lay on a marble-topped table next to his father's bronze nargile water pipe. The painted shutters that framed the lower-level courtyard windows had been painstakingly restored, as had the poplar ceiling beams and the tulip-and-pomegranate-themed wood panels that lay between the beams. Pillows had been arranged around the century-old hand-knotted Persian carpet.

They had purchased the house nearly two years ago, before the troubles had really started, and had put too much into it since to just pick up and leave.

Besides, reasoned Sami, while staying was not a safe option, neither was trying to flee the country with two young children and an entire extended family in tow. Fighting was raging across the city and, evidently, at the border crossings. They had no relations outside of Syria to turn to. He had no savings to speak of—it had all gone to pay for the house and renovations and bribing the historic preservation inspectors, and he had not been able to sell or rent out his old apartment in New Aleppo because of the protests. A permit to work in Lebanon or Jordan or Turkey would have been difficult to get a year ago; now it would be close to impossible.

And what was to say the house would not protect them if they stayed? It had survived earthquakes, the fall of the Ottoman Empire, the French occupation, World Wars I and II, the push for independence from France, and the wars with Israel. Plus, it was hidden. There were no windows that looked to the street. A winding alley, too narrow for cars, led to a single entrance. By design, everything faced inward. From the outside, there was no hint of the luxuries that lay behind Beit Qarah's thick stone walls. It had protected its previous owners, and it would protect them too.

"Then we stay," said Tahira. "At least for tonight. But you must hide until we are sure they are no longer looking for you, and we must be prepared to leave quickly if we need to. Rafiq's mother in Jarabulus called when she heard of the fighting, she has room for us."

Sami nodded, then he stood.

"Where are you going?" demanded Tahira.

"To talk to your sister."

As he reentered the courtyard, he put his hand up to shield his eyes from the sun.

"Aya!" he called sharply, addressing her from across the courtyard. She turned, looking wary. "Your protester friends—yes, I know you are one of them—some of them have connections to the Free Syrian Army, I assume?"

"I do not need to hear your accusations now, Sami."

"I am not accusing you. I ask because I need your help."

"What help?"

"I need for you to take a message to the Free Syrian Army—to tell them that I am willing to work for them. Heal their wounded and train their medics. But in exchange, Beit Qarah and my family will be protected."

The courtyard was silent for a moment. Up by the roof, a pigeon cooed. Then Sami's brother-in-law threw up his arms.

"*Allahu Akbar! Allahu Akbar!*"

No one joined Rafiq in the call. But Sami's four-year-old son spoke the words.

"Adam, no," said Sami. "You diminish yourself with such talk." Then turning to his brother-in-law, "I can assure you that my conversion regarding this matter has nothing whatsoever to do with God."

CHAPTER 18

Hannah ran to the Pullman Hotel, but the taxis were all gone, so she bought bottled water and the last three quince-and-pomegranate-stuffed kibbe patties at the hotel restaurant and began walking north. In the wealthy neighborhoods that bordered the University, Christian and Muslim housewives stood on their expansive balconies, sipping coffee and gazing south as though watching a display of fireworks. Some pointed with excitement when fighter jets buzzed the highland Kurdish district of Sheik Maqsoud and shook their heads with disapproval when the bombs dropped on Salaheddine.

Regime soldiers and armored cars were assembling around the Air Force Intelligence building on Nile Street. New graffiti had been spray-painted on buildings: *Assad or we will burn it!* Support the president and the regime, or we will burn Syria to the ground.

She walked for an hour. Gaziantep Avenue was clogged with cars, decades-old minibuses, and crowds fleeing on foot. Women in abayas pulled roller suitcases behind them. Men in flip-flops carried kids piggyback on their shoulders while lugging overstuffed plastic bags.

Hannah tried to hop on a minibus, but it was packed too tightly with bodies, as were the private cars, so she resigned herself to walking. She was young and wearing sneakers with good soles. She had food and water. No children. If anyone should have to walk, it should be her.

Fields of wheat and barley began where the city ended. Low-slung houses fronted by privacy walls anchored groves of fig, lemon, and olive trees. Modest minarets rose from neighborhood mosques. Salt from the sweat on her face stung her eyes. Her bra chafed, her feet ached.

She finished her food. Then her water.

It occurred to her that Oskar had likely traveled the same road not twelve hours earlier, only far faster. Farid would have been driving. Oskar would have been in the back seat.

Would the passenger seat have been empty?

The shithead. Even if he had been cheating on her, he could've at least had the decency to give her a ride.

She heard rumors there was more fighting ahead, in the villages on the way to Turkey, at a military airport. Everything was colliding, falling apart faster than she'd ever anticipated it could. At times she heard bombs exploding.

She tried to buy food at a store attached to a gas station that had no gas, but the shelves were bare. There was running water in the bathroom though, and she craned her head underneath a dirty sink faucet and drank as much as her stomach would hold, as mosquitoes bit the back of her neck.

By nightfall, she reached a town that lay nearly halfway between Aleppo and the Turkish border. Desperately hungry, she ducked behind a furniture store where several fig trees were laden with unripe fruit. She picked a fig, bit into it, and grimaced at the bitter taste.

Then Oskar called.

She stared at the caller ID for a moment, unsure whether she wanted to answer. She clicked the talk icon just before it went to her voicemail.

"Hannah?"

She didn't know what to say to him, so she said nothing. She'd never pegged him as a cheater. She thought he'd been better than that. Kinder than that.

"Hannah?"

It annoyed her how panicky he sounded, especially when she contrasted it with how she used to look up to him as being relatively unflappable. "I'm here."

"It's Oskar."

"I know."

"Where are you?"

She took a moment to respond. "Ah, somewhere north of Aleppo?"

"So you made it out. Thank God."

Thank God for what? thought Hannah. She may have made it out of Aleppo, but she was still in Syria.

"I'm in Istanbul," he added. "At the airport. On standby for flights to Copenhagen."

Well, good for you, she thought. Copenhagen was just a short drive, across the Øresund Bridge, to his family home in southern Sweden.

He paused long enough so that she wondered whether the call had been dropped, then asked, "Did you get my text?"

"Yeah, I got it," she said.

Was he even going to apologize for having left her? Or ask why she'd been delayed? She'd been detained, accused of being a spy, had walked halfway to Turkey, and now had no food. Did he even care?

"I didn't get a text back."

"I didn't know what to say."

"I'm sorry. I . . ."

"I know about Elsa," she blurted. "I read your emails. When I was trying to find you."

No one spoke for a long time.

Finally, Oskar said, "Hannah, it's—"

"It's what, not what I think? Don't insult me, Oskar."

"No, it is what you think, it's just . . ."

She heard something that sounded like a grown man trying not to cry. Which she thought was ironic, given that she was the one getting screwed over.

"Are you in pain?" she asked.

"Of course."

"Do you have someone meeting you in Copenhagen?"

As she posed the question, it suddenly dawned on her that the reason he'd been so eager to leave without her. He must have been worried she would try to accompany him back to Sweden. And then he'd have his two women in the same city at once.

"My mother."

Hannah rolled her eyes. His mother. Her phone beeped—a low battery alert. "I have to go."

"I'll call you when I get to Sweden. We have to talk."

"No, we don't."

"Hannah."

"I can't do this, Oskar."

"Hannah, we have to talk. And not like this."

He sounded desperate. She was too tired and hurt and hungry to care.

"There's nothing to talk about. No matter what you say, no matter what your excuse, I'm not spending any more time, much less the rest of my life, with a man who would do to me what you've done."

CHAPTER 19

Inside the Aleppo property registry office—a labyrinthine tangle of ancient filing cabinets, metal desks, and corded phones—Rahim Suleiman, still dressed in his black anti-riot uniform and laden with combat gear, sat outside the director's office in a wobbly, decades-old easy chair that had been placed next to a plastic fern.

His right leg, though bandaged with a field dressing, oozed blood out onto the scuffed, cracked leather. His expression betrayed no emotion.

He had arrived five hours ago, just in time to catch the lone clerk trying to slip out of the office, and yet he was still no closer to learning where Dr. Hasan lived. Unable to justify continuing to retain the junior intelligence officer who had assisted him at the hospital, he was alone.

Rahim checked his watch. His orders were to report to the Military Intelligence Directorate in two hours.

He waited five more minutes, then checked his watch again.

O you who have believed, seek help through patience and prayer. Indeed, Allah is with the patient.

He repeated this verse from the Quran twenty times in his head, then clenched his fist and thought: This clerk is useless! Over five hours to look up a simple address! With a government such as this, is it any mystery why people are protesting?

Minutes later, however, the clerk—a frail man with rimless glasses and a face marked by deep wrinkles and an overabundance of liver spots— hobbled out from the canyons of filing cabinets looking especially stooped, as though he had been bending over for far too long. With both his hands, he gripped a piece of paper.

Rahim stood, for though the man was just a clerk, and a remarkably inefficient one at that, his advanced age demanded that he be afforded respect.

"I have it, Lieutenant!" the clerk declared, both his voice and arms trembling as he offered the paper. "The address of your doctor."

Rahim took the paper and stared at it for a moment. "God bless you," he said.

———

As battles continued to rage in Salaheddine and other districts, sending sounds of gunfire and exploding mortar shells booming out over the city, Rahim raced to the wealthy New Aleppo district just west of the hospital—stopping abruptly outside a three-story, white-limestone building which, even though half the city had no electricity, was illuminated by a nearby streetlight. The third and highest floor was marked by a series of floor-to-ceiling windows that were framed by decorative pointed arches.

Rahim eyed the windows, noting with dissatisfaction that they were dark.

The common front door was locked, but Rahim used a combination jack-handle, lug-wrench bar from the trunk of the Peugeot to pop the latch. Upon limping up the interior stairs as quickly as he could, he arrived at the third-floor landing. Seeing that the heavy oak door was secured with both a latch and a dead bolt, he stepped back down the stairs and, using an oak baluster to partially shield himself from ricochets, set the firing selector on his AK-47 to automatic, and shot up the wood casing to the right of the locks.

The door popped open when he threw his shoulder into it. He stepped inside.

Light from streetlamps glinted off an expansive marble floor in what appeared to be a living room. But the room was empty save for a small circular table. Nothing hung on the walls. The windows had been stripped of their curtains.

Rahim moved cautiously toward the table, gun to his shoulder. The sound of his steps echoed off the hard walls and floors. On the table lay a stack of papers which he bent down to examine, using his cell phone flashlight for illumination.

It was an advertisement for an apartment. Four bedrooms, two and a half bathrooms, twenty-two thousand Syrian pounds per month—an absurd amount of money. Photos of the apartment—including the room in which Rahim was standing—had been printed under the description.

At the very bottom of the page was a number. He called it, but no one answered.

———

Rahim drove back to the University of Aleppo Hospital.

Finding no one at the reception desk, he grabbed the first male doctor he could find, brandished his military intelligence ID, and demanded to speak to someone who could tell him where Dr. Hasan lived.

A harried, portly man wearing blue scrubs stained with blood soon met him at the reception desk and introduced himself as Dr. Issa.

"Where is Dr. Hasan?" Rahim demanded, declining to shake Dr. Issa's hand when it was offered.

Gesturing with his already outstretched hand that Rahim should calm himself, Dr. Issa said, "What I came to tell you is that Dr. Hasan, he . . ."

"He what?" demanded Rahim.

Dr. Issa looked at the ceiling, then said, "He has been called to God."

The two men stood facing each other for an extended moment.

Rahim clenched his jaw. "How?" he demanded.

"I was not here, but I was told there was a misunderstanding of sorts this afternoon—"

"There was no misunderstanding."

"You know of this incident?"

"Do not evade my questions, doctor," said Rahim, unclipping the snap that kept his pistol secure on his belt holster. "You tell me Dr. Hasan has died. How?"

"He was shot!" cried Dr. Issa. "While trying to flee to Turkey. His wife called the hospital for help as he was dying. She needed an ambulance, but there were none to spare. It would not have mattered because he died well before any ambulance could have come, but still, I fear we failed him."

"I do not believe you. Where did this happen?"

Rahim placed his hand on the grip of his pistol.

"Lieutenant, please—"

"Where?" Rahim shouted.

"Castello Road!" cried Dr. Issa in a panic. "His wife said he was shot by rebels. I do not know whether it was an accident, or whether they tried to get him to join them and he refused or . . ."

Dr. Issa's stopped speaking as he glanced at Rahim's pistol.

"This Dr. Hasan, where is his home? And do not try to send me to his clinic next door as your colleagues did earlier today! That is not where he lives. Nor does he live in the apartment he owns in New Aleppo."

"He moved to somewhere near the old city, I think," said Dr. Issa, speaking quickly. "He mentioned it some time ago, but I have never been there. But he works so much, his clinic is like his real home."

"What is his number? His personal cell phone number. And the number his wife used to call you."

"I have it," said Dr. Issa, as though grateful to be asked to perform a task he was capable of performing. He retrieved his cell phone from the back pocket of his scrubs. "Here, I will look it up."

The number Dr. Issa provided for Dr. Hasan's wife matched the number Rahim had found at the bottom of the apartment advertisement. The other number was new.

"You will wait with me here," Rahim said.

He made a call to the Military Intelligence Directorate and asked a signals intelligence officer he knew to tap into the directorate's cell-site simulator network.

Ten minutes later he was told that Dr. Hasan's phone was still transmitting a signal somewhere in or near the northern portion of the Sakhour neighborhood, not far from Castello Road. And that the phone belonging to Dr. Hasan's wife was up in the town of Azaz, near the border with Turkey.

Rahim considered—if Dr. Hasan had been shot, it was plausible that his phone would have remained near the scene of the shooting. And if his wife had felt threatened, she might very well have continued to flee to Turkey, taking whatever children she had with her, perhaps relying on remaining family to bury her husband if it had not been done already.

It was impossible to say for sure, short of searching for the phone and the doctor in Sakhour. But Sakhour was, for the moment, behind enemy lines.

"If you are lying to me," said Rahim.

"By God, Lieutenant, I speak the truth."

Rahim studied Dr. Issa's face again, then checked his watch. He had ten minutes to get to the Military Intelligence Directorate. It would be just enough time. After his next shift, and after he had slept—he had already been awake for nearly forty hours—he would investigate further.

For now, he decided to accept that he had been patient, and God had rewarded him.

CHAPTER 20

Istanbul Atatürk Airport, Turkey

They almost didn't let him board. But he'd told them he'd come from
Syria, and that had bought him some sympathy.

"Are you ill, sir?" asked the airport assistant assigned to help Oskar
from his airport wheelchair to his seat on the plane.

"No. It's just my leg," he said.

But it wasn't just his leg. Despite popping as much extra-strength
Tylenol as he thought his liver could tolerate, Oskar was feverish, had a
splitting headache, and his chest wound was burning as though a live coal
were buried under his skin.

Breathing was a chore.

"You look pale. Are you sure you don't need a doctor?"

He wore a T-shirt over his hospital robe. His broken leg was extended
over the wheelchair footplate, nearly dragging on the ground, and he'd
tied his engineer friend's undershirt over the sutures on his leg where
blood had started to seep through the bandages.

"It's just the pain," he said. "I'll be fine."

The airport assistant helped lift him out of his wheelchair and onto
his crutches.

"Don't forget your passport, sir." The assistant picked it up off the
wheelchair, slipped into Oskar's hand, then asked, "You have someone
meeting you in Copenhagen?"

The other passengers were staring at him. Giving him distance, not wanting to contract whatever it was that he had. It occurred to Oskar that he'd lost track of his laptop.

"Yes."

It was the second time in his life he'd flown first class, the first time being the flight from Antakya to Istanbul. Given his height, and the fact that his leg was in a brace, it was the only way he could fit into a seat.

The stewardess brought him a blanket shortly after takeoff. He tried to sleep but could never manage more than an anxious semiconsciousness.

The idea that the woman he'd harbored secret hopes of marrying was leaving him seemed like something he'd dreamed up while sleeping off too many glasses of wine. Fucking Elsa.

He became paranoid, worried that people from Syria were following him.

Needles were pricking his skin, pricking his eyes. Those Syrian doctors, they'd messed him up.

God, his head hurt. He pulled the blanket tighter and forced himself to imagine what it would be like to lie under the birch trees in back of his mother's house. He tried to hear the rustle of the leaves and the chirping of the willow warblers, but whenever he started to nod off, the image of that boy Adel's last moments on this earth would form in his mind, and he'd get panicky and wake up.

The woman sitting next to him edged closer to the window. He didn't blame her. It wasn't just his leg, and the fact that he'd witnessed a murder. Something was terribly wrong with him.

2013

CHAPTER 21

Rebel-held Aleppo

Before the war, it had been known as the Omar Bin Abdul Aziz Hospital, named after a respected eighth-century caliph. Now Dr. Sami Hasan, and everyone else who worked there, called it the M2.

Nestled among apartment buildings in a poor section of the city, it was far smaller than the regime-controlled University of Aleppo Hospital and not nearly as well equipped. But the M2 had been built when the French ruled Syria, at a time when it was not considered profligate to add decorative motifs to an exterior facade or star-shaped inlay to the tile floor of an operating room, and so it had a certain faded elegance to it that the university hospital lacked and which Sami, its chief surgeon, had come to appreciate.

Indeed, there were many things about the M2 Sami had come to appreciate, not the least of which was the *dallah* coffeepot one of the nurses had donated to the staff room and that from the smell of it, had already been refreshed.

Sami opened his eyes and checked his phone. Seven fifteen in the morning. Which meant he had been able to catch five hours of sleep and explained why he was feeling particularly well rested.

He swung his legs off his narrow cot, poured himself a cup of coffee, and began washing his face and hands in a small utility sink. The bright, foresty smell of laurel oil in his wife's soap, paired with the feeling of the strong coffee settling in his stomach, made him smile. Yes, the winter had been interminable and bloody, but now it was nearly summer and after a year of war, the rebels were winning. In a month or two, Aleppo might be fully liberated.

He took another sip of coffee then stripped off his shirt and washed as much as he could under his arms without dripping too much water.

Because he had ten minutes before he had promised to be on the floor, he sat back down on his cot with his coffee in one hand and his cell phone in the other. After signing on to the hospital's satellite Wi-Fi and checking his email and text messages—nothing he needed to respond to—he opened an online version of *Le Monde* and quickly read through the headlines: protests had broken out in Istanbul, the economy of Greece was a mess . . .

When explosions sounded not far to the south, he sighed, clicked off his phone, and put on a clean pair of scrubs. Bypassing the aging elevator, he took the staircase up to the third floor, where he checked on a pregnant nineteen-year-old whose lung had been punctured by a piece of shrapnel.

Minutes later, ambulances and private cars announced their collective arrival with repeated beeps on high-pitched horns.

He returned to the ground floor, where the emergency room intake area had been divided into triage zones marked by colors—green for the walking wounded, yellow for those seriously wounded but not in immediate danger of dying, red for the wounded who would die soon without treatment, and black for those still alive but certain to die.

The first patient to arrive had been placed in the yellow zone and was bleeding profusely from a shallow laceration on the back of his head. Sami ushered him into an exam room and had just finished suturing the wound when three men—soldiers, dressed in battle gear—burst in, claiming that the brother of some Colonel Antar had been injured and was in need of immediate treatment.

Sami knew nothing of any Colonel Antar, much less the man's brother. He eyed the men, noting with dissatisfaction that they were armed. "This colonel's brother. Why wasn't he brought to a field hospital?" he demanded.

Sami was a supporter of the Free Syrian Army and had even performed work at their field hospitals during the first few months of the war for Aleppo. But this was a civilian hospital. If the regime saw armed soldiers being treated here, it would encourage them to bomb.

"The doctor at the field hospital sent him here because he was unable to treat him properly. Please, Doctor."

"First, you will get your weapons out of my hospital," Sami ordered, remaining seated.

"Doctor—"

"Now."

Two of the soldiers handed their rifles to the third, who left the room. Sami followed the remaining two soldiers into the triage zone, which was rapidly filling with wounded. Some had been brought in on metal gurneys, others had stumbled in on their own.

"There!" cried one of the soldiers, pointing to a man on a gurney.

Sami was determined to follow triage protocol. The life of a soldier was worth no more or less than the life of a civilian, and in any event, prioritizing the treatment of soldiers over civilians was another good way to put a target on the M2.

But the soldier in question was in the red triage zone and first in line, so Sami knelt beside him. He was maybe twenty years old. Long black hair, long eyelashes that were covered with dust. A prominent hawklike nose. Conscious, but barely.

"What happened?"

"The building collapsed and he was buried from the chest down. We had to dig him out."

"Bleeding?" Sami asked as he looked for external signs of the same.

"No."

"What is his name?"

"Abdul."

"Abdul!" said Sami loudly, as he pinched the nail bed of Abdul's right index finger and noted that the blood was slow to refill. "How do you feel?"

Moaning, Abdul said his stomach hurt. Sami palpated his skull and began to work his way down the rest of the body, which was colder than it should have been. When he got to the abdominal region just below the ribs, he detected swelling. Abdul winced.

"I need a FAST scan!" Sami called over his shoulder, making eye contact with a nurse's assistant.

Moments later, she produced a white ultrasound device that was connected to a wall outlet by a twisted extension cord. Along with the ultrasound, she handed him a half-full dispenser of hand sanitizer. "No gel," she said.

Sami frowned, but then squirted hand sanitizer on top of a probe, which he then used to shoot high-pitched frequencies into Abdul's abdomen. When, moments later, he observed a thick black stripe in the upper right quadrant, between the kidney and the liver, he said, "Prep the OR. Number two. You, you"—Sami pointed at a nurse, as well as custodian who was helping to lead a child into the green triage zone—"get him on the table." He hesitated for a moment. Supplies of universal-donor blood were limited, but there was no time to type and crossmatch Abdul's blood; the last of the rapid-test kits had been used yesterday. "And ready three units of O-negative, more if we can spare it."

———

As he was donning his operating robe, Sami's phone rang. The ringtone was Ravel's Bolero, which meant it was his wife calling.

He ignored it and began to wash his hands. Then she texted:

Call me now!!!!

Sami stared at the four exclamation points then pushed the callback icon and put the phone on speaker as he continued to scrub his hands.

"What is it?" he snapped when his wife picked up.

"We need you."

For a moment Sami stopped scrubbing. Tahira explained that fighting had broken out in the northern Syrian town of Jarabulus, where she and the children had been taking refuge since fall of the prior year.

"The regime is in Jarabulus?" asked Sami, alarmed. As far as he knew, they had been nowhere near that area of the country.

"No, this is some other group. Rafiq says they are telling people that Jarabulus is now part of a new nation, with new rules."

"What new nation?"

"The Islamic State of Iraq and al Sham. They frighten me, Sami."

Sami recognized the name. He took two deep breaths.

"They have been raiding homes," added Tahira. "Doing terrible things. I—"

"Go to Turkey," Sami said, interrupting. Jarabulus was a border town. Turkey was only a short walk away. "Get out. Go now."

Sami had long been comforted by the thought that by moving his family north and out of Aleppo, he had left them in a position to get out of Syria quickly if they ever needed to.

"Rafiq says they have already captured the border crossing and are not letting anyone pass."

Sami took another deep breath. "Wait for me. I will come as soon as I can."

———

Lacking assistants, Sami pushed open the door to the staff washroom with his foot and took care not to touch anything on his way to the operating room.

The patient had been hoisted up onto the operating table, and his clothes had been cut off. The anesthesiologist was sitting with her cart near the head of the table. A nurse was hastily rolling an instrument table into place.

"What am I prepping him for?" she asked.

They were poison, Sami thought, this group that had invaded Jarabulus. Poison to the rebellion, and certainly to his family. He had to leave. Now.

"Doctor?"

"Laparotomy."

"Is there something wrong, Doctor?"

"No."

"Your instruments are ready."

Sami conferred with the anesthesiologist as the nurse arranged surgical drapes over the patient so only his torso was exposed. Upon sterilizing the exposed skin, Sami made an incision from the patient's upper right quadrant, just below the ribcage, down to his belly button, using a scalpel to cut through the initial layer of skin and fat, but switching to surgical scissors to cut through the fascia and peritoneum.

Upon exposing the inner organs, it became clear that internal bleeding was indeed present. As he focused on finding the source, fear of what might happen to his family receded.

CHAPTER 22

Northern Syria, near the border with Turkey

Like the Mohammedans in the seventh century and the Mongols in the thirteenth, they came to conquer the Levant, but instead of horses, they rode pickup trucks. Chevys and Fords, Toyotas and Izuzus. Humvees stolen from the Americans. Kicking up dust and bouncing over ruts in the road, they blitzed up the Euphrates River Valley, taking towns by surprise.

Certainly five-year-old Adam Hasan, son of Dr. Sami Hasan, was surprised to see them when they roared into Jarabulus.

It was just after eight in the morning, the start of summer only a few days away. Adam, being an early riser, had woken at dawn, crept outside, and tried to light bits of newspaper on fire by directing a beam of the morning sun through a magnifying glass. But he had only been outside for a few minutes before his mother had pulled him back into the house told him not to leave the house at all for the whole day.

Which Adam had thought was crazy. He was allowed to play outside every other day, why not today? So, when his mother took her eyes off him to make a phone call, he snuck back outside. The morning sun had not yet crested the privacy wall that surrounded the house in which he was staying, and he did as he had done earlier in the morning—opened the gate and stepped into the road.

The first of the pickup trucks appeared just as his newspaper was beginning to smolder.

He stood to the side as they flew by him, more curious than scared. He counted one, two, three . . . At ten, he stopped counting. Most of the men inside the trucks wore black balaclavas or bandannas. They all carried guns. Some stood on the back of the pickup truck beds, holding onto the roofs. Others sat half in, half out of the windows.

When one of the trucks skidded to a stop in front of him, Adam thought to run back inside to his mother, but he was too mesmerized by the sight of the soldiers and the guns they carried, and the way the whole town suddenly seemed to be buzzing.

The soldier driving the truck that had stopped leaned his head out the window. He wore a patchy, untrimmed beard with no mustache, a floppy hat, and wraparound sunglasses. Unlike the others, his face was not covered with a balaclava.

"You should go back inside," he said, smiling as he spoke.

Adam nodded but found himself frozen in place.

"We are conducting operations," the soldier added. Then, when Adam still did not move, he asked, "What is your name?"

"Adam."

"I have a son, only a few years older than you. My son likes marbles, do you like marbles?"

Adam nodded. The soldier reached behind him, and from a cardboard box produced a small, dirty plastic bag filled with four glass playing marbles. He offered them to Adam.

Adam stared at the bag. One of the marbles was chipped, and something greasy glistened on the outside of the bag.

"Take it," said the soldier, when Adam hesitated. "It is a gift. And then you go back inside."

As Adam accepted the marbles, one of the soldiers in the back of the pickup truck extended the black flag that was affixed to the back of the truck. On it, crude white calligraphy had been inscribed above a white circle-like blob, upon which black calligraphy had been inscribed. Adam stared at the flag.

"What does it say?" demanded the soldier.

Although Adam had been able to read since the age of three, the writing on the flag was different than anything he had encountered in his studies.

He shrugged.

"I will give you a hint," said the soldier who had given him the marbles. "It is the *shahada*. The *shahada*," he repeated, upon observing Adam's blank expression. "Surely you must know this?" When Adam did not answer, he grew agitated. "There is no god but God, Muhammad is the messenger of God! This is the *shahada*! This is what is on our flag!" He pointed to the white blob. "Muhammad. Messenger. God. You have heard this, of course?"

"I think."

"You think? Are you Christian?"

Rebel-held Aleppo

"We are going to need that transfusion!" said Sami. "What is the delay?"

The anesthesiologist ducked out into the hall to investigate as the remaining nurse began suctioning blood away from the patient's exposed internal organs. Sami lifted the small intestines out of the patient's body, quickly inspecting them as he did so, but declining to run each section of the bowel through his fingers as he might have done had the situation not been so critical.

After glancing at the stomach—it appeared to be intact, but he could revisit that assessment if necessary—he slipped his hands under the patient's ribcage and gently exposed the liver. As he had suspected, it had ruptured and was now swimming in a pool of its own blood.

"More suction!"

Sami grasped the liver with both hands and began to compress it, focusing on the center of the large right lobe where the worst of the rupture appeared to be. After a minute of compression, he felt confident he had at least managed to isolate and contain the hemorrhage.

"For the third time, where is my transfusion?" he demanded, just as a man with two units of O-negative blood burst into the operating room. Sami turned to the nurse, who had put down her suction probe. "You must compress the liver while I pack it."

She exhaled then nodded.

"Tight enough to keep it from bleeding, but not so tight you cause another rupture. Get your hands in position. "On three . . ."

Sami counted to three.

They made the switch, and as the nurse stood over the patient, and the transfusion of universal-donor blood began, Sami sutured and tied off what bleeding blood vessels he could, then packed the liver in place with absorbent, sterile abdominal pads. When the nurse released the liver, Sami packed in two more pads to maintain compression. Then he sewed a clear plastic bag over the exposed entrails, connecting one side of the incision to the other with the bag. The suture thread he had used was black, and the stitches wide-spaced.

The result was not attractive.

"Bring him to intensive care," Sami said. "Type and cross-match him for blood, give him at least two more units, and keep him warm. I will finish with him maybe tonight, maybe tomorrow."

At that, he pulled off his gloves and rushed back to the triage room. Seeing no one waiting in the red section, he announced that he was leaving for the afternoon.

"What?" said the intake nurse. "But—"

"I am sorry," he said, "it is an emergency."

After stripping off his scrubs, Sami jogged back over to the pharmacy where threw his stethoscope and a collection of syringes and medications into a cardboard box. As he was racing out through a set of back doors adorned with iron scrollwork, he was almost bowled over by a soldier his size or taller wearing camouflage and a waist belt that held an empty pistol holster and a satellite phone.

The soldier gripped Sami's shoulders. "Abdul Antar! Do you know where he is?"

As the chief surgeon at the M2, Sami was not used to being manhandled. But because he was dressed in civilian clothes and realized the soldier could not know his position in the hospital, he chose not to make an issue of the affront.

"He is recovering from an operation," he said, disengaging.

"You have seen him? He is alive?"

"If it is the Abdul I operated on, then yes."

The soldier's eyes widened. "You are the doctor?"

"Evidently."

Sami began to walk away.

"Where is he? I must see him. I am his brother."

"The intensive care unit. But you may not visit him."

"I must! And I must talk to you about his condition!" called the soldier, who Sami assumed was Colonel Antar.

"The staff inside will help you," Sami called back as he reached the street, talking over his shoulder as he bunched his fingertips together and made the sign that patience was called for.

Minutes later, as he was halfway between the hospital and his home, passing through Qinnasrin Gate and into the old city, it occurred to Sami that he probably should have mentioned to Colonel Antar that he intended to perform a second operation on his brother—that he would never leave any patient in such a compromised condition forever. He hoped the nurses would know enough to deliver that message. In any case, it was too late to turn around.

CHAPTER 24

"I asked, are you a Christian?" the soldier in black demanded again, this time with more anger.

Not knowing what a Christian was, Adam did not know how to answer, so he was relieved when, from behind him, he heard his mother say, "Of course he is a Muslim, brother. And who are you?"

"The army of the Prince of the Faithful, of the Caliph of the Muslims. Your liberators."

"But this town has already been liberated."

"And now it is being liberated again."

"*Alhamdulillah,*" said Adam's mother. Thank God. With a stern warning never to disobey her again, she grabbed Adam's hand and pulled him inside the courtyard. The soldier with the patchy beard stared at them for a moment, then sped off.

Inside, Adam was served a breakfast of flatbread with yogurt and fresh cucumbers, as his Aunt Aya paced around the kitchen yelling something about traitors and cowards.

There was shooting outside. Adam knew it was shooting because he had heard plenty of it when he had lived in Aleppo.

When the soldiers in the pickup trucks came back an hour later, it was with megaphones. Everyone was instructed to come to the roundabout near the center of town. His Aunt Aya and mother closed the drapes on all the windows and told everyone to be quiet, but then the soldiers came by on foot, banging on the front door. Attendance was mandatory they said. Everyone must come to the roundabout. Anyone who was found inside their home would be considered an enemy of the Islamic State of Iraq and al Sham.

His mother dressed herself in a black robe, then brought Adam and Noora to the kitchen.

"When we go outside," she said, "you may see things you do not want to see. You may hear things you do not want to hear. But I will be with you, and you must stay right by my side and do exactly as I say. Do you both understand?"

What things? Adam wondered. But he nodded.

The wide, dun-colored streets of Jarabulus were shaded in places by locust and pine trees. Alternating blocks of black and white paint had been applied to the curb that lay between the sidewalk and the street, and as Adam walked to the roundabout in the center of town, he tried to step on only the black blocks.

"Adam!" his mother snapped when he got too far ahead.

It was a strange thing, Adam thought when they got to the square. Two men had been tied to wood crosses that in turn had been tied to telephone poles. According to his mother, the men on the crosses were sleeping. How anyone could sleep when tied up like that, Adam did not know, but his mother told him they had been working all night and were very tired.

Because there were so many people crowding into the roundabout, it was hard for Adam to see. Soon he found himself bored and staring at the pant legs of a man in front of him.

"Praise be to God! We ask God to grant us victory!" yelled a man near the center of the roundabout. Then, "The Prophet said you have to swear allegiance to a caliph before you die. And here today, you have the honor of swearing allegiance to the Prince of the Faithful, the Caliph of the Muslims, Abu Bakr al-Baghdadi! Takbir!"

"*Allahu Akbar!*" roared the crowd.

When his mother muttered *Allahu Akbar!* as well, he looked up at her, surprised, but she just glared at him, so Adam went back to staring at the legs of the man in front of him, wondering when they could go back home.

The man up by the roundabout started talking about two criminals who were apostates, but Adam did not know what an apostate was. Then the man who was yelling said all the children should come forward because they should see what happens to apostates.

Adam tried to push forward, but his mother stopped him with one hand and Noora with the other.

"We wait here," she said.

One of the men with guns insisted that they come forward though, so they did.

Adam saw three men. They were kneeling on the pavement. Green blindfolds covered their eyes. Directly behind the blindfolded men stood three more men, dressed in black. Even their faces were wrapped up in black fabric. Each man held a sword. In the center of the roundabout, two men held the black flag with the white writing on it.

Adam needed to pee.

"I want to leave," he told his mother.

"Shh," she said. "Whatever happens, you must not scream, do you understand me?"

"What are they doing?" he asked, but then, as the three men who stood behind the blindfolded men raised their swords, his mother covered his eyes with her hand. He heard thumping, then gasps.

"Let them see!" someone cried.

When his mother took her hand away, Adam observed that the three kneeling men had fallen to the ground and that their heads were no longer attached to their bodies. Blood had pooled around the pavement in front of their severed necks.

"With the help of God Almighty, we will free this land from Assad and the infidels and apostates!" yelled a man in black in front of the bodies. "And know you all, young and old, that if any of you harbor the enemies of God who would take up arms against us, you will be considered an enemy and apostate yourself! But if you should help us, and cast the enemies of God from your home and onto our swords, it will be taken as a sign of your allegiance to the Islamic State of Iraq and al Sham and to the Caliph of the Muslims, Abu Bakr al-Baghdadi, and you will prosper!"

Adam peed in his pants and felt great shame because he had not done that since he was his sister's age. He glanced at his sister. He wondered whether she had peed in her pants too and hoped she had.

"Are they sleeping?" he asked, but he was crying when he spoke because he knew they were not.

"No," said his mother.

One of the men held up a head and showed it to the crowd. Everyone was forced to walk past the bodies. As Adam walked by, one of the soldiers asked him, "What do you want to be, a jihadi or a martyr?"

Adam did not know what to say.

"Jihadi, I think," he heard his mother whisper as she gripped his hand so tightly that it hurt. She tried to pull him away, but the man indicated she should stop.

"And you, my little jihadi," he said, addressing Adam. "How many enemies of God do you know?" And then, "How many men live in your house?"

Adam's mother said her husband was a doctor, but he was working in Aleppo. And he was a devout Muslim, who would surely welcome the arrival of the caliphate.

"Let the child answer," said the soldier. "Adults lie with too much ease. With children, it is different." Bending down so that he was closer to Adam, he asked, "How many men live in your house?"

Adam swallowed.

"One, two?" asked the soldier. "You must tell me the truth, or surely, God and the Caliph will take your mother from you."

"My sister has a husband," said his mother. "But he is in Aleppo as well."

"Let him speak!"

"It is as my mother says," said Adam. And then, "I have learned the *shahada*." The man stood to his full height. "This is true?"

"There is no god but God. Muhammad is the messenger of God," said Adam.

"What is your name, little one?"

"Adam."

"You are very smart, Adam. If you see any enemies of God, you will tell me, will you not?"

Adam nodded. The soldier let them go.

———

Back at the house, Adam's Uncle Rafiq was sitting cross-legged on the orange carpet in the reception room. A rifle that looked like the ones the soldiers outside had been carrying lay near his feet. Aya turned on the reciprocating fan and knelt next to Rafiq and ran her hands through his hair. He explained that battle for the town was over. ISIS had won.

"Everyone is scared to fight them," he said. "A few of us tried. The rest ran."

CHAPTER 25

Sami found his mother, Maryam, in the courtyard of Beit Qarah, sitting at a wicker table, drinking black tea and smoking. Her long hair was wild and had an orange tint to it, the result of an insufficient supply of dye. She wore large, old hoop earrings and a bright green kimono-inspired robe. Two women, both dressed in black abaya robes and headscarves, accompanied her.

Three pointers with rubber tips lay on the table—to be used for moving playing cards to and from the center of the table.

When Maryam saw Sami, she startled, looking guilty for a moment, then recovering.

"I did not," she said, stubbing out her cigarette and raising her eyebrows, "expect you home until tomorrow evening."

It was hot in the courtyard, the air stagnant and heavy, and no water flowed through the marble fountain's bronze seahorse spouts. To the left of the fountain, a one-legged man sat in a plastic chair, huddled over a radio listening to a soccer match. A woman of perhaps twenty faced away from him as she nursed a baby.

Sami turned to his mother's table companions. "Sisters," he said. "So good to see you."

"And you, Abu Adam."

"You are both well?"

They said they were.

"I need the Mercedes," Sami said to his mother. "There has been an incident." He pulled a pill vial out of his pants pocket and placed it on the table. "Your blood pressure medication."

"What kind of incident?"

As Sami explained, his mother picked up her cigarette then put it back down. Her friends lowered their gazes in respectful silence.

"No one need leave Beit Qarah," Sami added. "There will still be room for everyone."

The house had become a homeless shelter of sorts. For relations and friends who had lost their homes in the war, for the wounded who had been discharged from the M2 but had nowhere to go to, for a mother and her daughter who were recovering from a sarin gas attack in Khan al-Asal . . .

Maryam's hands shook as she pocketed her vial of blood pressure medication. "The keys are in my wardrobe. You will have to buy petrol. The tank is nearly empty."

Sami kissed his mother on both sides of her cheek. "Thank you."

"Be careful."

———

The mustard-yellow 1989 Mercedes turbo diesel sedan was parked two blocks away in a garage that opened onto one of the few roads in the old city that was wide enough to accommodate cars.

It had belonged to Sami's father, and after his father died, his mother had refused to part with it. Too many memories, she had said—of the three of them driving across the Bosporus Bridge on their way to Greece, of racing through the Syrian desert on their way to Baghdad, of trying to find a parking spot in Jerusalem.

Sami had paid to have the battery replaced shortly before the war and was grateful that he had, given that his own Mercedes had been abandoned in the University of Aleppo Hospital parking lot, on the regime-held side of the city.

The car started on the first try, roaring to life and belching black smoke as he revved the engine.

Outside the city he raced north on the M4 highway, stopping only to buy diesel dispensed out of plastic jugs by roadside vendors and to present his Free Syrian Army papers at multiple rebel checkpoints. *The reckoning approaches, O you dogs of Assad,* read graffiti that had been painted on the front window of a roadside restaurant.

He turned left off route 216 before reaching the Euphrates. The dry rolling hills were barren save for scrub brush and clusters of olive trees, and they were crisscrossed by dirt roads.

The ISIS checkpoint he encountered just outside Jarabulus wasn't so much a checkpoint as it was two armed men harassing people by the side of the road. The black flag that flew from the back of their pickup truck was ringed with gold fringe, making it look a bit like an unattractive carpet.

Sami turned on the radio, fiddled with the old dial until he came upon a station that featured a nonstop recitation of the Quran, then pulled to a stop when instructed to do so.

The soldier who demanded to know where he was going spoke Arabic, but with an accent Sami didn't recognize. Tunisian, Sami guessed. Maybe Egyptian. The ISIS fighters came from all over the Middle East. From Europe too.

"I work at the M2 hospital in Aleppo, but I have family in Jarabulus," Sami said. "So, I visit the hospital in Jarabulus when I come to visit my family. I am going there now." He explained that he fought for no army, was affiliated with no militia group. When they demanded to know whether he was Muslim, he said, "Of course, brother."

"How many *rak'ats* are compulsory for the *fajr* prayer?"

Sami's mother was a lapsed Catholic descended from French bureaucrats, his late father a lapsed Sunni Muslim. So Sami had never been taught to pray, but Tahira and her family were practicing Sunnis, and he had witnessed them praying on countless occasions.

"Two," he said.

"And how many for the *zuhr* prayer?"

Sami knew the answer to that one as well, but he harbored doubts about the *asr* afternoon prayer. "Four. Brother, would you permit me to ask you a question?"

"What question?"

"May God protect you, but when the sand flies that are biting your toes and crawling up your pants infect you with the parasite leishmaniasis, how many milligrams per kilogram of body weight of the medicine I am carrying should I administer to you?"

The soldier looked down at his toes, which were exposed because he was wearing plastic sandals. And indeed, a few flies had gathered around his feet. Not sand flies, but Sami doubted the soldier could make the distinction.

"I am bringing this medicine to the hospital in Jarabulus," Sami added, pointing to the cardboard box that lay next to him on the seat. When the soldier instructed him to open it up, Sami did, exposing his stethoscope, several syringes, and a collection of tightly packed vials.

"This leishmaniasis," Sami said. "I am certain you know the disease, if not the name. The parasites, they get into the body, they cause the skin to blister, and the nose to run and bleed. Some grow very sick. I am sure you know some of your brothers who suffer from this illness. Surely the Caliph would not want Muslims to suffer with disease? Surely he would want me to complete my mission?"

"Open the trunk," said the soldier. "And get out of the car."

Sami did. They found no weapons, and they let him go.

———

The only thing different Sami noticed about Jarabulus, apart from the fact that there were fewer people on the street than usual, were the heads on spikes in the center of the roundabout.

The ISIS militants had left the heads there, tilted at odd angles, eyes closed, mouths agape. One man's tongue was sticking out. Surprisingly little blood, Sami noted, or signs that the heads had once been attached to neck. It was as though the necks had receded, turtle-like, into the victims' skulls.

There were no militants to guard the heads, just a couple of teenage boys, gawking and pointing.

———

When Sami arrived at the house where his family was staying, his children greeted him with ebullient bursts of "Baba! Baba! Baba!"

He let them grip his legs before hurrying them all—Tahira, Noora, Adam, Aya, and Aya's two children—into the Mercedes. Tahira and Aya had already covered themselves head to toe in black, leaving only their eyes exposed.

Then Rafiq showed up. With his AK-47.

Sami had never much liked his brother-in-law. But he considered that Rafiq still had two children to care for and that the patchwork of private roads around Jarabulus would likely allow them to evade the checkpoint outside of town. Besides, the Mercedes was almost certainly faster than anything the militants were driving.

"Get in the trunk," he said, adding, "If we are stopped and searched, do not wait to start shooting."

———

Much to everyone's relief, they arrived back at Beit Qarah without incident.

Before leaving for the M2, Sami retrieved a book from an alcove in the reception room and brought it to the courtyard where Adam was sitting on the pinkish marble floor, in the shade of a small pistachio tree. Although Tahira had pulled a plastic slide and a tricycle out of storage, Adam was focused on an old green vacuum that had stopped working a year ago. Brow deeply furrowed, he was raising and lowering an inner lever with his pudgy little hand.

"Have you fixed it yet?" Sami asked.

"Not fixing, Baba."

"Not fixing?"

"No."

"Then what are you doing to it?"

"Building."

"Hmm," said Sami.

He took a seat on the cool marble, leaned back against the fountain, and considered that when he and Tahira had first looked into buying Beit

Qarah, the courtyard walls had been covered with ugly gray stucco. Tahira had been right about what had been under them—sturdy, honey-blond limestone, bisected by bands of black basalt. Hewn stone that was as beautiful as it was thick.

These were the walls that would now have to protect his family until the war, at least for Aleppo, was over. Which would be soon, he hoped. A few months.

"I have something for you," he said to Adam. "This is a special book to me. Do you know why?"

Adam glanced at the book and shook his head.

"When I was a boy, not too much older than you are now, my family moved from Damascus to Aleppo. I hated moving. All I wanted to do was move back to my old house in Damascus and go to sleep in my old room, play with my old friends. But we could not move back, because my father had taken a job at a hospital here in Aleppo. So, I was very upset and very worried. But then my mother, your Mémère, bought me this book and taught me how to fold birds and animals, and it was very calming for me. It became my favorite book."

Sami started to explain what origami was, and that if Adam had been disturbed by what he had seen earlier in the day, the act of concentrating on something like origami might help to alleviate his mental pain. But before he could finish, Adam went back to fiddling with the vacuum.

Sami sighed then placed a hand on his son's shoulder. "I can see you are busy but know that the book is yours if you want it. I will leave it in your room."

———

Back at the M2, Colonel Antar was waiting for him in the entrance foyer, demanding to know where he had been and that Sami account for the condition of his brother.

"There is this, this—*thing*—sewn to his stomach. I can see inside it! This is not acceptable. You should never have left him like this!"

Sami scowled. "I instructed you not to enter the intensive care unit."

"I do not care what you instructed me to do, Doctor. This man is my brother. You must tend to him. Now!"

"Your brother," said Sami coldly, "came to this hospital not only with a ruptured liver, but also drained of blood and hypothermic. When I deem that he is strong enough to survive the next round of surgery, that is when I will perform it."

"When will he be strong enough?" the colonel demanded.

"When I say he is."

"And when you do operate on him, the bag—"

"Will be removed, of course. It is there to prevent infection while he gathers strength for the next operation. Your brother has a good chance of making a full recovery, Colonel—provided that you have not infected him—but I must be allowed to do my job as I see fit, just as you must do yours as you see fit."

Sami ascended a few steps then turned. "ISIS has taken over Jarabulus," he said. "When do they come to Aleppo?"

The colonel made a face. "Aleppo? No, do not worry yourself about that, doctor. ISIS will not come to Aleppo. The Syrian people, they reject these foreigners. You worry about treating my brother and let me tend to ISIS."

CHAPTER 26

Malmö, Sweden • One month later

Upon returning home from work at the Copenhagen office of the European Development Service, Oskar Lång found his fiancée, Elsa, standing in the kitchen of his third-floor walk-up. She was wearing a lavender tank top with spaghetti straps, the one that she'd taken to wearing with increasing frequency ever since he had remarked that it flattered her. Instead of her normal ponytail, she appeared to have blow-dried her blond hair. Her lips glistened with clear gloss.

"Well, hello, you!" he said. "This is quite the surprise."

"I hope you don't mind."

He let his leather messenger bag slip from his shoulder to the floor. "No, of course not. Good news?"

"I wanted to tell you in person."

She draped her arms around his neck, smiled, and gave him a quick kiss. Oskar observed that she'd placed her overnight bag on the futon in the next room. And that she had arranged flowers—three white-and-red peonies—in a beer-mug vase on the kitchen table.

"I went to the center this morning," she said, referring to the Sahlgrenska University Hospital Cancer Center, which lay three hours to the north in Gothenburg, Sweden.

"I thought your appointment wasn't until tomorrow?"

"They had a cancellation."

She kissed him again.

Oskar felt a small pang of regret for having given her the key to his apartment. It was six o'clock on a Friday, and he'd been looking forward to having the evening to himself.

"I'm so happy for you, Elsa."

"I'm so happy for us," she said.

At that, she took his hand and led him to the bedroom, in a way that made Oskar feel a bit like a dog on a leash. As they undressed and then climbed into bed, she talked about the traffic she'd encountered on the E6.

"Don't worry about me," she said when, after a few minutes of kissing, his mouth began to drift downward. She brought him back up to her lips, saying, "This is for you."

Oskar attempted to perform as though it were. Eventually, he climaxed; she didn't, but said not to worry about it.

"Are you sure?" he asked.

"I'm sure."

They'd known each other since preschool, so he knew better than to persist. Elsa handed him a wad of tissues.

As he was cleaning himself off, he said, "By the way, I told Nils I'd meet him at seven. For a run. Kungsparken to the marina. And back." They made eye contact. "Yeah, I know," he said. "Stupid."

"Can you cancel?"

Oskar sat up, scratched his head, and swung his legs off the bed. "I canceled last week," he said, adding, "He thinks he's helping me."

"If your leg hurts, just stop."

His leg hurt now. Just a dull pain, up by his hip, but it was always there. "I'll be back around eight, we can eat then."

For a moment Oskar listened to birds chirp outside his window. He reminded himself to remember to refill the suction-cup feeder he'd attached to the outside of the kitchen window, then he began to wonder—since she'd come to visit him this weekend, did that still mean he needed to go to Gothenburg to see her next weekend?

"What are you thinking?" she asked.

"How happy I am for you."

"No bad cells at all. Nothing. We can finally start to plan, Oskar.

Everything we used to talk about, it can still happen. You're better. I'm better. Maybe next summer we can . . ."

Her voice, sounding somewhere between ecstatic and weepy, drifted off. When Oskar didn't fill the silence, she added, "By then, it will have been over a year. I don't trust them, but if I'm still clear by next summer. Maybe June at your mother's house? We can rent a tent."

He stroked her hair. "We can."

"You're sure you don't mind adopting?" she asked.

"Of course not."

———

Oskar met his brother Nils at the base of a set of wide, gently sloping steps that extended into a pond that lay at the southern tip of a public park in downtown Malmö. A weeping willow stood next to the steps, and a family of geese rested under its branches. More geese were down by the water, waddling about in their own droppings.

Standing next to Nils, hands on hips as she stretched, was his wife, Birgit.

"I don't believe it," she exclaimed upon seeing Oskar. "You actually came!"

"Birgit!" said Oskar as he hugged her. "So good to see you."

That was a lie. He'd been hoping to talk to his brother alone.

"I owe you a hundred kronor," said Birgit to Nils. She laughed.

"Oskar," said Nils opening his arms. "I knew you'd show up, even if Birgit had her doubts."

The brothers embraced. Nils, like Oskar, was tall and lanky. But he was tanned, as was Birgit, both having been on vacation the last two weeks with the rest of Sweden. Oskar, having taken his vacation in the winter to be with Elsa as she recovered in Gothenburg, was pasty white.

"I actually used to run almost every day when I was in university," said Oskar, a bit defensively. When he'd been going for his bachelor's and, subsequently, his master's in engineering at nearby Lund University, he'd played on the soccer club and had frequently run with his clubmates.

"You're here today, and that's the important thing," said Birgit. "Have you stretched?"

"If you count the walk from my apartment, which I do," said Oskar.

"I need five more minutes," said Birgit, adding, "You shouldn't go light on the stretching! Much easier to prevent injuries than it is to recover from them."

Oskar stole a glance at the clock on his phone as he slipped it into the pouch encircling his bicep.

Birgit, dressed in tank top and spandex shorts, bent over to perform a stretch.

"You know," said Oskar, "I'm going to be slow, so I might just start out. You guys will catch up in no time."

"South around the Stora Dammen," said Birgit. "No cheating!"

———

Feeling sluggish and stiff, Oskar began to angle south as instructed. The gravel path merged with a paved bike path. An old woman with a rattling rear fender dinged her handlebar bell at him as she zipped by. A mother with two children in a bike cart also dinged her bell at him when he swerved to avoid colliding with some geese.

His brother passed him well before he'd even reached the traffic circle that lay between the beach and the park where they'd started their run.

Birgit came up behind him a minute later. Oskar noted she didn't appear to be out of breath or sweating.

"You go on," he said. "I don't want to hold you back."

"No, no—I promised Nils I'd stay with you! By the way, how is Elsa?"

"Complete remission. She just got the news."

"That's fantastic!" Birgit said. "Amazing, both of you, back as good as new. Now you two can finally get on with your lives."

Although it was late in the day, the Ribersborg beach was still crowded with beachgoers, fellow runners, and couples out for a late stroll. Birgit insisted on running on the beach itself, and Oskar labored as his feet, wide though they were, sunk into the coarse sand. He dodged clumps of seaweed gathered on the shore, children making sandcastles, a gaggle of drunk bikini-clad women laughing and dancing to Håkan

Hellström, and a woman in a burkini. Dogs and kids played in the cold water as the adults waded in up to their knees. Upon reaching the marina at the far end of the beach park, they ran back the same way they had come.

———

Twenty minutes later, egged on by Birgit who was now jogging backward in front of him, Oskar finished his run with a sprint, stopping where they'd started, in front of the willow tree next to the pond.

He was hyperventilating, his heart was pounding in his chest, and his bad leg ached, but by God, he didn't feel half bad. He would do this more often, he told himself. And he was glad he'd stuck it out for the full run rather than sneaking in a shortcut or stopping to swim. Running was good for him.

He leaned over, using a bench to support himself as he caught his breath.

"Are you okay?" asked a boy who was walking by with his mother.

Oskar gave him a thumbs-up and tried to smile but wound up breaking into a coughing fit. He gave the boy another thumbs-up as the boy's mother pulled her child away.

He was okay. The antibiotic-resistant infection that had spread from his rib to his blood was gone, and for the past few months, he'd finally started to feel as though his life was back on track.

As his chest heaved, he could feel where the operation to remove the infected portion of rib had been. It no longer hurt, but the scar tissue felt funny, as though someone were continually pulling at his skin.

He raised his head to the sky and the sun.

"Well done," said Birgit, patting him on the back and interrupting his thoughts. He was relieved to see that she was at least breathing heavily now, and sweating. When the run was finished, he could even concede that his brother was lucky to have married her.

Still, he thought, she was no Hannah.

2014

CHAPTER 27

Antakya, Turkey

On a warm spring day when the orange trees were beginning to bloom, nearly two years after fleeing Aleppo, twenty-six-year-old Hannah Johnson ducked out of the office at the Bonne Foi Aid Coalition at one in the afternoon and retrieved her aging Toyota Yaris from a parking garage in downtown Antakya.

As she raced out of the city, hurtling past cotton fields and a refugee camp for defectors from the Assad regime, she drank sweetened cherry juice from a box, blasted Turkish dance music over the crackly speakers, and let the wind tousle her hair while she stole glances at her Facebook feed. Her skin was tanned, her hands decorated with faded henna, and for good luck she wore a Hand of Fatima pendant on a leather cord. It had been months since she had brooded about Oskar—a two-week flirtation the prior year with a Turk who had proved himself to be as vain as he was beautiful had cured her of that—and she did not think of him now.

Two and a half hours later, she pulled up to the back of a dilapidated warehouse in Kilis, Turkey, where a young man named Osman helped her load fifteen overstuffed cardboard boxes into the back of her Yaris and then drove with her to the Öncüpınar border crossing.

After inspecting her Syrian passport, the Turks let her pass. Minutes later, in the zero-point zone between Turkey and Syria, a sweat-drenched Turkish Red Crescent officer inspected the boxes while she covered her hair with a paisley headscarf and zipped up her lightweight jacket to conceal her figure.

"You are lucky they let you through," he said.

Hannah shrugged. If they hadn't, she had been prepared to cross the border illegally. Osman knew a smuggler who knew a way through not far away. It just would have delayed her a few hours.

After a two-hour wait at the Syrian inspection building, a ragtag group of heavily armed twentysomethings who called themselves the Islamic Front asked that she scrawl her name on a piece of tissue-thin notepaper, to which they applied a stamp that read Free Syria.

"Welcome back, sister," they said.

———

On Hannah's first incursion into Syria, she had been met on the Syrian side of the border by a clean-shaven, exceptionally slender nineteen-year-old aid worker named Muhammad. This time, Muhammad met her again, but before they began to transfer her cargo into his Hyundai hatchback, he said, "I have bad news. The clinic has closed."

Behind Muhammad, on the other side of the road, mud-splattered cars were lined up waiting to enter Turkey. Luggage, cardboard boxes, and plastic bags had been strapped to roofs. People stood to the sides of their cars, killing time. Children sold diesel fuel in recycled bottles. Hannah's nose twitched at the acrid smell of rotting garbage and sewage that was drifting over from the nearby refugee camp.

"You mean for today?" she asked, speaking Arabic.

"No, permanently." Muhammad dipped his head to his shoulder, a little tic he had.

"What happened?"

"Dr. Malki left," said Muhammad.

"No one told me."

"I think he went to Turkey to be with his family."

Hannah bit her lip as Muhammad stood there with his hands in the pockets of his tight Euro jeans.

"When did this happen?" she asked.

"Two days ago."

"Huh," she said. "Why was I not told?"

Muhammad shrugged.

"You could have sent me a text, no?" she asked.

"There is another clinic," said Muhammad. "That ran out of anesthesia last night. If you are willing, we could bring the supplies there."

"In Azaz?"

"Farther south." Although Muhammad carried a cell phone, he also wore a showy silver watch on his wrist, and he checked it now. "We have time," he said.

Hannah stared at the boxes. She had agreed to bring medicine to Azaz, a dusty, low-slung town near the Turkish border, because Dr. Malki, the clinic supervisor, had done work for her employer, Bonne Foi. She trusted him in a way that she didn't trust other potential recipients of the medicine.

"Hmm," she said, recalling that a few weeks ago, in a town just south of Azaz, a British reporter had been kidnapped. She didn't think Muhammad knew she was an American—she'd insisted Bonne Foi not publicize it—but she couldn't be sure.

"Of course, I can make the delivery myself if you like," said Muhammad, perhaps sensing her reluctance.

Hannah wanted to trust Muhammad. On her prior trips, he'd been scrupulously polite and protective of her. His eyes, with their long, almost feminine lashes, had always struck her as kind. But part of her wondered whether he was just telling her the clinic in Azaz was closed so that he could sell the medicine on the black market. Bonne Foi was a small organization, with limited resources, and as a result was only paying him the equivalent of a few dollars a day. And Hannah was new at this. Since fleeing Syria, she had mostly confined herself to working on the Turkish side of the border—helping refugees transition from the refugee camps to private housing in Antakya, then serving as a liaison between French doctors on mercy missions and the Turkish refugee camps. She wondered whether Muhammad was trying to take advantage of her inexperience.

"That would be breaking protocol," she said diplomatically.

"I understand."

If the clinic really had closed, she wondered, why hadn't Dr. Malki texted her?

"Do you think," she ventured, "We could stop by the clinic in Azaz anyway?"

Muhammad smiled uncomfortably and dipped his head to his shoulder again. Hannah sensed he was embarrassed.

"Even if the doctor has departed, there may still be patients in need of medical supplies," she explained, hoping that would help them both save face.

"There are no patients," he said. "I was there yesterday."

"The nurses may be treating people. A new doctor may have arrived."

Muhammad glanced at the ground then at his car. "Okay," he said. "We go to the clinic."

———

Azaz had seen heavy fighting at the beginning of the war, but even though the charred shells of tanks still lay rusting in the streets and the central mosque was in ruins, Hannah knew the town had experienced only intermittent violence of late. So she was wholly unprepared for the scene of destruction that lay before her when Muhammad pulled up to the clinic.

Or rather, what had once been the clinic.

An enormous crater lay near where the entrance had stood. Above it, a telephone pole festooned with wires that were no longer connected to anything sagged at a forty-five-degree angle. On its periphery lay a porcelain sink that had stood in the clinic's common bathroom. Scattered around the sink were bits of brown-and-maroon-striped couch cushions, bright orange carpet fragments, the chrome base of an operating table, a shattered window frame, a woman's blouse stained with what might have been blood, and a pile of cracked china.

Without saying a word, Hannah stepped out of the car and over a downed wire. Her feet crunched on broken glass.

Muhammad followed her, hands in his pockets, kicking at the dirt with his pointy-toed dress shoes. He dipped his head to his shoulder.

"The regime blames ISIS, of course," he said. "But ISIS does not have fighter jets."

Hannah looked around. The adjacent buildings had also suffered damage, but the epicenter of the destruction was the clinic.

"This happened two days ago?"

A pair of goats and a group of school-aged children huddled under a sickly chinaberry tree, observing her from a distance. Aside from that, the street was empty.

"Yes," said Muhammad.

It had been a small clinic, really just a modest home that had been pressed into service when its owners had abandoned it. But the last time Hannah had visited, there had been patients, young and old, in every room.

"And Dr. Malki?" Hannah asked.

Muhammad shook his head. "They found him over there." He pointed to a pile of rubble next to the remains of a corrugated metal roof. Then he tapped out a thin cigarette and lit it.

"Why—" Hannah was about to ask Muhammad why he lied to her about what had happened, but as soon as she began to ask the question, she realized she could answer it herself. He'd lied because he was worried the medicine runs would stop.

Muhammad exhaled smoke and waved it away from Hannah's face. "I will be in the car," he said.

Hannah lingered, unable to pull her eyes away from the destruction. Near the pile of cracked china lay a fragment of teacup. She studied it from a distance, fixating on the delicate carnation design, then drew closer and realized she'd seen the same pattern teacup in her father's apartment, when she'd visited him in Aleppo, what, ten years ago?

She recalled the smell of sugared black tea stirred with a cinnamon stick, and the way her father used to call her the Princess of Aleppo, and eating baby eggplants drizzled with pomegranate molasses for breakfast . . .

After slipping into the back seat of Muhammad's car, she asked, "This other clinic. Where is it?"

"Aleppo," said Muhammad.

Hannah didn't answer. Yes, that was certainly farther south, she thought, knowing her mother and sister would be livid if they knew she was even considering it.

"It is underground, deep in a basement," added Muhammad. "No ISIS. In a district protected by al-Tawhid. Of course, now they call themselves something different." He shrugged. "I can show you the way."

Hannah still didn't answer. After leaving Aleppo she'd taken a job with Bonne Foi thinking she'd just help out with the relief effort for a few months. If she'd known that two years later she'd still be working for them, having only been able to afford to go home once in the interim, she wondered whether she would have ever accepted that first job offer.

But she had stayed, and one thing had led to another—an illiterate Syrian woman had needed help filling out the applications for an asylum process that promised to drag out for half a year, a family of five that had been swindled by their landlord and needed help navigating the Turkish legal system . . . More recently, a seven-year-old Syrian girl had become separated from her family during a botched illegal border crossing and had needed someone to escort her back from Turkey to the now-destroyed medical clinic in Azaz where her mother had been recovering from a bullet wound. The common thread had always been that Hannah felt needed.

"My brother was treated there," said Muhammad, interrupting her thoughts.

Hannah recalled that Muhammad had a younger brother whose lungs had been badly burned in a chlorine gas attack several weeks ago.

"He is still at this clinic?"

"No, he recovers at home. I am not asking for him."

"It would be okay if you were."

"He needs antibiotics."

"I have no antibiotics. Just anesthesia. And vaccines and dressings."

"I know."

Hannah was under no illusion that her little medicine runs were changing the world or the course of the war. Doctors Without Borders, Save the Children, the Syrian American Medical Society, the Red Crescent, Direct Relief . . . those were the organizations really supplying the aid.

But they could only do so much and were hampered by the fact that they were responsible bureaucracies, unwilling to put the lives of their employees and volunteers in too much danger. Whereas Bonne Foi was run by a collection of French Syrians who had proved far more willing to take risks. As a result, she was in a position to fill in a few of the gaps.

"Checkpoints?" she asked.

"Four, maybe five, I think."

"Who controls them?"

Muhammad listed a few rebel factions and claimed all were at least loosely affiliated with the Free Syrian Army. Hannah recognized some of the names, others she didn't.

"Will we have problems getting through?" she asked.

"No. Criminals used to control a checkpoint on Castello Road, but they were driven out months ago."

"These other groups. Will they steal the medicine? Or demand payment for letting us pass?"

"There is a chance, of course," said Muhammad.

Hannah knew she could hand the medicine over to Muhammad to deliver on his own, and she wouldn't be faulted for it. But it might jeopardize her ability to make future deliveries if she couldn't personally guarantee the chain of custody. No donors liked to think they might be funding criminal enterprises.

She calculated: it was six thirty now, and Aleppo wasn't far, but with the checkpoints, it could take a while. Would her car—which was really Bonne Foi's car—be safe parked in the Syrian border checkpoint lot where she'd left it? The border soldiers knew it belonged to an aid group and would keep an eye on it during the day, but the crossing closed at night.

She could always go back to the border and take her own car to get to Aleppo, but that would be a violation of Bonne Foi's policy. They didn't want their cars getting shot at, ruined by potholed roads, or commandeered by ragtag army units at internal Syrian checkpoints, so they forbade their workers from using them past the border.

"Can you get me back by tomorrow morning?"

"I have a cousin in Azaz," said Muhammad. "We go to Aleppo, come back to Azaz, you sleep at her house tonight, then early tomorrow I will take you back to the border."

"Okay," said Hannah. "Then we do it."

And so it was that, nearly two years after leaving Aleppo, Hannah found herself going back.

CHAPTER 28

Regime-held Aleppo • The next day

Rahim Suleiman opened his eyes at four thirty in the morning—a full fifteen minutes before he needed to get up. As a courtesy to his Iranian roommate, who lay snoring on a cot across the room, he reached across to the end table next to his bed, grabbed his cell phone, and clicked off the alarm.

A few minutes, he told himself. He could rest for a few minutes longer. To guard against falling back to sleep, he removed the earplugs he used to make the Iranian's snoring more bearable and placed them on the end table that stood next to his bed.

As a few minutes turned into ten, he did briefly drift back to sleep, but then heard what might have been coughing coming from his living room. Not wanting to cede the moral high ground of being the first to rise, he quickly swung his legs out of bed, grabbed his Makarov service pistol from the end table, and hobbled into the hall in his imitation-silk pajamas.

Upon placing his pistol on the kitchen table, he used the toilet, dusted himself with talcum powder, then ducked his head into the living room and confirmed with satisfaction that, in addition to the Iranian captain with whom he was sharing his room, the Iranian intelligence officer in the living room was still sleeping. As were the two bunked in what had been his daughter Zahra's room, before she and his wife and all the rest of his relations had fled to Beirut.

For fourteen days the Iranians had been living with him and for fourteen days he had risen before they had. This despite the fact that he was older than all of them. Surely, he considered, they must feel some shame.

Rahim made himself tea, ate a piece of stale flatbread topped with lukewarm yogurt, and checked the time. Sunrise in an hour.

He stood—slowly, so as not to pull out his back—then trudged into the living room and opened the window shade, revealing the Citadel looming above a dark gray haze in the far distance. The sight of the impregnable fortress, perched atop the same hill upon which the prophet Abraham had milked his cows, always cheered him. Held by the regime since the beginning of the war, her thick ramparts and crenellations had protected the city since the time of the Crusaders. Surely, he reasoned, she would not fall now.

On the eastern horizon, he perceived a hint of light, and it made him feel a little less lonely.

Rapping his knuckles on a glass-topped coffee table and speaking loudly, he said, "The sun will not wait!"

The eyes of the Iranian closest to him snapped open then narrowed.

Rahim had no sympathy. When the Iranians had first moved in, he had made it clear that despite their religious differences—they were Shia, he Sunni—regular dawn prayers would be observed. So they had been warned.

Turning to a twenty-year-old who likely would spend his day reconnoitering rebel positions in the bombed-out innards of the al Madina souk, he said, "Get up, Mahdi! God calls."

As the young man groaned, Rahim wondered if his son, Adel, would have exhibited such indolence, were he still alive. Rahim didn't think so. Unlike Zahra, who had been born lazy and still was, Adel had always been an early riser.

Rahim performed his ablutions at the kitchen sink, then retrieved his prayer mat, feeling invigorated by the hot tea in his belly and the cold water evaporating on his face. He unrolled the mat in the living room so that it was facing Mecca, then waited for his Iranian guests to join him. They soon did, leading Rahim to suspect that none had been particularly diligent in performing their ablutions.

Over the sound of the resumption of war, and as the Iranians each placed clay *turbahs* at the head of their mats, Rahim began to pray.

When he got to the bowing part—*Subhana rabbiyal adheem* . . . Glory be to my Lord—he felt the muscles of his lower back stretch ever so slightly, just enough so that there was a pleasant release.

The Prophet, peace be upon him, had been no fool when mandating prayers. To exalt God and stretch in the morning at the same time, this was genius, he thought.

———

Hundreds of checkpoints had cropped up all over Aleppo, on both the rebel- and government-held sides. Just to get to Military Intelligence headquarters later that morning, Rahim had to pass through five.

He did not mind the inconvenience. There were rebel spies and sympathizers all over the city. If the checkpoints meant that the government caught just one of them, and the counterintelligence division had indeed caught eighty-seven within the past week, then they were worth it.

Upon arriving at headquarters, he was displeased to note that the file containing his subordinates' prior-day intelligence summaries was not on his desk.

"Aisha!" he called to the secretary that had been assigned to him when he had been promoted to major. "I need—"

"It is under the al-Jalloum report."

"What?"

She repeated herself.

"I am not speaking of the al-Jalloum report!" snapped Rahim. Lazy and defiant this one was, just like his daughter. "As I have explained—every morning, without exception, I need the end-of-day collection reports for—"

"Look under the al-Jalloum report, Major."

Rahim, suddenly understanding, did. "I see," he said.

"Will you be needing anything else?"

"At the moment, no."

As a rule, the twenty-two intelligence officers Rahim commanded relayed actionable intelligence immediately, but less urgent matters were addressed in end-of-day reports. Rahim picked up those reports now and began to read. According to a sixty-two-year-old butcher who lived in rebel-held Aleppo but who had a son fighting for the regime, the rebel group Jaish al-Mujahideen had set up improvised hell cannons near the Huzeivh Mosque in the Bustan al-Qasr district. Meanwhile, in the rebel-held Sukari district, a mother with a daughter being detained in Aleppo's central prison reported that the rebel group Jabhat al-Islamiya had recently taken over two checkpoints that had previously been manned by the Free Syrian Army . . .

Rahim flipped through the pile of notes quickly, making notations of his own so that he would remember how best to distribute this raw intelligence to the appropriate air force targeteers and military commanders on the ground.

It was only as he was nearing the end of the pile, that he saw it. A single photo of a woman's face. Blurry, as though shot surreptitiously with a poor-quality camera phone.

It was face he was sure he recognized but could not recall from where. He felt he should be able to recall, though, because while he looked at hundreds of photos over the course of any given week—of rebel commanders, troop positions, artillery placements—rarely were they of women.

And this woman . . . There was something about her. Slender nose. High cheekbones. Understated beauty. She wore a paisley headscarf that covered all but a wisp of black hair.

Rahim closed his eyes and leaned back in his chair. Well, it would come to him eventually, and he began to read the file. The photo had been taken at the Maqam Gate checkpoint in rebel-held Aleppo. The woman, who had been carrying a Syrian passport had been identified as Hannah . . .

Rahim squinted as he tried to make out the last name. Johnson?

A Syrian? Named Johnson? Hannah Johnson? Rahim stared at the photo again.

And then he remembered. Adel's room at the hospital! The girl, the one who had told him about what had happened to Adel. But she had not been Syrian, she had been American! Seizing the report now with both hands, Rahim read as fast as his brain could process the words. The girl and her driver, a man named Mohammad Atwan, had passed through the checkpoint on their way to a medical clinic in the Sheikh Saeed district. They had been carrying medical supplies.

An American. Making runs into rebel-held Aleppo.

Rahim very much doubted she was only there to deliver medicine. Was she CIA? Delivering money perhaps? Or messages?

And then his mind veered toward darker thoughts. She had also been in Aleppo just days before the war broke out, had she not? Her excuse was that her boyfriend—she had been a loose woman, he recalled, sleeping with a man out of wedlock—was hurt, but had she really been there to scout the city? Had she known the rebels were about to attack? Could she have had anything to do with Adel's death? That had been the doctor's fault, of course, but she had been in the room. Had she known Adel was a member of the *shabiha*?

Rahim pounded his fist on the table.

"Major?" asked his secretary, looking up from his desk. "Everything is okay?"

He checked the file and noted which one of his officers had collected the information, and how.

"Is Sergeant Nassar at the prison today?"

Aisha leaned into her computer screen, typed for a moment, then said, "I believe so."

"Tell him I will be joining him shortly."

———

The Aleppo Central Prison lay north of center city at the edge of an industrial zone. Its imposing perimeter fence was topped with barbed wire and stained with rust, its multistory concrete form broken up only by the narrowest of window slits. Above it loomed a massive watchtower.

As guards waved Rahim through the front gate, he made the mistake of leaving the window of his UAZ 4x4 open and caught a whiff of something putrid, like a dead mouse rotting in a closet—the bodies they had buried in the east yard, he feared, slowly decomposing. He held his breath and rolled up the window, but the smell was already in his nose. Why they did not simply burn the bodies was beyond him.

From a 1970s-era office in the administrative wing of the prison, the deputy watch commander paged Sergeant Nassar. Twenty minutes later Rahim stood to the side as the sergeant and two prison guards dragged a naked prisoner out of a cell packed tight with bodies.

The prisoner's feet were purpled and bruised. Both of his front teeth had been shattered, and his testicles were grotesquely engorged, as though they, too, had been beaten.

The whole prison block smelled of urine, feces, vomit, and malnourished bodies afflicted with what Rahim had been warned was tuberculosis and typhoid.

Acting on Rahim's orders, the prisoner was deposited in an empty cell at the end of the hall, in which there was a small cot and a pit toilet.

Rahim produced a photograph of a young man dressed in a Free Syrian Army uniform and held it in front of the prisoner's face.

"This is your brother, no?" he asked.

The prisoner began to cry.

"Stop that," ordered Rahim. "For *inshallah*, you will come to cherish this day. I have been told that as a result of your brother's concern for your wellbeing, he has been providing us with certain valuable deliveries of information?" When the prisoner didn't respond, Rahim turned to Sergeant Nassar. "This is true?"

"Yes, Captain."

Speaking to the sergeant, but for the benefit of the prisoner, Rahim said with a flourish, "Then I am issuing the following order—this prisoner shall receive no less than two hundred fifty grams of flour every day for the next week!"

Rahim paused, giving the prisoner an opportunity to express his thanks. When none were forthcoming, he turned back to Sergeant Nassar, "Fortunately, an opportunity exists for this man and his brother to provide an additional service. This woman"—Rahim handed the photo of Hannah to Sergeant Nassar, who handed it to the prisoner—"was photographed by the prisoner's brother passing through the Maqam Gate checkpoint yesterday. She is of great interest to me."

Turning to the prisoner, Rahim said, "If your brother encounters her again, and can provide additional information regarding her location, you will be rewarded. And if your brother can capture her and deliver her to me, then upon my word of honor, you will be set free."

"Sir?" asked Sergeant Nassar, as though he might not have heard Rahim correctly.

"I will be posting a general alert later today to all my officers," said Rahim. "If this woman passed through the Maqam Gate once, it is possible she will do so again. And if this man"—the prisoner flinched when Rahim placed a hand on his shoulder—"successfully assists you in this matter, and that assistance leads to the capture of this woman, then he must indeed be set free. Is that clear?"

"Certainly, sir."

"And if my brother does not see this woman again?" whispered the prisoner, his voice barely audible.

"Then you must trust to God," said Rahim.

CHAPTER 29

Rebel-held Aleppo • One week later

The bomb had fallen in the center of the street, on top of a buried water main. Clear water now spilled out of a cracked pipe at the bottom of the resulting crater. Two boys were already splashing around.

"Wow," said Adam when he saw it.

"Wow," echoed Noora.

Sami looked up to the sky for at least the twentieth time that morning. Still detecting no sign of fighter jets or helicopters, he said, "Let me go first." He tugged gently on Adam's arm. "Do you hear? You must wait until I give permission. And keep your shoes on."

"Okay," said Adam.

Noora, Sami observed, was getting tangled up in her shirt as she tried to strip it off.

"Leave it on," he said.

He had seen the crater late the night before, on his way home from the hospital, but he inspected it more closely now for live electrical wires, sharp glass, or chemical contamination. Finding none—it was just brick rubble, slicked over by wet hands and wet feet—he waded in, wearing a collared shirt, plastic sandals, and long, black slacks. The water felt blissfully cool, especially in contrast to the heat that had settled over the city for the past several weeks. At its deepest it came to just above his chest.

"Come," he said to Noora and Adam. "But you must be careful, some of the bricks are sharp."

Before the war, Tahira had often taken Adam swimming. But his son had not been to a pool for years now, so when Adam approached the rim of the crater, Sami extended his arms.

"I will guide you," he said.

Adam, however, just jumped in, splashing his father in the process.

"Careful!" called Sami, worried that his son would sink or cut himself on the rubble. But Adam was already laughing and dog paddling to the side.

———

Sami stayed with his children until late in the morning, taking advantage of the fact that two Syrian-American doctors had recently arrived at the M2 on a mercy mission. Tomorrow, he had promised the Aleppo Medical Council he would visit a smaller clinic while the Syrian-American doctors tended to the M2, but today was his own. He had not seen his children in a week, and he intended to spend much of the day with them.

On the way back to Beit Qarah, he held Noora's hand, their shoes squishing with every step. The sun overhead was searing white. The Citadel gleamed.

Nothing had gone as he had hoped it would over the past year. ISIS had taken over half the city. Iran had come to the aid of the regime. The Free Syrian Army, once on the verge of victory, had splintered and was now floundering. But Beit Qarah stood in territory that was still controlled by neither the regime nor ISIS, and his family was safe. For a moment Sami allowed himself to hope that everything would soon right itself.

———

Upon returning to Beit Qarah, he found Tahira sitting in the shade of the iwan arch, sipping weak ginger tea. She wore a loose white robe and looked up from a book when he entered the courtyard.

They had both lost weight over the past year. Tahira's skin was taut on her cheekbones, giving her a distant, regal air when she pressed her lips together as she did now.

Ever since Aya and her family had fled Aleppo to brave the refugee camps, Tahira had taken refuge in his mother's collection of books—at least when she was not tending to the children or patients from the M2 who came to Beit Qarah to complete their recovery. Most of the books were in French, which Tahira did not speak, but there were Arabic translations of works by Gustav Flaubert, Colette, and Simone de Beauvoir. At the moment, she was reading *Madame Bovary*.

Before the war she had never been a reader, except for the romantic poetry of Nizar Qabbani.

"You were gone longer than I thought you would be," she said, looking up from her book.

Sami told her about the swimming.

"And now that they know this is possible, they will want to go again tomorrow, and then the day after that, and then what?"

It was a rare day that the children were permitted to leave the house.

"There will be nothing to go to tomorrow. The water will be shut off." Sami told the children to get out of their wet clothes. Turning back to Tahira, he asked, "Where is Mémère?"

"Her room. She was feeling lightheaded with the heat."

———

The thick walnut door to his mother's second-floor room was shut. Sami knocked quietly, waited a moment, then knocked again.

If it had not been so hot out, he might have simply let her be, at least for another hour or so. But given the temperature, and that she had been feeling lightheaded in the afternoon, he cracked the door open and poked his head inside.

She lay on top of the blue toile bedspread, head propped up on two pillows. A fan that had stopped working because the electricity was out sat on a nearby dresser.

Her mouth was open, as were her eyes. The air was perfectly still. As Sami observed the remnants of his mother's life—the gilded antique mirror above her marble-topped rosewood dresser, the reproduction Hiroshige woodblock print, the Victrola she'd inherited from her parents, the origami menagerie he had made for her when he was a young boy—he was struck with the sensation that he had stumbled onto the set of a play and could not remember his lines.

Lightheaded now himself, he walked to her side, grasped the underside of her wrist and felt for a pulse. There was none.

No chest rising and falling.

He dropped to his knees at the foot of her bed and buried his head in the bedcover.

CHAPTER 30

Copenhagen, Denmark

Oskar Lång was used to people not recognizing him, so he wasn't surprised when the principal engineer for the Middle East and Southeast Europe Development Group at the European Development Service's regional headquarters in Copenhagen received him with a skeptical frown.

"Can I help you?"

"I was told you were ready for me, Mr. Schultz?"

The principal engineer, a German in his fifties who split his time between Brussels and Copenhagen, wore rimless glasses and a thick mane of wavy salt and pepper hair. He did a double take, then smiled, shook his head, and said, "I must be losing my mind. Sorry about that, Oskar, it's just the new look—haven't gotten used to it yet."

They spoke in English.

"Can't say I'm used to it myself."

"Easy to comb in the morning, I bet!"

Oskar laughed politely. "It is that."

After Elsa had relapsed six months ago, Oskar had stopped using his hair-loss cream, at which point his head had begun to resemble a tree shedding its leaves in late fall. After her funeral two weeks ago, he'd shaved himself bald and started growing a goatee.

A new life, a new look.

Did he like his new look? He did not. But it was better than a comb-over, and he was too cheap to go the hair transplant route.

"Thank you for joining me today. Please, have a seat." Shultz gestured to the chair in front of his desk. "You weren't waiting long, I hope?"

"No, not at all." He'd been waiting for a half hour.

"Now, I see you've done some good work coordinating with the field engineers on the Cairo project. Spot on cost estimates, and . . ."

Shultz spoke glowingly of the work Oskar had been doing of late, making Oskar wonder what it was all leading up to. He'd already had his performance review for the year.

"So," said Shultz eventually. He placed both hands on top of his desk and exhaled.

"All of this is to say I have good news for you. You're being promoted."

Oskar was genuinely surprised. He hadn't applied for a promotion, and he hadn't heard one was in the offing.

"That's fantastic. Thank you."

"I thought you'd be happy."

"If you don't mind, sir—promoted to what?"

"Regional senior engineer. You'll be spending some time in the field, but mostly it will involve managing and coordinating with the field engineers—and keeping us here in Copenhagen and Brussels up to date, of course."

Us here in Copenhagen and Brussels? thought Oskar, his suspicions now raised. "And this position, sir. Where would it be?"

"Ankara, Turkey. We have an office there, as you may be aware."

"I am."

"You lived there for a time, no?"

"Ah—that was Antakya."

A silence bordering on awkward ensued.

"It's in southern Turkey," Oskar added. "South of Ankara, near the border with Syria."

"Well, great then," said Schultz. "You'll have the opportunity to explore a brand-new place. Human resources will walk you through the details. And there may be some hazard pay involved. Not that Ankara is hazardous, but you might get something extra out of it given the larger troubles in the region. Of course, if you have issues with existing leases you don't want to break, or other financial considerations, be sure to bring them up with human resources. I'm sure they'll find a way to work it out for you."

"They've been good to me in the past."

"Well then." Shultz nodded, signifying it might be a good time for Oskar to leave.

Instead, Oskar said, "I don't want to seem ungrateful, sir, and I really am flattered that you thought of me, but, ah . . . If I decided I wanted to stay put in Copenhagen, or move to Brussels even—would that be an option?"

He considered mentioning what had happened with Elsa, that he needed time to pull himself together in the wake of her death, but he didn't feel that he could do so without losing his composure.

"Not a good one, to be honest. You see, along with the good news of your promotion is the perhaps unwelcome news that we weren't planning on filling your current position once it becomes vacant."

Oskar let the news sink in. "You're saying my position is being eliminated."

"That's one way to put it. The larger truth is that it's part of an organization-wide shuffle that isn't eliminating positions here and in Brussels, so much as it is shifting them to the regional offices. Pretty soon they'll be kicking me out the door too!"

Oskar very much doubted that.

"You'll like Ankara," added Shultz.

Oskar doubted that too. "I'm sure I will, sir," he said. "Thank you for thinking of me."

2 0 1 5

CHAPTER 31

Northern Syria

It was Hannah's ninety-sixth medicine run. She knew the exact number because she had promised herself that she'd only do it until she got to a hundred. After that, she was going back to the United States to apply to grad school.

Her latest driver was twice her age, wore a kaffiyeh headdress and drove an old Isuzu van. They met on the Syrian side of crossing, which at first appeared to be little different from the Turkish side. Traffic and people clogged the roads. Animals grazed in adjacent fields. Markets were open. Checkpoints were manned.

But as they approached the outskirts of Aleppo, the veil of normalcy was lifted, revealing a landscape that reminded Hannah of black-and-white photos she had seen of World War II: the bombing of Dresden; the battle of Stalingrad. Pancaked buildings, burned papers drifting across pockmarked roads, twisted metal that looked like the remains of the Twin Towers.

The real death zone, though, was Castello Road, a narrow, hope-lessly exposed rebel supply corridor that skirted ISIS territory but was surrounded by the regime. It was the umbilical cord keeping rebel-held Aleppo alive, and as they pulled onto it at dusk, the driver gunned the engine. On one side of the road, an earth berm had been constructed to protect moving vehicles from snipers. On the other side lay buses that had been flipped upside down, craters left by barrel bombs, uprooted trees, burnt-out cars, and decomposing bodies that stank. Smoke from bombs that had fallen in the city curled up above the long black silhouette of low-slung buildings on the dark, eastern horizon.

By the time they reached Aleppo, night had fallen. Even if the Isuzu's headlights had worked, the driver wouldn't have used them because of the threat from snipers and airborne attacks. Hannah was constantly bracing herself, anticipating the impact of what she kept thinking were imminent crashes as they tore through the dark rabbit warren of rubble-strewn streets.

Upon arriving unscathed at a clinic in the al-Marjeh district, she and her driver tried to be quick unloading their delivery. But when they heard the regime helicopter overhead, quick turned to careless, and the driver slipped while stepping down from the back of the van.

He attempted to cushion his fall by extending his right hand.

Hannah rushed over to him. He was fine, he said, as he picked up his cell phone, which had slipped out of his front shirt pocket and clattered on the pavement. Perfectly fine! Except perhaps for his wrist. Which he believed was broken.

Observing that it was bent at a grotesquely unnatural angle, Hannah pointed out that he wasn't fine at all and insisted he be seen at the clinic.

The driver refused.

"This place is a butcher shop," he said dismissively. "But at the next hospital, there is a bone doctor who is excellent." After his cousin's arm had been nearly severed by a grenade fragment last year, everyone had been certain it would need to be amputated. "At this clinic they would have chopped it off for sure. But for the bone doctor, it was no problem. Now my cousin is back to fighting. Do not worry," he added, "I can make arrangements for someone else to take you back."

The plan had been for them to make a series of quick nighttime deliveries then scoot back to Turkey before dawn.

"No," said Hannah. "We stick together."

CHAPTER 32

Rebel-held Aleppo

"Can you save it?" asked the patient when Sami entered the operating room on the first floor of the M2.

Ignoring the inquiry, Sami turned to the nurse who was standing in for the anesthesiologist. "Why is she still conscious?" he demanded.

"Can it be saved?" asked the patient again, slurring her words. Her nose was bruised and misshapen, so her voice had a nasal inflection to it.

The answer, of course, was no. The bullet that had struck her leg had yawed and fragmented upon impact, so instead of passing cleanly through soft tissue and perhaps nicking bone, it had exploded like a fist punching through gelatin. Her tibia had shattered, and the muscles and ligaments attached to it had been shredded instantly. The pressure wave had opened a gaping cavity that had only partially receded. Sami had already determined that, given the circumstances, trying to save the limb would be pointless.

But to explain that to a partially anesthetized patient would be to invite chaos into the operating room. It was one of the reasons why, despite the supply of general anesthetics being perilously low, he had ruled out using an epidural to numb the woman only from the waist down. He needed her unconscious.

"Relax," ordered Sami. "When you wake up, we will discuss your recovery."

The woman's eyes drooped.

Sami adjusted the placement of the overhead surgical light and examined the makeshift tourniquet that had been applied just below the knee. He palpated the upper calf and considered the X-ray image. Bone and bullet had shattered the upper tibia, but better to leave the knee intact if he could . . .

Had he the time and the right tools, it might have been different. A properly sized intramedullary tibial nail. Or at least more external fixation devices—all of his were already in use. Enough antibiotics. A spare bed so that she could be properly monitored for several weeks while the fragmented bone struggled to heal. But he had none of those things.

He used a surgical marker to draw his cut line.

"Scalpel," Sami said a minute later.

He cut a ring with flaps around the circumference of her leg, just below the knee, and then used a cautery pen to staunch the flow of blood as he cut through muscle, fat, and tendon.

"Saw," he said when he was ready.

The reciprocating bone saw the nurse handed him made short work of cutting through the woman's tibia and fibula. Moments later, he deposited the severed limb into a plastic bag, so that it could be delivered to the woman's husband for burial.

———

The amputation, paired with the fact that the hospital cook had left for the evening and it had been seven hours since he had forced down a ten-minute lunch of French fries, fava beans, and chocolate, had left Sami in a foul mood.

So as he was removing his bloodied scrubs and washing up, preparing to go home for the first time in three days, it was without the slightest hesitation that he said, "No," when one of the nurses asked whether he could examine a patient who had injured his wrist. Especially since he had promised Tahira he would try to buy diesel fuel for the generator on the way home.

"Either Dr. Wasim can see him," he added, referring to a former veterinarian who, at the age of twenty-six, was now performing general surgery, "or he can wait until tomorrow. Assuming I have the time tomorrow."

"He works for Bonne Foi. He hurt himself while unloading supplies at the al-Marjeh clinic."

Sami shrugged. He didn't think much of Bonne Foi—they were too small to make much of a difference, and their deliveries were inconsistent. But with the security situation deteriorating, the regular shipments from Doctors Without Borders had become much less regular. Every bit helped.

"He wants to leave Aleppo before dawn," the nurse added. "The van he is driving is needed for more deliveries."

"That may be so, but to see him tonight is impossible!" Sami snapped. Then, flustered because he knew he had spoken too harshly, he added, "I have other commitments to tend to this evening. But tell him I will try to see him early tomorrow. First thing in the morning."

———

Sami finished changing, but the incident with the nurse gnawed on him.

Expecting immediate treatment at ten thirty at night during a time of war!

Such were his thoughts when he opened the staff room door and nearly collided with a woman in the hall.

"Pardon," he said, stepping to the side. But she stepped to the side at the same time he did, so they nearly collided again.

Annoyed, Sami placed his back to the wall, and while looking down at the floor, gestured with his arm that she should pass. "Go," he said sharply. "Go." She did not pass, however, and Sami soon saw that she was a young woman, with a face more attractive than most, and that she was staring at him.

"Dr. Hasan?" she asked, appearing taken aback. She pulled headphones out of her ears, and he caught a snippet of English-language rock music playing before she tapped her phone and turned it off. He noted that her hands had been decorated with henna.

Because they were close enough for Sami to feel uncomfortable, he leaned away from her. "Surnames are not used here. Dr. Sami will suffice."

"Of course, I should have known."

"It is a matter of safety."

"I understand."

Sami made as though he were about to leave.

"I always wondered what happened to you," the woman added.

Curiosity piqued—he recognized her but could not recall from where—Sami asked, "And how do I know you?"

"You treated my friend," said the woman, sounding eager now. Too eager, thought Sami. "Before the war, when you were working at the university hospital. He had a broken leg."

Sami considered. "I see so many patients," he said.

"He was a Swede, tall, as tall as you. In July of 2012. We both worked for the European Development Service." She stepped toward him and briefly touched his forearm. "It is so good to see you. After all these years."

"Hmm," said Sami, pointedly staring at his forearm.

"Oskar Lång was his name," she added, withdrawing her hand. "He left when the rebels attacked."

Sami pressed his lips together then nodded. "Oh yes, of course." He remembered the Swede. And now that he thought about it, he vaguely recalled someone pestering him with questions, and that—

"But you are American, no?" he whispered suddenly, with concern.

"And Syrian, my father was from Aleppo."

His voice still a whisper, he said, "But if you are American, of course it is too dangerous for you to be here. Why—"

Interrupting, she whispered, "Think of my nationality the way you think of your last name." Leaning in so close to him that he caught a whiff of peppermint lozenge her breath, she added, "Meaning it is something best not to mention."

"I would think not!"

"Unless," she said, her tone now cheerful and loud, "I am crossing from Syria into Turkey, and then it is useful because I have a Turkish work visa. By the way, in case you forgot, my name is Hannah."

They had been speaking in Arabic, but she pronounced her name in the English way.

He stared blankly at her for a moment before stepping out of the way to let a nurse carrying an infant incubator squeeze by.

"I was working for the European Development Service before the war," she added, "but now I am with Bonne Foi. We just brought you fentanyl."

"Ah."

"Not enough, I know." After a period of silence bordering on awkward, Hannah added, "I should be going."

Sami detested small talk and typically tried to engage in as little of it as possible. But as she was leaving, he found himself confronting an unfamiliar desire—to prolong a conversation.

"And how is your Swedish friend?" he asked, as she was turning away. "His leg, it healed properly?"

She turned back and, after using her tongue to reposition the lozenge in her mouth, smiled. "I believe so."

He nodded.

"The truth is," she added, "he is no longer my friend. I have not seen him in years."

Feeling as though he might have pried too deeply, Sami nodded mutely again then quickly asked, "You were looking for something?"

She blushed, then said, "Only for the bathroom."

Embarrassed—this was why small talk should be avoided, he admonished himself—he said, "The end of the hall."

At that he turned, assuming he would never see her again, and his thoughts turned to where he might buy diesel fuel at this time of night.

"Until tomorrow," she called.

"Tomorrow?" he asked, turning back to her.

"My driver, he injured his wrist, and he insists upon waiting to see you because you saved his cousin's arm. So I will see you again tomorrow morning."

Sami frowned, conflicted. And a bit chagrined. "Had I not committed to a prior engagement . . ."

"I understand."

"He is in much pain?"

"I think so, but he will not admit it."

Sami sighed then relented.

Twenty minutes later he showed Hannah and her driver an X-ray image that he had loaded to an old Lenovo laptop computer.

"The distal radius has been fractured," he announced. "Dorsal displacement of the fragments."

The driver, a middle-aged man who smelled of cigarettes and garlic, offered no response.

"Is that bad?" Hannah asked.

"Certainly, it is not good."

"But you can you fix it?"

"Given the level of displacement and position of the two fragments, to do so properly I would need to operate on his wrist, install a plate and screws—or if not that, at least pin the fragments into place. But I have no plates and screws, and what pins I have are too large for the size of the fragments in question."

"But you can do something?" asked Hannah.

"I can use a closed reduction method as best I can."

"What does that mean?"

"It means I can try to push the bones back into place without operating, then cast the injury. After that, it will be up to the patient to be careful not to displace the fragments."

"So, you can fix it?" asked the driver.

"Not as I would like, but if you are careful, you should regain full use of your wrist."

The driver offered his profuse thanks.

"The reduction must be done manually. It will be painful. You may wish you had not thanked me by the time I am through."

But the driver tolerated Sami manipulating the bones in his wrist without crying out or demanding any form of anesthesia, although tears did form in his eyes. He was again profuse with his thanks after Sami took another X-ray image and confirmed that the bone had indeed been set as well as it could be, short of surgery.

"The cast is thinner than I would like," said Sami, as he wrapped the wrist with fiberglass casting tape. "We use only the absolute minimum to provide rigidity. Because it will therefore offer you less protection, you will have to take care not to bang it, lest you dislodge the bone fragments, which will not begin to fuse for two weeks."

Upon finishing with the cast, Sami gave the driver detailed instructions on what he should and should not do. Then he stood and said good night.

"Wait," said Hannah. She flipped a lock of hair out her eyes. "Make a list."

"A list of what?" asked Sami.

"Of things you need the most. Medicines, supplies—like fiberglass tape! Or just tell me now, if you have no time to write it down. I may not be able to get them to you, but I will do what I can."

Sami began to explain that they were perilously low on propofol, and even fentanyl despite the Bonne Foi delivery of earlier this evening. And they would be out of atropine entirely as of tomorrow. Yesterday they had run out of vancomycin. And if they didn't get a supply of the polio vaccine in, well, that could kill more children than the war.

He was still speaking when one of the nurses interrupted. A new patient had arrived. A teenage boy with burns over half his body and a piece of shrapnel still protruding from his skull. Dr. Wasim wanted Sami's advice. Could he help?

Hannah left with a promise she would do what she could to meet Dr. Sami's needs.

Sami texted Tahira to say he would not be coming home that night.

CHAPTER 33

All week long, Adam Hasan had been hoping that the old man from the M2 who had been staying at Beit Qarah would leave. On Sunday, upon announcing that he was finally well enough to walk—thanks to Adam's father—he did.

Which meant Adam and his younger sister, Noora, would be alone in the house for the day.

Well, not completely alone. Their mother was still there. But she hardly counted anymore. At night she stayed up late reading books. During the day she slept with the shutters pulled tight, wearing a purple eye mask in case any light got through the shutters. She used to promise that soon she would take him and Noora on a vacation to Jordan to be with their cousins, but then one of their cousins died, and now she never mentioned Jordan.

So he was not worried that she would interfere with his plan.

"I have a great idea," he said to Noora, a few minutes after the patient had left.

Noora's eyes widened when he explained what he wanted to do.

"We can fly them all the way to the street," he added.

Looking worried, Noora shook her head vigorously. But when Adam turned to leave, she followed him anyway.

The door at the top of the narrow, stonewalled staircase that led to the rooftop terrace was locked.

"Wait here," Adam said.

From behind a sleek fur coat that smelled of mothballs, in an armoire that stood in the room where his Mémère used to sleep when she had been alive, Adam retrieved a large, black key.

Minutes later, he unlocked the door and bounded out onto the roof of Beit Qarah and into the bright sunshine.

Noora ducked her head out of the doorway but kept her legs firmly planted in the stairwell.

"Are you sure?" she asked.

"Look! Look! You can see the Citadel," he said.

The fortress's walls appeared to be floating amid plumes of smoke. The air smelled of smoke.

Adam took Noora's hand and pulled her out onto the tiled section of roof.

A breeze was blowing, ruffling Noora's hair. She leaned into it with outstretched arms.

Adam observed that most of the nearby roofs were intact like his was. A few had caved in—from the bombs, he knew—while others were cluttered with water tanks and rusted satellite dishes. On a roof in the far distance, a man with a gun was sitting on a pile of bricks. Adam squeezed between a stone parapet wall and a wrought iron railing. Noora followed, and they positioned themselves near the edge of an untiled section of roof that overlooked an alley near the entrance to their house.

The first paper airplane Adam launched from the roof flipped over in the wind and tumbled to the street below.

He cursed. That had been one of his best planes. He had gotten the design, a Concorde jet, from the back of the origami book his father had given him, and it had taken a long time for him to fold it. He had even put a small pebble in the nose of the plane so that it would fly straight.

"Throw it harder next time," said Noora.

"If you throw it too hard, it crashes." He had been practicing in the courtyard, so he knew.

Noora stepped close to the edge of the roof with the one simple, crudely folded plane she had made, pulled her arm back, and launched her plane into the air. Whether by luck or design—Adam guessed luck—the plane caught a burst of air that propelled it forward with a velocity that made Noora squeal and jump up and down as she clapped her hands together.

It shot down the narrow alley all the way to an intersection far away, at which point it turned, slowed as it circled around an invisible eddy of air, and then drifted out of sight.

"Whoa," said Adam.

"Where did it go?"

"Follow me," he said.

They climbed over waist-high walls and squeezed between rooftop buildings. A few times they had to jump over small gaps between buildings or take long detours to avoid having to jump over much larger gaps. On top of one roof was a garden; on top of another, a ceiling fan had been converted into an electricity-generating windmill. Halfway to their destination, a helicopter appeared in the sky, and they watched it race low over the eastern half of the city.

Upon arriving at the spot directly above where the plane had disappeared, Adam got down on his belly and stuck his head over the edge of the roof.

"Do you see it?" Noora asked.

"No," said Adam, and then his eyes fixed on a group of boys playing soccer in the middle of the road. He was pretty sure he knew one of them.

"Selim!" he cried. "Selim! Up here!"

One of the boys in the street turned, but he was looking in the wrong direction.

"Up here!" cried Adam. "On the roof!"

A small, stick-thin boy squinted at the roof. Adam waved excitedly. The boy pointed to Adam and said something to his friends. Everyone stopped playing soccer and looked up at the roof.

Adam waved again then asked whether anyone had seen the plane.

"Do you want to be on my team?" asked Selim.

——

Adam played soccer all afternoon while Noora and Selim's sister shared half a piece of yellow chalk and drew flowers on the cobbled pavement.

While the children played, two veiled women wearing formless, black abaya robes stood nearby chatting. Also standing watch, and occasionally kicking an errant ball back to the game, was a bearded, heavily armed man.

Every twenty minutes or so, Adam would promise himself he would leave after just one more goal was scored. But then a goal would be scored, and the other boys would encourage him to stay, and the game would keep going.

Finally, they got tired of soccer, but one of the boys had a bike, and they took turns riding it up and down a pile of rubble.

When Adam's mother appeared, at first, he did not recognize her. She was backlit by the sun, and her uncovered hair was wild and uncombed. She wore plastic slippers and a rose-colored terrycloth bathrobe over green silk pajamas.

One of the boys pointed at her and laughed. Adam laughed with them—until he realized who it was.

"Noora!" he cried.

His sister was on her hands and knees, trying to trap a wounded moth. She looked up. Adam scampered up the pile of rubble.

"Get down!" his mother demanded. She climbed up the front side, and Adam ran down the back.

The two women standing to the side giggled.

The armed man sauntered over. "*As-salamu alaykum*, sister," he said. Peace be upon you.

"*Wa alaykumu as-salam*," said his mother back, distracted. And upon you, peace. Then to Adam, "For an hour I have been looking for you!"

"The boy was perfectly safe," said the armed man. "I was here."

"And who are you?"

"Mrs. Hasan, you do not recognize me?" When it was clear she did not, he introduced himself as Ibrahim Antar and reminded her that she used to visit his father's cheese shop by the Antakya Gate. "My son, Selim, he is friends with your son," he added. "And your husband, last year he tried to repair the liver of my cousin."

Adam watched his mother cover the base of her throat with her palm, dip her head, and say that of course she recognized him, "It is just this boy

of mine, he makes me crazy," she said. Then she asked about his cousin—
he died three weeks after Sami operated on him, evidently—and his wife.

Ibrahim explained that his wife had been killed by a sniper early in the
war trying to cross to the regime-held side to visit her ailing mother, but
that no one need regret the will of God. *Inshallah*, he would soon marry
the wife of a martyr.

They turned back to Adam.

"He did not have permission to be outside," said Tahira. "That is why
I am so angry with him. Adam! Get down now!"

"Is this so?" Ibrahim directed his question to Adam.

Adam nodded.

"And you disobeyed your mother?" asked Ibrahim.

Adam nodded again.

Ibrahim sighed. "Had I known, I would not have permitted it," he said
to Tahira. And to Adam, "You must respect you mother more. Come here."

Adam did as instructed.

The blow came too quick for him to dodge. An openhanded slap to
the side of his head. He felt a scream rising in his chest and opened his
mouth, but for a moment no sound escaped. His ear was ringing, and it
burned. Finally, he began to cry.

"He is in pain now, but he will certainly be more obedient later, you
will see," said Ibrahim.

Adam felt his mother grasp his hand. Selim and the other boys were
all staring at him. He wanted to be able to stop crying but could not.

"I did not ask you to discipline my child!" cried his mother.

Ibrahim appeared taken aback by her outburst. "Then you should
discipline him yourself. So that he respects you."

"Noora!" said Tahira. "Come here!"

Noora took her place at her mother's side. Adam felt his mother grab
his hand and begin to pull him away. They had only taken a few steps,
however, before Ibrahim said, "One more thing, Mrs. Hasan. Next time
you leave your house, you must cover yourself."

His mother did not respond.

Adam, scared but filled with anger, called out, "My father is a doctor!"

By which he meant to say that, even though he was too small to stand up to Ibrahim, his father was powerful and respected, and that if he were here, he would surely do something.

His mother tugged at his arm. "You!" she said to him when they had turned the corner and the entrance to Beit Qarah was in sight. Her lip was trembling. "You will bring death upon yourself and your sister by saying such things."

Adam pulled his hand from hers, clenched his fists, and kept walking toward the entrance to their house.

He was not worried about getting himself or Noora killed. If they got hurt, his father would fix them. If someone tried to hurt them, his father would protect them. Adam was sure of it.

Because his father was a doctor.

CHAPTER 34

Rebel-held Aleppo • Three months later

By the time Hannah and her driver passed through the first of a series of checkpoints in Aleppo, darkness had settled over the city. The smell of wood fires, raw sewage, and dust was thick, the moon and stars obscured by clouds.

It was her 121st medicine run.

As always, they drove with their lights off. Every so often, empty bullet casings and broken glass made popping sounds under the weight of their tires, but Hannah could barely hear them because she was listening to music—mostly Enya, because it calmed her—on her earbuds while exchanging texts with her younger half-sister Allison back in New Jersey, having picked up a weak wireless signal once they'd reached the city limits.

From Allison she gleaned that their mother was applying for jobs at the Paramus Park mall, hoping to pick up work over Christmas because Allison's father, a lawyer named George Johnson, who was Hannah's step-father, was late on alimony payments.

What store?

Victoria's Secret.

OMG.

You should come home for Christmas.

Maybe.

"We are being followed," said the driver, interrupting her thoughts.

Hannah pulled out one of her earbuds, put down her phone, and leaned forward in the passenger seat so she could use the side-view mirror.

Her driver, whose wrist cast had come off a month earlier, was on edge because at the zero-point zone between the Syrian and Turkish borders, the Red Crescent had forced them to hand over two laptops that had been hidden at the bottom of a box of bandages. The laptops were needed at a hospital in Azaz, but computers and smartphones were prohibited because the regime considered them potential tools of war, and the Red Crescent didn't want to cross the regime. Then, two hours later, more of their supplies had been taken when they'd inadvertently passed through a Kurdish checkpoint, and the Kurds had demanded a tribute as the price of passage.

Which is why Hannah wasn't sure whether the driver was really seeing something or just being paranoid.

"I see no one," she said.

"Keep looking."

"Oh. There."

Not far behind them, but nearly swallowed by the darkness, a man on a bike had just passed in front of a dimly lit window, momentarily exposing himself. Hannah couldn't make out any of his features. She wasn't even sure it was a man—it could have been a boy, or even a woman.

Either way, she wasn't overly alarmed. They had been followed before, sometimes by Free Syrian Army soldiers trying to protect them, sometimes by Islamists who were trying to—and in some cases, did—rob them, sometimes by kids who were just curious.

She put her earbuds back in, settled back into her seat, and waited for another text from her sister to ping, but as they slowly made their way to the delivery point, she noted that the man on the bike continued to trail them. When a pack of barefoot teenagers stared them down, she wondered whether they were coordinating with the biker.

The driver pulled up next to a row of brown tents that had been reinforced with sandbags and set up to offer first aid treatment to victims of chlorine gas attacks. A scrawny man-kid with a patchy beard emerged from a door that led to the hospital. Hannah shut off her music and texted her sister.

> got to go

She then helped establish a bucket brigade from the back of the van to the hospital. One of the things that they unloaded first was a box of fiberglass casting tape, the same kind that Dr. Sami had used on her driver's wrist, and that Hannah had made sure had been added to the manifest.

She was about to ask whether Dr. Sami was working inside now—he had been splitting his time between the larger M2 hospital and this smaller clinic—when a whistling screech suddenly sounded. Hannah locked eyes with her driver.

"Down!" he cried.

She dove to the pavement, intending to roll beneath the van, but before she even hit the ground the explosion rocked her.

———

At first the only thing Hannah was conscious of was a ringing in her ears.

She thought she must be back in Antakya, sleeping in her studio apartment. So she rolled to her side, intending to hit the snooze icon on her cell phone alarm. She was so tired; she needed more sleep.

Then she realized she couldn't breathe, or at least not properly, because when she tried to inhale, she began to cough.

Her head throbbed.

For a moment she was confused because her head was resting on a hard surface, her hands too. She must have fallen off the bed, she reasoned. Strange, that hadn't happened to her in years.

Her eyes stung. She coughed again and tried to push herself up off the ground to get back into bed.

A stone wall not far from her crumbled to the ground. Sirens sounded in the distance. People began to scream. The dust was too thick for her to see far through it.

As she glanced at her legs and arms—to confirm they were still attached to her—she was struck by the paleness of her skin in the gloom. She touched her cheek with a finger. Her skin was so smooth, so thin. But it was that very same thin, nearly translucent skin that was holding the blood inside her body, like a flimsy plastic bag filled with water. A cut here, a cut there, and . . .

Hannah coughed a few more times then leaned back into a sitting position on the ground. Her ears were still ringing, her head still throbbing, and now her chest burned every time she tried to breathe.

The baby-blue Nike sneakers she was wearing hovered in the darkness, floating as though they were no longer attached to her feet.

She inspected her torso, then her arms and legs for signs of shrapnel wounds. Finding none, she wiped her hands over her face, hair, and neck and checked them for signs of blood. Nothing. After a few more deep breaths, she speculated that the pain in her head and chest must have been due to the concussive force of the blast.

Moans and cries for help sounded from the remains of the clinic. As she stood, a gust of air swept away some of the smoke and dust. Through the lingering murk, she saw that the chemical decontamination tents had been completely blasted away, exposing the drainage pipes underneath them. Where the clinic had been, small fires illuminated tangled bits of metal rods that had once been embedded in concrete. The Isuzu van had been thrown a full car length.

The side of the van facing the blast was dented and charred, and a spear-like section of stair railing had punctured the cargo bay. The driver's-side tire was burning, and the driver's window had been shattered. Had she been on that side of the van, she'd be dead.

Instead, entirely by chance, she'd been on the other side, and the metal cargo bay that had stood between her and the bomb had protected her, even as she and the van had been thrown by the force of the blast.

Her driver lay face down in the street. She pulled a few bricks off his back then shook him gently. When he didn't move or respond, she mustered enough strength to flip him over.

His forehead had been bashed in so that it appeared dimpled, and his neck was covered with blood, but she still felt his wrist for a pulse.

As she changed the position of her fingers, just to make sure she hadn't missed anything, it occurred to her that she was holding the same wrist that Dr. Sami had repaired.

———

She wasn't sure how long she sat there. It might have been a minute; it might have been twenty. The sirens grew louder, then stopped. Eventually a woman in nurse's garb asked if she was okay, and Hannah said she was. Two men in white helmets, khaki coveralls, and black boots, dragged her driver to a spot on the street where other dead men and women had been lined up in an orderly row.

She checked her phone; it had been badly dented in one corner and, although it would turn on, it wasn't picking up a signal. At this time of night, she doubted anyone from Bonne Foi would answer anyway.

At some point it occurred to her that she should be helping. So she stood, wobbled on her feet for a moment, and walked over to where the decontamination tents had once stood and where people were now picking through the rubble. She watched them, feeling useless, not knowing where to start or whether she'd be in the way.

One of the men in the white helmets was talking with a nurse who was anxiously gesturing to the remains of the clinic.

She inched closer and gathered that they were going to try to move the surviving patients to the M2, but that first they needed to evacuate the survivors and salvage what equipment they could.

"Where are you bringing the patients who need to be transferred?" she asked the nurse after the man in the white helmet ran off.

The nurse gestured across the street to five-story apartment complex.

"Where is Dr. Sami?" Hannah asked.

The nurse stared at the remains of the clinic, and Hannah followed her gaze. Half lay in ruins, just a crater surrounded by brick and twisted metal. The other half was still standing, looking a bit like a dollhouse the way so many of the interior rooms were visible. On one charred wall, Hannah perceived what she thought was the faint outline of a human form, a wartime equivalent of a sun print. A human leg, detached from the owner's body, lay on the periphery of the crater. Eventually, the nurse brought her hand to her mouth, said, "I would not know," and turned away.

———

Inside the section of the clinic still standing, it was hard to breathe because of all the dust and hard to see because the lights were out. A few of the rescuers had flashlights, and Hannah did her best to follow them in and out of the building. She helped pull a young child, wet with urine and barely clinging to life, from the rubble. She salvaged X-ray equipment, blood pressure monitors, infusion pumps, otoscopes, mismatched blankets, a sternal saw, a General Electric mammography machine, a vaginal speculum, two defibrillators, a stack of sponge bowls, a surgical stapler, a box of scalpel blades, a box of casting tape she had brought with her, and an anesthesia cart.

A Kawasaki front-end loader arrived, along with a dump truck. Men yelled into walkie-talkies. Someone started using a jackhammer on the collapsed portion of the building, trying to get to the dead below. A makeshift fire truck arrived, with a single hose and no ladders, and doused the sections of rubble that were still smoldering.

On every run back into the hospital, Hannah asked about Dr. Sami. No one had seen him.

She finally found him in the basement, on the side of the building that had survived the blast. He was standing in one of the recovery rooms, his back to the door. At first she thought he was just one of the rescue workers, but then, under the glow of the LED headlamp he was wearing, she was able to make out the form of a woman of indeterminate age who appeared to be unconscious. He had her on a regular hospital bed rather than an operating table and he was concentrating intently, peering through a set of surgical loupes as he stitched her stomach.

Hannah opened the door.

"Dr. Sami," she said quietly. He didn't react, so she called his name again, this time louder. "Dr. Sami, we are trying to move—"

He turned, blinding her with the glare of his headlamp. She put up her palm to block the light.

"What is it people find so difficult to comprehend about operating theaters!" he shouted. His voice was muffled because along with scrubs, hairnet, and surgical gloves, he was also wearing a mask. "Leave me be! I have told you I will bring her up when I am finished! *Ya Allah*," he added. Good God.

He turned back to his work, but as though God had chosen to respond, an explosion sounded. Hannah felt a burst of air pressure hit her as she flinched and covered her head with her arms.

"It is merely an oxygen tank," said Sami, unperturbed. "There were several in storage. You may expect more of the same."

Recovering herself, Hannah asked, "Is there anything I can do to help?"

Sami had been hunched over his patient, but now he stood and faced her again. Again, Hannah put up her palm to ward off the glare.

"You," he said, as though just recognizing her. "What are you doing here?"

"Delivering medicine. What can I do?"

Sami gestured to the woman on the bed. "My anesthesiologist has left. Can you take her place so that this woman will not wake in five minutes?"

"I can try."

"The correct answer is no, you cannot. Can you finish these sutures?"

"No."

"Then there is nothing you can do."

"Will you need help transporting her when you are done?"

Sami sighed then finished another stitch. He appeared to be arguing with himself for a moment. "Yes," he said eventually.

"Then I will stay until you are done, and we will move her together."

When Sami spoke next, he sounded more reasonable.

"There is one thing you can do for me, if you would be willing. Behind me, on the counter, is a sterile dressing. Open the bag in which it is contained, being careful—very careful!—not to touch the dressing inside."

Hannah found the bag and ripped open the top.

"Hold it open," said Sami.

Hannah did. Sami retrieved the dressing with a pair of forceps and applied it to the sutured abdominal incision point. Then he taped the dressing in place, removed his gloves, threw them to the floor, and put his hand on his patient's forehead.

"She is ready to be moved," he said.

"The basement recovery room has been destroyed," said Hannah. "We will have to take her through the back stairwell."

CHAPTER 35

Adam waited and waited for his father to come home that night. After he heard his mother slam her door sometime after midnight, he decided he would try to sleep too. So he drank half a box of room-temperature milk that was stamped with the flag of Saudi Arabia, then crept back down to the cool, stone-walled storage cellar beneath the kitchen where he and Noora had been sleeping for the past year.

When he woke again, it was still dark out. After drinking all that milk, he should have tried to pee before going to bed, but the inside toilets had not been working for months, so he had to go to a corner of the courtyard where his mother had pried up a tile and dug a hole.

As he was passing by the iwan, though, he heard a sound—like an animal panting. Afraid that it might be a soldier, or maybe a thief, he froze. A figure, bathed in cold moonlight, was seated on the floor of the courtyard, back to the fountain. Recognizing his mother, Adam almost called out to her, but before the words could form, he saw that she was hugging herself and still making that panting sound as she rocked back and forth.

For a moment, he thought he must be dreaming. He had seen his mother crying before. But never like this.

It occurred to him that if his mother was this upset, something must have happened. Something truly terrible.

And then he recalled that his father had not come home, even though his mother had been expecting him to.

The panic that started in Adam's mind radiated outward. He began to feel a tightness in his chest, as though a bully with strong arms were squeezing the breath out of him. Struggling to breathe, he began to hyperventilate. It occurred to him that he was starting to sound a little bit like his mother.

This house, Noora, his mother . . . if his father could be hurt . . . He felt his chest tighten even more. Everything, everything could be at risk.

"Who is there?" cried his mother.

For the briefest of moments, they made eye contact. "Where is Baba?" asked Adam.

"I do not know."

"Is he dead?"

"I said, I do not know!" screamed his mother, pulling her hair.

Adam ran.

CHAPTER 36

Hannah pulled more bodies from the rubble. She carted more boxes of salvaged medical supplies out of the clinic. When the nurse told her to hold a boy's hand, she held it; when Sami told her to find him a ten-milliliter vial of fentanyl for him, she found it.

By three in the morning, she was exhausted and unsteady on her feet, tripping over the bricks that littered the street. She'd had no food or water.

She didn't know how people like Dr. Sami did it, day after day. She could see him now, leaning over a badly burned woman. The decent thing to do would be to offer to help him, to do whatever he told her to, try to get him whatever he told her to get. But she needed sleep. And then she needed to get the hell out of Aleppo and back to New Jersey where she belonged. What a luxury it would be to slip into her childhood bed and curl up and go to sleep! The problems she'd experienced four years ago—her mother's divorce from her stepfather, her mother's subsequent drinking—and which had made her so eager to strike out on her own, seemed so trivial now.

———

There was no electricity or running water in the abandoned building where the surviving patients were being sheltered. Just debris—a coffee cup, a child's riding toy, a heap of soggy books and fashion magazines from Turkey, a pair of ripped sequined jeans, a cracked bottle of hand lotion, empty sardine tins that reeked.

In an empty apartment on the first floor, she threw a cheap, pink, machine-made area rug over a stained mattress and curled up into a fetal ball. Just a few hours of sleep, she told herself, that was all she needed. But she was too uncomfortable and cold to fall asleep right away.

Instead, in a sudden flash of what seemed like insight, she realized how lonely she was, and that led her to wonder what her mother and sister and old college and high school friends from New Jersey were doing. What would they think if they knew where she was right now? She always downplayed what she was really doing over here, always said she was being safe, working mostly in Turkey, that they needn't worry. Would they care if they knew the truth? Her mother and sister would. With her old friends, she suspected she'd been too emotionally and physically distant for too long for them to care much anymore.

As she wrapped her arms tighter around herself, she pictured her childhood home. It lay in the shadow of the Phillips 66 Bayway oil refinery but on a tree-lined street, with a little backyard where a nearly squirrel-proof bird feeder hung from a Japanese maple. She saw house finches gathering at the feeder and her mother in the basement, tossing an ice cube into the dryer to steam her clothes, while upstairs her sister Allison applied purple eye shadow in the bathroom. Allison smelled of peppermint-scented nicotine vapor and wore skin-tight jeans and a sweater that showed a decent amount of cleavage. She was getting ready to go out, having finished her waitressing shift at Chili's. "Do you want to come with me?" she would ask.

"Maybe next time," Hannah would say. "I have to study tonight."

"You need to get out more, sister."

"I know."

———

When the attack came, it was almost as sudden as the bombing had been. Hannah had no chance to run, no chance to really fight, although she'd always imagined that if faced with such a situation, she'd be a fighter.

The man clamped one hand on her mouth and another on her neck. He jammed her lips into her teeth and dug his fingers into her neck.

She couldn't breathe, couldn't even cry out. When she tried to knee him, she wound up kneeing air. When she tried to bite his hand, he pressed his palm down so hard that it felt as though the top of her jaw would separate from the bottom.

It was dark. She couldn't see. She managed to suck a bit of air in through her nostrils, but it wasn't enough.

The last thing she remembered, as she was struggling to remain conscious, was the feel of his wet breath in her ear.

CHAPTER 37

When the sky began to lighten, someone distributed weak tea and almond shortbread biscuits. A man from the Aleppo City Medical Council announced that ambulances to transfer survivors to the M2 would be arriving soon.

Sami cut away a melted polyester abaya robe that had fused to a woman's leg and smelled of burnt fat. He elevated the woman's leg, covered the wound with sterile plastic wrap, then administered morphine and an IV bag of Ringer's lactate. Noting the rigidity of her burned thigh, he made an incision through the leathery brown skin, cutting all the way down to the fat so that the wound could swell without cutting off circulation.

As he was readjusting her IV drip, a woman who had once specialized in dermatology but now, like him, performed general surgery, said, "Did you hear that?"

"Hear what?"

"That," she said.

Sami concentrated, and this time he heard what he thought might have been a muffled, high-pitched scream.

Other people were staring.

The dermatologist began walking toward a hallway opposite the staging area. "There," she said. "There it is again."

She began to jog toward the sound. Sami followed her down the hall and out the back of the building where a large young man with sunken cheeks and infected sores on his face was laboring to carry what looked like a pink carpet over his shoulder. A pair of baby-blue sneakers protruded from the carpet, and they were kicking in tandem, like a horse bucking.

Sami, recognizing those sneakers, was about to intervene when two of the white-helmeted rescuers tackled the man.

Hannah rolled off her abductor's shoulder and hit the ground with a thud as her head connected with a rusted car fender. As the gash on the top of her skull began to bleed, Sami unwrapped her from the pink carpet.

He quickly pressed his hand against her head.

"Relax," he said. And then, yelling to the men who were pummeling her abductor, "I need bandages!"

CHAPTER 38

Regime-held Aleppo

Rahim had been searching for her for over a year, ever since seeing that photo of her passing through the Maqam Gate checkpoint.

At times there had been leads. In January she had been seen passing through a checkpoint in Bustan al-Qasr, in May through a checkpoint in Sheik Saeed. But her schedule was seemingly random, and when she had been observed, the people doing the observing had been unable to pursue her without exposing themselves as regime spies.

Until yesterday.

Until a young man with a father in the Aleppo Central Prison had inspected Hannah Johnson's Syrian identity card, and—placing his father's well-being above his own—had abandoned his post and followed her to a medical clinic in the Nayrab Gate district.

The plan had been to bring her to safe house that lay not far from the point of abduction. The whole operation should have taken less than ten minutes. But three hours after Rahim had given his final approval, he had still heard nothing.

At eight thirty in the morning, as he sat at his desk on the third floor of military intelligence headquarters, his cell phone chimed.

Instead of his man in rebel Aleppo, it was his daughter Zahra calling from Beirut. She wanted money. Or rather, his wife wanted money but had charged Zahra with obtaining it.

Rahim agreed to send what he could that afternoon and to increase the amount he sent her each month. He suspected that God was testing him, and that a show of generosity on his part would soon be followed by good news regarding Hannah's capture.

It was not.

By late morning he was exasperated. And angry—angry at the rebel spy who was supposed to have abducted Hannah, angry at his daughter, his wife, the rebels, the war, and himself.

A few minutes before noon, his secretary Aisha knocked on his door then poked her head in without waiting for his response.

"Abu Halabi still waits, Major," she said, referring to a prominent accountant who was under investigation and whom Rahim had instructed to arrive at eight in the morning.

He tapped a finger on his desk. "Keep him here until four," he said. "Then reschedule him for eight tomorrow morning. Inform him that I am reviewing new information regarding his case."

Aisha closed the door.

Rahim picked up a pen that lay on his desk, threw it across the room, and then, because he could think of nothing else to do, opened the last text message he had received from his spy in rebel-held Aleppo. Attached to it were several photos of Hannah. Rahim had already studied them at home before arriving at his office, but he did so again now.

There she was straining to lift a computer monitor and helping to lead someone to safety at the clinic that had been bombed. There she was securing a patient to a hospital bed.

When he tried to enlarge the photographs, he was unable to make out any of the details. Partly because the pictures had been taken at night, partly because his phone, which he had bought before the war, was of poor quality.

It occurred to him that now that he was at work, he could transfer the photos to his desktop computer and view them on the monitor.

When he had, that was when he noticed, in the back of one of the grainy photos, on the periphery of where light from the rescue effort dissolved into darkness, a man who made him suck in a quick breath and clench his fists.

He dipped his head closer to his computer screen and squinted just to make sure. Then he leaned back and looked at the man from a different angle and punched his left palm with his right fist as he recalled being told by a doctor at the University of Aleppo Hospital that Dr. Sami Hasan had been shot dead on Castello Road while trying to flee to Turkey. When he had come back to the hospital a week later to investigate further, the head of human resources at the hospital and three of the nurses who had worked on the orthopedic ward had also sworn that Dr. Hasan had died, offering his shuttered nearby clinic as evidence.

Deceivers, every one of them, thought Rahim.

Because there could be no doubt. There he was, the doctor who had killed his son and lied about it, standing—as alive as could be!—next to the American girl.

CHAPTER 39

Rebel-held Aleppo

Nauseous and with a persistent ringing in her ears, Hannah crouched in the back of a pickup truck, trying to steady herself while applying pressure to the bandaged wound on her head.

Upon reaching the M2, where soldiers were busy reinforcing the entrance with sandbags, she was led to the green triage zone, given a prayer mat to lie down on, and told to wait.

From time to time, she saw Sami, surgical gown stained with blood, pulling people out of the red triage zone as though he were some faith healer choosing those worthy of being saved. She refused to bother him—he had more important things to do than tend to her—but four hours after arriving at the hospital, he noticed her and did a double take.

"Why are you still here?"

"Where else should I be?"

"I told Dr. Wasim to bring you to the doctors' quarters!"

She shrugged. No one had told her not to be here, so what did he expect?

"Look at me," he said, as he crouched down on his haunches.

She did.

His surgical mask had fallen around his neck, revealing a face peppered with stubble. The features of that face—his eyes, nose, mouth—seemed unnaturally large as he leaned into her.

"Your pupils are fine," he announced. "Are you nauseous?"

"Some."

"Headache?"

"Yes."

"Where are you?"

"At the hospital."

"What hospital?"

Hannah knew exactly what hospital she was in, but . . . This was ridiculous, she thought, because at the moment she couldn't remember what they called it.

Before she could answer, Sami asked, "What day of the week is it?"

Hannah couldn't answer that question because she was still trying to answer the first.

He briefly lifted the bandage from her head and examined the wound. "There is residual bleeding, but not enough to be of concern. I will tend to you when I can. Until then, you need to rest." He leaned into her ear again. "The doctors' sleeping quarters are in a basement next door. It will be safer there."

He led her down a flight of stairs, through a tunnel, and into a small room where a dozen mattresses had been thrown on the floor in front of shelving packed with medical equipment and supplies.

"You may use that one," he said, gesturing to one of the cots as he shut the door behind him. He opened a cabinet and shook out two pills. "Tylenol. For the headache. Take them, then wait here until I come back. It may be hours, so I suggest you lie down. Let your brain rest. I suspect a mild concussion."

"Why did you bring me here?"

He looked at her as though she had completely lost her senses. "Because you are an American, of course! Which means you are worth money. That is almost certainly why someone tried to kidnap you. So, you will stay here until I treat you, and then you will call your people and return to Turkey and never come back." He opened another cabinet. "There is bread, bottled water. Some sweets. Have what you wish."

Despite the nausea, Hannah forced herself to drink half a liter of water and eat a handful of chocolate-covered wafers. Later, as she lay down and listened to the voices and beeps and clatter of the hospital operating at full tilt, it occurred to her that the pillow smelled like Sami did. Then she noticed that, propped up on the sill of a ceiling-high window blocked with sandbags, was a photograph of Sami, two young children, and an attractive dark-haired woman. The woman was leaning into Sami, her head resting on his chest.

———

Hannah woke that afternoon to the sensation of a nurse rocking her shoulder. Her headache had subsided, and she was hungry.

"Dr. Sami is ready for you," said the nurse.

The nurse led her to an operating room, but instead of mounting the table, she was told to sit in a wingback chair, one that looked as though it had been plucked from a dining room. Dr. Sami sat behind her in an identical chair.

"I need to inspect the wound," he said, and without waiting for her to respond, began unwrapping the bandages. He announced that he would need to shave and disinfect a small portion of her scalp prior to suturing the cut with ten or so stitches.

"The top of the skull is not a particularly pain sensitive region," he added, "but I can offer you a limited amount of local anesthesia should you require it."

Hannah wanted to shout that of course she required it. Maybe the top of *his* head wasn't sensitive, but hers sure was. It hurt now, in fact. But she also sensed that, above all else, Dr. Sami was a practical man, and he would not have offered her the option of going without anesthesia if he hadn't thought she was up to it.

"Thank you, but that will not be necessary," she said.

"Very well then. This will hurt," replied Dr. Sami.

CHAPTER 40

After making short work of suturing Hannah's skull wound and ordering her back to the doctors' quarters, Sami turned to his next patient, the woman with the burned thigh.

As with most burns, the damage was inconsistent. In places, the outer layer of skin peeled off when he pulled at it with tweezers, revealing the weeping red dermis beneath it. In other places, every layer of the skin had been burned to a leathery brown color. And in some sections, the burn had extended down through the fat and muscle, leaving the flesh mottled with patches that were either sickly white or charred black. The leathery brown sections he removed by slicing away the skin with graft knives, as though he were peeling an apple. The black and white sections, he cut out with scalpels and scissors, being as careful as he could to maintain as much of the original contour of the thigh as possible.

The wounds bled copiously, which was reassuring for Sami because it was indicative of viable tissue beneath. He was acutely aware that the M2 was short on blood, and he cauterized the bleeding vessels as quickly as he could. As he worked, the nurse who was assisting him—and who had not been in the room when he had tended to Hannah—gossiped about the American woman who had survived a kidnapping attempt and was still in the hospital. Had Sami heard of this?

In fact, he had, Sami said as he tried to compensate for a dull skin-graft knife by making extra-long slicing motions.

"Evidently the Mukhabarat," said the nurse, "were the ones who tried to take her."

"The Mukhabarat? Are you sure?" asked Sami, stopping for a moment to face the nurse.

She picked out a piece of burnt skin that Sami had just sliced off. "I was told they caught the kidnapper and questioned him."

"I see," said Sami, as he went back to slicing.

Upon removing the burnt tissue and washing the wound with saline, he harvested a thin layer of skin from the patient's unburned thigh, perforated the harvested skin in a way that rendered it an expandable mesh, and sewed it in place on top of the wound.

Two hours after starting the operation, and after dictating post-operative instructions and donating a unit of his own blood, he returned to the doctors' quarters to find Hannah sitting cross-legged on the floor. Watching her concentrate intently as she tapped away on a dented phone reminded him of how persistent, and sometimes annoying, she had been three years ago when advocating on behalf of her Swedish boyfriend.

"You have a connection?" he asked, as he retrieved a bottle of water from the cabinet.

"I did. But not now."

Wireless networks that originated in southern Turkey had sprung up all over the rebel-held zone, and there was a thriving business in Turkish SIM cards. But the towers that handled the Turkish signals were frequently targeted by the regime, and the reception was inconsistent. The hospital used password-protected satellite Wi-Fi, so that they could consult with doctors in Europe and the United States, but he was not about to let her clog up that system with frivolous YouTube videos.

He took a long drink of water, feeling a bit weak from having donated blood.

"Thank you again," she said.

Compliments always made Sami uncomfortable, so he usually ignored them, as he did now. "You were able to contact your people?"

"Yes."

"When are they coming for you?"

"Tomorrow, I hope."

"You know where you are now?"

She flashed him a tired smile. "The M2. But the day of the week remains a mystery. Not because of my head, I always lose track."

"Wednesday."

"I would have guessed that."

Sami squatted down so that he was her level. "Let me see your eyes."

She opened them wide for him and leaned into his space.

Ordinarily, Sami's proximity to a patient was not something he paid much mind to. If he needed to examine someone's eyes, he got close enough to examine their eyes. If he needed to examine a shrapnel wound in their buttocks, he got close enough to examine their buttocks. There was nothing immodest or unprofessional about it, the occasional protest from deeply religious women—or their husbands—notwithstanding.

But he could not help, at that moment, being intensely conscious of how close her face was to his. So close that he could see her pores, and the downy hair on her cheek, and a small mole underneath her pierced ear.

"Still normal," he announced awkwardly, standing quickly as he did so. "But I have bad news."

He told her that he had heard that Mukhabarat had ordered her kidnapping and that people in the hospital already knew she was an American.

"How would the Mukhabarat even know I am here?" Hannah asked. "I never go to the regime side of the city."

Sami shrugged. "They monitor the checkpoints. They have spies in our hospitals. I would be surprised if they did not have a spy here. But the danger to you now is not only from the Mukhabarat. The rebels here, many are Islamists. Al-Nusra. Nour al-Din al-Zenki. Some sympathize with ISIS. If it becomes widely known that you are an American . . ." He exhaled. "What I mean to say is, it would be best if your people came for you tonight."

"I have been told that is not possible." Hannah replied.

"But tomorrow?"

"I think."

Sami considered all the medicine that Hannah had delivered over the past year, all the patients that medicine had saved. "Wait here," he said.

He left the room, retrieved a black niqab veil from a collection of clothes that had been salvaged from the dead, and returned a minute later.

"Put this on," he said. "You will come to my house. My wife will care for you until your people come. It will be safer than staying here."

CHAPTER 41

Hannah followed Sami through a sandbag tunnel and out the rear of the hospital. She wore the veil Sami had brought her, while he wore a gray baseball cap, a fraying red jacket emblazoned with the symbol of the German soccer club Bayern München, and Adidas sneakers that had holes in them.

She thought he looked more like a someone who might sell diesel fuel on the side of the road than one of the last orthopedic surgeons still practicing in Aleppo.

"Every day I take a different route home," he explained, calling over his shoulder. "Impossible for your enemies to learn your routine if you do not have one."

He was tall and his natural pace was fast—faster even than Oskar's had been, and he'd been the tallest man she'd dated—so she found herself struggling to keep up, regularly taking two steps to his one. Her head and neck ached, she felt weak, and the niqab restricted her vision, so although she knew Aleppo well, she quickly lost track of where they were.

She was too proud to ask him to slow down though, and he didn't seem to realize how fast he was going, so instead, she kept pushing herself even as they doubled back on their tracks.

Just past a still-functioning barbershop, they ducked down a narrow alley lined with corrugated metal fencing and into a bombed-out apartment building

She followed him up a narrow staircase defaced with graffiti which read *La ilaha illallah*—There is no God but God—and which popped out on top of what he said was a neighbor's roof. From there, they made their way over low stone rooftop parapets, passing rows of carpets that had been hung from clotheslines to provide blinds from snipers.

The sun had set by the time they came to a roof marked by what appeared to be the remains of a raised garden. Even in the weak light, Hannah could see that while perhaps a good idea in the abstract, the garden had caused the center of the roof to sag, suggesting the ceiling beams below hadn't been able to handle the weight. Pigeons roosting on the periphery of the roof were cooing. Hannah pulled off the niqab.

"My mother and my children brought the dirt up," Sami explained, "but when my mother passed away, we had to give up on the garden." Noticing Hannah's condition, he added, "You are okay?"

Hannah took a moment to catch her breath. "Of course."

To avoid talking, she fished her phone out of her back pocket, powered it up, and noted she was now picking up a weak signal.

As she texted the Turk in charge of logistics at the Bonne Foi warehouse in Kilis, Sami unlocked the door to an interior stairwell.

"Baba!" cried a voice.

From the stairwell bound a gangly, gap-toothed boy with shaggy brown hair and a face that, despite the lingering baby fat on his cheeks, reminded Hannah of Sami's.

The boy's pants barely reached his ankles, suggesting a recent growth spurt, a lack of new clothes, or both. He had used gold and blue magic markers to draw what looked like armor on both his forearms.

Sami descended the stairs, and when he got to the bottom, the boy bear-hugged his waist.

"Where have you been, Baba? It has been five days."

"I was working," said Sami as he placed a hand on the boy's shoulder. "There was a small problem. Where are Noora and Mama?"

"Noora is in the ribat. Mama has left to buy food."

Once Hannah had also descended the stairs, Sami said, "This is Adam, my son."

Hannah bent down to Adam's level.

"This is our guest," said Sami to Adam." And you must be extra kind to her because she has been helping to bring medicine to the hospital where I work. Her name is Hannah, and she will be staying with us until her friends can pick her up."

"*As-salamu alaykum*, Adam," said Hannah.

"*Wa alaykumu as-salam*," Adam said back, quietly but politely. He turned back to his father. "Would you like to see the ribat? We made it much bigger."

Sami said he did, and Hannah followed them down a long stone-walled hallway. Along the way she paused in front of a wide window with a long marble sill. Below the window lay an expansive but cluttered courtyard. There were riding toys that looked too small for Adam, a deflated soccer ball, a plastic playhouse with a red plastic slide affixed to it, random pieces of scrap wood, an exterior wicker table with matching wicker chairs, a new-looking generator with a Medusa-like tangle of multicolored extension cords snaking away from it, and several rain buckets that had been placed under roof drains. Fraying, knotted ropes were strung between a decent-sized laurel tree, a fountain, and the plastic playhouse; ripped sheets had been suspended between the ropes, forming a rudimentary child's fort.

Eventually, Hannah noticed that under all the clutter was a marble-tiled floor and that the fountain was made of marble and indigo blue tiles and the walls of the courtyard were striped with golden limestone and black basalt in the *ablaq* style. The main entrance to the courtyard was marked by a two-story-tall pointed iwan arch that could have been a museum piece.

She eyed the bronze seahorse spouts on the fountain.

This was one of the old Ottoman-era houses that Aleppo and Damascus were famous for, she realized. Before the war, she and Oskar had looked into staying in one that had been converted into a boutique hotel, but it had been far too expensive.

Sami had stopped to wait and was staring at her, looking tired.

"You have a beautiful home," she said, and then followed him down to the courtyard.

———

Sami left to find his daughter and soon reappeared with a small girl in his arms.

"And this is Noora," he said.

The girl's long brown hair had been tied into pigtails, and she had decorated her arms with the same gold and blue markers that Adam had used, only it had come out looking more like an attempt at abstract art. Instead of acknowledging Hannah, she buried her head in her father's neck.

"Noora is a shy one," said Sami.

"I get shy around strangers too," Hannah said to Noora.

"Did Mama say how long she would be gone?" Sami asked Adam.

"No."

"When did she leave?"

"Last night."

"Last night?"

"Yes."

"You are sure?"

"After I went to sleep, she woke me to tell me I must watch Noora."

Sami froze. "You spent all day alone? Just you and Noora?"

Adam nodded as Noora hugged Sami tighter.

Furrowing his brow, Sami asked, "But who made you breakfast? And lunch?"

"I know how to turn on the generator," said Adam, his pride evident. "And how to fill it with diesel. Only one-half liter per day! I cooked bulgur and cauliflower."

"You are certain Mama left to purchase food?"

"And a new phone because her old one stopped working."

"And where did she say she would get these things?"

Adam shrugged.

"Is there food for dinner?"

Chest puffed out as though he were answering a question in front of a classroom, Adam said, "We have bulgur, olive oil, and milk."

"What can I do?" asked Hannah.

"Find an empty room to sleep in. I must look for my wife."

CHAPTER 42

When Sami locked the doors behind him, the *ka-chunk* of the locks engaging echoed through the stone hallways of Beit Qarah. Noora began to cry.

Hannah sat cross-legged on the marble floor in the front foyer and rested her back against the wall. Her head was pounding.

After a time, she professed to be hungry. Which wasn't true—in fact, her stomach was still upset. "Is anyone else hungry?" she asked.

Adam didn't answer. Noora's crying shifted to whimpering.

"The only problem," added Hannah, "is that I am very bad at cooking food."

She was about to ask for Adam's help in cooking dinner, when Noora ran away. Hannah heard a door slam. She looked at the floor, then at Adam. "Do you know where she went?"

Adam shrugged. "The ribat, I think."

"What is the ribat?"

Adam ran away, but then came back with a flashlight. "Come. I will show you."

———

Hannah had seen hints of Adam and Noora's enthusiasm for constructing sheet forts—what Adam called ribats—in the courtyard, but in the kitchen cellar they had outdone themselves. Save for a section where

Sami slept, the entire room was covered with overlapping white sheets suspended from ropes tied to limestone pillars and wrought-iron hooks. The effect was to form a second, much lower ceiling.

From her perch on the stairs, Hannah had the sense that she was on top of a mountain, peering down at clouds below her. The sheets reflected the beam of Adam's flashlight.

"Follow me," he said, and he dropped to his knees and ducked into an opening between two sheets.

As when she'd first entered the Beit Qarah, Hannah had been struck with the sense of passing through a portal into another world. But this was the inner sanctum, even more secluded than the house itself was.

The children had covered the floor with cardboard, so they could crawl around without hurting their knees. Once inside, vertical sheet walls divided the space into several rooms. The walls had been decorated with magic marker drawings—some just scribbles, others clear depictions of airplanes and houses and flowers and people. Similar drawings on recycled scrap paper had been hung from the sheets with a hodgepodge of paper-clips, pins, and nails.

Filtered light cast strange shadows over everything, and because Hannah had brushed against the sheets when she'd entered the fort, all the shadows were quivering.

"These are my planes," said Adam.

He retrieved a spare LED flashlight that could be charged with a crank handle and handed it to Hannah. She turned the handle and pointed the resulting beam of light at a mobile-like collection of more paper planes than she could count. All of them had been decorated with either magic markers or paints, and each had been individually suspended from the sheet ceiling with sewing thread.

"You made them all?" asked Hannah.

"Yes."

Adam kept his own flashlight trained on the planes, so Hannah obliged him by crawling closer to examine his work. They weren't just your average paper planes. These were intricate origami creations involving complex folds.

"Where did you learn to do this?"

"I have a book. But most I made myself. Special designs. Follow me," he said, then crawled around another sheet wall.

Noora was on the other side, surrounded by dolls. Some were in plastic cradles, one sat at a circular table that had been fashioned from a tambourine. In Noora's arms lay a large doll dressed in a glittery shirt. The doll's long hair was dark brown like Noora's and had been arranged into two pigtails. Noora was brushing the ends of the doll's pigtails with a plastic comb.

"She is so pretty," said Hannah. And then, "Her hair reminds me of yours."

Noora just kept combing her doll's hair, making the same repetitive motion again and again.

"Adam and I were going to make dinner. Would you like to help us, or would you prefer to stay here?"

Noora didn't answer. Hannah had seen kids go mute because of the war. The stress became too much to bear, and they retreated into themselves. It was a defense mechanism, the mind trying to protect itself. She wondered whether something like that was going on with Noora. Maybe she just didn't like strangers.

"I think she wants to stay here," said Adam.

———

In the kitchen Hannah marveled at the long granite countertops. Above them, hand painted tiles depicting cypress trees formed a backsplash. A shiny brass gooseneck faucet serviced the wide, stainless-steel double sink. Under the countertops lay open cedar shelving filled with copper pots and pans, and on them sat a stainless-steel microwave and espresso maker. French doors opened out onto both the courtyard and the dining room. The four corners of the ceiling were marked by intricate honeycombed *muqarnas* vaulting. A flat-screen television hung from one wall.

Sami had been lucky that the place hadn't been looted, Hannah thought.

The open shelving underneath the countertops was largely bare, though, and the appliances were no longer being used. Instead of the main refrigerator, a dented, far smaller one had been set up in front of it. On top of the stove lay a single-burner electric hotplate. Hannah guessed that the portable generator wasn't strong enough to run larger appliances.

"Okay," she said, "so, what do we do first?"

Adam showed her the sealed container where they stored the bulgur and the plastic water jugs that they kept out in the courtyard.

They poured water into a pot and mixed the bulgur into it. As they were waiting for the water to boil, Hannah inspected the cabinets and found a can of tomato paste, some olive oil, and an onion. She wasn't much of a cook, but as a girl she'd often helped her mother make spaghetti sauce from scratch and remembered that the recipe had called for tomato paste, olive oil, and onions. Granted, it had also called for fresh tomatoes and sugar and basil and half a dozen other ingredients, but they would just have to make do.

"You are a very lucky boy, Adam," she said.

"I am?"

"Yes. Because tonight we are going to have a special treat I call bulgur spaghetti."

CHAPTER 43

No one at the local market had seen Tahira.

In the sandbag-reinforced basement of a nearby bakery, where the clay ovens were still warm, and the tile floors dusted with flour, the baker told Sami that he hadn't seen her in months, not since bread deliveries had been taken over by the local council. Nor had the baker's sister, who lived in a neighboring block. Nor had the brother-in-law of this sister, who evidently used to buy soap from Tahira's family.

By ten at night, Sami had three loaves of flatbread—but no Tahira.

Unwilling to give up, he began walking the empty streets. Fighter jets roared above, but they were dropping their bombs far to the north. When he did encounter people, he described his wife, said she may have been looking to buy a phone—had they seen her?

No one had.

When Sami arrived back at the alley that led to his front door, instead of pulling out his keys, he leaned against the alley wall, slid down to the ground, and looked up into the dark sky.

Something terrible had happened to her, he thought. There was no other explanation. Adam was only seven years old; Noora, five. She never would have left them alone all day intentionally. What if one of them had been injured? Or if looters had broken in? Or if the generator had caught fire?

Unless . . .

Unless, Sami considered, she had become too depressed to care about the children. Unless she had—

Sami forced himself not to think it. But he knew she had been close to the edge. And that he had largely ignored the signs, trusting that she would find a way to pull herself through.

He stayed in the alley for what felt like an hour, resting, perhaps even drifting off to sleep for a moment. Having been on his feet nearly nonstop for the past thirty-six hours, he was exhausted.

And then Tahira came back.

She was wearing soft-soled shoes, a black abaya, and a black headscarf, so Sami didn't see her until she was almost on top of him. But he did recognize her smell—it was a laurel-scented perfume that she had favored before the war, it smelled like her soaps—so when she saw him and startled, he knew it was her.

She asked what he was doing in the alley.

Sami swallowed then pressed his lips tightly together. He was so relieved to see her, so grateful that she was still alive. "Waiting for you, of course. Where did you go?"

She brushed by him on the way to the front door, inserted her key in the lock, cursed when she could not get it open.

"Tahira," he said, "Wait."

She tried the lock again and again cursed.

"Let me," he said.

"I can do it!"

He placed a hand on her shoulder. "What happened?"

"Nothing," she said, sounding ashamed.

"But the children were alone. All day."

"I had intended to come back earlier. I was delayed."

Her voice cracked. Sami felt her shoulder tremble beneath his hand. "Tahira, where were you? Adam said you were buying food, but . . ."

He let his voice trail off. She was not carrying any food.

With her mother, sister, and all her close friends gone, there were few people he could think of she might have gone to visit. For a moment he considered—could she be seeing another man? Even with his extended absences, he did not think it possible. But then, why this?

She met his question with a question of her own. "And where were you last night?"

He told her how the hospital had been bombed and that he was sorry—he should have texted her. He had not intended to cause her pain.

"You must not worry about any pain you might cause me, Sami, you must worry about your work!" she cried. "I have heard it said that you are worth one hundred soldiers, and I believe it. As for the children, I am sorry they were left alone, but it was for them I left."

"To do what?"

When she declined to answer, Sami repeated the question then said, "The children need you, Tahira."

"I know that. And I am trying, Sami!"

He brought her face to his and tried to embrace her. When she failed to respond, he lifted the door handle a hair, which allowed the lock to disengage. As he opened the second of the two locks, he said, "I must tell you, we have a guest. I anticipated you would be home when I brought her here."

CHAPTER 44

Hannah and the children ate the bulgur in the sheet fort, from bowls decorated with blue fleur-de-lis. After they were finished, Hannah made up a story about two young chickens named Prince Abdullah and Princess Lila who discovered a secret room that brought them all the way to a chicken shopping-mall paradise in America known as the Paramus Park Souk where, because they were phenomenal tambourine players, they were able to make a lot of money which they used to buy pistachio *ka'ak* pastries and—

When Hannah heard a door opening upstairs, she stopped speaking midsentence.

"Baba!" cried Adam.

Hannah followed Adam and Noora out of the sheet fort and up the stairs where she saw Sami standing behind a conservatively dressed woman who was a good deal shorter than him. It took her a moment to realized that this woman, with her hollowed-out cheeks and troubled frown, was the same smiling, attractive woman Hannah had seen in the photograph at the hospital.

"Mama, where were you?" asked Adam. He hugged her, and while she didn't turn him away, she didn't hug him back. Noora lingered in the background.

"You should be in bed," said Tahira. Her voice had an edge to it.

"Hannah was telling us a story," said Adam.

Sami gestured to Hannah with an open palm. "This is our young guest that I was telling you about." He introduced her and explained she worked for a relief organization that had been helping deliver medicine to hospitals in Aleppo, and that she had been the victim of a kidnapping attempt during which she had been injured.

"I am so grateful for your hospitality," said Hannah, wishing that she had thought to put her headscarf back on before leaving the cellar. The necessities of war had upended traditions in ways large and small, but she still sensed that Sami bringing an unfamiliar woman home was not a welcome development. Upon receiving no response, she added, "I hope to leave tomorrow, I only wait for a call from my driver."

"I am going to bed," said Tahira.

———

Hannah slept for nine hours. When she awoke, she wriggled her toes in the clean sheets that Adam had found for her, feeling a little guilty because she was so dirty.

The room was dusty, but aside from that, it was easy to imagine that she was in an upscale hotel. The refinished shutters that looked out onto the courtyard had been pulled shut, but rays of morning light filtered past the louvers, casting a striped shadow on the thick marble sill. Above her, in between exposed beams, the ceiling had been painted with stylized tulips and pomegranate blossoms. The interior limestone wall that bordered the courtyard had been sandblasted clean, as had the other three walls of exposed fieldstone.

From the courtyard, she heard the rumble of a generator and smelled diesel smoke.

Her head was tender to the touch where Sami had stitched it up, and her neck and torso sore from the fight with her kidnapper. But she felt well otherwise, and knew she was lucky to be alive. Still hanging from a leather cord around her neck was her silver Hand of Fatima necklace. She'd bought it two years ago at a bazaar in Antakya, because many— Jews and Christians included, though it was named after Muhammad's daughter—considered it to be a sign of peace and good luck, and she'd been hoping it would bring her both. As she clutched it now, she considered that perhaps it had.

She dressed quickly, putting on the same soiled, blood-spattered clothes she had been wearing for the past two days. Upon throwing open the shutters, she observed Adam in the courtyard, sitting in a patch of sunlight next to a collection of blue plastic jugs filled with diesel fuel. He appeared to be folding a paper airplane.

"I guess you woke early," she called. "May I help make breakfast?"

He made a few more folds, focusing intently. "There is bread with oil," he said.

"Is your father awake?"

He nodded.

"Do you know where he is?"

"Hospital."

Adam finished a few more folds, then held up his new paper airplane and smiled. It had bat wings and reminded Hannah of the shape of a stealth bomber. "Amazing," she said. "And your father—when did he leave for the hospital?"

"A long time ago."

"Where is Noora?"

"At the Paramus Park Souk, playing with chickens," he said. This was followed by giggling.

———

Hannah was able to get a weak cell phone signal on the second floor and learned that her new driver had left Azaz at dawn and hoped to meet her just outside the old city, near the Qinnasrin Gate, at ten.

Which was in twenty minutes. She texted him that she'd be there.

Before leaving, she rejoined Adam in the courtyard. The sun had come out, and he was wearing a collared short-sleeved shirt that was too small for him, concentrating as he repeatedly threw his new plane into the air. After each throw, he'd make small adjustments to the folds.

The generator had been shut off, but the smell of diesel fuel lingered.

"I have to leave now," she said.

"But you need to finish the story."

"I bet you can finish it. You have a good imagination."

"It will not be the same."

"No, I suppose not." Hannah waited until Adam retrieved his plane, then asked, "And where is your mother?"

Adam led her to a massive door off the courtyard that had been decorated with a sixteen-point star and reinforced with black, wrought iron straps.

"In there," he said.

"Could you knock?"

He did. No one answered.

"You just have to go in," he said.

Hannah didn't want to do that, so she knocked harder than Adam had.

When no one responded, Adam yanked open the door. "Mama!" he yelled, loud enough that Hannah flinched. "The guest woman leaves!"

Tahira was lying on a bed in a raised section of the room, a pillow propped up behind her back, the glow of her phone illuminating her olive skin. The shutters to the courtyard had been closed tight, and she'd draped sheets over them.

She shielded her eyes from the new light that spilled in from the doorway.

"I only wanted to let you know that I am leaving," said Hannah. "Thank you so much for your hospitality."

"Close the door. Now."

Hannah did. She then said goodbye to Noora in the cellar, and Adam followed her to the front foyer.

"Are you going to help Baba at the hospital?" he asked.

Hannah bent down. "Probably not. I plan to go home. To America."

"Oh."

She nodded, suddenly filled with a sense that she didn't want to leave this little boy. Struck with an idea, she cocked her head, squinted at him, and said, "I bet you would know how to use a cell phone if you had one."

"I use Baba's sometimes."

"You know how to make calls and send texts?"

He nodded.

She retrieved her phone from her back pocket and turned it on. "This one is a little dented, but it still works. Would you like to have it?"

Her real phone was back in Antakya. This was just a cheap backup she used when traveling in Syria. She purposely hadn't stored financial information, photos, or much else on it. Mainly it was just downloaded music.

Eyes wide, Adam nodded again.

"I will give it to you, but before you use it, you must ask your mother or father whether it is permitted. Okay?"

Adam agreed, so after taking a minute to delete a few recent texts and enter her name and the number for her real phone into the contacts, she handed him the phone and charger.

"If you ever want to call or text me—or maybe not me, but maybe you have other friends, or family you want to get in touch with—if you want to call me or them, now you can."

Hannah promised herself that, once back in Antakya, she would go online to replenish the minutes on the Turkish SIM card that was in the phone.

"Thank you," he said, and he patted his heart quickly and bowed his head.

She wanted to hug him, but instead lightly placed a hand on his shoulder and asked him to lock the door behind her.

He said he would.

"Okay then, Adam Hasan. You take care of yourself."

She turned, but at the last moment, she quickly slipped her Hand of Fatima necklace from her neck and placed it around his.

"An extra gift, to protect you," she said, then left.

CHAPTER 45

Ankara, Turkey

"A toast then!" said Oskar, lifting his glass. "To good friends becoming better friends."

His date, a petite brunette named Melinda, smiled modestly and tipped her head, "To good friends becoming better friends."

They clinked glasses. Oskar took a sip of his wine. Melinda did the same.

They were seated at a table for two in an old Ottoman-era home that had been converted into an upscale restaurant. Above them, dried sumac-berry branches hung from age-blackened wood beams. The orange flicker of a candle in the center of the table reflected off their wine glasses. The air smelled of cinnamon.

At twenty-four, Melinda was five years his junior. She was British, Oxford-educated, and fluent in Turkish because her mother had been a diplomat. She worked in the international trade department at the British embassy in Ankara, where they'd met at an embassy reception.

"Imagine what it would have been like to live in this place," said Melinda. She shuddered dramatically. "Freaky."

"I don't know," said Oskar, contemplating her use of the work *freaky* and wondering if their age difference might be more of an issue than he'd thought. "Maybe not so bad."

"But it's so dark!"

"It is that."

"So," said Melinda, after they had reviewed the menu. "I understand that you were posted to Syria before the war." Wide-eyed, she placed her elbows on the table and rested her chin on the back of her hands as she stared at him.

"I was."

"Tell me about it."

"There's really not much to tell," said Oskar.

"Tell me about it anyway."

"I was a field engineer. We were trying to develop a site for an urban park that was going to help revitalize a local neighborhood. Then the war came, and I left."

"I was in Istanbul when the protests broke out there in the summer of 2013, that was really something," said Melinda, and for the next half hour, prompted by Oskar's tepid questions, she spoke of her experiences in the Turkish capital, exaggerating her brushes with violence.

As she did so, Oskar considered that his wine, a white clay-pot-fermented *kvevri* from Georgia, was quite tannic. He further considered that, while his last sexual partner had been a tattooed Romanian aid worker who'd left him with a case of chlamydia, at least there had been no postcoital emotional entanglements to deal with. He found himself wishing the same could be true in this instance, should any physical intimacy develop. He sensed, however, that Melinda harbored different expectations.

It had been a mistake to accept her invitation to dinner.

Interrupting his thoughts, Melinda asked, "So when did you leave for good?"

"Sorry?" Oskar turned to her, mildly embarrassed that he'd lost the thread of the conversation.

"Syria? When did you leave?"

"Oh, right." He took a sip of wine. "Summer of 2012."

"But the war had already started by then, no?"

"It had, in parts of the country at least. It came late to Aleppo. But still, we hung on longer than we should have."

After he spoke, he realized that the use of pronoun "we" instead of "I" must have sounded strange given that he had never mentioned Hannah.

"That sounds so brave."

Oskar sensed she was receptive to hearing him recount some valiant act. A few years ago, he would have been happy to supply such a tale, and to tell it with false modesty. But not now.

"It wasn't," he said. "It was stupid."

2016

CHAPTER 46

Rebel-held Aleppo

They came to bomb ISIS, or so they claimed. To their credit, they did.

KAB-500Kr glide bombs fell from Sukhoi and MiG fighter jets, 3M-54 Kalibr cruise missiles were launched from ships as far away as the Caspian Sea, Kh-101 cruise missiles were released from massive Cold War–era Tupolev turboprop bombers that rumbled so loudly in the sky they rattled window panes and dishes . . .

But they also claimed that they were not there to take the side of the Assad regime, and that was a lie because their bombs fell not only on ISIS, but also on the Free Syrian Army and her allies. In Raqqa and Homs, and then in Aleppo. Just a few, at first. Then hundreds. Then even more.

———

When the Russians entered the war, joining forces with Assad and the Iranians, Sami redoubled his efforts at the M2. If he had treated twenty a day before the Russians started bombing, then he would heal thirty a day now, he resolved.

Tahira dealt with the situation differently. In February of the new year, Sami found out exactly how differently.

He was between operations at the M2 when he received the call. Because the Bolero ringtone had indicated it was his wife, he was surprised to hear a male voice.

The man explained that his name was Abdul, and it was essential that Sami come to the town of Kafr Hamrah. Immediately.

After taking his phone from his ear and staring at it for a moment in confusion, Sami asked, "Why do you call me on my wife's phone?"

"Out of necessity, sir. When can you come?"

Sami heard what sounded like a woman wailing.

"Where is my wife?"

"Here."

"I must speak with her."

"Yes, yes, of course," said Abdul. Then, "But perhaps this is not possible. There was an incident."

"What incident?" Sami asked. Then, "Are my children there as well?"

"I believe not."

A part of Sami's brain registered the import of what the man was saying, but a larger part did not want to admit it. He felt as though he were floating. "Perhaps I have not been clear," he said. "I am a doctor. I have patients in need of care. To leave would be to—"

"If you want to retrieve your wife, Doctor, you must come to my shop in Kafr Hamrah!" He blurted out a street address, then said, "By God, I am sorry."

"Is she hurt?" Sami asked, but the man had already hung up.

———

Sami stood outside the operating room for a moment. His legs began to tremble.

Retrieve your wife. What did that mean?

"Dr. Sami," said one of the nurses. "They are ready for you."

Sami felt his chest tighten, gripping him first with steady pressure then with a ferocity that left him breathless.

"Dr. Sami?"

He tried to wave the nurse away with one hand as he braced himself against the wall with the other.

"Are you not well?" she asked.

He straightened his back and inhaled once, then again. "I must leave."

He walked back to Beit Qarah. A frail pensioner whom he did not recognize at first, but then realized used to be friends with his mother, lay bundled in shawls, napping in the front reception room.

Upon waking, she claimed not to know where Tahira had gone. "She tells me nothing, that one."

"Then why are you here?"

After suffering a coughing fit, she explained that Tahira had begged her to watch the children until the evening. But that was all she knew.

Adam and Noora were in the courtyard, using chalk that Tahira had bought them to draw on the floor. It was cold and damp. Leaden clouds hung low in the sky. They were both wearing puffy winter jackets that had been repaired with tape.

"When did Mama leave?" he asked them.

"This morning," said Adam.

"Did she say where she was going?"

"Look, Baba." Adam pointed to one of his chalk drawings. "Look how fat the chicken is!"

"Adam! Did Mama say where she went?"

"To a secret place. But she said she would take us there soon."

Sami glanced at Noora. She had barely acknowledged him.

"I need to leave," he said to Adam. "To find Mama. Can you make dinner?" Adam said he could.

"It is cold," Sami added. "Do not wait to go inside until you are freezing."

It was cold inside too though; there was not enough diesel to run the space heaters for long, much less to power the main heating system. Sami had bought a small, wood-burning stove, but there was little wood to burn save for the furniture, and it had not come to that yet.

"Okay," said Adam.

"Put on your winter hat. You must set a good example for Noora."

———

He walked, then hitched a ride with a private car. The driver tailgated a dump truck, using it as a shield from potential snipers in front of them, so the air stank of exhaust.

Some stretches of the road they followed were purgatorial visions of ruin—bombed-out buildings, twisted metal, blasted date palms—but in others, street vendors huddled around garbage-bin fires sipping hot *sahlab* drinks, selling cooking oil from giant plastic tubs. Pretending life was normal.

The farther Sami traveled from the familiar neighborhoods of old Aleppo, the more untethered from reality he felt.

A mist had descended over the northern stretches of the city, and soon it began to drizzle, then rain. The air was cold enough that he guessed the rain would turn to snow that night. The apartment complexes showed no signs of harboring life within, but it was impossible to tell whether that was because they were abandoned, or simply because the inhabitants were huddled in the inner rooms, far from the windows.

Two hours after leaving the M2, Sami reached a muddy parking lot packed with cars and vans in various states of disrepair. The lot lay in front of a two-bay garage. One of the bays accommodated a collection of grease-laden pneumatic tools and a large, purple air compressor, the other, a green Fiat sedan. In the back of the garage, a dented brass samovar sat atop a small wood stove.

Rainwater dripped down Sami's forehead and into his eyes. It was four thirty in the afternoon. The sky was darkening.

"*Salaam?*" he called, not even certain he was in the right place. There were no street numbers or signs. He had been directed to his current location by a diesel-fuel vendor who had claimed that his nephew worked at the garage.

"*Salaam?*" he called again.

From behind the green Fiat came the clang of metal hitting concrete. A teenage boy slid out from under the trunk of the car, his face, hands, and orange sweatshirt smudged with grease. His gray ski cap had been pulled down low on his forehead.

Sami gave his name and said he was looking for Abdul.

"Stay here," said the boy.

Sami ducked into the garage. On a work bench, a collection of ratchets, pneumatic tools, and wrenches caught his eye, and it occurred to him that, on some level, what he did and what the people who worked in this garage did was not so different.

A door at the back opened. The woman who appeared was either elderly or prematurely aging, Sami could not tell which. A thick, woolen shawl and a woolen headscarf that she wore over a lighter headscarf weighed heavily upon her.

She gestured that he should follow.

Paths had been cut between piles of rusting car parts behind the garage. The woman led Sami down one that ended at a collection of tires that had been piled up against a deteriorating limestone wall. At the base of the wall, lying face up and covered with a sheet that was once white but was now translucent because it was soaked with water, lay a body.

On top of the body sat an abnormally thin, one-eyed cat with patchy fur.

"Tsk, tsk," cried the woman. She darted toward the cat, which had backed off but appeared reluctant to leave. "Tsk," she hissed, kicking feebly in the cat's direction. The cat just backed up a bit more so that it was crouched between two tires.

"Who is this?" demanded Sami.

"May God have mercy," she said.

Sami dropped to his knees in the mud and bowed his head. When he pulled back the sheet, an involuntary cry of despair escaped his lips.

"*Inna lillahi wa inna ilayhi raji'un*," the woman chanted softly and repeatedly. We belong to God and to him we shall return.

Tahira's eyes were closed. Blood had pooled in the mud on the right side of her body. A brief examination revealed that two bullets had pierced her torso.

The first had penetrated her chest on the left side, shattering her first rib. From the placement of the exit wound near her spine, Sami guessed that the bullet had nicked the upper lobe of her left lung, perforated her left subclavian artery, and passed through her lower trachea. The entrance wound of the second bullet was between the fifth and sixth ribs and had likely pierced the left ventricle of her heart.

He clasped and unclasped his fists as he considered what must have been uncontrollable hemorrhaging of the subclavian artery, perhaps a collapsed lung, blood rushing into the pleural cavity . . .

It began to rain harder.

She would not have died immediately; her heart would have tried to keep beating.

He continued to kneel by her side. Night fell. He remembered how she looked in her white gown on their wedding day, the sweet expression on her face as she had held Adam in the hospital room hours after his birth, and the crushing bouts of anxiety and apathy that had consumed her of late. Eventually, he crossed her hands over her stomach, pulled the sheet back over her body, and stood.

The cat had returned. Having seen animals feeding on the dead before, he scooped up a handful of pebbles and tossed them near the cat's paws.

"Go," he whispered gently. "Not this one."

———

The old woman was waiting for him in the garage, sitting on the wicker chair next to the wood stove and a lit candle. The chair that held her was no larger than normal, but she made it seem so.

"She was placed there with respect," she said quietly, as she brought her hands to her heart. "Covered and facing Mecca."

"And where is Abdul?" Sami demanded.

"He has gone home."

It was irrational, he knew, the anger he felt rising. But his inner voice was shouting at him, insisting that Tahira's death was a grave injustice, that someone needed to acknowledge that injustice and pay for it.

"How did it happen?"

"There was fighting. On the road to Khanasir."

"What was she doing on the road to Khanasir?"

"Going to the other side, of course."

"The other side?"

"Of the city. She has a friend there she visits."

And then Sami understood—understood why Tahira had been

sneaking off, and why she had been hiding it. She had been visiting regime-held Aleppo. Making an all-day trip, down to the south through dangerous stretches of no-man's-land before crossing to regime-held territory and coming back north.

Upon being questioned, the woman revealed that Tahira had first hoped to stay in an apartment she claimed she and Sami still owned in regime-held Aleppo, but finding it occupied by soldiers, she had turned to a friend who had offered her and her children a spare room.

Had Sami not known this? It would have been better for his children, of course. Tahira had been planning on moving them soon. This last trip had been to make the final preparations.

Sami pictured Tahira sitting on a bench in the park off Saadallah al-Jabiri Square, in the shadow the statue of the poet Khalil Al Hindawi. Maybe eating at a café by the Queiq River, sitting across from med students preparing for the national exam. It was true the regime-held side of the city was no paradise—every day the rebels bombarded it with jury-rigged gas-canister bombs that they shot from homemade cannons—but the range of the cannons was limited, and the rebels had no air force. Sami imagined that on the regime side, she and the children would have been able to live without the same degree of daily fear.

She would have felt horribly guilty leaving him though, taking the children with her to live with the enemy. So, she had kept her plans secret. He wanted to tell her he would not have tried to stop her. That it would have been enough just knowing that she had pulled herself back from the edge and was trying to do what was best for the children, and that the children were loved. She could have trusted him with her secret!

"Who was fighting when she was killed?"

"Daesh," she said, using a common term for ISIS, "attacked a checkpoint. Your wife and Abdul and two others were trapped. Two of Abdul's passengers were shot. One was your wife."

The woman paused for a long time, then said, "You must have family. That can help you."

"No."

"And yet, she must have parents."

"Her mother still lives. But she is in Jordan, with her sister. They are all gone, her family. They left two years ago." As Tahira and the children should have, Sami thought. He should have encouraged her to leave then, to have taken the risk. "I have my children, but . . ." Sami's voice trailed off.

"She must be washed. And you must to buy a *kafan*. And bury her. I can arrange to have people help you with this, if you wish."

Sami resisted the idea of Tahira being buried in the Muslim way. But he knew that every Ramadan, she had fasted, or had at least pretended to, along with her mother, sister, and brother-in-law. And that on the Eid al-Fitr feast that followed, she had always prayed and sung songs with her relations as her family had done for generations. It was true that, even before the war, her attendance at Friday prayers had been intermittent, but her dedication to the family meals that had followed—stuffed grape leaves! stuffed intestines! stuffed eggplant!—had been something approaching absolute.

There was no doubt in his mind that she would have wanted a traditional funeral.

So he turned to the woman, exhaled, and said, "I would be grateful if you knew people who could help. The cemetery in Aleppo where her relations are buried is full. Is there one near here that we can use?"

"It is not a cemetery, but there is some land where we can dig a grave."

———

The woman's grandson ran to get help, and soon Tahira was laid out in the garage on a table. A few sticks were added to the wood stove. *Dua* death prayers were chanted. Buckets of clean water were brought in, and the body washed three times, as Sami sat outside on an overturned crate.

After Tahira was washed, she was dressed in a five-piece white-cotton *kafan* burial robe that the old woman managed to buy from a friend. It cost Sami every last cent he'd brought with him.

Two men Sami had never seen before brought her to a patch of land that lay next to what had once been a busy road, next to other newly dug graves. The rain had turned to wet, clumpy snow, and the men slipped while lowering her body.

More prayers were offered.

"Oh, God, elevate us in faith, obedience, and piety . . ."

When the woman assured him that only other Muslims had been buried in the makeshift cemetery, Sami thanked her for her help and for being so thoughtful. The teenage boy and the two men helped him dig the grave. It took a long time and his hands were cold, blistered, and filthy before they were through. When they moved the body close to the grave, in preparation for lowering Tahira into it, Sami fashioned a dirt pillow under where her head would lie and left fist-sized clumps of dirt under where her chin and shoulder would rest.

She was laid on her right side, her face looking toward Mecca, then buried.

Although the grave was unmarked, Sami found a collection of old bricks by the side of the road and arranged them in the form of a rectangle at the head of her grave. He noted the angle and distance from it to a nearby street sign.

One day, when they were older, he imagined he would take the children there.

———

He walked back to Beit Qarah that night—trudging for hours through the darkened, battle-scarred city—never becoming completely lost but sometimes straying from the most direct path. The snow had turned back to rain, transforming what little had accumulated on the ground to slush. By the time he fell onto his mattress in the cellar, still fully clothed, wet, and freezing, it was three in the morning. He was exhausted but still could not sleep.

He did not go to work the next day, or the day after that. He burned a prized beechwood couch his mother had brought with her from Damascus in the wood stove.

He did not wash. Nor did he eat.

Adam asked him, "Baba, what is wrong?" and "When is Mama coming home?" but Sami could not bring himself to answer.

"Later," was all he said. "We will talk later."

———

They came for him on the third day. Two representatives from the M2, nurses Sami had worked with for a year, along with a rebel commander named Ibrahim Antar.

Ibrahim was a cousin of one of the nurses and claimed that Tahira and his own late wife had been friends. They had known each other from the cheese shop, by the Antakya Gate. Ibrahim had brought his son Selim with him, and within minutes Adam and Selim were playing soccer in the courtyard.

"As our wives were friends, so are our sons, as you can see," said Ibrahim.

Sami could not see because he did not bother to look.

The nurses and Ibrahim extended their sympathies and asked what they could do to help. Then they asked when Sami intended to return to work because he was sorely needed at the hospital.

He could not return to work, Sami said, because he had to care for his children.

But Ibrahim offered a solution. "My mother, she lives on a farm outside of Aleppo. She cares for Selim and his sister and several of his cousins. I am certain she would welcome your children as her own."

When Sami didn't respond, Ibrahim added, "It is far from the battle lines, much safer than Aleppo. And of course, it would be easy for you to visit whenever you wanted."

Sami said he would consider it, and then did nothing of the sort.

That night he told the children about the death of their mother, that she had died trying to find them a better home. Adam became despondent, Noora mute. Sami attempted to console them but instead, wound up ruining part of their sheet fort when he tried to squeeze into it.

He burned the tulipwood foyer bench that Tahira had bought just before the war. And the shoe rack that had stood next to it. They ran out of bulgur.

Five days after Tahira died, he was again visited by the nurse who was Ibrahim's cousin, only this time she was accompanied by a bleary-eyed Dr. Wasim who, after asking for Sami's advice concerning a patient whose jaw had been shot off, begged Sami to return.

"This Selim boy, you like him?" Sami asked Adam that night.

Adam said he did, though he did not care for Selim's father.

"If Selim's grandmother were to care for you, and I were to visit often. What then?"

Adam shrugged. "Maybe," he said.

His mother was a sweet woman, Ibrahim assured Sami the next day. She lived an hour west of Aleppo, in the farmhouse Ibrahim himself had lived in before the drought that had ravaged Syria had forced him to go to work at his uncle's cheese shop in the city.

Sami visited the house. It was modest, but it had heat, there was food, and Ibrahim's mother appeared to be responsible and willing to help.

Within a few minutes of arriving, Adam and Selim were holding hands and taking turns riding Selim's bike. Selim's young cousins flicked marbles in the dirt and played blind man's buff with stick swords.

Arrangements were made.

Sami would continue to work in Aleppo, and he would visit his children every week or two. Tahira, he hoped, would have approved.

"*Mashallah*," concluded Ibrahim. God has willed it.

Sami doubted very much that the offer had anything to do with the divine, and he was leery even then about what he recalled was Ibrahim's affiliation with Ahrar al-Sham, a rebel group which hoped to impose an Islamic state upon Syria. But he reasoned the war had led to many strange alliances of convenience—even the Americans were supporting many of the radical Islamists—and therefore, he would not judge Ibrahim too harshly for supporting them as well.

CHAPTER 47

Antakya, Turkey • Ten days later

Hannah was finally going home.

Not because she wanted to—even after nearly being kidnapped by the Mukhabarat, she had continued to venture into Syria, although she had limited her medicine runs to day trips in and around Azaz. But two weeks ago, the Turks had refused to renew Bonne Foi's registration permit. Which meant her work visa would not be renewed either. Other aid groups were getting kicked out or forced to hire only Turkish workers.

The message was clear: the Turks were done with playing host to the do-gooders of the world. So, having nowhere else to go, she was headed back to live with her mother and sister in New Jersey and apply to graduate school.

But before she could go, she needed to get her suitcase zipped up, a task she was finding was a little bit like trying to stuff a big balloon into a small box, in that pushing on one part just caused another to pop up.

She tried sitting on the top of it, which helped, but the gap was still too great, so she flopped over and pressed her chest against the lid. That method gave her a better purchase on the zipper, but she still couldn't advance it more than halfway.

Her purse and carry-on daypack were stuffed tight, and she was already planning on wearing her bulkiest shoes and winter jacket, the pockets of which she'd stuffed with socks, so the suitcase had to fit the rest.

Taking a deep breath, she executed a little belly flop onto it. Just as she managed to advance the zipper a bit more, her phone, which lay on the bed, rang.

Unwilling to release the suitcase lid and have it pop back up, she ignored the call and instead, shifted her weight on the suitcase lid in a way that allowed her to advance the zipper farther.

As she took a moment to catch her breath before shifting her weight yet again, her phone pinged, indicating a text had come in. Then it rang again.

Worried that it might be the airline alerting her of a change in plans or her sister saying that she could not, in fact, pick her up at Newark when she landed, she reached for the phone, but her arms weren't long enough.

Cursing, she stood, grabbed the phone, and swiped the talk icon without looking at the caller ID.

"'Allo?" she said.

No one responded.

Forced open by the pressure, her suitcase unzipped on its own. She sat back down on the lid.

"'Allo?" she said again, then in Arabic, "This is Hannah, who is this?"

It was one thirty in the morning, a taxi was coming for her at six, and she wanted to get at least a little sleep. She came close to hanging up. In another second or two she would have. It was only the faintest of sounds that prevented her from doing so. The wind, or maybe static on the line.

"Is anyone there?"

More silence, then, "Can you come here?"

The voice seemed too low to be a woman's and yet still too high to be a man's. The connection was crackly, and Hannah wasn't even sure she'd heard correctly.

"Who is this?"

"Adam."

"Adam—" Hannah was about to ask, Adam who? But she realized she recognized the boy's voice. "Is this Adam *Hasan?*" she asked, emphasizing his last name.

"Uh-huh."

"Adam Hasan the great paper-airplane maker? The great ribat-builder of Aleppo? That Adam Hasan?"

"Uh-huh."

Hannah bit her lip and considered that, although she'd continued to replenish the prepaid minutes on her old phone, she hadn't heard from Adam since she'd given it to him. She'd texted him once, to make sure he had her number, but he'd never responded. Which was perfectly normal, she'd thought. A boy his age had better things to do than text some strange woman he'd only met once.

What wasn't perfectly normal was that he was calling her now, at one thirty in the morning.

"Well, hello, Adam," she said. "This is Hannah. Do you remember me?"

"Yes. Can you come here?"

Assuming he meant his house in Aleppo, but confused as to why he would ask, she said, "That would be very difficult. You see, I am in—"

"I want to go back to Beit Qarah."

Hannah lifted herself off the suitcase and placed a hand on her forehead.

"You are not at Beit Qarah now?"

"No."

"Then where are you?" When Adam didn't answer, she asked, "Is your father or mother there?"

"No."

"Who is with you?"

"Noora. But she is on the ground."

Hannah rubbed her temple and began to pace. "If Noora is on the ground, where are you?"

"On the roof. I climbed for the phone. So it would work."

———

Bit by bit, Hannah pulled out the pieces of the story. Adam's mother had died. He and Noora had been sent away to live in the country where an old sheik at the local mosque had made him get up before dawn for prayers and memorize parts of the Quran. The sheik had mocked Adam for his poor pronunciation and had smacked him in the face when he had neglected to speak the introductory *Bismillah*—In the name of God, the Most Gracious, the Most Merciful. Then yesterday, Selim's grandmother, Sitto, had stolen the Hand of Fatima necklace Hannah had given him, so he had stolen it back, and he and Noora had snuck into a van bound for Aleppo. They had snuck back out when he thought they had arrived, but now he was not so sure they were in Aleppo, and his father would not answer his phone, so could she please come help him?

"Listen, Adam," said Hannah, "I need you to do something very important. I need you to climb back down off the roof and find an adult who can tell you what city or town you are in. Can you do that?"

"I think everybody is asleep."

"Look for the best house on the street. Go to that one with Noora and knock on the door until someone answers. Tell them you are lost, that you need them to tell you what town you are in. Do not hang up the phone while you are doing this. Try to keep talking to me. But if we get disconnected, call me right back. Okay?"

"Okay."

———

Hannah had barely been able to hear Adam to start with, and the cell phone signal gave out completely when he left the roof. She tried calling back but got his voicemail. She left a message and sent a text, then returned to packing as though nothing had happened. After finally getting her suitcase closed, she went online and checked if her plane was still scheduled to depart on time. It was.

This wasn't her business, she told herself. Adam probably wouldn't even call back. He'd call his father, and his father would come for him.

Adam called her back.

"We are near Andzara," he said.

"Hold on," said Hannah. She rushed to unzip her purse and grab a pen and a twenty-lira Turkish banknote because she didn't have a piece of scrap paper.

"How is that spelled?"

Adam, sounding as though he might be near tears, said he didn't know.

"Are you with an adult now?"

"Yes."

"May I speak to that person?"

———

Hannah tried calling Sami one more time. After getting dumped into his voicemail again, she locked her bags in a storage bin in the basement of her apartment complex, then paid forty euros to postpone her flight. When the taxi came for her at six in the morning, she had the driver bring her to the Bab al Hawa border crossing instead of the airport.

The olive groves north of Antakya were bare, the sky was gunmetal gray.

At the crossing, she waited five hours before reaching the border control point. The whole time, she worried she'd be turned away. They didn't let private citizens cross at will anymore.

The Turks asked whether she was going to Raqqa, to marry an ISIS fighter.

She showed them her Bonne Foi identification, which she'd pulled from the garbage bin, and said she was on a charity mission to reunite two missing children with their father.

The guards said she was foolish to cross, but if she wanted to be a fool, then they wouldn't stop her.

Outside the Kah refugee camp on the Syrian side of the border, she found a group of Free Syrian Army soldiers on their way to Aleppo who drove her the better part of the way to the village of Andzara for free.

Adam and Noora were kicking a soccer ball outside of the two-story stone farmhouse when she got there. The house bordered a dormant cotton field and was on the outskirts of the village.

Adam wore a woman's shawl around his shoulders as though it were a cape. He was a constant, lanky flurry of motion, kicking the ball, racing after it, throwing it in the air, keeping it suspended with kicks from his knees. Noora was standing nearby, looking ridiculously vulnerable in her pink boots and pink pajamas and puffy winter coat, kicking the ball back whenever Adam sent it her way.

A rickety water tower stood on the roof of the house. Parked to the right of the front door, next to a three-wheeled car and a rusty irrigation tank, was a bright red tractor that had weeds growing around its tires.

Adam noticed Hannah first. He waved and ran toward her.

Hannah waved back as she kept walking.

When Adam skidded to a stop in front of her, he was all smiles. "*Salaam*," he said.

Hannah noticed he was still wearing the Hand of Fatima necklace she'd given him.

"*Salaam*," she said back.

"You took a long time to get here," he noted.

"Yes, it did take a long time," she said. "You must have been worried."

"Did you bring a car?"

She explained that she didn't have a car.

"Then how will we get to Beit Qarah?"

"I guess we will have to figure it out."

CHAPTER 48

Rebel-held Aleppo

When Sami opened the first of his two doors and heard the faint sound of voices, he thought squatters must have broken in.

The fact that he could also hear the plaintive voice of the Lebanese diva Fairuz singing *I Loved You in the Summer* drifting down from the second floor and that he recognized the crackle of his mother's 1980s-era speakers told him the squatters had invaded not just Beit Qarah, but his mother's room.

Although exhausted, having slept at the hospital the four nights prior and having worked all but six hours of the last forty-eight, he found that he was not too tired to be enraged by the violation. If it had been his room, that would have been one thing, but for strangers to be soiling his late mother's things . . .

He did not care whether they were heavily armed ISIS thugs or just homeless waifs. Whoever they were, they could have found perfectly adequate shelter in any other part of the house. Furious, he inserted his key into the second of his two doors and yanked it open.

In three and a half years of war, he had never neglected to remove his street shoes when entering the house, but he did so now. As he ascended the steps to the second floor in the dark, taking two at a time, he noted that the generator in the courtyard was running—on his supply of diesel, no doubt. He wondered whether there would even be any food left in the kitchen.

The extension cord that ran from the generator to his mother's room had prevented the intruders from shutting the door all the way. So when he yanked the door open, the squatters did not notice. They were facing away from him, huddled together on his mother's Aubusson rug, looking at his mother's collection of albums that were spread out on the floor. Edith Piaf stared up at him. A single dim light blazed in the corner.

"Get—"

He was about to shout, "Out!" when he realized he was staring at his own children. And the American woman.

——

Adam and Noora sprang up as one and ran to their father.

Sami stepped back, confused, his mind and body still primed for an outburst of anger. His children grabbed him and pulled at his waist. It felt as though they were trying to climb up him, as they might a tree. He wobbled a bit, off balance and speechless. The Fairuz record skipped.

"Baba, where were you?" asked Adam.

Sami looked down at his son and Noora.

"At the hospital," he said, still incredulous. "Why are you here?"

As he observed the smile on Adam's face falter, he realized that those were the wrong words, that he should be hugging both his children back, expressing concern for them and telling them how good it was to see them. But he had been so tired and angry a moment ago, and so confused now.

"We wanted to come home," announced Adam, still sounding cheerful, but also a little defensive.

"I thought the boy Selim, he was your friend? What happened to the arrangements?"

Adam shrugged.

Sami eyed Hannah. Her long, black hair was uncovered. Her abaya had been casually thrown into a corner of the room revealing a form-fitting blue fleece athletic top. "And you?" he asked.

"When they could not reach you, they called me," she said, giving Noora's shoulder a squeeze.

Sami had planned to be back at the M2 by seven the next morning and to sleep at the hospital tomorrow night. There was nowhere near enough food in the house to feed everyone. The idea was that the children would be cared for in the country, and now—

"Adam and Noora," said Hannah brightly. "I imagine your father is surprised to see me and has many questions about how we got here. So, perhaps he and I could talk while you two arrange your beds?" As they trudged out, she added, "Leave the door open."

Sami held his tongue as Hannah explained what had happened. He already felt oafish and unrefined in her presence—he was at least a head taller than her and had not shaved in a week—and was hesitant to make himself appear to be more brutish by expressing anger. So when he finally spoke, it was only to explain that the battery on his phone had died, which is why he had not answered any calls. And to express concern that, after the kidnapping attempt, she had dared to come back to Aleppo.

"The checkpoints are watched," he said. "You know this."

"Are you working tomorrow?" she asked.

He opened his palms. "Of course."

"And you are determined to stay in Aleppo?"

"Yes. Yes, of course. I will find someone else to watch Adam and Noora. Someone who can come to the house. They are attached to Beit Qarah. I see now it was a mistake to have moved them."

"I can stay a few days, if that helps."

If she could, Sami said, and if she promised to stay inside and not risk going through any more checkpoints, then yes, he would be grateful.

———

The next day, Sami called Ibrahim.

There was no easy way to tell him that Noora and Adam had run away, or that Sami had no intention of forcing them to go back. The insult, even delivered diplomatically, was evident.

"Of course, your children are used to finer accommodations," said Ibrahim. "It must have been difficult for them living in such conditions."

"It was not the conditions, I assure you. My children, they simply—"

"Having a home such as Beit Qarah to oneself during wartime is important, to be sure," said Ibrahim. "I must tell you," he added, "my mother informed me that, because your children have been raised with little discipline, they lack proper respect. I speak candidly because I know you are too busy to see this."

"I am indeed," said Sami, "and I am ashamed at the trouble I and my children have given your family. Please tell your mother I will forever be grateful for the assistance she offered me in my time of need."

Ibrahim paused then said, "*Inshallah*, I will tell her. And as for you, what will you do now?"

"What I have always done."

"So, the M2. You will not be leaving it?"

"Of course not."

"And who will watch your children?"

"I am in the process of making arrangements."

"I will send men tomorrow. So that whatever arrangements you make, your children will be protected."

"That will not be necessary."

"What is necessary," said Ibrahim, his voice hardening, "is for you to focus on your work, and you will not be able to do that if you fear for the safety of your children, Doctor. I speak from experience. If you recall, earlier in the war when you feared for your children, my cousin died."

"What do you mean by that?"

"My cousin Abdul Antar, God grant him rest, brother of my cousin Colonel Umar Antar, God grant him rest. You treated Abdul at the beginning of the war. He had a liver injury. But you left in the middle of the operation to retrieve your children—from Jarabulus I was told. Three weeks later my cousin had pains, then he died."

Sami vaguely recalled having operated on a man's liver around the time he had rescued his family from ISIS in Jarabulus, but he had performed so many similar operations that he could not remember the particulars of this one.

"If he had pains, why did he not come to see me?"

"A soldier does not have that luxury, Doctor."

"Three weeks after the operation, he was back to fighting?"

"After two weeks."

"Then that is why he died! Because he did not follow my instructions."

"I do not blame you, of course."

"And yet, you do."

"It was God's will to take Abdul and then Umar, not yours. But now God and Syria need all of you, Doctor. The tyrant must be defeated. For the good of your children and all the children of Syria. Please keep that in mind."

———

The next day at dawn, three soldiers from Ibrahim's Islamist Ahrar al-Sham militia group showed up at Beit Qarah unannounced. They bore bread and cheese and dried apricots.

One of the soldiers said he had been instructed to accompany Sami back and forth from the hospital and that from then on, Sami would always be provided with protection. In fact, at least one soldier would perpetually stand guard outside the entrance to Beit Qarah, and another would be posted on the roof.

It was a courtesy, they said, given the important role Sami was playing in sustaining the rebellion.

"I do not want any soldiers near the hospital," said Sami.

"They will be dressed in civilian clothes," said Ibrahim. "And we will bring no weapons inside the hospital. The regime will bomb anyway, of course, but we will respect the will of the medical council."

It occurred to Sami that the soldiers could just as easily be used to prevent him from leaving Aleppo as they could be used to protect him. But he did genuinely worry about Adam and Noora's safety, and planned to stay in Aleppo anyway, so he decided that ignoring the soldiers and going about his business as though they were not there would be the path of least resistance.

CHAPTER 49

A week after Adam and Noora returned to Beit Qarah, a cease-fire was declared. Badly needed supplies suddenly flowed into the city. Hannah agreed to stay a bit longer. Her mother was beside herself, her sister was furious at her, and what friends she'd had in high school and college no longer expected to hear from her. The pull of the children was simply too strong.

She bought tomatoes, cauliflower, potatoes, green beans, and cabbage. Chicken, lamb, and eggs. Cumin and tahini. Fresh oranges, pomegranate, and grapefruit juice. Rosemary syrup and even jelly beans. When leaving the house, she veiled herself and avoided checkpoints, but she didn't try to avoid contact with all people. Indeed, upon returning home from shopping one afternoon and observing an elderly neighbor outside of her apartment, willowy and blinking in the bright sun as though emerging from hibernation, she invited the woman into the courtyard where they ate lunch and drank tea.

Spring was nearly upon them. The light lingered longer in the early evening sky, and the air grew warm.

Old men sat outside playing backgammon and smoking apple-scented tobacco from nargile water pipes. Adam and Noora wore T-shirts. There was talk of reviving the rooftop garden and maybe trying to fix the leak in the roof.

Hannah grew accustomed to the routine of the house. Waking up at dawn. Making breakfast while Adam ran the generator. Teaching school lessons to the children, fixing the leaky sink in the bathroom—all it had needed was a few twists with a wrench—washing clothes in the bathtub, cleaning the courtyard, helping Adam build a mousetrap—he swore there were mice in the cellar, although she'd never seen evidence of them.

At night she told the children stories about the two precocious chickens having adventures in the Paramus Park Souk.

With the cease-fire, the incidents of trauma wounds at the M2 plummeted, then two foreign doctors arrived on a mercy mission, so Sami had more time to himself. He wasted most of it pacing around the courtyard, ostensibly paying attention to his children but looking more like a caged beast who didn't know what to do with all his time and energy.

A few times—when Hannah prepared tea, and the children were playing in the cellar—he tolerated her questions.

She learned that his father's family had lived in Damascus since the 1700s, and that his parents' marriage had caused quite the scandal because his mother, a descendant of French colonialists, had been raised Roman Catholic, while his father had been a Sunni Muslim.

And even though he hadn't asked her, he listened politely when she told him that her own father, a Syrian named Eli Samaan from a Sunni merchant family, had died in Aleppo before the war, leukemia, and that he'd been a con man of sorts, almost making it big in the United States selling electronics, buying a Cadillac, and marrying an American wife, but ultimately reduced to running back to Syria, tail between his legs, to peddle secondhand stereos in the al Madina souk.

Had Sami ever heard of her father, ever bought electronics from his shop in the souk, maybe when he was a boy? No? Well, she wasn't surprised, but he should get used to the last name Samaan because it had been her original last name, before her mother had remarried, and she intended to take it back again someday when she had a chance to file all the paperwork.

On two occasions Hannah even got Sami to express what she gauged to be genuine interest in a conversation, once by inquiring as to whether he had heard that Einstein's gravitational waves had been observed—he had, he read *Le Monde* on his phone when he could—and a second time when she mentioned that in Antakya, she had watched a program on gene therapies that were finally beginning to show promise. Had he heard of this?

Indeed, he had, he exclaimed, then proceed to speak—at great length—about it.

———

The matter of her lingering presence came to a head near the end of March, after she had been there for two weeks.

Sami came home early that evening, with news that the sister of a nurse who worked at the hospital was willing to move in and watch the children.

He made the announcement when they were all seated at the kitchen table. Hannah had made a lamb stew with a sauce of sour cherries.

"It came as a surprise," he added. "I had spoken with this nurse over a week and a half ago, and she had indicated her sister might be interested, but I had not heard from her since."

Three beeswax candles, set upon an overturned olive-jar lid, burned silently in the center of the table.

Adam gritted his teeth and squinted.

Hannah glanced briefly at Sami then studied a paisley pattern in the tablecloth. "And this woman—what do you know of her?"

"She and her son lost their home last month. Before the war, she was an elementary school teacher, and she has some nursing skills, so we may begin using Beit Qarah as a recovery ward again."

He explained that patients too well for the M2, but too injured or ill to be released, had sometimes been brought back to Beit Qarah to recover, and Tahira had overseen this process.

Hannah wanted to protest that there was no reason patients couldn't be brought back to Beit Qarah now, that she could manage. Instead, she held her tongue, and told herself that it was better this way, that she couldn't stay here forever, and that repairing relationships in America should be her priority. The longer she stayed, the harder her eventual departure would be for her and the children.

"Excuse me," she said, trying to smile and failing as she pushed her chair back from the table and stood. To cry over this news would be absurd, but she could feel the tears coming anyway. "I will be right back."

———

Later that night, after helping to put the children to sleep in the cellar, she found herself alone in her room off the courtyard, staring at the ceiling, listening to Enya through earbuds, and wondering—what if? What if she were to go to him now?

Would he laugh at her? Push her away?

She pulled the bedsheet up under her chin, turned to her side, tucked her knees up into her waist, and pulled her forearms to her chest.

She'd seen the way he looked at her—the quick glance followed by studied indifference when they were drinking tea and talking. And she knew what it meant when men looked at her that way. In that sense he was no different from Oskar or half the men she'd worked with at the International Aid Coalition.

But would he perceive an advance as just a pathetic attempt to stay on as a nanny?

There would be truth to that, but it would be a half-truth.

She glanced at the door to her room. It was cracked open a hair. A sliver of light from a crescent moon extended to her bed. She closed her eyes and imagined what it would be like to touch him, to run her finger across his large, full lips. To run a finger across his chest. To feel his weight. He was thin, but he would be heavy anyway because he was so damn tall.

Oskar had been the last man she'd slept with, and that was four years ago now. With Oskar it had been easy, because Oskar was just Oskar. She remembered how he would always gently tease her about her wild *knull-ruffs*, post-sex hair, and how they'd laughed about it when looking in the mirror together, whereas with Sami . . .

The idea of him placing his hand on her abdomen caused her to shiver with something that fell between pleasure and desperation. She imagined the coolness of his palm, the roughness of the callouses on his fingertips, the pressure on her belly button. She placed her own hand on her belly button, held it there for a moment, then let it slide lower. The familiarity of her touch, the knowledge that it was her hand and not his, and the utter lack of real intimacy it implied, made her want to cry again, and she stopped.

Distraught, her thoughts grew dark. She recalled her father's old Peugeot sedan and how when it was breaking down, he was always searching for replacement parts at the souk, but the replacement parts he found never seemed to be quite right. They'd work, but not as well as the original.

And that, she realized, was exactly what she was hoping she could be for Sami and Adam and Noora. A lousy replacement part.

———

When Hannah awoke she wasn't sure what time it was, but it was still dark out. She assumed Sami had long since drifted off. The time to approach him had passed. Tomorrow she would meet the new woman, approve of her, and leave Aleppo for good.

She was hungry, having eaten little for dinner, so she swung her legs out of bed and walked barefoot across the cool marble floor. Her hair was tousled. She wore sweatpants and a loose-fitting cotton T-shirt.

Although intending to visit the kitchen, she noticed that the court-yard was bathed in moonlight, so she took a moment to step into the center of it and look up at the sky.

At first she didn't see him. He was so quiet, and his dark form seemed to be an extension of the wicker furniture. Then he shifted slightly, and she startled.

"*Salaam*," he said.

He was seated on the wicker couch and had been leaning forward with his arms resting on his thighs, but now he straightened.

She wasn't sure whether the thumping in her chest was a result of having been startled, or because it was him, here in front of her. She turned to face him, taking quick sips of air.

"What are you doing here?" she asked. Her voice was barely a whisper.

He held her gaze. She felt frozen in place.

"You will be tired for work," she said.

"Not very." His voice was deep, and calm.

She hugged her arms to her chest. She'd been shot at while racing down Castello Road and she hadn't been particularly afraid. She'd pulled people from rubble knowing it was possible, or even likely, that the regime would strike again at any moment. Compared to that, there is nothing to be afraid of now, she told herself.

But she was. He intimidated her.

She sat next to him on the wicker couch.

"*Salaam*," she said.

They made eye contact and held it. Then Hannah slowly took his hand in hers and, encountering no resistance, guided his hand to her cheek. Their foreheads and noses touched.

"I want to stay with you and the children," she said, breathing the words into his mouth, breathing him in.

Their lips touched. He kissed her, and she kissed him back.

"Then stay."

He guided her to his lap as she steered his hand from her cheek and up underneath her shirt to her bare breast. She shivered, and they kissed again, deeper this time, then he wrapped his arms around her waist and lifted her up with ease.

Hannah laced both her legs around his waist. She pressed her whole body close against his as she buried her face in the crook of his neck. In her bedroom, when he finally slipped inside her, the sensation was both better and worse than she'd imagined. The stubble on his chin was so rough. For the second time that night, she began to cry.

"I know I am just a replacement," she whispered to him afterward, as they were lying side by side, staring at the drifting moon shadows on the fieldstone wall opposite the bed. "For what you lost."

Instead of denying it, as she'd hoped he would, he instead noted that he used replacement parts all the time in medicine. Replacement kidneys, hearts, livers. There was no shame in being a replacement, he said.

Replacements, in fact, were quite useful.

It was so unromantic, so not the answer she was hoping for, that she couldn't help but laugh. And fall a little bit in love with him.

CHAPTER 50

Regime-held Aleppo • Four months later

The cease-fire collapsed in April, and the airstrikes and artillery barrages resumed. In the Sukkari district, the al Quds hospital was hit, killing the last pediatrician. Newborns choked on dust. White phosphorus from incendiary munitions burned deep holes in flesh. Up north by the Turkish border, ISIS advanced.

The Russians began using cluster bombs, and Rahim helped generate the target lists for those bombs.

Indeed, that was his intention when, early in July, he picked up the handwritten intelligence report—one of many that had been delivered to his desk that morning—and began to read that two days ago a young man with a broken arm had attempted to pass through a checkpoint in the Ramouseh district of regime-held Aleppo. Because the soldiers at the checkpoint had suspected that the man's papers were forged, he had been detained.

Under interrogation the detainee had revealed that until being wounded in an aerial bombing attack a week ago, he had fought for the al-Nusra rebel group. Detailed information about al-Nusra positions in the Malah district, near Castello Road, had followed. Rahim dutifully noted the positions, with the intention of forwarding the information to the targeteers.

It was not until the end of the report, however, that Rahim's pulse quickened, and he sat up in his chair. For that was where he read that, when asked who had casted his arm and where, the detainee had claimed to have been treated at the old Omar Bin Abdul Aziz Hospital near the

Maqam Gate, and that the man who had set and casted his arm had been exceptionally tall and known to all as Dr. Sami.

———

Three days later Rahim woke up an hour before sunrise. Feeling exceptionally vigorous, he stuffed himself with flatbread, white cheese, and apricot jam. After waking the Iranian intelligence officers who were still quartered in his house and downing two cups of strong black coffee, he performed his morning prayers with great enthusiasm. By seven he was dressed in his uniform, Makarov pistol at his side, ascending the steps to his office with an eagerness that had been unflagging ever since he had learned that Sami worked at the M2.

Today his optimism was rewarded.

The intelligence report had been filed at four in the morning. As had been the case the prior two nights, Dr. Sami had been observed at the M2 by the spy assigned to watch him. But this time, instead of spending the night there, the doctor had left at three thirty in the morning and had proceeded on foot through the Qinnasrin Gate and into the old city— stopping only when he had come to a locked door at the end of alley, the GPS coordinates of which were attached to the report.

When his secretary Aisha showed up at ten after eight, Rahim first upbraided her for being late, then ordered her to provide him with military grid maps, the ones that were comprised of photos taken on low altitude bombing runs.

Minutes later he sat back in his chair and sighed.

He had always envisioned buying a house in the country for himself someday. Maybe in the fertile Orontes Valley between Aleppo and the sea. Nothing that was unduly expensive—he knew his station in life was largely settled—but he had long pictured being able to save enough to purchase a house with a small courtyard. He would be content, of course, with a concrete fountain instead of marble. As long as he could hear the water running. It would be his own little private paradise, where his grandchildren and nieces and nephews could play.

That dream had receded further and further out of reach. He was now middle-aged, had no savings to purchase a house, and even if he were to stumble upon a fortune, the idea of his daughter bringing her children—assuming she ever were to marry and have them—to a house that he owned seemed far-fetched at best given that she, and his wife, still blamed him for Adel's death.

So it was particularly painful for him to observe that, near the end of the alley where the Dr. Sami had last been observed, was a house organized around a spacious central courtyard and that in the center of this courtyard was a fountain.

It was one of the old houses, of the type that was renowned in Aleppo and Damascus and usually had a name. Beit Ghazaleh. Beit Wakil. Beit Achiqbash. The type of house that Europeans would pay to dismantle and reassemble in museums simply because it was so beautiful; the type of house that in centuries past, would have sheltered a rich merchant or foreign consul or a pasha of the Ottoman Empire. When an ambassador from Constantinople paid Aleppo a visit, he might be hosted in such a place.

Only now, Rahim suspected, it sheltered a doctor.

Curiously enough, half the courtyard was covered with a tent-like structure. While it was common enough for people to hang rugs and other blinds around their houses to protect themselves from sniper attacks, Rahim had not heard of people taking such precautions in interior courtyards. Did the fact that the inhabitants of this house had done so suggest they thought themselves important enough to be specifically targeted by airborne attacks?

Perhaps. A top doctor might merit such protection.

He forced Aisha to loan him her reading glasses—ignoring her protests that his fat head would ruin them—and expanded the image on the screen as he leaned toward it and squinted.

Upon closer examination, he noticed several other relevant details: a green rectangle on one of the roofs adjacent to the courtyard; a child's slide and furniture inside the courtyard; and the presence of a man on the rooftop who appeared to be wielding an automatic rifle.

The man on the roof with the gun suggested the house was guarded.

As for the green rectangle, Rahim assumed it was a rooftop garden, not uncommon on either side of Aleppo, given the frequent food shortages. As of a week and a half ago, when the photo had been taken, it appeared to have been growing vigorously. Given that it had been a particularly dry spring, it was a certainty then that the garden was being regularly watered.

A busy doctor would not have the time to tend to a garden like that, though. So assuming this was where Dr. Hasan lived—and Rahim thought it probable, given the poor state of the adjacent buildings and the assumption that Dr. Hasan would not stoop to living in anything less than a small castle—the likelihood that he was living alone was slim. Indeed, the plastic slide in the courtyard suggested a child, or perhaps several, still lived with him.

Which in turn suggested the presence of a wife.

And why would Dr. Hasan's wife and children not be living with him? It was true that most people of means had fled the city, but the doctor had chosen to play the role of a martyr, and the wife of a such great man would never abandon him. Unlike Rahim's own wife, who had fled to Lebanon.

———

Rahim spoke with a clerk at the property registry office, impressing upon him the urgency of his request, and that the Military Intelligence Directorate would not look kindly upon excessive delays. A mere four hours later, he learned that the house in question was still listed as being owned by a man who had allegedly purchased it in 1982 and whose name meant nothing to Rahim. He ordered the clerk to research the matter further, and learned that in 2010, a bill of sale had been signed and money exchanged. The sale had been noted, but the transfer from one owner to another had not been recorded due to unresolved claims against the title.

The names of the purchasers listed on the copy of the bill of sale agreement were Dr. Samir Hasan and Tahira Hasan.

The fact that Dr. Hasan had seen fit to give a woman equal property rights only confirmed Rahim's dismal opinion of his character.

———

The interrogation report he submitted later that day to be reviewed by a targeting committee was marked as urgent and, along with the precise GPS coordinates of Dr. Hasan's home, contained the following passage:

Aerial photographs of residence reveal presence of armed militants. Al-Nusra Front intrusion into al-Jalloum district suspected. Much of inner courtyard intentionally shielded from view, suggesting presence of high-value targets. Immediate action recommended.

Rahim knew the regime and the Russians were hungry for targets. And while the M2 had been bombed early in the war and again in 2015— and Rahim would certainly advocate for a strike now—it had a maternity ward, so the decision whether to strike it again would be a political one, made at the highest levels.

But a private residence? To add that to the targeteers' list would be an easy affair.

CHAPTER 51

Rebel-held Aleppo

On the morning of July 15, Hannah woke at dawn, made breakfast for the children and the eleven overflow patients from the M2 who were staying at Beit Qarah, then left the house pushing a wheelbarrow, intending to pick up a shipment of Mercy Corp food baskets by the Qinnasrin Gate.

When she got there, however, she was told that all deliveries had been suspended due to fighting near Castello Road. For now, it was too dangerous for the trucks to pass.

Later that morning her inventory of what food remained in Beit Qarah revealed they only had enough to last for three days. After that they would have to make do.

Make do with what, she wasn't sure. Tomatoes, green beans, and potatoes from the rooftop garden could supply her and the children with perhaps half of what they needed to survive, and she could and would cut back on her already limited rations, but she had lost so much weight that her clothes were baggy on her frame and the garden couldn't begin to feed all the patients.

So as the children fought over who got to play with a large, bright-blue marble and the patients lay convalescing in the courtyard, shaded by the iwan, Hannah sat up on the rooftop terrace researching the hoops Sami and his children would need to jump through if ever they were to try to immigrate to the United States.

Just in case.

She quickly became entangled in a web of acronyms and numbers—

Section 214(b), Form I-130, Form I-589, Form I-730, USCIS, USMLE, Form DS-260, Form I-864 . . .

After an hour, the better part of which was spent waiting for webpages to load, she determined that the chance of Sami and the children being granted refugee status was a crapshoot at best. Only a minuscule number of Syrian refugees were being let in.

Option B was for her and Sami to get married, at which point she could legally adopt the children. Which she was perfectly willing to do. But even then, there was good a chance that visas for Sami and the children would be denied, especially if the US immigration service suspected she and Sami had married for the sole purpose of obtaining a visa.

As she was reading of one family that had been separated for over two years, Adam called, "Hannah! Hannah!"

She approached the edge of the roof and looked down to the courtyard. Noora was quietly sobbing. "What happened?"

"Noora hurt her knee!"

"Badly?"

"Maybe not."

Hannah left the roof. Noora, she discovered, had scraped herself while going down the plastic playhouse slide backward on her belly. While Hannah helped to clean out the grit, an explosion—frighteningly close—shook the entire house.

Adam dove under the wicker couch in the courtyard. Hannah reflexively flinched and tried to cover Noora.

For a moment following the blast, everything was silent. Then a shard of glass fell from one of the windows that looked out onto the courtyard and shattered on the hard marble. Dust that had been dislodged from the limestone walls drifted down. The rebel soldiers up on the roof began to yell back and forth, trying to ascertain where the bomb had struck.

Noora, who had stopped crying momentarily, began again in earnest. A burn patient who had been lying on her side, on a bed that had been pulled into the courtyard, moaned.

Hannah resumed breathing then examined the courtyard. The four walls were intact. The children and seven patients in the courtyard were unharmed. She brought a sixty-seven-year-old man dying from bladder cancer some water and brushed dust off the face of a forty-year-old woman who had lost her husband and both her arms in a cluster-bomb blast. Then she embraced Noora, who was still sobbing, and grabbed Adam's hand. "Hey," she said. "No one got hurt."

"Did it hit our house?" asked Adam.

"No," said Hannah. But it was close, she thought.

"Should we go downstairs?"

Hannah hesitated. On the one hand, the kitchen cellar was the closest thing they had to a bomb shelter. On the other, it was also the closest thing they had to a crypt.

"For now," she said, "that might be best."

One of the rebel soldiers from the roof appeared. He had an AK-47 slung across his back and was balancing what looked like a rocket-propelled grenade launcher on his shoulder.

"What was hit?" Hannah asked him.

"A building on the other side of the alley."

Hannah said she would help. There might be wounded. But the soldier ordered her not to leave the house. She didn't think he had the right to order her to do anything, but then the sound of fighter jets flying high above the city intensified.

Twenty minutes later more bombs exploded. The ground shook, but not nearly as much as during the earlier attack. When Hannah checked on Adam and Noora, she found them inside their sheet fort, with Adam reading an Arabic translation of *Harry Potter and the Sorcerer's Stone* out loud to Noora.

Sirens, muffled by the walls of Beit Qarah, wailed.

A few hours later, and after conferring with the soldiers on the roof, Hannah asked Adam to start the generator, then let both children play in the courtyard while she administered medicine, changed bandages, and cooked dinner. Bombs were going off all the time, she reasoned. The children couldn't hide underground forever.

———

When the third attack came, at least they had a warning. First there were sirens, then calls from the roof. Hannah ran out from the kitchen to the courtyard and heard the faint *thump-thump-thump* of a helicopter and caught a glimpse of one of the soldiers on the rooftop aiming his gun at a distant point in the sky.

"Adam! Noora! Into the cellar!" she screamed.

Noora started running, but Adam was nowhere to be seen. Hannah glanced up at the sky. In the corner of the rectangular patch of blue that was visible from where she stood, she saw a regime helicopter, its nose tilted down as it raced toward them.

Directly toward them, she noted and was suddenly gripped with fear. She held her breath as she glanced at the old man with bladder cancer and saw the look of fear on his face too.

"Go, go!" said Hannah as Noora ran past her. "Go to your bed!" Then, "Adam!"

She ducked into the kitchen, but he wasn't there. She ran into the living room and then the kitchen yelling for him. The sound of the helicopter grew louder. At the stairs to the second floor, she hesitated for a split second—torn.

"Adam!" she yelled again, and then charged up the steps.

She pulled open the door to his old room. It was empty. Then she heard a faint sound coming from the end of the hall. Music. It was Fairuz singing. Adam had been told by his father not to use the stereo by himself so that he wouldn't scratch Mémère's old records. But he'd been so mesmerized by the music . . .

Sirens were blaring. One of the soldiers who'd been on top of the roof raced past her.

Hannah sprinted to the end of the hall and yanked open the door to the yellow room. Lying on the floor, with his head next to the speaker as he tried to solve a broken Rubik's Cube, was Adam. His eyes widened with a look of guilt when he saw her.

"I was—"

She grabbed his hand before he could finish, yanked him into her arms, clutched him tightly to her chest, and ran down the steps and across the living room. As she stumbled on the rug, she fell to her knees and, through a window, caught a glimpse of the helicopter hovering far above them. She could make out the Syrian flag on the tail and the desert camouflage paint job. Its rotors appeared to be slowly moving backward, an optical illusion that mesmerized her for a fleeting moment. Hanging below it was a large black cylinder. Shots were being fired from a machine gun mounted to the helicopter. The sound filled her with terror.

Adam shrieked. One of the patients in the courtyard screamed. Another chanted *Allahu Akbar* . . .

Hannah ripped open the door to the cellar, slammed it shut behind her, raced down the steps as fast as she could, and threw Adam to the floor at the entrance to his tent fort.

"Go to your bed!"

The children's beds had been arranged under a low arch, between two support pillars—Hannah had been told that Tahira had chosen that spot because she'd thought, if the worst ever did happen, it would be the safest, strongest place to be in the whole house.

Adam scurried into the tent fort. Hannah dropped to her knees intent on following him, but then the blast hit.

CHAPTER 52

They called them barrel bombs.

And indeed, many were made of old metal barrels, only instead of oil or chemicals the barrels were packed with massive amounts of explosives, nails, used ball bearings, and any other metal scrap that was close at hand.

Sami was on the third floor of the M2 when he heard the latest one detonate.

At the time it even occurred to him that the blast must have been near Beit Qarah. A bit to the south from the sound of it, perhaps near the Qinnasrin Gate.

Although moderately worried, he was not alarmed.

A blast near Beit Qarah was, if not a daily or even weekly event, by no means a singular one. And anything other than a direct hit—the odds of which were low, even given the recent escalation of hostilities—would not do much damage.

Just the same, he tried to call Hannah, as he had when he had heard bombs going off near Beit Qarah earlier in the day. But this time there was no answer. To reassure himself, he jogged up to the roof of the M2 to try to get a better sense of what had been hit.

And that was when he saw the trail of black smoke curling up from a point that was a bit to the north of the Qinnasrin Gate. Just about where . . .

He ran.

Out through the sandbag-reinforced entrance, down Said Bin Al Ass Street and into the narrow alleys of the old city. As he drew closer to his neighborhood, he heard men shouting. The dust was thick. The heat from the blast lingered.

He coughed and lifted the collar of his shirt to his mouth, and he told himself that the odds were good that, even if the house was damaged, Hannah and the children would be okay and most of Beit Qarah still standing.

Moments later, he stopped short, his black leather shoes skidding on the cobblestones. Then he fell to his knees.

The front of Beit Qarah had been utterly pancaked. The rear still stood, but most of the walls that faced the courtyard had been blown away, exposing the interiors of the rooms. Electrical wires dangled from ceilings. Where a stairway once stood, all that remained was a handrail hanging from a single post. He could see his own bedroom and the remains of the bed he had shared with Tahira. The kitchen, the living room, the dining room—all those had been reduced to rubble. Flames licked up from where the front reception room had been.

"Noora!" he cried. "Adam!"

He tried to lift himself off the ground, intent on moving toward the destruction, but for a moment it was as though he were made of stone. He was unable to move his arms; his knees felt glued to the ground.

He swallowed, blinked, took a breath, forced himself to stand, and stumbled toward the smoldering pile.

"Noora! Adam!"

His gaze fixed upon a little patch of painted ceiling, and he began to climb up the pile of rubble toward it. Underneath the ceiling fragment, he found a gilded seventeenth-century glass mosque lamp that used to hang from the *iwan* in the courtyard. Tahira had moved it to the main reception room during the renovations, and it had never been reinstalled.

Half of it had shattered, but half was still intact.

He reasoned that if even a part of something that fragile could have survived the blast, then it was possible that Noora and Adam . . .

He surveyed the ruin again. Where the courtyard had been, there was now a crater.

The entrance to the cellar staircase had been directly off the kitchen.

It would have been . . . Sami took a moment to get his bearings, then his eyes focused on where he thought the entrance to stairwell must lie, buried under the rubble.

He turned to a cluster of men standing on the periphery of the destruction. "There is a storage cellar. We used it as a bomb shelter. If my children and my"—he did not know how to characterize Hannah—"the woman who cares for my children, if they heard the helicopter before the bomb dropped, they would have run to it." He half stumbled, half crawled to a section of rubble and heaved a limestone block off the top, exposing a section of roof covered with dirt and mangled tomato vines. "We need to start digging here." He threw off several more blocks and bits of wood.

After maybe ten minutes, he stepped back to catch his breath and noticed two men in white helmets staring at him.

One of them held a dust-covered human arm in his hand.

Sami examined it and determined it did not belong to Hannah or his children.

"Please!" he pleaded with the men. "Help me dig!"

They did.

Soon, though, they heard another helicopter. When Sami eyed the sky, he saw it screaming over the Citadel, headed straight for them. A black barrel swung beneath it.

"Go!" said the men in white helmets.

Sami refused, preferring to die with his children, but the men in white helmets pulled him away.

CHAPTER 53

Brick by brick, relying solely on touch because the darkness was absolute, Hannah tried to clear away the pile of rubble at the base of the steps. But it was as though she were trying to remove grains of sand from below the narrow neck of a sand-filled hourglass—the more bricks she pulled away, the more slipped down the stairwell.

Still, she kept digging until the earth shook when a second barrel bomb detonated. A few pieces of stone from the arched ceiling tumbled down, and she covered her head with her hands and crouched into a ball.

"Are you okay?" she called to the children, coughing as she spoke, because the dust was so thick.

"What was that?" asked Adam, still inside the sheet fort with Noora.

"Maybe people above trying to get to us," she lied.

The second bomb had created more dust, and she coughed again then slipped back into the sheet fort, which had turned out to be a stroke of genius because the sheets acted like a dust filter. As a result, the air inside the fort was much easier to breathe.

She slid between Adam and Noora on the bed. With an arm around each of their shoulders, she said, "I imagine they are working very hard up there."

It was smoky, even in the sheet fort, and terribly hot. Hannah worried that the fire would spread to the cellar.

"Should we yell again?" asked Adam.

"I think we can wait," said Hannah, coughing.

The act of shouting all together in the dark and receiving no response had unnerved Hannah as much as it had the children, so she had resolved to keep quiet unless they genuinely heard something from above.

"I think it was a bomb," said Adam, sounding worried. Then he coughed.

"Maybe," allowed Hannah, trying hard to sound upbeat and calm. In truth, she was terrified. The first bomb had collapsed half the ceiling and the wall closest to the courtyard. She didn't know how stable the rest of the ceiling and walls were. Her lungs hurt. "But if it was, it seemed like it was pretty far away."

She felt around again for the windup flashlight that the children usually kept near the bed but now was nowhere to be found. After cursing under her breath, she suddenly recalled seeing . . .

"Adam!" she said excitedly. "Last week you were exploring Mémère's armoire. The bottom drawer. Do you recall?"

"No."

"I am not angry with you; I only ask because you were using a flashlight. Do you remember?"

"Maybe."

"Adam, please."

"I was looking for more records."

"The flashlight—what happened to it?"

"It is in my pocket," he said and produced it. When it wouldn't turn on, he confessed that he had removed the batteries to make a device that, when paired with steel wool, could light paper on fire. They were in a shoebox inside his fort in the courtyard, he said. He promised to get them for Hannah once they got out of the cellar.

They lay in silence for a time. Hannah guessed it was around nine o'clock. The sun would already have set.

She wondered—what if no one was looking for them? Sami would come eventually, but what if he stayed at the hospital tonight? And when he did come home, would he think to look in the cellar, or would he just assume they were dead?

Would the smoke get worse? Would they have enough food and water?

Water, good God, she realized, they didn't have *any* water! How stupid of her! That should have been the first thing she thought to keep stored in the cellar.

Hannah's anxiety spiked. Her breathing rate increased, but it was painful to take deep breaths. She told herself she had to stay calm, that if she didn't panic, the kids wouldn't. But then she pictured the pot of bulgur she'd left on the hot plate. She'd been about to serve dinner. They were probably too upset to think about food now, but they'd get to thinking about it soon enough.

She gave both children a squeeze and said she was sleepy, which was another lie, but she thought if she could get the kids to go to sleep early, it would buy her time before they complained of being hungry.

Adam said he wasn't tired.

Noora said she wasn't either.

"We could just rest then. Being very quiet with our eyes closed."

After an hour or so, the children did drift off to sleep. But Hannah couldn't. Thinking about how much of the house might have collapsed on top of the cellar made her feel claustrophobic. She could hear the children breathing, and it made her worry again about the air supply. Her hands were sweating.

She crawled back out of the sheet fort and pulled more bricks off the pile of rubble that lay near where she thought the staircase must be, but then she ran into a wall and realized she had been digging in the wrong place.

Noora stirred.

"How will they fix our house?" she asked, sounding worried.

Hannah didn't answer at first.

There is plenty of air down here, she told herself. You're not in a sealed compartment.

But it was still smoky.

"Shh," she whispered. "Adam is sleeping."

"Quiet, Noora," said Adam.

"I need to go to the bathroom," said Noora.

Hannah took three breaths. "Does anybody here want to hear a chicken story?" she asked, then told them about how Prince Chicken

Abdullah and Princess Chicken Lila learned how to travel secretly though the air vents at the Paramus Park Souk, the better to spy on a group of terribly misguided chickens who were stealing sugar-coated fennel seeds from a candy store and how they out-negotiated a rich mustachioed rooster from Damascus, resulting in a purchase of one million purple sheets and the biggest piece of paper in the world. They used the sheets to build a giant sheet fort and they folded the piece of paper into a giant origami spaceship that they glued to the roof of the sheet fort. The wind on top of the sheet fort was so fierce that it caused the origami spaceship and the sheet fort to lift off the ground and fly around in the—

Hannah stopped speaking in midsentence, thinking she might have heard something above them.

"I wish I was like Prince Abdullah," said Adam as he rearranged himself on the mattress.

Hannah, still listening intently, said, "You are."

"But I am not a prince."

There it was again—some thumping perhaps? Maybe a voice? But Hannah couldn't be sure. It was possible her mind was playing tricks on her.

"How do you know you are not a prince?" she asked.

"Because Baba is not a king."

"He is almost like a king, no? He is one of the best doctors in Aleppo, which is very much like being a king, I think. And your mother, she helped make the best soap in Aleppo, which is almost like being a queen. And Beit Qarah is like a palace."

"I mean a real king," said Adam.

"If you go back far enough in your history, maybe to your father's father's father or further, you would find somebody you are related to who was a real king."

"Oh."

"I mean it. If you go back far enough, we are all related to each other. Even the two of us. So, I am certain that you, Adam Hasan, are related to a real king."

He was quiet for a moment then asked, "Really?" in a way that to

Hannah seemed so innocent. And trusting. It was the trusting part that made her ache.

"Really," she said, but then thought—there! There it was again! A distinct thumping. It was hard to tell for sure, but it was conceivable that it was coming from near the cellar entrance. She held her breath.

"What happened to the origami spaceship?" asked Adam.

Distracted, and still concentrating on what was going on above, Hannah exhaled then said, "The wind blew so hard, it sent it and the sheet fort into outer space." She listened again, thought she heard a muffled banging, and then had an idea. "But there was a problem," she said quickly. "All the electricity got disconnected when the sheet fort lifted up from the ground, so there were no lights, and all the little chickens who had been playing in the fort started getting scared. So Prince Abdullah and Princess Lila started singing to them, which made everyone feel a lot better." She gave them both a squeeze. "Hey, you know, besides being a prince and a princess, the other thing that makes you two a little bit like Chicken Abdullah and Chicken Lila is that you are both pretty good singers."

"I am pretty good," admitted Adam.

"And I would like to hear you both sing now, just like Chicken Abdullah and Chicken Lila in the story. What should we sing?"

"*Shadi*," said Adam immediately.

It was the Fairuz song he had been listening to just before the barrel bomb exploded and would not have been Hannah's choice because the song was about a boy and a girl who used to play together, and then a war comes, and the boy goes off to watch the fighting and is never seen again. But she didn't think Adam and Noora associated the song with their own plight.

"That is a great song," said Hannah. "Should we sing it together?"

She felt the children nodding next to her.

Moments later, their three voices rang out loudly in unison.

A long time ago, when I was a young girl, a boy used to come from the nearby woods, his name was Shadi . . .

CHAPTER 54

The alleys in the old city were too narrow to accommodate the type of construction vehicles that could tear through debris quickly, but one of the white helmet men had a jackhammer, and he used it to break large sections of collapsed walls into pieces, and then everyone came together and used pry bars to lift the pieces off the pile.

Sami's hands were shredded and bleeding, his lungs filled with dust. Some of the wood ceiling beams that had been smoldering under the wall burst into flame when exposed to air.

It was shortly after breaking apart a particularly large section of wall, that Sami thought he heard a snippet of one the songs his mother used to sing to him at night when he was a boy.

Shadi was lost forever, snow fell and melted for twenty times, I grew up, and Shadi remained the boy I knew, playing in the snow . . .

At first he thought his mind must be succumbing to sadness and exhaustion-induced dementia. But then he saw that the men around him had stopped and were listening, too, looking around them as though trying to ascertain where the sound was coming from. It was hard to tell, it seemed to be from everywhere, resonating in strange ways both beneath and above the rubble. Sami briefly wondered if one of his mother's Fairuz records had been playing when the bomb hit and somehow had managed to keep playing, but that was improbable to the point of being fantasy. In any event, what he was hearing sounded nothing like the clear, plaintive voice of the real Fairuz.

In fact, he noted as he concentrated on the song, whoever was singing clearly could not even carry a tune; the lyrics were being shouted more than sung.

Sami turned, prepared to ask whoever was attempting to sing to please, please desist—did they not know they were trying to listen for people trapped under the rubble?—when a cheer erupted. And then another and another, and then Sami looked down, and understood.

Excavation efforts were redoubled. An hour later the serpentine tunnel that had been dug through the collapsed stairwell had reached the cellar.

When Sami first saw the top of Noora's head, her dark hair rendered gray with dust, it reminded him of a baby crowning at birth. As she slipped easily between the final blocks of cracked limestone, he slid his hands under her armpits and pulled her to him and just held her close for a moment—wincing because of the pain in his hands.

Adam's little fingers appeared moments later, gripping the stone. One of the white-helmeted men bent down to pull him through, but he popped out before any assistance could be rendered.

Sami embraced his children.

"Were you scared?" he asked them, his voice cracking. He had never felt so humbled in his life.

"Some, Baba," said Adam.

"You are so brave, both of you."

Adam turned back to the hole. "Hannah!" he called.

Her hands appeared. Two men attempted to pull her out, but even though she was a slender woman, another limestone brick had to be dislodged with a pry bar before she was able to squeeze through.

Finally liberated, she stood there, supported by one of the men in the white helmets, blinking and shielding her eyes from her rescuers' headlamps. Her jaw was set, her prominent forehead thrust forward. Her face and every other inch of her body was covered with a thick layer of dust, rendering her ghostly pale except where she was bleeding from a small cut on her forehead. The blood had trickled down past her eye and dried on her cheek. Adam hugged her waist. Noora wriggled out of her father's arms and hugged her legs. She hugged them both back. Sami stood before her, hands at his sides.

"Thank you," he said.

They stared at each other for a moment.

"I want to go home," said Noora.

No one spoke at first. Finally, Sami said, "We are going to a new home. Far away from here."

"Not a new home. Our home," said Noora.

"Come," said Sami. "For now, we must go to the hospital."

CHAPTER 55

The bombing of Beit Qarah had been preceded and followed by a flurry of aerial attacks throughout the city. The M2 was in a state of chaos, the emergency room overrun, the staff rooms and doctors' quarters occupied by patients.

When Sami stumbled through the entrance, people called out to him, assuming he was there to work. But for the first time in his life he felt truly, physically incapable of working, even if he had wanted to.

He searched for a quiet place where his children could sleep for the night, but even the sleeping rooms for the doctors were now filled with patients. Then one of the plainclothes Ahrar al-Sham soldiers who had reported to Ibrahim Antar, and who had accompanied Sami and his family back to the M2, said that there was a place nearby that they could use. He had already called Ibrahim.

Sami accepted, and when he, Adam, Noora, and Hannah arrived at the small three-room apartment, they were given water, flatbread, and a small room to themselves. By four in the morning, they had all collapsed on the dirty, child-sized mattresses. Sami's only accommodated his torso.

Although blankets had been nailed to the molding above the one window, Sami woke up at dawn anyway.

His thoughts were in turmoil, but what was really preventing him from sleeping was the pain in his hands. Upon stumbling to the bathroom, past an Ahrar al-Sham soldier who was smoking in the hall, he examined them.

While most of the white-helmet volunteers had been wearing gloves, Sami had not. His hands, at that point, had been the least of his concerns.

They were a big concern now. Both were swollen. His fingers felt like fat, stuffed kibbe balls, and it was painful to bend them. But it was the bruises and lacerations on his palm and the undersides of his fingers that really worried him. He had known he'd been bleeding as he dug—that the shards of limestone, glass, and tile were sharp—but he had not realized how deeply and badly his hands had been cut. Last night he had been in pain, but too tired and distraught to care.

A few of the cuts were deep enough that, had he seen them on a patient, he would have advised stitches. But even with the right tools and equipment, he was in no condition to perform such delicate work.

He could at least wash his hands, he thought. Upon discovering that the faucet was dry, he prevailed upon a soldier in the hall to bring him a pitcher of water, then did his best to clean out the dirt and gravel, gritting his teeth and willing himself not to cry out.

"I must go to the hospital," he informed the soldier when he was done, speaking sharply because he was still in pain. At the M2 he could sterilize and dress his wounds. And he felt duty-bound to tell his colleagues in person he was leaving Aleppo. There was a chance he would return—in a month or two, if he could find Aya and Tahira's mother in Jordan, and they were able to care of the children. But for now, the M2 would need to make do without him. "Should they wake up, you will tell my family I will be back shortly?"

In the small kitchen behind the bathroom, he observed another soldier, bearded and with stringy long hair, heating water on a stove next to a sink filled with unwashed dishes. A box of noodles had spilled on the counter. The door to the kitchen had a hole in it. No decorations adorned the walls. Save for several prayer mats, the living room was bare. The whole apartment smelled of body odor. Sami assumed some of it was his own.

The soldier in the hall ashed his cigarette onto a ceramic saucer. "I will find someone to take you,"

"That will not be necessary," Sami snapped. "I need only that you tell my family where I have gone when they wake."

"Wait." The soldier pulled a phone out of his pocket, dialed, and ducked out of the apartment.

Sami had no intention of waiting, so he gently roused Hannah.

"I must go to the M2," he said. "But I will return shortly. When I do, we make preparations to leave."

Upon exiting the bedroom, another soldier said, "Okay," and gestured to Sami with his gun. "We go."

"Get out of my way," said Sami.

———

At the M2 Sami ignored the greetings and shouted entreaties and headed straight to a supply room where he opened a bottle of Betadine antiseptic. After trickling it over his wounds, some of which began to bleed again, he informed Dr. Wasim and the nurses he encountered on the ground floor that he was leaving Aleppo for at least a month, maybe more.

The news spread quickly; so quickly, in fact, that as Sami was striding past the sandbag-reinforced chemical decontamination tents, he was approached by the plainclothes Ahrar al-Sham soldier who had escorted him to the hospital.

"Doctor," said the soldier, sounding anxious as he struggled to keep pace. "I must inform you that Commander Antar, he requests that you wait."

Sami ducked around a man who was using a wheelchair to transport boxes filled with saline solution.

"You know the Commander, I believe?" pressed the soldier.

Still walking, Sami asked, "You refer to Ibrahim?"

"Yes, yes. He requests you wait."

"That is not possible."

"He arrives shortly."

"And yet, I must leave now," said Sami without breaking stride, knowing that Ibrahim would try to dissuade him.

"I must insist," he said.

"No, I must insist," said Sami.

The Aleppo he had known had been a city of manners and civility, of *hammams* and hidden caravansaries, of universities and soccer stadiums. A city in which Sunni, Shia, and Alawite Muslims, along with Christians,

Jews, Druze, nonbelievers, and everyone in between had lived together in at least relative peace. To walk through the souk was to hear languages from all corners of the world. But that city was dead, and the idea of forcing his family to watch the regime and Islamists like Ibrahim and ISIS fight over the corpse of the city he had once loved, filled Sami with revulsion. If he could, he would come back to do what he could to heal the people who were trapped here, but he would no longer force his children to be counted among the trapped.

The soldier continued to trail him. When three more soldiers suddenly arrived, they seized Sami.

He managed to rip an arm free and shove one man down, but the others tackled him and grabbed his legs and lifted him up. He punched one in the face, but then someone clubbed him in the head, and he was half carried, half dragged to an empty corner market where the shelves were bare, but the brightly colored sign above the entrance still advertised pineapple-banana fruit smoothies and Coca-Cola.

They threw him into a defunct walk-in refrigerator in the back of the store and told him to wait. Sami cursed them. He reopened the wounds on his right hand by pounding on the locked refrigerator door.

Outside, one of the soldiers began to sing a song about what an asshole Bashar Al Assad was. The others clapped to the beat and laughed at the lyrics. Sami smelled cigarette smoke.

Hannah would be waiting for him. Wondering where he was. Worrying that he had broken his word and instead of leaving, had decided to resume work at the hospital. The children would grow anxious.

He grabbed an empty fruit crate, flipped it over, and used it as a chair. After a minute, he stood, cursed the guards again at the top of his lungs, and kicked the crate at the locked door.

He was genuinely incredulous. The regime targeted doctors all the time, but Sami had never heard of any rebels—ISIS excepted—treating one of their own doctors like this.

———

Ibrahim yanked open the door a half hour later. He appeared to be unarmed. Sami had gone back to sitting on the fruit crate, using a wall as a backrest, but now he stood.

Ibrahim closed the refrigerator door behind him. "You must have some understanding of our position, of course?" he said eventually.

Sami stared at him with contempt.

"You understand," continued Ibrahim, "that this is a crucial point in the war? You may have noticed that the fighting has intensified." Sarcasm had slipped into his voice. When Sami again declined to reply, Ibrahim added, "Perhaps I have misjudged the situation. Perhaps you do not fully understand our position because you have been so focused on your medicine. So let me explain it to you, Doctor. Aleppo is nearly surrounded. The city hangs by a thread. And do you know what that thread is?"

Sami still remained silent.

"Castello Road," said Ibrahim. "That is the one remaining road in and out of the city. One road! Every day, we fight to keep it open so that we can continue to receive food to eat, weapons to defend ourselves, and medicine that you can use to heal our people. And every day, the regime tries to close it off!" His clenched fists trembled for a moment before he released them and ran a hand through his hair. "*Inshallah*, they will not succeed, but the truth is, they have taken the high ground above the road and people are worried. Even my fighters." He lowered his voice so that it was barely above a whisper. "Some even talk of surrender. Now, if they see you, the famous Dr. Sami leaving, after staying for so long, what message will that send to our people?"

"Even if I were to stay, I could not work." Sami raised his hands.

Ibrahim stared at Sami's swollen and deformed palms for a moment, then his eyes narrowed. He exited the room, and when he returned, he was gripping a piece of narrow wooden shelving.

He cursed, then swung the shelving at Sami's midsection. The board wasn't particularly heavy, though, and Sami absorbed the blow then tackled Ibrahim, pinning him to the wall and using his forehead to headbutt Ibrahim in the face.

The other soldiers raced in. One of them clubbed Sami on the head with an AK-47. The rest kicked him.

"So, the big doctor is not so strong after all!" one of them said.

Sami kicked the man's the knee joint, sending him tumbling to the ground.

"Not the head," said Ibrahim. Then, "Hold him."

The soldiers did. Ibrahim punched Sami in the gut until Sami slumped over and Ibrahim tired.

Heaving from having exerted himself, Ibrahim shouted, "You think you owe nothing to us? You think it is coincidence that you are still alive? People like you are the reason for this war! People like you who think you deserve more than everyone else. People like the tyrant Bashar! You turn your back on God and live in your house when others have nothing. Are you even a Muslim, Doctor?"

Sami spit out a mouthful of blood. "I am a rationalist."

"A rationalist. Meaning you think that because I am a Muslim, I am not."

Sami did not answer.

"Meaning you think you can leave us whenever you wish, giving nothing back."

"I have given plenty back, you fool. And after I bring my family to safety, I will return and give more. Not to you, but to my patients."

"And you think if I let you leave, you will be free to take your children and go where you wish? Castello Road is under fire. You would take your children on this road? You would risk their capture by the regime? The regime will kill you in an instant if they capture you. Do you know that, right now, there is a man in the Mukhabarat whose mission it is to find you? You and your family are targets, Doctor. Even if you flee to the refugee camps or Turkey, the regime will worry that you will return, and so, you and your family will still be targets." Ibrahim spit at Sami's feet. "If you work hard for us, your American whore and—"

In the recesses of Sami's brain, a warning signal had flashed. The hairs on the back of his neck tingled, and the pain in his stomach vanished.

"What Mukhabarat officer?" Sami demanded.

Ibrahim appeared surprised that Sami would care to ask. "He is a major. In Military Intelligence," he said dismissively.

"I mean," shouted Sami, "what is this man's name?"

"You think I lie? His name is Rahim Suleiman."

Sami put his hands on his knees to prevent himself from toppling over. "And how do you know this?"

"Because we interrogated the man sent to capture your American whore last year, and then we interrogated another regime spy who was working at the hospital last week. Both men were sent by this major."

"And you did not think that was important to tell me?"

"Tell you what? You know the regime targets doctors."

"You did not think this Suleiman might find a way discover where I live? Might order a bombing?"

"That has always been a risk. For any of us. What would you have had me do, build you a new home to live in until we could be sure your old one was safe? This is what I offer you, Doctor. If you work hard for us, your children will be well cared for here in Aleppo. You will be allowed to see them—at least once a week. But if you try to leave with them, if you try to turn people against me and my men, I cannot guarantee their safety."

"You disgust me," said Sami.

"Guard him until you receive word that the children and the American have been moved," Ibrahim said to his men. "Then bring him back to the hospital and see that he resumes his work. I do not care how much his hands hurt."

CHAPTER 56

Regime-held Aleppo

Rahim clicked on a file containing the post-action photos of Dr. Sami Hasan's house.

Upon reviewing them, he slumped back in his seat, pressed his lips tightly together, turned his head to the ceiling as he closed his eyes, and clasped his hands together.

Alhamdulillah, he thought. Praise be to God.

The destruction was near total. The house lay in ruins. The courtyard was a crater, the vegetable garden that had mocked him, nothing but dust. After the war this house would not be rebuilt, it would be bulldozed.

Had anyone been inside—and why would they not have been?—they would have been incinerated in the blast.

Alhamdulillah.

He imagined the next time he spoke to his wife he would ask her whether she recalled the doctor who had killed their son.

"How could I forget him?" she would say.

Then, he would tell her what he had done to the doctor and his family.

Rahim considered calling his wife now but decided against it. He would visit her in Beirut. She would not want him to come, but he would make some excuse as to why the trip was necessary.

She would look at him differently. Even his daughter would. Her eyes would widen, and she would ask, "But how? How were you able to do this? How did you hunt this doctor?"

"What else could I do?" he would say. "After what he did to Adel?"

To be sure, it would reflect better upon him if he could tell them with certainty that Dr. Hasan no longer walked this earth. Indeed, it would be an affront to God and the memory of his son if the doctor had survived.

But not as much of an affront as it had been yesterday.

Not as much at all.

CHAPTER 57

Rebel-held Aleppo • Two weeks later

Two hundred fifty thousand people, most of them civilians, were left stranded behind enemy lines when the regime captured Castello Road. The flow of supplies, already slowed to a trickle, stopped entirely.

Hannah knew nothing of the particulars because she was not permitted to know. But she could hear the bombs falling and see the daily allotment of bread diminishing. Every day of her captivity in a basement apartment somewhere in rebel-held Aleppo, she looked for a way to escape—and every day she concluded that the risk was too great.

Until the first of August.

That was the day when two things changed. The first was that, instead of the usual heavily armed soldier, one of Ibrahim's many nephews showed up to stand guard. He claimed to be seventeen but looked closer to fourteen. Bowl-shaped haircut, crooked teeth, armed with a pistol instead of an AK-47. Only a bit taller than Hannah.

He began his shift by attempting to engage Hannah in conversation, speaking English with a heavy accent as he spoke about an uncle who had moved to New Jersey in the 1990s.

Hannah pointedly kept her back to him as she poured two half-glasses of milk, emptying the carton. But the boy persisted.

"My uncle, he drives a Chrysler 300. I have seen pictures. I think this is very good car?"

"I wouldn't know."

"But you know the Chrysler? This is a good car?"

Feeling overheated and mildly dizzy, Hannah bent over and placed the back of her hand on her forehead. It must be the clothes, she thought. Even when she was inside, Ibrahim's men insisted she cover herself with an abaya and bulky headscarf.

There was no furniture in the basement apartment, just a few mattresses and cushions and carpets. Nowhere, save the floor, to sit. In the adjacent room, Adam and Noora were arguing over Hajj, a dreary Arabic board game that attempted to teach kids about the pilgrimage to Mecca all Muslims were supposed to make at least once in their lives.

The boy stepped closer to her. "You are sick?" he asked.

Hannah had been around people who could eat garlic hummus by the bucketful and still smell like rosewater, but there were others whose bodies processed it in such a way that the garlic seeped out of their pores, giving off a sour and rancid smell. This boy was very much one of the latter.

She forced herself not to retch. "I'm fine," she said.

"Can I—"

"You can leave me alone and let me make the children lunch. That is all I need you to do."

"Okay, okay," he said, laughing, either not grasping or not caring about the depths of her revulsion. "But first I must know what you think of the Chrysler. You must tell me honestly."

Hannah picked up a serrated butter knife that her captors had deemed too small and dull to pose a threat. She used it to cut a small piece of stale flatbread in two equal portions and said, "Perhaps you have heard that women are much different in America than in Syria. That we are much more forward. Especially in relationships."

Hannah didn't think that was true, but she assumed the boy would think it was.

"Yes, I—"

"For example, one American woman, when her boyfriend mistreated her, she cut off his . . . well, I don't want to say the word, but it is the part of your body you use when you go to the bathroom."

The boy's smile vanished.

Hannah showed him the dull butter knife. "It's true. She felt she was being mistreated, so when the man was asleep, she"—Hannah made a slicing motion with the knife—"cut it right off. Then threw it out. Doctors tried to sew it back on, but I don't think it worked very well after that. I wish to say that I very much admire this woman. If a woman is being bothered by a man, even a young man, she should not tolerate it, don't you think?"

"Ha ha," said the boy soldier, sounding uncomfortable. "Maybe they should tolerate it a little."

"Ha ha," said Hannah. "Maybe not."

The boy soldier retreated to a corner in the other room. He said he was going to practice memorizing a section of the Quran, but Hannah soon observed him tapping away at a video game on his cell phone.

Meanwhile, the children's argument in the other room had devolved into a brawl. Noora had tried to bite Adam, and Adam had pushed her down. Now, both were shouting at each other.

Hannah knew she should go in there and break it up, that on some level that was what they expected and wanted her to do. Instead, she just stood there, both hands on the counter, bent over, unable to move.

Their lunches were ready. She just needed to feed them what little she could and get on with life, make it to the next day. Ibrahim didn't appear to want to kill them or sell them to ISIS. Things would work out.

But just at that moment, she couldn't see anything working out. The smell of garlic body-odor seemed to be everywhere, even in her lungs, choking her, making her lightheaded.

Her stomach felt bloated.

She slumped onto a dirty carpet that lay on the kitchen floor, toppling a vase of plastic flowers that should have sat on a kitchen table but instead had been pushed into a corner on the floor. She just needed to rest. For a minute or two, that was all.

God, what was wrong with her? Was it just the stress of captivity?

She exhaled deeply.

That was when it dawned on her. Of course. She recalled how sensitive her breasts had been that morning, when she'd been putting on her bra—further evidence of her condition. And should she really be surprised?

———

The calculus, Hannah decided, had changed.

Food was running short. She was losing weight at a time when she should be gaining it. Escaping wouldn't get any easier given her condition.

The apartment consisted of two bedrooms and a kitchen from which everything had been removed save for a gas stove, dry sink, and a sliver of countertop between the sink and stove. The bathroom was a waterless pit toilet outside the apartment, at the end of long hall at the edge of a bomb crater.

In one bedroom, Adam and Noora had gone back to playing Hajj, having eaten their lunch and resolved their argument; in the other—which also doubled as an entrance hall—the boy was still tapping on his phone.

Hannah got down on her knees, crawled behind the stove, unscrewed the copper line that led from the stove to the small silver gas canister, then smacked her fist on the kitchen countertop.

"And what is wrong?" the boy asked.

"Nothing!" Then a minute later, "Dammit!"

"What is this problem?"

"Nothing," she said, but a few seconds later she smacked the countertop again.

The boy entered the kitchen then stopped short, his eyes were wide. Hannah had let her headscarf slip to her shoulders.

"It refuses to start," she said in Arabic, pointing to the stove.

The boy nodded and quickly turned away from her face. "And where is the lighter?"

"There." Hannah pointed to where it lay next to the sink.

The boy lit the lighter and turned on the one burner that worked. Nothing happened.

"No gas," he said.

Then he eyed the small canister that was wedged behind the stove.

"They changed it yesterday," said Hannah.

"Yes, but it is not full, I think."

"It was."

"You check it is connected properly?"

"I would not know how to do this. Do you?"

"Yes, of course."

"Then perhaps you should look at it." Hannah's palms were sweating. She'd never been a good liar. "I wish to make tea."

The boy made his way to the back of the stove and slipped to his knees.

"It is connected correctly?" asked Hannah. She positioned herself directly behind him, taking short shallow sips of air and recalled feeling the same way once when she'd been teetering at the very tip of a high diving board, at a pool in New Jersey. She'd told herself that she was going to jump, so she was going to jump—and she had—but God, she hadn't wanted to.

"Ah, I see the problem! It is not screwed in. I will—"

Hannah aimed for the gap between his buttocks and kicked with every ounce of strength she possessed.

There was no loud cry of pain, just a barely perceptible bleat followed by a rapid stiffening of the body.

A split-second later, she yanked the boy's pistol out of his belt holster, confirmed that the safety was off—she'd learned a few things about guns in Syria—took two steps back, aimed and, speaking in Arabic, said, "If you cry for help, I will shoot you. Nod your head if you understand."

The boy whimpered as he pushed himself out from behind the stove.

"I am waiting for a nod," said Hannah. The gun felt absurdly heavy in her hand, but her head was clear. She was no longer lightheaded. "You have two seconds. One—"

The boy nodded, then fell to the ground in a fetal position, gripping his crotch.

"Sit facing the wall, hands extended behind your back."

The boy sat, but—perhaps remembering Hannah's story from earlier—kept his hands on his crotch.

"Hands behind your back!" whispered Hannah, adding, "I promise I will not hurt you if you comply."

The boy slowly did as instructed. Hannah retrieved a clothesline that had been strung up between two nails in a corner of the kitchen. She put the gun on the floor behind her, so that if he tried to fight her, she could get to it before he could get to her, and then bound his hands.

"Why do you do this?" The boy cried, angry and indignant, as though they'd had an understanding and she had betrayed him.

"Because you were mistreating me and the children."

"How did I mistreat you?"

"By doing what your uncle told you to do."

"We were protecting you."

"No, you were holding us hostage."

Hannah finished tying the final knot, then she tied the boy's hands to the handle of the stove door. It was a lousy attempt to restrain someone. Under two minutes—that's how long she estimated it would hold him should he try to escape.

"The men outside, they will not let you leave," said the boy, still facing the wall.

She took his cell phone and confirmed that she could use it without entering a password.

"If you tell them I am coming, or if you try to untie yourself and stop me, I will come back and shoot you. Right there." She tapped the top of his head. "You understand?"

He nodded, but her threat turned out to be unnecessary. Even though in the past there had always been someone—usually an older man with an AK-47 rifle—sitting in the hallway, today it was vacant.

She stepped out of the apartment then turned back, put a finger to her lips, and waved to Adam and Noora that they should follow.

On the floor above, she heard yelling. Instead of exiting the way she'd been led into the apartment days earlier, she grabbed both children by the hand and turned toward the pit toilets, worrying that at any moment the boy soldier would call for help.

"Eww," said Adam, holding his nose.

Hannah whipped around, gave him a look, and put her finger to her lips again. They crept past the toilets and began climbing around the remains of a collapsed portion of the apartment building.

After picking their way down, around, then through the rubble, she saw a splash of white sunlight illuminating a partially blocked alley and hurried toward it.

The street was deserted. High overhead, a fighter jet roared. It wasn't a coincidence that her only jailer today had been a young boy, she guessed. Everyone else must be off fighting. The end must be near.

"We have to go fast now," she whispered to the children. "Can you do that?"

They both nodded, then Hannah began to run.

CHAPTER 58

Because the M2 had suffered bomb damage and was undergoing repairs, Sami had been transferred to the M10 hospital in the Sakhour district, northeast of the Citadel. Established early in the war in a three-story, concrete-framed Ministry of Health building that had since been fortified and partially moved underground after its top two floors were bombed, it was now the primary trauma hospital in Aleppo.

There, he had bandaged the deep cuts on his hands and treated the smaller ones with an antibiotic ointment that had had the effect of rendering the newly formed scabs flexible.

The unbearable had become bearable. He had gone back to work. Supplies were running dangerously low, but they resterilized needles, washed surgical drapes that should have been thrown out, used nerve blocks instead of general anesthesia. When Hannah called, Sami was checking on a thirteen-year-old boy who had lost a leg to a cluster bomb munition and was recovering in the intensive care unit without the benefit of morphine or any other painkiller.

She explained what had happened and where she was.

"Give me a half hour," he said.

"Be careful."

"There is no need. With you and the children free, I have nothing to fear."

As he was leaving the M10 via the stairs that led up from the underground emergency room, an older man who had been helping with patient intakes followed him out.

"Dr. Sami!" he called, looking flustered. "Dr. Sami, please wait!"

"I must speak with you," said Sami, when the man—who wore a pink rugby shirt but was really one of Ibrahim's soldiers—drew close.

"Commander Antar has requested—"

"I do not care what Ibrahim has requested. We must talk."

Sami gestured to what had once been a park and where, despite being scarred with several deep bomb craters, several tall cedar trees still stood.

As the soldier's gaze drifted from Sami to the park, Sami swung his gloved fist into the man's face.

Two hospital orderlies who had been lugging boxes of sutures from a nearby underground medical supply warehouse ran over.

Sami explained to them that Commander Ibrahim Antar of Ahrar al-Sham had kidnapped his family and had been holding them hostage for two weeks. A few minutes earlier, such a declaration might have led to Hannah and the children being harmed. Now, it simply resulted in the Ahrar al-Sham soldier's teeth being kicked in.

CHAPTER 59

The vast cemetery lay due south of the Citadel and east of the M2 hospital. The dirt road that snaked through it led Hannah to a green-domed mosque, which stood just a block away from the newly reopened M2 hospital, which in turn was just a short walk away from the Qinnasrin Gate where she'd agreed to meet Sami.

When she and the children were finally in sight of the gate, they hid behind an abandoned drainage pipe in a patch of undeveloped land that lay just south of the walls of the old city.

While waiting for Sami, Hannah tried to call the Bonne Foi warehouse in Kilis, Turkey, hoping that maybe someone had remained after the main operation had shut down—someone with connections to either smugglers or the Turkish Directorate General of Migration Management. Someone who could help get them the hell out of Syria.

The line had been disconnected.

So she looked up the number for Bonne Foi's headquarters in France, and she even spoke with a woman who was sympathetic to her plight but had no connections to the Turkish ministry officials who could determine whether Sami and the children would be allowed entry into Turkey.

Hannah asked if they at least still had a copy of her American passport on file. Because all of her identification had been destroyed, buried under the rubble of Beit Qarah, and if she and Sami and the children just showed up at the Turkish border without identification, then confinement in one of the unofficial refugee camps on the Syrian side of the border would be the best they could hope for.

They did not.

After hanging up with Bonne Foi, she tried the European Development Service at their regional office in Ankara, hoping that she might still know someone there who could vouch for her and help arrange for Sami and the kids to be granted temporary protection status by the Turks. EDS was a bureaucratic behemoth with deep ties to nearly every country in the Middle East, and even though the satellite office in Antakya had been shut down, they were still active in Turkey.

Four years ago, she'd been in frequent communication the office in Ankara. With a bit of luck, someone might remember her.

———

"Well, would you at least know where I can reach Greta Becker?" Hannah asked after she'd explained her predicament and was told there was nothing the European Development Service could do for her. "I used to report to her."

"No."

"What about Clara Braun?" Clara had been Greta Becker's boss. Hannah had met her once, five years ago.

"No."

"Is it possible to look any of these names up? To see whether they're still with the company, and if so, where?"

"Employee records are confidential. I'm sorry, the connection isn't that good, your voice is going in and out. What did you say your name was?"

"Hannah Johnson," she said slowly, practically yelling into the phone. "I worked for the company until 2012. In Aleppo. We were trying to develop a park just outside the old city."

"Oh, sure. I heard about that project. Lucky you."

"I'm sorry to press like this, it's just that I'm a bit—" She was about to say desperate, but then she glanced at Adam and Noora. They were sitting on either side of her, staring at her. She didn't think they understood any

English, but she didn't want to worry them more than they already were. "It's just that I could really, really use some help."

Her voice began to crack. The cell phone had only been holding a nine percent charge when she'd started the call.

"I understand that, but I just don't see how—"

"What about Oskar Lång?" Hannah asked, interrupting.

A pause. "And what is your relationship to Mr. Lång?"

"We worked together for two years." After another pause, this one longer than the first, she said, "We know each other. He'll want to talk to me, I swear. Do you know where I can reach him?"

"Hold on."

Enough time passed that Hannah worried that the connection had been severed. She checked the battery level on the phone—it was down to seven percent.

CHAPTER 60

Ankara, Turkey

Oskar noted with satisfaction that the site of the infiltration basin for the energy-efficient waste disposal center in Sivas Province, Turkey had been excavated on schedule. Good, good, he thought, skimming over the email.

The administrative assistant he shared with three other engineers poked her head into his office.

"Someone on line six who wants to speak with you. She claims to be a former colleague."

Oskar had started wearing low-magnification reading glasses the month prior; he glanced over their imitation tortoiseshell frames now.

"Does she have a name?"

"Jana something. Says she worked with you in Aleppo, before the war."

Oskar furrowed his brow and stared past his computer screen. Jana . . . no, to the best of his recollection he had never worked with a Jana.

Then it hit him that Jana sounded a bit like . . .

"I'll pick up," he said. As soon as the door to his office closed, he took a deep breath, pushed line number six, and said, "Hi, this is Oskar Lång."

———

The shock of hearing her still-familiar voice, paired with the revelation that she was in Syria when he'd assumed she'd been living in the United States these past four years, prevented him from immediately grasping the full nature of her predicament.

"So it would be me, Dr. Sami Hasan, his son Adam, and his daughter Noora," she said, the words tumbling out of her mouth with a speed he found hard to keep up with. "You met Dr. Hasan four years ago—he was the one who set your leg. It's a long story, but we're seeing each other now, and I've been caring for the two children he had with his wife, and I may be pregnant with his third child. I'd be willing to marry him and adopt his children, if it helps."

At that, Oskar took off his reading glasses and leaned over his desk, one hand on his forehead, the other pressing the phone to his ear. He felt his face flush. At some point, he realized Hannah had stopped talking and was waiting for him to respond.

"Oskar?" she said.

"I'm sorry, it's just . . ." He inhaled, then exhaled. "It's just that I'm trying to wrap my head around the fact that you're in Aleppo again, and . . ." He paused.

He'd tried to contact her two years ago, after Elsa had died. But she'd changed her phone number, her old EDS email had been shut down, and she'd left no forwarding information. She used aliases for Facebook and Instagram, he'd recalled, but she'd changed whatever those aliases were, so he hadn't been able to find her online, and he'd tried hard. He'd even mailed a letter to her childhood home in New Jersey.

No response.

But he'd never forgotten her.

"My battery on this phone is about to go, Oskar, can you help me? Will you try?"

She was still speaking quickly, and the connection was bad. He felt flustered.

"You're—you're seeing the doctor who set my leg?" Oskar stuttered. "How . . ."

"We met again after the war broke out. Oskar, please."

Virtually married. Possibly pregnant. Completely unavailable. She hadn't called him because she cared about him or had been thinking about him. She just needed a ticket to get into Turkey.

And she would never come back to him.

But he still loved her. More, although it pained him to admit it, than he'd ever loved Elsa. He realized that now, hearing her voice again.

"Yes," he said, "Yes, of course I'll help you. Let me give you my cell number, so that if we get disconnected, you can call me back directly. Are you ready?"

He recited the number, wrote hers down when she gave it to him, then said, "Give me an hour or two to see what I can do."

After Hannah hung up, Oskar just sat there, staring at his phone.

The Turkish government was distracted and in turmoil, having just crushed an attempted coup. But he figured if anyone could find a way to get Hannah and her adopted family into Turkey, it would be Clara Braun, a woman both he and Hannah had indirectly reported to when they were in Aleppo. She was now a deputy director of the Middle East and Southeast Europe Development Group, and the most well-connected person he knew in the company.

He picked up the phone, called the human resources department in Brussels, and asked to be put through to her.

CHAPTER 61

Rebel-held Aleppo

Hannah stared at the number she'd scribbled in the dirt. Oskar, she thought. After all these years. She quickly transcribed the number to the phone she'd stolen from the boy.

"Who was that?" asked Adam.

"Somebody I used to know."

"Will he help us?"

"I hope so."

She scanned the road beyond the drainage pipe for signs of Sami. That was when she realized that they were just a stone's throw away from what she and Oskar and so many others had, before the war, tried their best to make into an urban park. Just beyond a half-collapsed building that had been covered with a fraying blue tarp, sewer drains had been dug according to Oskar's specifications. She recalled architectural drawings that had depicted pedestrians holding ice cream cones strolling through landscaped gardens, and she contrasted those drawings with the weedy piles of rubble that lay before her, and—

"Adam! Noora!"

Sami's voice boomed across the broken ground.

The children rushed out to greet their father. Hannah followed a step behind. She and Sami exchanged a long look. She took his hand.

"We should leave now," she said. "On foot if we have to. I have a friend in Turkey. He may be able to help us if we can get to the border."

"Castello Road has been taken," said Sami.

"Then we will have to find another way out."

"There is no other way."

Noora said she was thirsty.

———

They went back to their old neighborhood.

The old woman with whom Hannah had shared tea during the cease-fire invited them into her small ground-floor apartment. She had only a half-liter of water, so Sami fetched several more from a nearby public well.

With the city surrounded, no one—save for the enterprising few who were melting down oil-based plastics—had any diesel to run the generators, but the old woman knew of another neighbor who had a small solar charger.

Making use of the last light of the day, Hannah huddled at the end of a west-facing street and, bathed in sun, charged her phone as much as she could. Sami used half of the remaining charge on his phone, calling people, trying to find a way out of the city.

At dusk, as the children lay together on a threadbare couch in the living room, staring blankly at the concrete floor, and as the old woman embroidered a waistcoat by candlelight in what passed for a kitchen, Hannah and Sami talked outside on the front stoop. He told her about Rahim Suleiman's role in her kidnapping and possibly in the bombing of Beit Qarah. She leaned into him, placed a hand on his thigh, and whispered that, by the way, she suspected she was pregnant.

"How many weeks?" he asked.

She did the math in her head again, just to be sure. It was around the beginning of June that she'd run out of pads and had needed to make do with a baby's blanket she'd cut up into squares. So around fourteen days after that . . .

"Six, maybe seven? I could just be late."

But she didn't think she was late. He had never pulled out, and she had never asked him to.

He sighed. Which wasn't exactly the reaction she was hoping for, but she knew he wasn't a man given to outpourings of emotion.

"You are upset," she said.

"On the contrary. I am relieved."

She faced him. "You are?"

"Of course."

"Why?"

"Because it ties you to Adam and Noora. And they will be safer that way."

"So you wanted this?"

He shrugged. "Want is a complicated word. Suffice it to say, I was not opposed to it. I thought that was evident."

Hannah didn't answer.

"I sensed you were not opposed either. Did I misjudge the situation?"

Hannah held his gaze for a moment then stared down at the ground, thinking—did he always have to be like this? This calculating? Would it be too much just to say he was happy, for her and for them, and that he cared for her, and leave it at that? "No. I guess not."

———

After the children went to sleep, Hannah phoned Oskar back.

He had made progress, he informed her. Great progress! If they could just get to the Bab al Hawa border crossing anytime from tomorrow evening on, he could meet them there with an official letter from Turkey's General Directorate of Migration Management that should allow her, Sami, Adam, and Noora to enter Turkey on a provisional basis, after which they could begin the process of obtaining replacement passports.

"Thank you, Oskar. Thank you so much."

"Thank Clara," he said, referring to their former boss. "She was the one who fixed it. Now you just need to get to the border, and there's good news on that front too—they're opening corridors from the rebel side of Aleppo to the regime side. So that civilians can escape the fighting. The regime has promised safe passage. It was on the news."

"But it wouldn't be safe for us," said Hannah. She told him about Rahim Suleiman, the father of Oskar's roommate at the University of Aleppo Hospital before the war, did he remember? "He hates Sami, and maybe me. So we can't go to the other side of Aleppo, we have to find another way."

"But Dr. Hasan didn't kill that man's son," said Oskar.

"Well, not on purpose," said Hannah.

"No, I mean he didn't kill that boy on purpose or accidentally."

"He mixed up the medications, Oskar. I was there."

"But that's not what killed the boy. And I know, because I was there."

"What are you talking about?"

CHAPTER 62

Ankara, Turkey

Oskar was seated on a bench in Kugulu Park, cell phone pressed to his ear, half watching an old man throw breadcrumbs to collection of white swans in a man-made pond.

But in his mind, he was in Aleppo, and it was 2012. His fever was just beginning to spike, evidence—although he didn't know it at the time—that the infection in his rib, the infection that would nearly kill him, was spreading to his blood . . .

———

Four years earlier • Aleppo University Hospital

A nurse entered Oskar's hospital room. Wide hips, red lipstick, painted eyebrows. Yellow scrubs paired with a black headscarf that made her look a bit like a bumblebee.

Oskar put down his phone.

"I need Tylenol," he said, in poor but passable Arabic.

"Yes, of course," answered the nurse brightly as she brushed by Oskar on her way to Adel, who lay behind a curtain that divided the room. "Very soon. Very soon."

"Do you mean very soon as in an hour?" demanded Oskar, as the nurse ducked behind the privacy curtain. "Or very soon now?"

The pain in his leg was intense.

"One hour, I think, would be best. Now is too soon."

Oskar was as annoyed as he was desperate. The nurse in question hadn't been the one who'd given him Tylenol earlier in the day. So how could she know it was too soon?

"Are you sure, because—"

"Please, sir. I will tend to you shortly."

Oskar picked up his phone again. Maybe the nurse from earlier in the day had communicated his medication schedule with this nurse? It would have been a first, but it wasn't inconceivable.

It was only because he lost a life in the *Candy Crush* game he was playing that he looked up a few seconds later. When he did, he squinted and frowned.

The chrome paper towel dispenser affixed to the wall opposite his bed had been hung in such a way that it inadvertently served as a mirror of sorts, allowing patients to see around the privacy curtain from one side of the room to the other. The angle wasn't quite right, and the reflection was dull and wavy, but when Oskar leaned to the side of the bed to put down his cell phone, he saw the nurse had her fingers pressed down on either side of Adel's throat.

At first, he thought he had to be mistaken. Surely, she was just taking Adel's pulse or feeling his lymph nodes.

He squinted at the paper towel dispenser, wishing his mind wasn't so cloudy. He didn't trust himself.

"Hey!" he called out.

The nurse looked around, appearing confused as to how Oskar might be able to see her. Sounding stressed, she said, "Sir, I must tend to this patient. I will bring you Tylenol in an hour."

Oskar stared at the hazy reflection. The nurse appeared to be compressing the carotid arteries on either side of the boy's neck.

"What are you doing?!" called Oskar in Arabic. Then, "Stop that!"

The nurse kept her fingers firmly in place.

"Get the hell off him!" Oskar yelled in Swedish, then he grabbed his cane, which was propped up next to his bed, and used it to whip open the privacy curtain.

There was no doubt. The nurse, her fingers still pressing down on Adel's carotid arteries, glared at Oskar. Oskar tried to push himself out of bed, but before he could extricate himself from the sling that kept his leg elevated, the nurse grabbed a used catheter needle from the top of the garbage bin and was on Oskar a second later.

She pressed her fingers into Oskar's wounded chest with one hand and with the other, jammed the tip of the needle into the corner of Oskar's eye.

The nurse was a full head shorter than Oskar, but it didn't matter. Oskar's broken leg kept him anchored to the bed and the pain in his chest was raging. When she poked the corner of his eye with the catheter needle, Oskar froze.

"Fight me," she said, whispering directly into Oskar's ear, "and I will see if I can reach your brain."

For a moment, neither spoke nor moved. Then the nurse cast a glance to the closed door, as though afraid someone might walk through it at any moment, and whispered, "If you say a word of this to anyone, as God is my witness, I must kill you. Do you understand me?"

Oskar couldn't speak.

The nurse dug her fingers into Oskar's chest wound, applied more pressure to the catheter, and repeated her question, sounding more frantic this time.

Keeping his head perfectly still, Oskar managed to whisper a single word in Arabic. "Yes."

"You will find a way to leave Syria," she said. "Today. You understand?"

"Yes," whispered Oskar again.

She released him, stood, then tossed the used catheter needle back into the garbage.

Oskar was trembling. He observed the nurse was as well.

"Even if I say nothing," said Oskar, as the nurse yanked the privacy curtain closed, "to anyone, ever—people will still see this! There will be an investigation. You cannot hide this."

She gesticulated with her hands, in a way that made Oskar wonder whether she was crazy. "And who do you think will investigate?"

"The police!" said Oskar.

"Wrong!"

"Or the boy's father. He works for the government."

"Who do you think did this? Do you think I awoke today and decided to"—she lowered her voice to a whisper—"take the life of one of my patients? Out of spite? The government—the Mukhabarat!—forced me to do this because they found out he"—she gestured with her chin to Adel—"was spying on his father. They came to my home; they made threats. I have children," she pleaded.

Oskar observed how rattled the nurse appeared, perhaps on the verge of tears, then asked, "Does the boy's father know this?"

"No! The Mukhabarat did not tell him. Will you?"

Oskar didn't answer.

"Better for him to think his son died from a car accident or from a medical mistake than to know the truth. Go home, Mr. Lång. This is not your business. This is not your war."

———

Oskar, upon finishing his story, listened to the sound of Hannah breathing on the other end of the line.

"Why didn't you tell me?" she asked eventually.

"I was sick."

"You got better."

Oskar pressed his lips together as he searched for a credible lie that wouldn't reflect poorly on him. Finding none, he opted for the truth, "I was ashamed. For leaving you the way I did. For allowing myself to be bullied by that woman. I didn't want you to know."

"Oh, Oskar."

"And there was also Elsa."

It all came out. His childhood romance with Elsa, the breakup with her before he left for Syria, sleeping with her before her bone marrow transplant in Paris. The second relapse. The funeral. The utter awfulness of it all.

"I didn't tell you about her," Oskar said, "because I was afraid you wouldn't take me back if you knew. And I planned to come back to you, after getting Elsa through the rough part of her transplant in Paris. And then I got hurt. And the war happened. And that fucking nurse happened. And Elsa never got better, at least not really."

He wanted to add that he considered abandoning her in Syria to be the biggest mistake of his life, that he'd tried to find her after losing Elsa, but he didn't think that would be fair. She'd moved on from him a long time ago.

CHAPTER 63

Rebel-held Aleppo

Later that night Hannah told Sami how the nurse had been the one to kill Rahim's son, Adel.

She did it as they lay side by side on a living room carpet that smelled of cat urine. They had no sheets or pillows. The children were sleeping by their feet. Through an open window, she could see the sky and had been hoping to catch a glimpse of at least a single star, but there was too much smoke in the air.

"It is like this whole war," Sami finally said, several minutes after she had finished.

She turned to him and raised herself up on an elbow. "How do you mean?"

"Misinformed. Misguided. Irrational."

She touched his cheek. "But surely it makes you feel a little better?"

"Why should it? The boy still died. She must have cut off the blood supply to his brain just long enough to kill him, instead of giving him an overdose of morphine so there would be no evidence of excess drugs in his body," he speculated, as though the logistics of the crime, not his belated absolution from having caused the death of a child, was what truly interested him. "Or evidence of missing morphine. I wonder if she switched the labels in the pharmacy or whether it was truly just a mistake?"

"Either way, that boy did not die by your hand, Sami. It makes a difference."

"Too many others have been killed or saved by my hand for it to mean anything to me anymore."

Hannah suspected he was speaking more out of frustration than conviction, but she couldn't be sure. She hadn't seen what he had.

"This nurse," she said. "Did you know she was Mukhabarat?"

"No. Farrah was a good nurse. I liked her. But I suppose I should have guessed. After the war broke out, did you know many of the nurses brought their families to the hospital at the university? Not because they were sick, but because they had no electricity or food at home. They used up half of the patient rooms, pushing out regular patients, but because they were Mukhabarat, they were permitted to stay."

"Rahim has no reason to hate you, Sami. He should know this."

"At this point, Hannah, it matters little. The damage has already been done."

———

That night, the fighting just southwest of their position was intense. Adam and Noora woke up in the middle of the night, scared and asking to go to the cellar, not realizing that there was no cellar to go to.

Hannah worried that if the city stayed surrounded, things would only get worse. That food would run out, that the bombings would intensify. She didn't think it inconceivable that the regime would slaughter everyone who remained on the rebel-held side. They had the city surrounded. The rebels showed no signs of being willing to surrender, and the Russians had no shortage of bombs.

In the morning, the regime dropped leaflets which fluttered like confetti to the ground and blew through the ruined streets, getting stuck in the gaps between the piles of rubble and swirling beneath the wreckage of burnt out cars, hanging like laundry from tangles of electric wires.

People picked them up, but upon realizing what they were, threw them back to the street and stepped on them.

More regime lies, they said. More tricks. They were not humanitarian corridors; they were death corridors.

In the early morning, while the children slept, and as the sounds of homemade rebel cannons mixed with the sound of starving cats fighting each other in a nearby alley, Hannah and Sami examined the map on the back of one of the leaflets.

"There might be safety in numbers," said Sami. "If thousands are crossing."

Hannah's eyes widened. "No! It will never be safe for you there, even if you were to make your peace with Rahim. They would kill you because of who you are!"

"I meant for you. And the children. Not me. If you were to call your friend Oskar, and he were to tell the American embassy in Ankara that you plan to cross, there at least might be a diplomatic cost to mistreating you."

"No," said Hannah. "We stay together."

"You would deny the children food for this purpose? Why? How does that benefit them?"

Hannah took a long time to answer because she was so torn up inside. "I will do as you think best," she said. "But I would much rather we stick together. The children need you."

"We split now and reunite later," said Sami. "That is what I think is best."

CHAPTER 64

More than anything, Adam just wanted to go home.

He had been scared the night before when he needed to go to the bathroom; it had been so dark. And he had been hungry when he had woken up, but no breakfast had been offered, and Hannah had told him not to ask the old woman for food. He knew that Hannah and his Baba had no food either, which worried him a lot. After they started walking, he asked whether there was anyone who could sell them food.

"Not yet," said Hannah.

"Soon?" asked Adam.

"I am not sure how soon," said Hannah.

"I need you to be strong, Adam," said Sami. "Can you be strong?"

Adam said okay, but what he thought was, how could he be strong if he had nothing to eat?

He thought again of Beit Qarah. He remembered the way the smooth handrail to the cellar felt under his palm, the way the door to Mémère's yellow room squeaked a bit when it opened, how he liked to lie on the floor in the living room in a patch of sun under one of the windows and look up at the painted ceiling. He remembered harvesting a giant, purple eggplant from the rooftop garden and climbing the laurel tree in the courtyard. He knew that the house had been damaged, but he also knew his father was a doctor and good at fixing things. So he thought maybe Beit Qarah would get fixed soon and everything could go back to the way it was.

Noora said she was tired, so Baba picked her up and carried her. Adam thought that was unfair, but after looking at the expression on his father's face, he decided not to complain.

In the middle of one road, men wearing plastic sandals and sleeveless undershirts were burning tires, claiming that the black smoke would help shield them from the bombs. The smoke got in Adam's lungs, and he began to cough until Baba pulled him to a spot where he could breathe. On another road, a crowd had gathered around a tiny Russian plane—they called it a drone—that someone had managed to shoot down. Even though he was scared, Adam wanted to see it so that he could get ideas for his planes, but Hannah would not let him get close.

Eventually, they came to a stop at an intersection.

"Is this it?" asked Hannah.

Baba gestured for everyone to wait, then poked his head around the corner of a mustard-yellow building that had weeds growing out of cracks in its walls.

Hannah looked around the building as well. "Maybe it will open this afternoon," she said.

Across the street, a woman dressed entirely in black, wearing oversized designer sunglasses, held the hand of a little girl who—despite the heat—wore a bright red coat. Adam waved to the girl.

"Have people been crossing?" Hannah called out.

The woman in black shook her head.

"Are we trying to cross?" asked Adam.

"Maybe," said Hannah.

"Why?"

"It might be better on the other side," said Hannah.

Adam hoped that better would mean more food. He began to dream of the *kanafeh* cheese pastry Hannah had bought him during the cease-fire and how sweet and delicious it had tasted. He could eat ten squares of it now and still not be full.

Baba pulled out one of the leaflets that had fallen from the sky and consulted the map with Hannah.

Gunfire erupted. It did not appear to be directed at them, but then a group of rebel soldiers ran over and waved them away. The soldiers told them to go home and that it was not safe for them this close to enemy lines, that there were snipers.

———

They walked. Adam felt the longing for Beit Qarah intensify so much that his stomach hurt. He would give anything to be in the courtyard right now! Hiding in his sheet fort or helping Mémère with her garden or listening to Fairuz in Mémère's yellow room . . .

Mémère! How he missed her.

Thinking of his grandmother made him think of his mother, and all of a sudden, he began to cry. He had not thought of his mother in so long, he could barely remember what she looked like, but he had such a need to see her now—even if she was in one of her sad moods. He remembered the way she would grip his hand so tightly when they were outside Beit Qarah.

"Hey there," said Hannah. She put his arm around his shoulder. "Not much farther now. You can do it."

But no people were crossing at the next place either, and the sound of gunfire near the line of control was intense.

Noora began to cry, because even she knew that meant they were trapped.

They went back to the M2.

Though its facade was pockmarked, its windows shattered, and whole wings had been entirely destroyed, most of the old building still stood and thus had been reopened. Arrangements were made for Hannah and the children to stay in a nearby apartment while Sami worked at the hospital. Ibrahim, they learned, was dead—killed fighting to keep Castello Road open.

Hannah hated the idea of being confined to the new apartment, though, and said it was no different than being imprisoned by Ibrahim. So although she stayed there with the children during the day, she began bringing them to the M2 at night. While they slept in a sandbag-reinforced closet near the intensive care unit, she served as a nurse's assistant.

Her efforts were not nearly enough, nor were Sami's. The city was still surrounded. Patients died for lack equipment, antibiotics, anesthesia, electricity, and care.

But a week later, when thousands of rebels banded together and launched a lightning attack on the regime lines just to the southwest of the M2, everything changed.

For several days the near constant sound of jet fighters and artillery fire sounded like distant thunder, bouncing off of cloud formations. A Russian Mi-8 helicopter was shot down and the pilot's naked body dragged through the streets. The M2 was busier than it had ever been. Finally, over the roar of the Russian and Syrian jet fighters, a convoy of trucks, brilliant, white semis filled with supplies, blasted through a new gap in the regime lines.

The siege had been broken.

The first delivery of medicine in nearly two weeks arrived at the M2 at four in the morning, and that was when Sami turned to Hannah and said, "Gather your things and the children. We are leaving for real this time."

He again told Dr. Wasim that he would return as soon as his family was established Turkey.

Do not be a fool, Dr. Wasim said. If you make it to Turkey, stay there.

———

They trudged through the narrow alleys of the al Fardos district and then Sheik Saeed. Sami carried a leather satchel across his shoulder and wheeled a suitcase behind him. Even at dawn it was hot, and his long-sleeved Oxford shirt quickly grew stained with sweat.

Along the way they encountered militants who tried to advise them.

"When the gap narrows, do not venture near the cement factory, it is still held by the regime."

"The center of Ramouseh is safe, but to the west, near the artillery base, it is not."

"Keep close to the cement factory, there are Iranian forces entrenched near the fuel depot."

"Stay clear of the river."

"If the railroad is always to your left, all will be well."

While crossing under the M5 highway, they joined with a seven-year-old girl and her mother.

"Stop," said Sami when they arrived at the narrow isthmus between the rebel-held section of the city and the wider rebel-held regions beyond.

A fuel depot lay directly to their right, behind a high brick wall. Its enormous circular storage tanks were intact but contained no fuel. To their left, across the corpse-laden Queiq River, loomed the cement factory.

Gunfire could be heard near the cement factory, and swirls of dust rose up from the gravel pits behind it. In front of the factory lay a smoldering Russian-made T-72 tank that was missing one of its treads. In a swath of rebel-held territory across from the factory, militants were milling around atop flat roofs. Far to the west, two helicopters were hovering near an artillery base that, until a week ago, had been occupied by the regime.

But there were other civilians in front of them, and they appeared to be passing through without incident.

"Wait here until I tell you to come," said Sami.

He edged forward through the sunbaked, weedy strip of land that ran parallel to the wall that encircled the fuel depot, keeping the railroad to his left as he had been told to do.

No one shot at him or ordered him to go back. If there were Iranians still entrenched at the fuel depot, behind the wall, he saw no evidence of it. He advanced a bit more, then gestured for the others to follow. They did, and with Sami leading the way, they made it past the fuel depot and into a blasted-out wasteland of what used to be a residential area. Now it was little more than a collection of rubble, old oil drums, charred tires, and garbage.

The whole area was riddled with dusty, narrow trenches. An Iranian rial bill blew past Sami's feet.

Not far ahead lay a protected path between a collection of buildings that were still standing, and just beyond that, the wider expanse of rebel-held territory. They were so close to being free of the city.

"Quickly," he said.

And then came the shot. A single crack that was closer and louder than the intermittent volleys of AK-47 fire sounding from the cement factory. The girl behind Sami cried out. Her mother screamed.

"Get down!" yelled Sami to Adam and Noora, but Hannah was already pulling them into a trench.

Another shot sounded, then from behind them came the rapid *pop-pop-pop* of AK-47 fire. Sami slipped into the trench next to Hannah and his children.

"Keep their heads down!" he said to Hannah, but then he lifted his own above the lip of the trench.

The mother was on her knees, wailing, completely exposed. Her wounded daughter lay at her feet, bleeding from her arm and making goat-like bleating sounds. Sami crawled on his belly to the girl and pulled her into the trench.

As Sami ripped the girl's pink tracksuit open, exposing her wounded arm, a group of five rebel soldiers vaulted over the trench, raising their AK-47s above their heads as they fired on automatic.

Ignoring the gunfire, Sami observed that the bullet had passed through the girl's triceps and did not appear to have impacted the humerus bone.

"Give me your veil!" he said to the mother. And when she appeared flustered, "I must use it as a bandage."

She removed it, revealing long, dark hair and a face marred with a bruise on her right cheek. Sami placed her hands over the wound on her daughter's arm.

"Squeeze," he said, and then began ripping the veil into long strips. The girl wailed, but Sami told the mother to keep squeezing.

Noora was crying.

Not far from the trench, the five rebel soldiers had taken cover behind a pockmarked concrete wall that had once been one side of a house. They wore sleeveless t-shirts and bandanna-like head coverings and were laden with ammo pouches. One wore a surgical dust mask; another had brought a wood box filled with loose AK-47 rounds and was frantically loading spare magazines while the four others fired at the smoldering T-72 tank that lay in front of the cement factory.

The bullets were as thick as a bee swarm and they pinged as they hit the tank.

Sami eyed the rest of the trench and concluded they should have been traveling in it to start with because it appeared to lead all the way to the protected section of path ahead.

"Go!" he said to Hannah. He gestured with his chin down the trench as he continued to apply pressure to the girl's arm. "I can catch up. Take the children. Run!"

Hannah eyed the trench then began to shepherd Adam and Noora down it. Sami turned to the girl. Her straight, brown hair had been pulled into a ponytail that was only barely held in place by a Donald Duck barrette. A small scab above her eye had been picked off and was bleeding a little. The sequined, rainbow-colored butterflies on her tracksuit were stained with blood. For a moment he was transported back to the beginning of the war, when he had failed to save his nephew Omar. He recalled the cerebrospinal fluid, the seizure, and Aya's despair. For this child, though, things would be different.

He finished ripping the veil into strips, and then fashioned a pressure field dressing out of the strips and applied it to the girl's arm. The trench was too narrow for his shoulders, and his hands and arms stirred up dust as they banged against the trench walls.

As he was finishing, the gunfire from the AK-47s abruptly stopped. He heard a whoop and an, "*Allahu Akbar!*" and surmised that the sniper who had shot the girl had himself been shot.

"It hurts now, but you will be fine," Sami said as he placed his palm on the girl's forehead. He turned to the mother, "She must be seen at a hospital, of course, after we are through. The wound must be properly cleaned and dressed. But the prognosis is excellent." Upon sensing her skepticism, he said, "I am a doctor, so I say this with confidence. We must move now."

The mother and daughter and Sami crawled down the length of the trench. To their right, more rebel supply trucks were racing down a road that appeared to have been bulldozed clear. When the trench ended, Sami helped lift the girl up into an alley that led straight south.

He ran to catch up to Hannah and Adam and Noora. After a minute, he thought it odd that he had not reached them yet, so he ran faster. He popped out at the end of the alley and started bearing to the right, toward the road that led straight out of the Ramouseh district and into the heart of rebel territory.

"Adam! Noora!"

He scanned the fields in front of him.

"Adam! Noora!"

He ran forward, all the way to the road, then doubled back and asked the woman and the girl whether they had seen his family. He asked the same question of the rebel soldiers who had shot the sniper in the tank.

"They were following the tracks," one of the soldiers said, pointing to the railroad. "But they were going the wrong way."

"What do you mean the wrong way?"

The soldier pointed. "That territory is held by the regime."

Sami recalled that early on, they indeed had been told to keep the railroad tracks to their left. But that was only until they got to where the city ended, and the fields began. After that they needed to bear off to the north, to reach the road that ran out of Aleppo.

Surely Hannah had known that! Surely she would not have . . .

But how well did she really know the city? And why had he not told her to wait for him when she got to the fields? He had assumed he would catch up to her long before then, but he should never have sent her off without instructing her on where to stop!

For the next five hours, Sami searched for them. In between searching, he called Hannah's phone twenty, thirty times. She never answered.

Finally, he fell to his knees and screamed.

CHAPTER 66

One wrong turn! Such a simple mistake. There had to be a way to fix this, Hannah thought.

After nearly falling on top of regime forces hiding in the trenches next to the railroad tracks, she had begged the officer in charge to let her and the children go. To overlook her mistake. To give her a second chance.

"We pose no threat. We wish only to go to Turkey."

"Take her to the others," said the officer to one of his men, after confiscating her cell phone.

They were marched at gunpoint to a Russian cargo truck that was idling next to a water treatment plant.

"Please," Hannah pleaded with the soldier who'd been assigned to guard them. When she looked over her shoulder, she could see the dormant fields that marked the start of rebel-held territory. In minutes she could be there.

They asked for her papers. She explained that she had none, that they had been lost in the bombing of Beit Qarah, but if they would only let her—

"Climb up," said the soldier.

When she hesitated, looking longingly toward the rebel-held territory, he poked her in the small of her back with the barrel of his rifle.

The cargo truck was packed with other detainees.

"I want to go back to Beit Qarah," said Noora.

"Where are they taking us?" Hannah asked the other detainees.

An old man shrugged. A child cried. No one gave her an answer.

It was hot in the truck, and there was no water. Sami had been carrying it all in his satchel.

"Where are you taking us?" Hannah demanded of the soldiers guarding the rear of the truck.

"Quiet," they said.

———

Their first stop was a processing center near the international airport. Television cameras filmed them waiting in line. Hannah and the children were given water and rosewater sweets.

She held her head high and told herself that she had been through worse than this, that she would find a way to make things right. She recalled a night long ago with Oskar, dinner at the Baron Hotel in downtown Aleppo, the same hotel where Lawrence of Arabia and Agatha Christie and the Shah of Iran and Ataturk had dined. She'd heard that the hotel had survived the war on the regime side and resolved that, if the regime showed them mercy—and from the reception they were receiving she thought maybe, just maybe, they would—she would take the children there and let them order whatever they wanted.

It would be okay.

She gave them her real name and said she was an American, and pregnant, and that the United States embassy in Ankara was expecting her to show up on the border with Turkey, and if they would only let her—

"Walk forward," said the soldier who fingerprinted her.

Flanked by Adam and Noora, and grasping their hands tightly, she did.

At the end of the line, where there were no cameras, she was herded into the back of a prisoner transport van.

Fifteen minutes later the van pulled up to the entrance of a four-story cement building surrounded by a high wall topped with rusting concertina wire. The air smelled like rotting corpses.

"Get out," said the soldier who yanked open the back of the van, "and line up next to the wall."

CHAPTER 67

Regime-held Aleppo

The rebel advance notwithstanding, supplies in regime-held Aleppo were still plentiful, so Rahim did not hesitate to make what had become a weekly sojourn to his favorite restaurant just off Saadallah al-Jabiri Square.

He did tell himself that he must exercise restraint when it came to the green olive, red pepper, and lemon appetizer—not in consideration of any wartime restrictions so much as his waistline—but his willpower to resist fresh olives had always been limited, and he soon lost count of how many he popped into his mouth while half watching the news on the flat-screen television that hung in the corner.

In the beginning of the war, the state broadcasts had depressed him, given the gap between what he knew to be reality and what was being reported. He had wanted real progress, not propaganda! But now it was different, he thought, as he put down the sprig of mint he'd been fiddling with and stuffed another olive into his mouth. Now the rebels, despite their recent advance in Ramouseh, were truly suffering.

Now the news reports did not ring nearly as false to him as they once had.

The noose was tightening! Regime troops and Hezbollah reinforcements were flooding in to help close the gap in Ramouseh. And anyone whom God had deemed to make stupid enough to still be living in rebel-held Aleppo after all these years deserved what was coming.

A few of them, apparently, were trying to get out. Admitting the error of their ways and throwing themselves upon the mercy of the regime.

On the television, he observed a woman in a black abaya clutching a newborn as she was being processed by the army. They would be granted safe passage, said the newscaster, to the rebel-held city of Idlib. Fine, Rahim thought, if a few women and children managed to escape, surely that was also God's will and for him to begrudge them the opportunity was churlish.

Go, he thought. *Ma salama!* Go in peace!

He plucked another olive from the bowl and resolved to double the alms contribution he made each year to the poor and orphaned. Then glanced at the screen again and froze, the olive poised before his lips.

She wore jeans, a loose-fitting blouse, and sneakers. Her purple head-scarf had slipped off the crown of her head, which she held high, exposing much of her long, black hair. A veil lay carelessly over her shoulder, as though it had been pulled away from her neck.

For a half-second, Rahim's interest was centered purely on the woman's beauty. To see such a lady emerge from the ashes of rebel Aleppo made him feel something akin to shame.

Then she turned, so that for a moment she was directly facing the camera. Rahim leaned forward. No, he must be mistaken . . .

He kept staring, leaning toward the screen, but her head was again turned from him as she was questioned by soldiers. He focused on the shape of her chin, the curve of her ear.

Then the camera panned away.

Rahim closed his eyes. Had it really been her?

Yes. He was sure of it.

He grabbed his cell phone, pushed his chair back, and stood. He had to alert his superiors so that they could question her! Question her about Dr. Hasan! She must not be released!

But as he pulled out his wallet and searched for the waiter, hoping to hail him for the bill, he paused and considered the image of the American woman and the fact that she had clearly been caring for two children. Four years ago, she had shown him a kindness by telling him that Dr. Hasan had given Adel the wrong medication.

Rahim scratched his temple and stared at the television, then glanced at the single olive that remained in his bowl.

He had already taken his revenge upon the doctor. That was what mattered.

"Sir, your meal," said a voice—his waiter's—from behind him. The waiter moved the olive bowl to the side and slid a plate of lamb kebab with Aleppo pepper in front of him. When Rahim continued to stand, he asked, "Was there something you needed, sir?"

The doctor's house was in ruins, Rahim reasoned. The doctor himself, likely dead. At this point, what was the girl to him? Even if she was an American spy, what did it matter? The rebels were losing, which meant the Americans were losing.

Rahim recalled that the Prophet, peace be upon him, had been renowned for his kindness, even to non-Muslims. But especially to women. Rarely were women evil, he thought. Unsophisticated and misguided? Like his wife and daughter? Yes. Ruled by emotion? Of course. But almost never evil. That was the province of men.

So was it asking too much to show a bit of kindness to the American woman? Surely doing so would not in any way alter the course of the war.

He recalled a passage from the Quran that had always struck him as profound.

Cursed are those who perform the prayer,
unmindful of how they pray, who make of themselves a display,
but hold back the small kindness.

"No," said Rahim, sitting back down and returning his cell phone to his pocket. The American girl was not his concern. Maybe she would find happiness with her rebel friends in Idlib and maybe she would not, but he would not personally make life more difficult for her.

"No, this will be fine. I have everything I need."

CHAPTER 68

There was no light in the cell, just a door with a barred window. The cinder block walls were stained dark from oily human hands. There was no toilet. No cot. No blankets. No food.

Wails from women caged in neighboring cells reverberated down the dimly lit hall.

"They must be injured," Hannah said when Adam and Noora started to cry. "But I am sure people are trying to help them."

The number they assigned to her was 11735.

The next morning a guard banged on the door with a club.

"Stand!"

She stood. The children stood with her. If she were cooperative, she thought, maybe they would go easy on her.

"Step back from the door!"

Boiled potatoes were left for them on a metal try, but the potatoes had little insects crawling over them, so Hannah made a game with the children of who could pick off the most. Noora won, but only because Adam had retreated into himself and wasn't playing, and Hannah didn't count half the insects she killed.

That night, two cells down, Hannah heard the slap of truncheons hitting flesh, the sound of clothes ripping, then meek protestations and men grunting—whether from the struggle to hold the woman down or the rape itself, she couldn't tell.

She sang songs to the children and told them more lies.

The next day, Adam began screaming that he wanted to go back to Beit Qarah, and when the guards ordered him to stop he told them to eat shit, so one of the guards beat his hands until they bled, and made him stand for six hours outside the cell.

Hannah had never felt so devastated. She didn't know what they wanted from them. She didn't know why they were there.

That night, no dinner was offered. The children cried.

From the indirect light that spilled in from a single basement window at the end of the cellblock hall, Hannah guessed that it was dawn of the second day when two interrogators—both older men with leaden eyes and gnarled fingers—came for her.

Noora gripped her legs and screamed for her not to go. Adam lay in a fetal ball in the corner.

The prison guards locked their hands on her arms and marched her to another cell and made her kneel on the concrete floor while they asked her questions. Save for lying about who the children's father was—a topic which didn't seem to interest them anyway—she gave honest answers.

She told them that she had dual US and Syrian citizenship, and that the embassy in Ankara would verify her US citizenship. She told them she had been delivering medicine for Bonne Foi, and when Bonne Foi was pushed out of Turkey—

"So you admit to aiding the terrorists! To bringing them medicine!"

"No!" she cried. The only people she had been aiding were the two children with whom she had been detained. And did they know that she was carrying the unborn sibling of those children in her womb? Surely they would want to show a woman in her condition mercy!

They said they did not believe she was an American, and that they would be calling no embassies. After tying her hands to a rusty metal ring on the wall, they beat her legs with truncheons until her knees gave out.

"You came to the regime side of Aleppo without identification," they said, "because your real name must be known to us."

She said she had already told them her real name, that she used to work for the European Development Service, and they should investigate this. In fact, she had been detained at a checkpoint in 2012, surely, they had a record of—

"We need the names of the al-Nusra officers you worked with."

"I was an employee of the European Development Service before the war. And then I transitioned to delivering—"

They twisted her breasts until she howled with humiliation and pain, bludgeoned her with a truncheon, then dragged her by her hair to a cell where a guard was using a broom handle to sodomize a female inmate whom they had bent at the waist and stuffed into a car tire. "That will be you," they said, "unless you begin cooperating."

Hannah made up names.

"You must do better than that," they said, adding that they had ways to force women who were pregnant to miscarry, but that to do it, Adam and Noora would be taken from her and she would be sent to one of the prisoner hospitals, and that was not a place one wanted to go.

There were crematoriums attached to the hospitals. Did she know that? Because there were too many bodies to bury, they just burned them by the thousands. Surely she didn't want that for her unborn child?

CHAPTER 69

Rebel-held Aleppo

The day after losing them, Sami woke up with a start before dawn, in the bottom of a trench in the Ramouseh gap.

Not knowing what else to do, he walked back to the M2 and put on his scrubs.

That night the nurses, observing his condition, grew worried. Dr. Wasim insisted that he rest. But to rest was to think and to think was to despair. So he performed a partial nephrectomy on a woman who had been shot through the kidney; he repaired a section of a soldier's perforated bowel; he extracted a rotted tooth from the mouth of a septuagenarian butcher; he assessed the condition of an eleven-year-old girl suffering from scoliosis; and he called doctors and nurses he knew at the M10 to ask whether any of them had a brace. No one did.

He tried calling Hannah again. And again. And again.

The next morning, he tracked down her friend Oskar in Ankara. But Oskar had not heard from her either. Nor had the American embassy in Ankara.

"She may have been detained," Sami said. "By the regime. We became separated, and she went the wrong way."

"Oh, God, no," said Oskar.

Near the end of the second day, Oskar called Sami back and said he had heard from the American embassy—the Assad regime was denying that they had detained her.

Sami did not believe it. The regime lied with as much forethought as it took to breathe. They lied about using barrel bombs and chemical weapons, about targeting hospitals, killing children, and intentionally starving their own people.

They lied about everything.

He tried to reason with himself. He told himself there was nothing he could do to change what had happened, that acceptance of this reality was the only rational way forward. That he just had to wait, stay calm, and see what fate delivered.

Reason failed him; he sank deeper into the abyss.

He was certain the regime was holding them. Either that, or they were dead. There was no other explanation. Even if she had lost her phone or not been able to charge it, she would have found a way to get a message through. To him, or to someone at the M2.

What frustrated him most was the knowledge that there was nothing he could do for them.

Nothing.

He repeated this to himself time and time again, to the point where it was beginning to drive him mad.

As he was amputating a soldier's arm right up to where it met the shoulder, however, cutting through the bone and wiping the blood spatter off his surgical glasses, he realized he had been kidding himself.

Of course, there was something he could to do for them. If only he had the courage to do it.

Regime-held Aleppo

At first Rahim thought he was being played.

It was true that ever since the first of his multiple promotions over the course of the war, his secretary Aisha had, at least to his face, treated him with respect.

But he still remembered the eye rolls he had endured prior to the promotions. Certainly, she had made little pretense of respecting him then. He suspected that, appearances to the contrary, she harbored little respect for him now.

Which is why when she told him who was trying to reach him, he suspected a ruse.

"Who gave you that name?" he demanded.

He was seated at his desk. She stood in front of him, clipboard in hand. Squat and arrogant. Crooked teeth.

"The man himself, Major," she said, appearing confused by his tone.

"That man is dead."

She exhaled and shrugged.

"Then it must be someone impersonating him."

Rahim perceived the hint of an eye roll. His eyes narrowed.

"You are certain that a man by that name called this office and asked to speak with me?"

She made a clucking sound with her tongue then said, "He called the main number for the Military Intelligence Directorate in Damascus. They transferred him to our office in Aleppo, who transferred him to me."

Rahim smacked his fist on his metal desk.

"He said he had information for you," added Aisha, "and that you would recognize his name. Of course, I asked him—what was the nature of this information? But he refused to give it. I am sorry if—"

"When did he call?"

She shrugged. "An hour ago?"

"And you did not think to come to me at once?"

"I was working on the transcribing the interrogation tape you gave me last night. If you will recall, you asked me to complete it by no later than nine this morning." She gestured with her head, performing a little bow as she did so, to the sheaf of papers that lay on his desk which she had handed to him upon entering his office. "I did not want to disturb you twice. He did leave his number, sir. I wrote it down for you."

———

Rahim stared at his phone for a full five minutes but could not bring himself to pick it up.

He drummed his fingers on his desk then rearranged the back-support pillow he had wedged into the crook of his chair.

The problem was that, two nights ago, he had broken down and called his wife in Beirut, to tell her that the doctor's home had been destroyed and that the doctor and his family had almost certainly been killed. His wife had not admitted it to him, but he could tell she had been pleased. Later in the conversation, she had confided to him that things were not quite as well in Beirut as she had let on. The refugees were driving up rents, the price of groceries was too high, and the food was nothing like it had been in Aleppo.

He had allowed himself to envision a time in the not-too-distant future when his daughter, wife, and his wife's parents—and perhaps even his brother and his family!—would all return to Aleppo and he, triumphant after driving the rebels from the city and avenging the death of his son, would resume his rightful place as the head of the family.

With all of his promotions, he might possibly even be able to afford to buy a house.

This recent development, however, it threatened everything. The doctor appeared to still be alive. Which meant he could not credibly claim to have adequately avenged his son. And surely, the doctor was not reaching out to him now to wish him well.

Rahim sighed. Then frowned. Then concluded that God had clearly seen fit to send the doctor back to him, and even though he had not asked for, much less wanted, such a gift, who was he to question God's will?

He sighed again, then picked up the phone and dialed.

CHAPTER 71

The knock came in the middle of the night, on the fourth day of their captivity.

"Stand!"

But Hannah would not stand.

Nothing she had told them, nothing she had done, nothing she had promised to do—none of it had mattered. So she would not stand now because she knew the pain and debasement would come anyway.

The children lay next to her on the floor. Adam stirred. A key turned in the lock.

"Get up."

Hannah curled tighter into herself. A hand grasped her arm. A boot kicked her bare foot.

Although her interrogators had made good on their promise to violate her, they had not yet made good on their promise to kill her unborn child. So when they pulled her up from the floor that night, she feared it was for that purpose, and she bit down on the hand that clasped her arm.

Noora screamed. Adam flailed his arms. Another guard entered the cell. Hannah kicked at his genitalia, but he grabbed her foot and twisted her leg so that she fell.

Together, all three guards dragged her out of the cell and brought her to a room that was bare save for two chairs and a fourth man.

Hannah attempted to charge the new man—a young sergeant with a weak chin and trim mustache—but one of the interrogators swept her feet out from under her, and she fell back to the floor. They bound her hands with plastic zip ties, hoisted her into one of the chairs, and zip-tied her feet to the chair.

It hurt for her to sit.

"I would advise you to save your energy," said the new man to Hannah. "At least until you hear what I have to say."

She tried to spit at him, but he had taken the precaution of standing too far behind her for her aim to be accurate.

Turning to the prison interrogators, the new man said, "Leave us."

"Sergeant Nassar, I would not recommend—"

"Go."

They left, and for a moment it was quiet, quieter than Hannah had ever remembered it being in the prison before.

The sergeant stepped from behind her and into her field of vision. The way he eyed her made her want to crawl into a corner. She leaned back in the chair, so that her loose prison robe fell flat to her chest.

"Please do not do this," she whispered eventually.

Her voice was gravelly. It sounded to her as though someone else entirely, some strange third person in the room, were speaking. And it enraged and mortified her to ask this man for mercy when she knew none would be offered. But she still felt compelled to try.

"I am here to arrange for your release," he announced. "A prisoner exchange has been arranged. For you and the children."

Hannah listened to herself breathe. She feared he was lying—dangling a carrot in front of her nose, fully intending to invent some reason to pull it away.

Unless they had finally realized that she had not been lying about being an American. Was that what this was all about?

"Why?"

The sergeant shrugged. "You must be important to the rebels. Either that, or the person the rebels are exchanging for you is important to us."

That was when Hannah figured it out. Her stomach flipped. Her face flushed. "No," she said. "I will stay here. I do not wish to be transferred."

"I am afraid you do not have a choice."

"I will fight it!" she screamed. "I am an American, and the American embassy in Ankara knows I am here! Call them; I am not lying! They will get me out! I do not need or want your fucking transfer!"

She spit at him again, and this time hit her mark.

The sergeant stared at the glob on his chest then said, "The decision has already been made."

CHAPTER 72

Rebel-held Aleppo

Sami visited the ruins of Beit Qarah.

It was as bad as he had remembered. The courtyard was completely gone. No sign whatsoever remained of the seahorse fountain or the lovely iwan. He considered that the house had endured the Ottoman Empire, the French Mandate, both world wars, and all the decades of rule and misrule Hafez al Assad—only to be destroyed by Hafez's sniveling eye-doctor son.

It hardly seemed a worthy end.

A few of the rooms at the rear of the house remained partially intact. In the one corner of the kitchen that remained standing, the honey-combed vaulting that Tahira had loved so much still clung to a fragment of the ceiling. The room that Aya and her husband Rafiq had occupied at the beginning of the war, and where he had first made love to Hannah just a few months ago, still had three walls and what looked like a relatively stable portion of roof over it.

He would rest there tonight, Sami decided.

That resolved, he took a slow walk up the rubble, stepping over a fragment of his father's nargile water pipe. Sami recalled passing clean water through the hose as a boy, cleaning the glass. Breaking apart the sticky tobacco so that it would burn properly, poking tiny holes in the tin foil that covered the ceramic pipe bowl, so that the tobacco would burn correctly. Most people would have simply poked holes at random, but Sami had always formed his in the shape of a perfect spiral.

He had been the best at it, his father had said.

A patch of yellow caught Sami's eye. His mother's room.

He pulled away a few pieces of limestone. Underneath one, he found an origami rhinoceros that he had made as a child. The paper was sun-bleached, but the folds were still perfect, or nearly so. Next to the rhinoceros, and covered with shards of glass, lay an origami elephant. Remembering how he had folded them, he collapsed both so that they were two-dimensional and slipped them into his back pocket.

In another section of rubble, beneath a ceiling fragment decorated with passion flowers and Damask roses, he found Descartes' *Meditations on First Philosophy*, a book he had purchased from the Shakespeare and Company bookstore in Paris when his parents had first brought him to France over twenty years ago. Near the book was a photo of Tahira that had been taken shortly after their wedding, along with a broken section of a hexagonal end table that had sat to the left of their shared bed. He placed the book and photo to the side, then excavated enough of the table so that he was able to remove the contents of one of the interior drawers: among the contents was the bill of sale for Beit Qarah.

———

The dry but fertile Aleppo Plateau extends west from the Orontes River Valley near the Mediterranean Sea, all the way to the Euphrates River Valley in north-central Syria, to the steppe in the southeast where it touches the tip of the vast Syrian Desert. The land is not completely flat but instead undulates in gentle waves, broken up by olive orchards and grain fields.

Some of those orchards extended all the way to the southern tip of rebel-held Aleppo. Sami began walking toward them before dawn, past the M2, through the vast cemetery that lay to the east of the M2, then turning south.

The air smelled of smoke—from the war or perhaps farmers outside the city burning their fields in preparation for the next planting.

Not being familiar with that part of the city, where the buildings abruptly ended and the fields began, he drifted too far to the north. When the sky began to lighten, he corrected his course and began to jog. The satchel that hung from his shoulder bounced against his hip. His left knee hurt.

As he got closer to the line of control, he watched for signs of rebel positions. A half-built overpass spanning the M5 highway loomed to the west. To the east were bombed-out farm buildings. But the path between those two landmarks appeared to be clear—just as Rahim had said it would be.

When dust plumes from cars speeding through olive orchards on the southern side of the M5 highway appeared, he ducked into a dry irrigation ditch. The dirt was soft and slipped into his shoes.

A bare, sunbaked patch of land separated the ditch from the M5 highway. In the predawn haze, he could just make out where two cars and a van had come to a stop in the middle of an olive orchard that lay on the opposite side of the M5.

He waited a minute then climbed out of the ditch and began to walk toward the highway, hoping that the regime forces on the other side would assume that he had brought a squad of rebel soldiers with him, ready to back him up should anything go wrong.

At the edge of the asphalt, he stopped, raised his hands briefly above his head to show they were empty, and then rested his palms on the top of his head. As he peered into the orchard on the opposite side of the highway, he observed more soldiers than he could count, crouched behind trees, aiming their rifles at him. Two Russian-made Ural cargo trucks with huge knobby tires were parked behind the two cars and the van that he had observed arriving.

Moments later, Hannah and the children appeared from the back of the van. They formed a human chain, with Hannah in the middle, holding both Adam and Noora's hands.

The children looked much the same as when he had left them; they even appeared to be wearing the same clothes. But Hannah's shoulders were stooped, and she was limping—so badly that she could barely walk. Her hair was uncovered and tangled. The formless, black robe she wore was too big for her. As she drew closer to the highway, Sami could see that her cheeks and eyes looked puffy.

He walked to the center of the highway.

When they drew close, Adam pulled his hand from Hannah's grip and raced toward him. Noora followed close on Adam's heels.

The sun had just crested the horizon and was bright in Sami's eyes. It made him blink as he struggled to focus on his children.

Adam tumbled into his arms.

"Adam," said Sami. Then, "Noora, come here."

The three embraced. Sami noted that there were raw lacerations on the back of Adam's hands.

He looked up. Hannah was there, watching as she silently wept.

"You should not have done this," she whispered. She pressed her lips together and held back more tears.

"There was no other way."

"There might have been. You should have waited. They will hurt you, Sami. They are horrible, horrible people."

"Shh," he said, finger to his lips as he glanced down at the children. "We have little time, but I must know—did you tell Rahim Suleiman about his son?"

"What does that man have to do with this?"

"You have not seen him?"

"No."

"Good."

"Whatever leverage you think you have, it will not work, Sami. These people—"

"Shh," he said again.

"Baba," said Adam. "I want to go home."

"And you will go home, my son. Not to Beit Qarah, but to a different home. Hannah is going to take you there."

A shot rang out. Hannah cringed. Sami glared at the cars.

"They said not to stop," said Hannah. "Noora, Adam, you must say goodbye to your father."

The children refused, instead clutching his legs tighter. Hannah moved to pull them away.

Sami brought his hands to his heart. "I have presents for the children," he said. He knelt, and the act of doing so, paired with the promise of a present, caused Adam and Noora to disengage from him.

From the satchel that hung from his shoulder, Sami extracted the origami rhinoceros and elephant figures he had folded as a child.

"Do you remember these?" he asked his children. "Your Mémère kept them in her room, on her dresser. I folded them as a boy. Now they are yours." He gave the rhinoceros to Adam and the elephant to Noora. To Hannah, he gave the satchel. "There is water and bread. Some money. Head to the M2. They will be expecting you. I am sorry I could not do more. I wanted to get you to Turkey."

Hannah began to cry again. "Oh, Sami." Another warning shot rang out.

"There is also the original bill of sale for Beit Qarah. And my last will and testament. The children will inherit the house." Sami held up his hand. "I know there is nothing to inherit, but maybe someday the land under the ruins will be worth something, and they can contest it if they wish. Keep all of this safe for them. Please. I have written the names of their relations on their mother's side, I would be grateful if you could find my wife's sister Aya, but I have also signed a document entrusting the children to your care. It will help that you bear their sibling."

Sami began to back away. Adam tried to follow him, but this time Hannah held him tight.

"I am sorry, my little prince," she said in English, speaking as much to herself as to Adam. "I hope one day you will forgive me for this."

"Come back, Baba! Come back!" cried Adam.

Sami turned away from his son, put his hands on top of his head, and began the long walk to the cars.

CHAPTER 73

From the moment Rahim saw Sami's son and daughter, he wished he had not come. He had always liked young children, and he had fond memories of his own children from that age—when they had still looked up to him as their hero, when disrespect could be punished with a swat to the backside or by taking away a toy.

Those had been simpler times. Better times.

It brought him no joy to see Dr. Hasan's children be deprived of that.

Which is why, long before Dr. Hasan had said his final goodbye, Rahim had turned from the scene and slipped into the passenger seat of a sedan that would be trailing the prisoner transport van. He was only there as an observer anyway; although he had initiated the process and had pointed out that the doctor was an extremely valuable asset, a special operations squad was handling the exchange.

Besides, he no longer had any desire to speak to Dr. Hasan. No desire to gloat. It was enough that God had arranged things as he had.

Rahim sighed, thinking *allah yisahellik*. May God make things easier for those children. Outside the car he heard a flurry of footsteps and, "Both hands behind your back."

Two special operations soldiers opened the rear doors of the van that was parked in front of him. As Dr. Hasan was shoved toward the van, Rahim dipped his head, not wanting to make eye contact.

He wished he had shot the doctor in the halls of the University of

Aleppo four years ago. That would have been cleaner. More honorable. This thing, though, involving the children . . .

"Major Suleiman! I have information for you. Look at me!"

Rahim raised his head, not sure at first who was addressing him. Then he observed Dr. Hasan craning his neck over his shoulder, looking right at him. Rahim returned the doctor's stare for a moment then turned away.

"I can tell you how he died, Major! It is not how you think! Your son, Adel—he was murdered, but not by me! I can tell you who did it!"

Rahim looked up again, now confused. The soldiers who had been stuffing Dr. Hasan into the van paused and looked to Rahim for guidance. Rahim suddenly felt self-conscious, as though he had been thrown upon a stage.

He also felt tricked. It was as he had feared. The doctor's claim that he was turning himself in solely so that his children and American girlfriend could be released had been a lie. There was some ulterior motive. The man was dangerous. Poison.

Rahim licked his lips and glared at the doctor. He turned his attention to the soldiers holding the doctor.

"What are you waiting for? Take him away!"

But he had already been bitten by the snake. The venom was even then poisoning his mind. Rahim knew it, and he was certain the doctor knew it as well.

Regime-held Aleppo

They bound his hands and chained him to the metal floor of the van.

"Where will you take me?" asked Sami.

The soldier who sat next to him clubbed him in the face with the butt of his pistol.

After bouncing along a rutted road that cut through a long olive orchard, they popped out onto a paved road and began making their way north.

Through the low front windshield, Sami could see well enough. As they skirted what had once been the bustling international airport, he recalled leaving from the very same airport on a trip to Dubai with Tahira, just before the war. Mémère had watched the children. He and Tahira had waited in line to ascend the Burj Khalifa, the tallest building in the world, and he pictured now that hazy point at which the skyscrapers of Dubai met the surrounding barren desert. He had bought a necklace for Tahira in the gold souk, they had stayed at the Four Seasons Resort, right on the Persian Gulf.

The Shaykh Najjar industrial zone north of the airport, where six years ago Sami had toured the manufacturing facility of a medical device company, was now nothing more than a wasteland of pulverized rebel tunnels, flattened concrete, and chemical factories. The streets were empty save for soldiers, the palm trees in the weedy road median covered with white dust.

When they pulled up to the Aleppo Central Prison, just past the industrial zone, it struck Sami as strange that he had lived his entire adult life in the city and had never really noticed the prison before. Yet it had always been there.

———

They called it a welcome party. Three men. Car jumper cables. A battery. A hot pad used to warm tea plugged directly into a wall socket and applied to his face.

He screamed and could smell his flesh burning. At the same time, he thought about all the work that would be required to properly debride his wounds. He wondered where, were he performing the restoration work himself, he would choose to harvest the graft skin. His buttocks perhaps. Or his right thigh, which they had left untouched.

An interrogation session followed, during which an electric stun gun was applied to his genitals. Over several hours, Sami made up information about rebel positions in and around Aleppo.

Either they did not notice his contradictions or did not care.

More beatings followed. The pain was like nothing he had ever experienced. It was beyond pain, the equivalent of an eardrum-splitting, madness-inducing wall of high-pitched sound that never ended.

Once he tried to run away, but he made it no more than a few cells down the hall. One of the guards shattered his right kneecap with a hammer.

That night he was shoved into a cell packed with other prisoners, even though there were empty cells nearby. There was no room to lie down. He could sit only by pulling his long, bony legs up into his chest, but the pain in his right knee was so great that he instead stood on one foot most of the night, using the back wall as support. There was no bathroom, just a few plastic Pepsi bottles that were quickly overfilled with urine. The smell of feces and vomit and urine caused him to vomit. One of the prisoners, whose body was riddled with electric-drill holes that were weeping blood, died.

Not long after, Sami considered his kneecap. It appeared to be a severely displaced fracture—he could slot a finger between the two main bone fragments—and the repair would have to entail surgery. To prevent his thigh muscle from pulling the upper fragment from the bottom one, he would do well, he thought, to apply a figure-eight tension band.

Yes, that was exactly the way he would do it.

The next morning, Rahim came for him.

———

"You claim to have information about my son," said Rahim in a nearby cell, sounding weary—and wary.

"Yes."

Sami sat on the floor, his injured leg extended in front of him. Rahim stood in a corner, his hands folded across his chest. He wore green army fatigues and a canvas belt; a Makarov pistol hung from a holster on the belt.

"And what is this information?" demanded Rahim.

"I will need for you to arrange safe passage for myself and my family. To Turkey," said Sami.

"You seek to trade information about my son for this safe passage?" asked Rahim, sounding incredulous.

Sami closed his eyes and swallowed. "*Inshallah*," he said.

"A man who has surrendered himself to God would not attempt to trade such information. He would give it gladly."

"Then evidently I am not that person," said Sami.

"Four years after my son dies—four years!—you come to me, not to apologize, but to bargain? No, I will not bargain. You can rot here, Doctor. And in a day or a week or a month, when your body has given out, I will give thanks to God that you are dead."

"I did not keep the truth from you four years ago," said Sami wearily. "It was only recently that I learned it myself."

"And yet you would keep it from me now."

Sami did not answer.

Rahim opened the door of the cell, let himself out, then locked it back up.

"It was the Mukhabarat," called Sami, as Rahim was walking away.

Rahim reappeared. "What is this nonsense of which you speak?" he whispered.

"It was the Mukhabarat," repeated Sami. "Your own men. They found out that your son was a rebel spy, found out that he was spying on you.

So they ran over Adel in the street, and when he survived, they forced a nurse to kill him. There was a Swedish patient sharing the room with your son. His name was Oskar Lång, and he was there when your son was murdered, he tried to stop it."

"No," said Rahim.

"It is true I gave him medication that he was allergic to but only because someone switched the labels. When the allergic reaction your son suffered was not enough to kill him, he was murdered by one of the nurses. I had nothing to do with his death. I thought I did—but we were both being lied to."

For a minute that felt much longer, neither man spoke. Sami listened to Rahim's labored breathing. Outside the prison, someone was honking their car horn.

Eventually Rahim asked, "And what was this nurse's name?"

"Farrah al-Mahmoud," said Sami. He remembered her. Cheerful. Efficient, walked quickly down the halls with a wide-hipped waddle.

"You had better not be lying to me now, Doctor, because if you are, hell would be a mercy compared to what I will do to you."

CHAPTER 75

Rahim called his daughter.

"Is it true?" he asked.

For a long time, all he could hear was music playing on the other end of the line. People laughing. An announcer encouraging people to dance.

"Zahra," he said to his daughter. "You must answer me! I must know!"

He was standing in a squalid bathroom next to the prison cafeteria. It had been the only place he had been able to find a bit of privacy.

"Yes," said Zahra finally. "Yes, it is true."

Rahim moaned.

"Adel believed in the cause!" added his daughter, sounding as though she were weeping. "He joined Freedom Torches after the father of one of his friends was murdered. He would make the flags for the protests. There is probably still some fabric in the old water tank. That was his hiding place."

Rahim slowly pounded the base of his fist against the bathroom wall as he looked up at the ceiling.

"Did your mother know then?"

"No."

"Does she know now?"

"No."

"And you? Were you spying on me as well?"

"Of course not, father," she said, but in a way that made Rahim certain she had been and was now afraid to admit it. Afraid of what he might do to her.

"Why do you call me with these questions?" she demanded.

Because it was God's will, of course, thought Rahim. It was all part of God's will—his actions, and Zahra's and Adel's. Even the doctor's. And yet while he thought this, still he whispered, "It was pointless what Adel did, what you did. Do you see that now? Do you see what has come of it? The rebels were never going to win. You only brought more death."

She hung up on him.

Rahim drove back to what had once been his home but which for years he had thought of simply as barracks. Breakfast dishes were piled in the sink, it was brutally hot because there was no electricity for air conditioning, and it smelled of men. The kitchen table sagged where one of the Iranians had sat on it. But for a moment he was able to see past the grime on the walls and recall what it had been like to come back to a home smelling of spiced lamb, the laughter of children, and the sound of music drifting up from his brother's flat below.

By the time he reached the attic, he was breathing at twice his normal rate because of the heat and the exertion of climbing the narrow ladder. The rusty water tank sat in the corner, looking much the same as it had twenty years ago when he had stopped using it. Rahim and his brother had talked about polishing the interior and sanding down and repainting the exterior, but instead, they had gone in together on a smaller plastic tank.

He unscrewed the cap on top, peered inside and saw his wife's missing scissors—she had blamed him for their loss—atop a pile of green fabric. He quickly screwed the cap back on. He exited his flat without locking it and drove straight to the military intelligence headquarters building.

His colleagues were nothing if not good record keepers. Because everyone lived in fear of being accused of being disloyal, the men of the Mukhabarat were careful to record their actions so that later they could turn to the records as proof of their fidelity to the regime.

The nurse had a file. And in that file was a record of a payment of ten thousand pounds having been made to her three days after Adel had died.

The payment had been recorded as *hospital services: Adel Suleiman* and had been authorized by a Major General assigned to the Aleppo division of Military Intelligence.

So that was what his son's life had been worth. Ten thousand Syrian pounds. Barely enough to buy two canisters of diesel today, a piddling sum even back then.

More payments for hospital services had been made to the nurse. But in 2014, she had been transferred to a prisoner hospital and in 2015 had been tried and put to death for smuggling out evidence of medical malpractice—a euphemism for torture—that had occurred at the hospital. As for the Major General who had signed Adel's death warrant, he had been killed in 2015 by hostile fire near Damascus.

So there would be no opportunity for revenge, even if he had been able or inclined to take it.

Rahim wondered how many of his colleagues had been secretly laughing at his grief, the way his daughter doubtless had been. Had his secretary, Aisha, been in on the lie? Certainly, she had not seemed shocked, or even curious, when she had handed him the file.

The world as Rahim knew it began to slip through his fingers, dissolving into air.

Why had Adel done this to him?

He remembered his son watching the news of the protests on television. And asking questions. *Baba, what will you do to stop these criminals from protesting?* And after a protest had been broken up at the university, and four students killed, *Baba, what will happen to the students who were taken prisoner? Where will they be held?* And when a general strike in Aleppo had been announced, *Baba, what will be done to break this strike?*

Rahim had assumed the questions to be evidence that his son looked up to him. He had even thought Adel might have wanted a job working in military intelligence alongside his father.

Breathing became difficult. His vision was impeded by drifting pockets of bright light. Outside his office, his coworkers chatted and laughed.

———

Rahim was not even sure he would be let back into the prison. Sami was not his prisoner, and the interrogation division of military intelligence had questioned his need to be there earlier that day.

But when he insisted that the doctor had information about rebel checkpoints that his operations group was monitoring, he was given half an hour. His identification was entered in the visitors' log. The locks to the prison were opened.

Sami was pulled from the overcrowded group cell back to the cell where he and Rahim had met earlier in the day. The burns on his back and face were weeping. His knee had swollen tight.

"In exchange for the information you gave me about my son, I am prepared to show you mercy," said Rahim.

Sami sat on the floor in the same place he had that morning.

Rahim stood over him. Sweating. Trembling.

"You are ill," said Sami, momentarily forgetting his own travails as he observed Rahim the way he might a new patient.

"You will not be going to Turkey," Rahim said. "You know that."

Sami looked at the ground then up to Rahim. "Yes."

"Are you ready?"

"Give me your phone," Sami demanded. "So that I may send a message to my children."

Frowning, Rahim looked flustered for a moment, but then he handed Sami his phone. "Be quick."

Sami sent Hannah an email but addressed it to Adam and Noora. He told them that he loved them, that if there was one thing he wished for them it was that, despite all they'd been through, they would find a way to be happy and kind. Given the pain raging throughout his body, it was an action that felt more dutiful than genuine, but he hoped Adam and Noora would not perceive it that way. For a moment, as he held the phone, his thoughts turned to Tahira. He allowed himself to remember her bouncing baby Noora on her hip, her gold bracelets jingling on her wrists, and the smell of laurel in her hair when she had stood on her toes to kiss him. He wished he could send a message to her too.

He handed Rahim his phone. "Thank you."

"Do you wish to stand?" asked Rahim.

"No."

Rahim unholstered his Makarov pistol, stepped to the side, and took aim with his extended arm.

"Stop," said Sami, scoffing, facing Rahim. "From the front. If you shoot where you are aiming, you risk penetrating only the frontal lobe. I have treated patients who have survived such a shot, and it is not a fate I wish for myself. From the top of the forehead aiming down. And shoot twice."

"I would prefer not to face you when I do this."

"And yet you must."

Rahim raised the gun again, quickly aimed, and pulled the trigger.

The shot entered Sami's head through his forehead and exited near the brain stem. Bits of his bone and blood spattered the wall behind him. As instructed, Rahim fired a quick second shot into Sami's temple.

From the end of the hall, he heard one of the guards cry out in alarm.

Sami slumped to the ground. Before the guards could arrive, Rahim sat next to him, placed the pistol in the doctor's right hand, slid the doctor's lifeless index finger onto the trigger, and then pointed the barrel at his own chest so that it was positioned over his heart.

"Forgive me," he said, speaking only to God. His family, he hoped, would hear that he had been killed by a prisoner. Which in a sense, he thought as he pulled the trigger, was true.

CHAPTER 77

Rebel-held Aleppo

It took Hannah all day to stumble back to the M2.

Adam and Noora grew sunburned and hungry. Upon arriving at the hospital in the late afternoon, she collapsed near a withered chestnut tree that still stood not far from the entrance.

The next morning, she woke up on a cot in the basement, surrounded by other patients. An IV drip led into her arm.

"Where are the children?!" she cried, panicked, trying to stand. But from under her bed Adam and Noora appeared.

Later, she checked her phone and read the email from Sami.

———

She stayed in Aleppo. Not because it was the wise thing to do—although she thought it might have been, given the relentless battles raging on either side of the Ramouseh gap—but simply because to risk capture again was unthinkable.

Two weeks later, the gap closed.

In September, the regime bombed the M2 and the M10 on the same day. By then, Hannah was working as a nurse, and the children were sleeping at the M2 with her. After the bombing, they fled to a nearby clinic established to temporarily replace the M2.

In October, when chlorine gas from an attack on an adjacent building wafted into the clinic, and Noora's eyes began to burn, they ran all the way back to the M2 which by then had been patched together yet again. Hannah had trouble keeping up because of how much the child inside her had grown.

In November, the regime dropped all pretense of not targeting medical facilities and bombed the M2 and M10 out of existence with bunker-buster munitions. Grains of dust blasted through the hallways like buckshot. It was only by chance that Hannah, Noora, and Adam survived.

In December, as the air turned cold and people burned plastic bottles and the clothes of the dead to stay warm, the last of the remaining food rations were distributed. Thousands of people who had nowhere else to go began to starve.

The regime and their Iranian and Russian allies pushed closer. The end, Hannah thought, was near. People burned their valuables—not for warmth, but so that the regime soldiers would not get them.

And then the Red Crescent announced that a deal had been struck.

———

They did not look like victims as they poured out of the bombed-out buildings at dawn on that December morning. Most of the women wore black, and although their sunken cheeks suggested death camps and famine, their robes were clean. They carried handbags and had dressed their children in puffy winter coats and rubber boots. A few held bright umbrellas to shield themselves from the cold rain.

Hannah had used a fork to comb Adam and Noora's hair and, with the help of a cracked mirror, her own. She'd cleaned their faces and fingernails with water from a puddle in the street, so determined was she that they not see her broken.

Then word spread that the Iranians had scuttled the deal, that there would be no buses to take them to rebel-held territory outside the city. Pride gave way to fear and desperation as the shots rang out and the artillery fire resumed. They ran back into the abandoned building where they had been taking refuge and huddled in a bathtub as the sky darkened with smoke.

The next morning, they were told the deal was back on. Hannah washed the children again, and this time, with thousands of others, they boarded a green bus—one of many in a convoy.

Fourteen hours later the bus began to move.

At the first checkpoint, just past Ramouseh, a soldier said they were welcome to get off in regime territory, and if they did, they would be treated well. Some people laughed. No one got off.

In the rebel-held city of Idlib, they got off the bus and were given food and shelter. But the next day, Hannah and the children began walking to Turkey.

"There is no reason to go," people said. "The border is closed."

That wasn't quite true. An ambulance here or there would be allowed to pass. Or the occasional humanitarian convoy. But for the vast number of refugees huddled at the border camps—for the farmers and schoolteachers and electricians and bakers and imams and electricians and doctors, and for their children—for them it was true.

People said they should stay in Idlib.

"Will you help us get to the border anyway?" Hannah asked.

People did.

A ride, a glass of water or black tea. An extra jacket for Noora from a woman who had lost a daughter. By late afternoon they had reached the outskirts of one of the camps.

The mud Hannah had remembered from prior trips was worse than ever. It soaked into their sneakers and chilled their toes, but the children walked onward without complaint. Step by step, past bikes with bent tires, and sewage ditches, and a collection of ragged blue-tarp tents where the human spillage that had bubbled out of the overflowing main camp had collected.

Shooting pains rose up Hannah's leg with every step she took.

As they started down the final strip of road that terminated at the border, the three of them reached for each other's hands, forming a human chain.

They knew how to do this.

"You should turn back," said a barefoot boy who was kicking a deflated soccer ball against a wall. "They will not let you through."

Whitewashed walls marked with graffiti and topped with chain-link fencing funneled them toward an arch. The sign that read *Syrian Arab Republic* had been removed. A small pentagonal gatehouse stood to the right of the arch, but no one appeared to be inside it.

Beyond the arch was a large traffic sign. Against a blue background, the sign displayed the red and white Turkish flag and a single word: TÜRKIYE. Beyond the sign stood a white gate, more Turkish flags, and Turkish soldiers.

Hannah and the children kept walking, under the Syrian arch and right up to the border where Turkish soldiers ordered her to stop. They wore camouflage pants and body armor.

You may not pass, they told her.

But I am an American. As you can see, I am pregnant, and these are my children. You have to let me through.

You have to.

They asked to see her passport. If she had an American passport, then yes, they would let her and the children through.

She explained that she did not have her passport, but if they would just call the American embassy, it would all get sorted out. She spoke in English, to prove she was an American, and she said she had a Swedish friend who was working with the American embassy in Ankara. She had spoken to him yesterday, and he was trying to arrange for asylum for the children in Sweden, and he might even be waiting for her on the other—

They began to shoo her back toward Syria.

Go, they said. No passport, no passage. One tapped his gun.

You have to leave.

She refused. "We have come so far," she said.

"Others have come so far as well. To let you all in is impossible. Now go."

And then, from far behind the border, a voice. "That's her! That's her! Hannah!"

Hannah turned to the voice, which sounded familiar. Standing next to a gatehouse inside Turkey, were four men. Two were Turkish soldiers and two were civilians wearing suits.

The taller of the two civilians was a bald man with a beard. In his hand he clutched something that was blue and roughly the size of a small paperback book. He was leaning forward and being restrained by the two soldiers. She didn't recognize him.

"Hannah!" the bald man yelled again. "It's Oskar. I have your passport!"

THE END

ACKNOWLEDGMENTS

This novel was more of a collaborative effort than any other I have written. At the top of the list of contributors to thank are those who lived in Aleppo, or contributed to the relief effort, and shared their stories with me.

Mahmoud Hallak was barely a teenager when the Assad regime tortured and murdered his father, Sakher Hallak, a prominent, highly esteemed doctor who practiced in Aleppo. In the year after his father's death, Mahmoud helped organize anti-regime protests in the city. Early sections of the novel were influenced by his experience.

Hani Hamou was working as a waiter at the tony Club d'Alep in downtown Aleppo, living in an apartment with a beautiful view of the Citadel, when the war came. A married father of three, he and his family endured deprivation in wartime Aleppo before hazarding a dangerous crossing from Syria to Turkey. Hani, his wife Yaldiz, and his children—Daryn, Kamber, and Mohamed—helped me better understand what it was like for a family to live in a city at war. The wonderful meal Yaldiz prepared after our discussion made its way into the book as well.

Dr. Zaher Sahloul, a former med-school classmate of Bashar al-Assad who now practices as a pulmonologist in the Chicago area, made many trips into rebel-held Aleppo in order to lend his expertise to the afflicted. He helped me better understand what it was truly like to undertake the harrowing journey along the Castello Road, and for what it was like for a doctor to practice in the horrific conditions of wartime Aleppo—particularly at the M10 hospital. Dr. Sahloul served as the president of the Syrian American Medical Society (SAMS) from 2011–2015, and currently serves as the president of MedGlobal, an organization, "dedicated to a world without healthcare disparity." I encourage anyone interested in supporting medical relief efforts in Syria and other countries to consider contributing to either of those organizations: www.sams-usa.net, www.medglobal.org. A portion of the profits from of this novel will be donated to relief organizations.

In the case of the following two individuals, pseudonyms were used so as to not put that person or their family at risk, but their contribution to the book was substantial and must be noted:

In 2012, Qasim al-Noury graduated from medical school at the University of Aleppo and began his post-graduate training as a resident at the University of Aleppo Hospital. When the war broke out, he continued to practice at the hospital, and helped treat victims of the Khan al-Asal gas attack. In 2014, he crossed to rebel-held Aleppo via the infamous *Maabar Almawet* (Corridor of Death), and then braved ISIS checkpoints to cross into Turkey. Many of his observations were woven into the fabric of the novel.

When I met Yusuf Baştürk in Turkey in 2017 near the border with Syria, I think he was worried I was a spy, and I was worried he might be secretly affiliated with ISIS. But I needed a guide, and he needed a job, so we got past our fears—to my great benefit. Yusuf took me safely to the border towns and camps and shared with me his experience working as a logistics officer for NGOs operating on the Syria-Turkey border.

In terms of helping massage my inchoate ideas into a novel, no person deserves more credit than my agent, Richard Curtis. His sense of when to encourage me to run with an idea, and when to gently lead me away from literary pitfalls that I am blind to, was exceptional. I am eternally grateful for his guidance, honesty, encouragement, and friendship. His contribution to this book cannot be overstated. Indeed, it would not be a book at all without him.

My profound thanks to Rick Bleiweiss and the rest of the team at Blackstone Publishing, for believing in this novel and helping to bring it to a wider audience. Those thanks extend to my editor Peggy Hageman—not only for helping to refine the language, but especially for suggesting revisions that helped me see key characters and crucial early scenes in a new light. I'm also grateful to Duaa Alhou, for reading this novel with an eye toward ensuring that my portrayal of Syrian characters and culture was authentic.

The assistance I received from family members was also considerable. My wife, Corinne Mayland, read the earliest draft of this book and—thankfully—helped disabuse me of the notion that it was anywhere near finished. My cousin Dr. Alyssa Green specializes in emergency medicine and has participated in medical aid missions abroad; she helped me refine the medical sections of the book. My sister, Dr. Beth Mayland, also helped with the medical sections, in addition to providing excellent editorial advice. My mother, Nan Mayland, worked for many years as a nurse in a pediatric intensive care unit; she, too, helped with the medical sections and provided key advice in terms of the logistics of administering medicine in a hospital environment. My cousin Kathy McIntyre lived in Syria for several years; her experience as an American woman in Syria helped me shape Hannah's character. My brother, David Mayland, read an early copy of the novel and provided valuable feedback.

In addition to the direct help I received from the people noted above, in researching the novel I turned to books by other authors. Of particular note: *My House in Damascus: An Inside View of the Syrian Crisis* by Diana Darke; *The Crossing: My Journey to the Shattered Heart of Syria* by Samar Yazbek; *A Disappearance in Damascus: Friendship and Survival in the Shadow of War* by Deborah Campbell.

Databases and reports that were publicly available online and which informed the novel include: *Mapping the Conflict in Aleppo, Syria*, an analysis prepared by Caerus Associates with support from the American Security Project and First Mile Geo; *Illegal Attacks on Health Care in Syria*, an interactive map and report prepared by Physicians for Human

Rights; the PubMed databases made available through the National Center for Biotechnology Information; Forensic Architecture's investigation into the bombing of the M2 hospital; *The Lost Treasure of The Polychrome Wooden (`ajami) Interior of Ghazalyeh House, Aleppo, Syria*, an examination of an Ottoman-era house written by Rami Alafandi and Asiah Abdul Rahim (Elsevier Ltd.); *Aleppo Conflict Timeline*, a report published by The Aleppo Project through the Shattuck Center on Conflict, Negotiation and Recovery at Central European University's School of Public Policy; *"It Breaks the Human": Torture, Disease and Death in Syria's Prisons* published by Amnesty International; *Deadly Detention: Deaths in Custody Amid Popular Protests in Syria* published by Amnesty International; and *Human Slaughterhouse: Mass Hangings and Extermination at Saydnaya Prison, Syria*, published by Amnesty International.

Professional journalists and citizen journalists, too numerous to mention individually, also made an enormous contribution to my understanding of what was happening in Aleppo. I am indebted to them.

And finally, I am grateful to my wife Corinne, and my children Kirsten and William for helping inspire me to write this book. Much of this novel was informed by the people who experienced unimaginable loss in Aleppo firsthand. I have not, a condition for which I am grateful. But as I read of the tragedy unfolding in Aleppo, and then as I wrote this book, a near constant consideration was how profoundly and permanently broken I knew I would be were I to experience even a fraction of the loss that so many others have, and that those feelings would stem from all the love and worry and pride that's wrapped up in my being a parent and a husband. And so it was that my own family, and my relationship to them, also became a part of this story.

Dan Mayland is an author and professional geopolitical forecaster, helping nonprofit, private, and government organizations navigate a changing world. His Mark Sava spy series was informed by his experiences in the Caspian region and Middle East. Raised in New Jersey, Mayland now lives in Pennsylvania with his wife and two children, in an old stone farmhouse he and his wife have restored.